King's Captain

Also by Dewey Lambdin

The King's Coat

The French Admiral

The King's Commission

The King's Privateer

The Gun Ketch

HMS Cockerel

A King's Commander

Jester's Fortune

King's Captain

An Alan Lewrie
Naval
Adventure

Dewey Lambdin

THOMAS DUNNE BOOKS

ST. MARTIN'S PRESS

NEW YORK

A THOMAS DUNNE BOOK.
An imprint of St. Martin's Press.

KING'S CAPTAIN. Copyright © 2000 by Dewey Lambdin. All rights reserved. Printed in the
United States of America. No part of this book may be used or reproduced in any manner
whatsoever without written permission except in the case of brief quotations embodied in
critical articles or reviews. For information, address St. Martin's Press, 175 Fifth Avenue,
New York, NY 10010.

www.stmartins.com

Book design by Kathryn Parise

LIBRARY OF CONGRESS CATALOGING-IN-PUBLICATION DATA

Lambdin, Dewey.
  King's captain : an Alan Lewrie naval adventure / Dewey Lambdin.—1st ed.
    p. cm.
  ISBN 0-312-26885-8
  1. Lewrie, Alan (Fictitious character)—Fiction. 2. Great Britain—History, Naval—18th
century—Fiction. 3. Saint Vincent, Cape (Portugal), Battle of, 1797—Fiction. I. Title.
PS3562.A435 K49 2000
813'.54—dc21   00-031764

First Edition: December 2000

10 9 8 7 6 5 4 3 2 1

This one is for...

Tom C. Armstrong, "your humble poet" as he calls himself, who, disguised as a mild-mannered writer/producer on Music Row for many years, a sometime songwriter, sometime book reviewer, sometime teacher/mentor to a new generation of writer/dreamers, a veteran of the old *Smothers Brothers Show*'s stable of comedy writers, *and* a poet ... serves the best, bottomless pot of coffee, along with a sympathetic ear for scribblers around Nashville such as myself, and has an abiding faith that talent will be recognized and appreciated. For Tom and his incomparable Beverly, and may God bless your encouragement.

Full-Rigged Ship: Starboard (right) side view

1. Mizzen Topgallant
2. Mizzen Topsail
3. Spanker
4. Main Royal
5. Main Topgallant
6. Mizzen T'gallant Staysail
7. Main Topsail
8. Main Course
9. Main T'gallant Staysail
10. Middle Staysail

11. Main Topmast Staysail
12. Fore Royal
13. Fore Topgallant
14. Fore Topsail
15. Fore Course
16. Fore Topmast Staysail
17. Inner Jib
18. Outer Flying Jib
19. Spritsail

A. Taffrail & Lanterns
B. Stern & Quarter-galleries
C. Poop Deck/Great Cabins Under
D. Rudder & Transom Post
E. Quarterdeck
F. Mizzen Chains & Stays
G. Main Chains & Stays
H. Boarding Battens/Entry Port
I. Cargo Loading Skids
J. Shrouds & Ratlines
K. Fore Chains & Stays

L. Waist
M. Gripe & Cutwater
N. Figurehead & Beakhead Rails
O. Bow Sprit
P. Jib Boom
Q. Foc's'le & Anchor Cat-heads
R. Cro'jack Yard (no sail fitted)
S. Top Platforms
T. Cross-Trees
U. Spanker Gaff

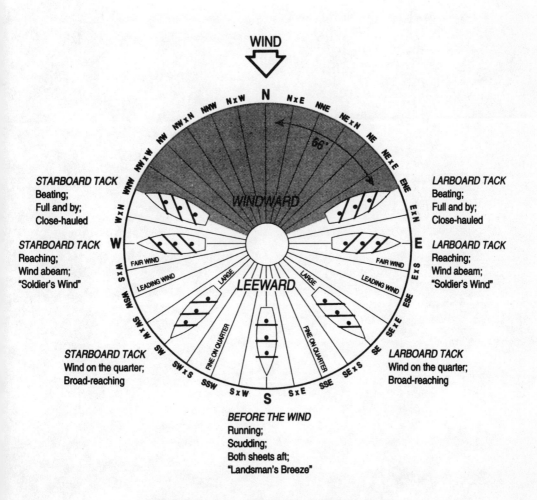

POINTS OF SAIL AND 32-POINT WIND-ROSE

Non unquam tulit documenta fors maiora,
quam fragili loco starent superbi.

Never did Fortune give larger proof,
on how frail ground stand the proud.
—*TROADES,* 4–6
LUCIUS ANNAEUS SENECA

PROLOGUE

Visa ratis saevae defecta laboribus undae,
quam Thetidi longinqua dies Glaucoque repostam
solibus et canis urebat luna pruinis.

She beheld a ship outworn
with the toils of the savage Sea,
long since offered up to Thetis and Glaucus,
which passing Time had scorched with its suns
and the Moon with her hoarfrosts had worn.

—*ARGONAUTICA*, BOOK II, 285–87
VALERIUS FLACCUS

*T*here was a thunder 'pon the sea.

Crash and bellow, a deep, continual tympany-drumming which went on and on 'til the waters on this slightly foggy, coolish day shivered as if in terror, and the winds, already nothing to boast of from out of South-of-West, were shot nigh to stillness. Winds failing and the long Atlantic rollers beguilingly rippled and fractured like an ocean of shattered glass fragments. But it wasn't the wind that did it—it was that thunder.

They could feel it, a gun-thunder which had quailed the winds and waters, rumbling upwards from the sea itself, as if some drowned volcano had cleared its throat numberless fathoms below; and their ship shook to that thunder, vibrated and trembled, humming in enforced harmony.

A game lass was their little ship, a plunger and a "goer" most of the time. But she was now worn just about out from *too* much daring and *panache,* too many hasty but vital errands and patrols, and nothing like a proper refit despite rare port-calls at Gibraltar, Lisbon, or at Oporto. Coming apart at the seams, she was; those seams weeping weary salt tears which had her hands at the bilge pumps every morning before breakfast; her oaken flesh and bones baked sere and dry as old toast—and not enough paint, tar, or oils left for even a "lick and a promise" either. Her bottom was foul, and she trailed a verdant jungle of vinelike weed and green slime from her quick-work—slowing her, so that she now lumbered like a dowager with the gout, instead of dancing upon the winds like the light-footed darling she once had been.

Yet her standing and running rigging, her towering masts, still stood in a lean Bristol fashion, her spars and yards were yet sound, and her sails—though much patched—still curved sweetly wind-full. Though her captain *had* considered frapping her roundabout with lighter kedge or stream-anchor cables, like a truss or corset, to remind her *how* to hold together for just a bit longer.

But slowed as she was, as frail-ing, her crew could load and fire three broadsides in less than two minutes, could still cajole her to "dance" at the peak of their expertise, gained in three years' continuous service together.

So she stood, near the end of the battle-line as it sailed on Sutherly, with the lead ships just starting to tack about Nor'west to double back on the two converging packs of foes they faced—a repeating frigate to pass messages or aid a ship which might be disabled.

HMS *Jester*—sloop of war, 18—still served.

Though again, to her captain's mind (and a rather *chary* mind it was at that moment, thankee!) being on the lee-side didn't particularly mean the "safe" side of the battle-line. Off *Jester*'s lee bow, down to the Sou'east, there were about eight or nine Spanish ships of the line, with accompanying frigates, and coming up slowly to merge with another pack. And that pack, good God! Seventeen, at the least, tall-sided, ugly brutes they were: two-decker 68s, 74s, and 80-gunners; some of them three-deckers, and one monstrous *four-decker* flying more admiral's flags than sail-canvas it seemed. And so stuffed with guns that every time she lit off a broadside, it looked like a mountain blowing up!

And here *they* were, curling about into a rough Vee, sandwiched like a forlorn nut between two arms of a *nutcracker*; fifteen warships of Admiral Sir John Jervis's fleet—formerly the Mediterranean Fleet before they'd been run out of that sea the previous summer—all just about as bad off as *Jester* in material condition when you got right down to it, yet blithely standing into danger as though they were about as fresh as new-picked daisies. Or as belligerent as a rutting bulldog!

With their artillery crashing and bellowing, making that thunder . . . sending shock waves through the sea.

"I can make out, sir . . ." Lieutenant Ralph Knolles attempted to say, as he took off his hat and swiped both forearms of his coat at his hair and brows. A bad sign that; usually, *one* nervous hand over his blond locks was sufficient sign of worry.

"Aye, Mister Knolles?" Commander Alan Lewrie replied, sounding almost calm in comparison.

"Beyond, sir." Knolles pointed towards the Spanish Fleet. "It may *not* be a convoy. About eight or nine more rather large ships over yonder . . . to the West-Nor'west. Do they *all* assemble, sir . . . well!"

"Two-deckers, d'ye think, sir?" Lewrie frowned, stepping to the starboard side of his quarterdeck, leaning on the bulwarks, and raising his telescope for a look-see. The smoke from all the gunfire was thick, a sulphurous, reeking mist which hazed the day even worse. More than a few British line-of-battle ships stood between him and the ones Knolles had sighted too, their gun-smoke and towering masts and sails obscuring what little he could see. But he could barely make out three-masters yonder, well up to weather and almost hull-down from the Spanish line.

Least an hour or more off, he thought, *sailin' large, to come down to join?* He couldn't tell.

As if we need more, he sneered to himself; *already got a bloody Armada here anyway! On its way North to join the French Fleet waitin' at Brest, the Dutch Fleet too. Transports, most-like. Carrying troops for an invasion of Ireland. Or England!*

And if Admiral Jervis threw away his ships in this action, then what hope did Lord Bridport and the Channel Fleet at Portsmouth have to stop them? Or even get word of their coming in time to . . . ?

Takin' this lot on's like a horsefly deliberately landin' on a game-table; sure t'get swatted! Lewrie speculated. *Has t'be done, no error. Growl ye may, but go ye must, and all that . . .*

"Cah-*rrisstt!*" was Lewrie's sudden, un-captainly comment. And a rather *loud* comment it was too.

In his telescope's ocular, he'd just discovered the fore-end of a ship of the line which *wasn't* crossing right-to-left, sailing obediently in the battle-line. He was looking at the beak-head and figurehead, the cutwater and frothing bow-wave below an out-thrust bowsprit and jib-boom of a warship—pointing right at him!

"Hands wear ship!" Lewrie yelped, eyes wide in dis-belief, as he lowered his glass in shock. "Helm hard a'weather!" Seen with normal vision, un-enlarged, wasn't much better as she bored direct for his *Jester*. HMS *Captain*, third but last from the tail end of the line, was swinging *out* of line alee and loomed close enough to trample them, if *Jester* didn't get out of her way!

"The *Captain*," Mr. Midshipman Hyde gawped.

"Commodore Nelson," Mr. Midshipman Spendlove supplied.

"That . . . *bugger!*" Lewrie opined, as his crew sprang to loosen braces and heads'l sheets. He heard Lieutenant Knolles and Bosun Cony barking urgent orders, felt the deck shift under his feet as his ship heeled to wear about, falling off the wind, spared a second to observe that things were well in hand. Then spared a longer glower at Nelson and his two-decker.

No one left the sacred order of the line of battle, no one, not ever! The Fighting Instructions were nigh to Gospel, and God pity the fool who disobeyed them. To turn away leeward, away from presenting a broadside to those Spanish warships, that could be called Cowardice in the Face of the Enemy—a hanging offence!

"Bugger!" Commander Lewrie snarled again. Not only was Nelson swinging clear of danger . . . he was forcing *him* to swing clear too!

Jester had been a cable to leeward of the line when HMS *Captain* began her turn, a fairly wide one to retain her speed. Being a smaller ship with smaller sails than a liner, she could cut a smaller radius of turn. So they ended up close together, once both ships had worn about to larboard tack, with the scant winds crossing their left-hand sides, for *Captain* was standing on almost Easterly to build back up to speed. They were within shouting distance.

Lewrie stood by the larboard bulwarks, hands fisted and akimbo on his hips, wondering just how *much* of what he had to say to a man who had just quit the line he could get away with.

Damn 'im, he's still *a Commodore!* Lewrie fumed to himself.

"Hoy, *Jester!*" came a high-pitched, slightly nasal shout from a runtish little dandy by *Captain*'s starboard rails. The dandy's hands were cupped round his mouth. "Follow me into clear air for signals!"

"Hoy . . . sir!" Lewrie replied, deliberately delaying his "sir." "And what . . . ?"

What the bloody Hell you think yer playin' at? was Lewrie's real question. He amended it though, regretting the necessity.

"Where are you *going* . . . sir?" he bellowed instead.

"No time to explain!" Nelson hallooed back, sounding infinitely pleased with himself, damn' near laughing with joy in point o' fact! "Before they join both bodies astern of us in the Nor'east! Follow me, *Jester!* We're off to *glorrryyy!*"

"Cack-handed, brainless bloody . . . cavalry charge . . . pip-squeak!" Lewrie grumbled in a harsh mutter, his face stretched into a toadying rictus of a smile. "Death or glory, mine arse! Mine arse on a bloody . . . *bandbox!*"

Then the *Captain,* with her longer waterline and taller, wider sails aloft, was surging past, beginning to turn even more Westward as wind filled her rigging and her greater speed returned.

"*Do* we follow him, sir?" Lieutenant Knolles wondered, still aghast.

"Christ, I don't . . . Christ! He's . . . !"

Captain was now aiming to pass *between* the last two ships of the line, *Diadem* and *Excellent,* to shorten the distance she'd have to sail to engage the entire Spanish Fleet!

"He's gone lunatick!" Lewrie breathed in awe.

But he's right . . . damn 'im! Lewrie had to admit to himself. *Do we hope Collingwood's on a run o' luck today and doesn't collide!*

"Have a prayer . . ." Sailing Master Mr. Buchanon moaned, crossing his thick fingers for luck as Captain Collingwood's *Excellent* seemed to shy, dithering whether to shorten sail, back the tops'ls to brake . . . or haul her wind and leave the line too.

"Aye, we'll follow, Mister Knolles," Lewrie sighed. "*Well* alee of *Excellent,* mind. Somebody has to do signals. Old Jarvy to Nelson or vice versa. Clap him in irons . . . ? This gap's too narrow, and closing. They'll merge, if we don't . . . get past us without a real fight. Haul taut to windward, Mister Knolles, course Nor-Nor'west."

"Aye, sir!"

"And Mister Buchanon? Do you *keep* those fingers crossed."

"Oh, aye, Cap'um," Buchanon rather soberly assured him. "Now 'til Epiphany, if 'at's what it takes. God help us, we're in for th' most *confounded* scrape!"

Lewrie shared a quick, quirky, and sardonic smile with his stolid Sailing Master, then turned away to look outward once more. The small batch of Spanish ships to leeward were almost level with them now and level with the tail end of the British line, which was still labouriously wheeling about one after the other . . . at a point which seemed to Lewrie's fevered imagination to be *too* damn' far South to be of any comfort.

To the West, Captain Troubridge's *Culloden,* at the head of that wheeling line, was almost level with the rear of the Spanish main body. Again, too far to windward to be of much immediate use to them. Apart from the fleet and its palls of gunfire, they were in clearer air, in undisturbed, un-roiled winds which cupped the sails taut and full, the two lone ships who'd disobeyed. Now going like Cambridge coaches!

Aft . . . Was *Excellent* dithering again, he wondered? Coming off the wind to wear, he hoped most fervently? Was *Diadem* too . . . ?

Forrud—over *Jester*'s larboard bows. There lay the Spaniards at which they charged, like naive house-terriers at an enraged bull on their first day of a country weekend. A very menacing and formidable pack of Dons they looked too! Though not in any particular order, he also noted. Though it must be said that at that moment Lewrie would have grasped at *any* straw of encouragement, no matter how frail. They were bunched, more like three ragged lines overlapping each other, and not a well-ordered in-line-ahead. Earlier, Jervis's line had shifted from two cruising lines into one battle-line, crossing the Dons' bows, while they'd come to do battle in three or four columns, as if to bore through in several places at once. But they'd been shot *out* of that plan—if plan it had been.

They could only fire the guns of those which were nearest, Lewrie grimly decided—*only* the first six or so! That, unfortunately, seemed to be more than enough to swat *Captain* away, for it included that four-decker which that moment erupted again in a ragged broadside he could almost count.

He quit when his tally rose over 60-odd guns along her starboard beam—times two equaled a sum too terrible to contemplate. He felt like a headache was coming on.

Yet, like a city-bred terrier too stupid of the consequences of tackling a huge farm animal, *Captain* opened fire as she neared the middle of that nearest line-of-battle, delivering a well-timed broadside from her 32-

pounders and 18-pounders that pummeled her target like an Alpine avalanche of boulders.

Fresh gunfire came, this from *Culloden* as she cruised up close to the tail of that nearest rank of Spanish ships. Sails were flying loose, puckering to round-shot; t'gallant and royal masts and yards at odd angles as they fell and tangled along the tops'ls and the fighting-top platforms; and timbers and bulwarks screamed, man-sized slivers of oak blown high as their main-course yards from that hopeless pummeling.

"Sir, deck there!" the main-mast lookout shouted down. "They be turnin'! D'ye hear, there! Head o' th' line's turnin' North!"

A fresh broadside from HMS *Captain* as she stood on, as if she'd pierce through between enemy ships to get at the second line, if that's what it took, hazing and becoming slightly indistinct as she sailed into the sour battle-fog of spent powder. One poor, lone, 3rd Rate 74, sure to be blown to flinders the very next instant, but she had daunted her foes and made them turn away! That gap would not close anytime soon; there was still time for Old Jarvy to complete his tack about to the North, bringing more ships into action—in perfect order. Lewrie was pretty certain the Dons had hauled off to sort themselves out into one long battle-line; but from where he stood that instant, it looked like the Spanish had no stomach for a real fight—and were flinching from the flea-bites of a single ship!

"Daft little bugger," Lewrie whispered in appreciation. "There's method to his madness, aye . . . *Still* mad as a hatter though."

"It's . . . !" Knolles gulped, as if witnessing the Second Coming.

"A cheer for *Captain*, lads!" Lewrie bade in a quarterdeck roar, ". . . a cheer for Commodore Nelson . . . he's showing us the way!"

His crew obeyed gladly, sure they were witness to one of those rare miracles, whooping and tossing their hats into the air and overside, no matter the cost of replacements that their Purser, Mr. Giles, would dun them for once soberer heads prevailed.

Lewrie looked astern again for aid. Several other vessels had taken Nelson's cue; for here came *Blenheim* of 98 guns, *Prince George* of 98, with *Ocean* and *Irresistible* in their wakes to re-enforce the insanity; still out of gun-range, far astern of *Culloden* but spreading more sail, letting fall their powerful courses, which were usually brailed up during battle to prevent accidental fires from the discharges from their own guns. And HMS

Victory—Old Jarvy's flagship—was in the process of wheeling about, tacking ponderously slow but sure, exposing her tall, bluff sides. Would those powerful ships arrive soon enough though, Lewrie fretted? Turning back to look at *Captain,* Lewrie could see her snuggling up close to a large Spanish two-decker, guns ablaze and ripping pieces off her with every shot. Taking fire too, taking damage but shrugging it off. The Spanish ships weren't firing quickly, none of them—nothing like three broadsides in less than two minutes.

"Poor practice, their gunnery," Lewrie commented.

"Slow, sir. Damn' slow, aye!" Knolles agreed. "Two or three *minutes* 'tween broadsides, not . . ."

"Mister Crewe!" Lewrie bellowed for his Master Gunner.

"Sir!" that worthy barked back from the waist.

"A broadside, Mister Crewe. I know it's too far for a hope of hitting anything, but the Dons yonder need a little *more* discouraging."

"Sir, uhm . . . !" Knolles blanched.

It was the accepted, gentlemanly practice for repeating frigates or auxiliaries near the battle-line to keep mum, their gun-ports closed, and they wouldn't be fired upon by the more powerful liners in return. To open their ports though, run out and fire upon larger ships, allowed them to be re-considered as fair game. And an 18-gun sloop of war with 9-pounder popguns had no business even placing herself near stray shot, much less inviting quick destruction.

"Bloody insane, ain't it, Mister Knolles?" Lewrie said, with his mouth screwed up, and an eyebrow raised. "But . . . there seem to be *bags* of insanity about today."

"Long as we don't take ourselves *too* serious, sir." Lieutenant Knolles shrugged, feeling fatalistic. His captain was wearing his bemused look, that wolfish, "Oh, what the merry hell," smirk. And his eyes . . . eyes that Knolles had come to be able to read; they were blue, or they were grey, by mood or temper. Had they steeled themselves flinty cold-grey, he would have been trembling in his boots, for when Commander Lewrie was out for blood, and there was hell to pay . . . Thankfully, this time he saw that they remained placidly, rake-hellishly blue.

"We'll not go plungin' into range of those monsters like we're a 1st Rate, no, Mister Knolles," Lewrie assured him with a chuckle and a wink.

"But we *will* make them look astern and see blood and thunder comin' down on 'em."

"Ready, sir!" Crewe reported.

"Blaze away then, Mister Crewe. Blaze away!"

It was impossible, really; nearly a mile-and-a-half separated *Jester* from the nearest Spaniard, and had her guns been able to shoot that far, with the elevating quoin blocks all the way out and the gun breeches resting on the truck-carriages, 9-pounder round-shot could do no more than *doink!* against thick oak sides and bounce off.

But out ripped their puny broadside, a bow-to-stern rippling of sound and fury, higher pitched and lap-dog sharp, compared to the great-guns of *Captain* or *Culloden*. But those puny iron balls *would* sing through the air, whistle and moan, and they *would* raise splashes where they struck—might even skip a time or two like a well-flung river pebble. They'd get *someone's* attention, or divert it.

"Short," Mr. Knolles noted, seeing the trout-splashes.

"Well, of course," Lewrie snickered.

"Bloody hell!" several gunners crowed from the waist, standing to peer over the bulwarks and gangway, through the open ports to spot the fall-of-shot. "Cowards, cowards!" someone began to sing-song.

Nothin' t'do with us, Lewrie thought, goggling as he saw the line of Spanish ships begin to peel apart; we *couldn't've . . . !*

The head of that line, their van group, was arranging itself in proper line-ahead at last, but hardening up to the wind to spare those astern from collisions—and inclining more to the *West*-Nor'west! The further column which had their guns masked by the nearest were stretching out into line as well, the ones nearest *Jester* back and filling, whilst those further North were making more sail, making room for those astern. And bending *away!* Leaving the smaller pack near *Captain*, including that massive four-deck flagship, by themselves, a bit to leeward!

"Mister Hyde, hoist a signal," Lewrie snapped. "Any one'll do, as if Nelson sent one. Dons can't *read* it, but . . . Mister Crewe, serve 'em another! Helmsmen, do you ease a spoke'r two a'weather. Let her fall off the wind a bit."

And open the range, he told himself; *so we don't sail right into that mess—get too close—and get squashed like a cockroach!*

"Ready, sir! On the up-roll, lads . . . steady . . . *fire!*"

Their slight turn away swung their broadside to point in the general direction of that monstrous four-decker. Mile-and-a-half, it was, for their 9-pounders—Range-To-Random-Shot. And this time that useless-as-dried-peas broadside struck the sea within half a cable of her waterline—flying tortoise-slow by then, Lewrie suspected—the iron round-shot cripple-skipping even closer a time or two.

She fired back!

Such a stupendous, sudden explosion from all her decks of guns that sailors whooped with delight for an ignorant second or two; that they'd somehow struck a weak spot and blown her sky-high!

"Uhm, errr . . ." Mr. Knolles said again, stoic but corpse-pale.

Oh, shit! was Lewrie's prime thought.

Moans and roars, sounds of tearing silk, irate witches' screams, and heavy surf crashes that went on and on, rustling overhead, beyond the bow and stern! Great pillars and feathers of spray leaped skyward, and the oceans boiled and frothed with more surf noises, as if *Jester* had conjured up a tropical reef at the entrance to a lagoon! Hundreds of yards to windward though . . . nowhere near her.

And once the shock had worn off, as chagrined gunners and gangway brace-tenders got back to their feet after flinging themselves down instinctively, *Jester*'s crew began to jeer their hapless foes.

"Uhm, Helmsman . . . two more points off the wind'd suit," Lewrie shakily ordered, marvelling that he *hadn't* pissed his breeches.

"Aye, *aye,* sir!" the senior quartermaster agreed, enthusiastic.

"Well," Lewrie crowed, clapping his hands and trying to justify his arrant stupidity, "*that* should draw their teeth for four or five minutes at any rate. A good broadside wasted, and them slow as treacle at reloadin'. Spare *Captain* her attention too. Mister Crewe, do you secure the larboard battery for now. Reload and stand easy."

"Aye, aye, sir!"

"Five minutes more, we'll have some other ships up to us," Lewrie went on, pacing aft to peer at the reinforcements which were positively bounding over the sea by then. "Mister Hyde? What signal flags are we flying?" he asked, craning his neck to look aloft up the mizzenmast.

"You said anything'd do, sir, so I grabbed the first four near to hand, sir." Hyde smirked. "Accident, really, but it's . . . It, uhm . . . means . . . 'Start Excess Water,' sir."

Lewrie looked aloft once more, hands on his hips, shaking his head in wonder, and began to bray with laughter! "Take it down, Mister Hyde . . . take it down. 'Fore the others think we're passing the word from Nelson to pump out and lighten ship. Run up more, as if we were speakin' the flagship. Meaningless strings of rubbish, mind, no real legible orders to anyone. Serve 'em gibberish, to keep our Dons on the hop. Good, God . . . 'Start Excess Water'! Hah!"

"Aye, sir." Hyde chuckled.

"Well, we won't be trying that on again anytime soon," Lewrie told Knolles, once he'd paced back to the nettings overlooking the waist at the forrud end of the quarterdeck. "Discretion above valour is our watchword. How is *Captain* faring?"

"Her fore topmast's shot away, sir, but it appears she's gunnel-to-gunnel with one of theirs. And boarding her!" Knolles relished to relate. "A real neck-or-nothing day, sir."

And by five in the afternoon it was over. The Spanish never managed to unite, and the smaller body of ships which had lain to leeward had turned about and sailed off to the South, out of sight. The bulk of the main body had limped away towards Cadiz, with the British squadron too cut up to pursue But it was a day of victory.

For the Spanish had left behind four ships: *San Ysidro*, a 3rd Rate of 74 guns; *San Nicolas*, a 3rd Rate 80, which Nelson had first engaged and boarded; the *San José* and *Salvador del Mundo*, both 2nd Rates of 112 guns! All defeated by slipshod sail handling and collisions, by horrendous casualties, and extremely poor, and slow, gunnery.

For a time, the flagship of Vice-Admiral Don José de Corduba, that four-deck monster the *Santissima Trinidad*, had struck her colours too, after being totally dis-masted, forcing the Spanish admiral to transfer to a frigate. A last-chance rally 'round 4:00 P.M. though had driven the British off, so the Spaniards could tow their flagship away. The largest warship in the world of 136 guns, the only four-decker anyone would *ever* build, and she'd almost been taken as prize—by the ferocity of Nelson and his 74-gunned HMS *Captain!*

"There, there, bad noises done . . . no more gun stinks," Lewrie told his cat, Toulon, as he carried him in his arms, cosseting and stroking him. The black-and-white ram-cat had spent the day far below decks on the orlop with Aspinall and the Ship's Carpenter, Mr. Reese, bottled up and moaning as gun-thunder echoed and thrummed 'round him. Now he was famished for attention and "pets," mewing plaintively, pawing, kneading "biscuits" for comfort. *"Mmmah-whahh!"* he entreated, muzzle under his master's chin.

"Big, timorous baby, yes I know . . ."

"Signal, sir!" Midshipman Spendlove announced. "Our number from the flag!"

Followed by "What Sort of Lunatic Are You?" I shouldn't wonder, Lewrie told himself with a rueful shrug.

"It's 'Captain Repair on Board,' sir," Spendlove concluded.

"Very well," Lewrie replied, turning to call out to his First Officer, "Mister Knolles? Take us down to *Victory* and lay us under her lee. Mister Cony? Ready my gig and boat crew. Best turnout, Cox'n Andrews."

"Aye, sah . . . best rig," his Jamaican coxswain answered. "We'll be ready, sah . . . as hon'some as Sunday Divisions!"

Handsome they were, half an hour later, when they rowed him over to the flagship, tricked out in clean check shirts, slop-trousers, and brass-buttoned, short, blue shell jackets. Ably competent too, hooking onto the starboard main-chains at the first try, oars tossed upright as one, as Lewrie made the long ascent up boarding battens and man-ropes to the upper deck.

A fresh-scrubbed side-party greeted him with twittering bosun's pipes, the slap of stout shoes on oak planking, horny hands on Brown Bess muskets, and a glittery whirl of swords presented in salute, winking in the wan winter sunset.

"This way, Commander Lewrie, if you please," an officer bade.

Up to the broad quarterdeck, where a group of senior officers stood, hats off and chortling like they'd just left a good comedy back home in Drury Lane and were waiting for their coaches to take them to some even more diverting entertainment: Captain Robert Calder and Captain Grey, Fleet Captain and the Flag Captain of HMS *Victory;* Rear-Admiral Parker off *Prince George;* Vice-Admiral The Honourable William Waldegrave off *Barfleur*—Admiral Hood's old flagship during the Revolution—Vice-Admiral Charles Thompson off *Britannia;* and Lewrie's recent squadron commander during '94–'95, Commodore Horatio Nelson, cheek-by-jowl with the gruffly gracious Admiral Sir John Jervis, K.B., a dour old tar who (*there's a wonder,* Alan goggled!) seemed almost congenial for a change. 'Twas a wonder what a victory would do.

"Sir John, gentlemen," the lieutenant announced. "Commander Lewrie of the *Jester* sloop."

"Lewrie . . . ah!" Old Jarvy grumped, doffing his large cocked hat as Lewrie did his, his head tilted back a bit to peer (rather dubiously, did Alan imagine?) down his fine-sculpted nose. "*Heard* some about you, sir. 'Deed I have," he pronounced, most disconcertingly.

That *don't sound promisin',* Lewrie quailed, not knowing how he might respond. *Just how much* has *he heard? And which bits?*

"Your servant, Sir John," he cooed instead, making a "leg."

"Well?" Old Jarvy barked, still holding his hat high over his head though Lewrie had lowered his to his side. "Did you? 'Start your water'? And was that before or *after* the *Santissima Trinidad* fired?"

"Oh!" Lewrie brightened instantly, much relieved to hear the chuckle which rose from Sir John, see the puckish grin on his phyz . . . to receive much the same sort of cheery approbation from the rest, all those senior and august commanders! "I'm certain more'n a few of our people did, Sir John . . . *immediately* after. For myself, 'twas a close run thing. I didn't anticipate such a response . . . certainly not her *full* attention."

"A fellow who yanks the lion's tail, sir," Admiral Jervis said, with a touch of high-nosed frost, "simply must expect a clawing!" He twinkled, snorted—actually making a jape! Almost but not quite as full of jollity as an affable compatriot and nothing like the flinty, humourless disciplinarian he was reputed to be, who could give anyone a case of the runs by simply glaring at him.

Admiral Jervis clapped his hat back on, stepping closer to take Lewrie's hand and pump away at it quite vigourously for a brief time, as the rest tittered polite appreciation for their commander's jest.

"I'll caution you, Commander Lewrie, about making a *career* of tom-foolery," Sir John added, pursing his features nigh to an actual admonishment, "but 'twas a splendid gesture nonetheless. You, Captain Troubridge in *Culloden* . . . Commodore Nelson . . . Was it disobedience of my signalled orders . . . ?" he posed, detaching his hand from Lewrie's.

Christ, am I for it after all? Lewrie shivered again.

Distressingly, now his hand was free again, Admiral Jervis doffed his hat high aloft once more, making Alan twitch in indecision.

". . . then it was a most forgivable disobedience, hmmm?"

"Thankee, Sir John," Lewrie muttered, dumbstruck. *That hat . . . !*

"Your casualties, sir, your damage?" Admiral Jervis asked more softly, coming closer, and glooming up in grim expectation.

"Why, none, sir," Lewrie declared. "No damage either. They couldn't shoot worth a . . . they were very poor at *long*-range firing."

"Close-in, though . . ." One of the senior officers sighed.

"But still, slow as 'church-work,'" Little Nelson chortled with glee. "Else we'd never have been able to stand within pistol-shot for as long as we did, sirs. Yank the lion's tail indeed, Sir John. Got *Santissima Trinidad* to waste a month's worth of shot and powder on his ship . . . 'stead of mine. My thanks, Commander Lewrie. When he was of my squadron at Genoa, sirs, I found none more expeditious and slyboots than Commander Lewrie when it came to befuddling our foes."

"No casualties . . . and no damage," Sir John mused heavily. "I do declare. Good, though. Good. 'Tis been a bloody-enough day."

"Well, for the Dons, much worse, sir," Nelson prattled on. "I must think they suffered ten times worse than us. You've been aboard the prize-ships, seen . . ."

"Aye," Sir John grunted, clapping one hand behind his back to pace himself back to his usual taciturn grumpiness. "So you may sail off towards Cadiz and 'smoak' the dispositions of their remaining warships, sir?" He directed this to Lewrie.

"Aye, Sir John," Lewrie said automatically. "Though . . . we are a *tad* worn down, sir. I was hoping to careen her, re-copper her bottom. A short spell in port before . . ." *Should I doff my hat to him too?*

"You've been in commission since . . . Captain Calder?"

"Three years, this month, Sir John," Calder supplied, off the top of his head.

"We shall make other arrangements then," Sir John said, almost mournfully. But instantly there was a twinkle in his eyes. "Lewrie, today is Valentine's Day. I shall make you a present. Remain under my lee 'til I send you written orders."

"Aye, aye, sir."

"And, well done, Lewrie. Damn' foolhardy, but well done."

"There was a lot of that going round today, sir. I think it must be catching," Alan allowed himself to jape.

". . . called the *San Nicolas* my 'Patent Bridge for Boarding First Rates,' ha, ha!" Nelson could be heard to titter in his high voice. "Up and over, without a pause, 'board the *San José,* d'ye see."

Lewrie cocked a chary brow at that statement; Nelson was never a shy man when it came to taking acclaim—he'd seen that preening side to him before. And he most-cynically suspected no one *had* called it that yet— Nelson had made it up himself. For his vaulting vanity!

Damn' fool! Lewrie sighed. *Never knew when to stop troweling it on!*

Servants were sporting trays of drinks 'round, and Lewrie snagged himself one and took a welcome sip of a very good claret. Old Jarvy's best, he imagined, saved for a rare occasion such as this.

"By the by, Commander Lewrie," Captain Calder purred, stepping over to him. "Just before this little set-to, we received some mails for the fleet. I do believe, should you speak to our First Officer, he has yours ready to hand."

"Mail, sir!" Lewrie enthused. It had been weeks since he'd had news from home. "I can't think of a single thing more to make this day any more perfect."

"Uhmm . . . is that some *cat* hair on your coat, sir?"

Nearly nine o'clock of the Evening Watch and almost time that all glims and lanthorns were doused for fear of fire in the night hours. Even a captain had to heed the Master At Arms. There was still time, though, to race through just one more letter from his wife, Caroline, back home in Anglesgreen, then give them all a slower, more loving perusal the next morning.

   He swiveled and craned under the swaying overhead lanthorn for the most light at his desk, idly stroking a sleeping Toulon, atop the attractively crinkly discard pile of other mail from chandlers, tailors, bankers, and such, tucked up all Sphinx-like.

> *. . . has purchased three hundred acres of Land, talked of*
> *running up a manse, just by the old ruined tower*
> *where long ago we pledged our mutual Love . . .*

Lewrie flipped back a page or two, looking for a clue. Was this some new botheration from Harry Embleton or his father, the baronet? That was Chiswick land, just by his own rented acres, land he stood a chance to inherit (his brother-in-law, Governour, for certain) once old Uncle Phineas Chiswick went "toes up" (and, pray God, soon!). Phineas would never sell a three-hundred-acre tract off whilst living and would likely find a way to tuck it in his coffin and hoist it off to Perdition with him! Just for spite! In fact, he'd rather *die* than give away a single blade of grass to a passing drover's goat! Ah . . . !

> *. . . to England, and has been making the most*
> *perfect Hooraw in the village since. And he*
> *now lodges on* Us, *until he discovers suitable*
> *quarters; which, as I am certain you understand,*
> *Dearest, has caused no end of Upset . . .*

Must be further back, Lewrie puzzled. If her brother, Burgess, had returned from service with the East India Company army, Caroline would be over the *moon* with joy, would never express reservations, even if he came back sick, lame, or bankrupt! More like, he could lodge with Phineas and his mother in that drab pile, with Governour and Millicent at their new house.

   "Now where the deuce . . ." Lewrie grumbled half-aloud, sorting out the fronts and backs of the hefty letter. There came the crisp clang of two bells up forrud, the stamp of boots, and a musket butt from the marine sentry at his main deck door, almost at the same instant.

"Master At Arms, sah! Reports 'darkened ship,' sah!"

"Christ on a *crutch!*" Lewrie yelped.

"Sah?"

"Very well . . . carry on then . . . Jesus!" Lewrie barked back.

> *. . . the proper Respect and Deference due your*
> *sire, and most of all, Dearest, that tender*
> *Consideration I feel bound to show Brigadier*
> *Sir Hugo as my father-in-law, though, until his*
> *un-looked-for arrival, we had never met.*

"My bloody father!" Lewrie muttered. "Aye, dark, alright. Dark and gettin' darker!"

> *I pray you, though, Alan, should you have any*
> *suggestions as to how to finesse this matter,*
> *I beg you write at once and tell me . . . what shall*
> *I do with your father?*

Load those pistols I left in my study was Lewrie's first thought; *send to the blacksmith's for a gross of chastity belts* was his second. Then—best yet—*run!*

BOOK ONE

*Non equidem invideo; mirror magis; undique totis
usque adeo turbatur agris.*

Well, I grudge you not—rather I marvel;
such unrest is there on all sides in the land.

—*The Eclogues,* I, 11–12
Virgil

CHAPTER ONE

*I*t should have been a glad day. Yet to Lewrie it seemed to be one of
infinite sadness. Though the harbour waters were sparkling and glittering,
the skies were fresh-washed blue, stippled with benign and pristine brush-
stroked clouds; the sun was bright; and the day was just warm enough to
be mild, yet not hot enough to be oppressive; and gulls and other seabirds
swooped and dove and hovered with springtime delight . . . it was his last
day. The morning he surrendered command of HMS *Jester.*

Admiral Sir John Jervis's Valentine's Day "present," following the Battle of Cape Saint Vincent, was a quick dash into Lisbon for two days Out-
of-Discipline, an aboard-ship revel with the Portugee whores and
something approaching a monumental drunk for all hands. And once the
last doxy had been chivvied ashore, the last smuggled wine bottle tipped
overside, and the last thick head had returned to normal use, they had
stripped *Jester* of top-masts, stores, and artillery for her first careenage since
Leghorn, the middle of '95. Tons of weed, slime, and barnacles had been
sluiced, swabbed, chipped, or fired off her hull; and what little they could
do to replace missing copper sheets, or tar over and paint over, had been
performed before re-floating her, giving her that long-delayed "lick and a
promise" above the waterline, before re-stocking her, re-arming her, and
setting her masts up anew.

It was only then that Lewrie could announce to his men that they were off for Portsmouth to de-commission; off for Home and England! And *Jester*'s decks had rung with whooping cheers and tears of joy!

He'd wished *he'd* known sooner; four hands had trickled off from the working parties, entered on ship's books as "Run." Had they known earlier that *Jester* was bound for England, they might have stayed on to see their families again and collect the pay owed them, which was nearly eighteen months overdue, which, given the times and the Navy's slack accounting system, was actually a little better-than-normal delay.

Then again, two of them had been Italian volunteers, or some of those Maltese seamen who'd been hired-out by the Grand Masters of Malta in '93, after Hood had taken, then lost, the French naval base at Toulon.

Lewrie was certain that their "fly" Purser—the young, bespectacled Mr. Giles—was cackling in glee somewhere aft in a stores room over their departure. Not only had they decamped without their meagre pay, but their shares in the prize-money which *Jester* had accumulated since '94. Finding a way to make absent men "chew tobacco"—purchase slop-clothing, hats, tinware, and such on a two-year spending spree as profligate as . . . as drunken sailors—to help make his books balance, Lewrie was mortal-certain! Or sign their pay over to him in total? Forge documents that he was their executor selected to hold any share of prize-money for them? Their only bloody *heir?* Lewrie had scoffed.

There was little he could do to their benefit. And, after all, they'd "Run"; taken "leg-bail" from the Fleet, from shipmates, and from his command. Now they were most-likely dead-broke and desperate for a berth in any merchant ship that'd have them, throwing away sums that for a poor sailorman were damn'-near princely! The Devil with 'em . . . damn' fools!

So he'd demurred and *hadn't* cocked a wary brow at Giles, letting him have his unofficial "due." He needed him too badly to anger the smug little "Captain Sharp," not at the last moments of a commission when his own accountings and financial records were to be scrutinised by a platoon of petti-fogging Admiralty clerks! Not if he didn't want to have some bear-trap snap shut on his arse, all unsuspecting, years later!

His cabins were stripped bare, but for guns, carriages, and the black-and-white chequer painted on the sailcloth deck covering. Ragged and scuffed, the paint scrubbed half off beneath the gun-trucks. The many light canvas and deal partitions were stacked to one corner like a set of abandoned doors or used-up stage-sets. His chests were now in a hired boat alongside. Toulon, strenuously objecting to it, was caged in a wicker basket which Aspinall held—rather carefully, he noted, for Toulon was hissing, spitting, hunkering, and licking chops like he wished to *nip* the fool who'd ordered him in there. Or whichever fleshy idiot got within slashing distance.

Lewrie huffed a huge sigh of finality. Even after they'd come in, there'd been nigh on ten days' worth of nattering with Vice-Admiral Sir Peter Parker's staff, in charge at Portsmouth, with the criminals at HM Dock-yards, with the bewildered twits at Gun Wharf, who'd given him permission to keep his French 8-pounders (which equalled British Long-Nines) instead of waiting to exchange for the proper 6-pounders his vessel rated . . . and now vowed they had never known a *thing* about it, and who the deuce did he think he was playing fast and loose with their records? Didn't he know there was a war on?

There'd been a blizzard of paperwork; all the forms, ledgers, and logs, the fill-in-the-blanks documents for Sick & Hurt Board, Victualling Board, Ordnance Board, powder and shot expended, in action or for gun-drill, with many "tsk-tsks" and mournful shakings of heads over *wasting* precious munitions without good reason. Back-stays shifted; spars lost or cracked; lumber, nails, and screws used for repairs—how *necessary* were the repairs to ship's boats or bulwarks, and had the Carpenter or Bosun allotted *too* many board feet, too many bloody *screws!* to restore a shot-through cutter. Marines, accused of using too *little* boot-black or pipe clay, whilst using too many flints, expending too much powder and ball, and losing one whole musket and *two* bayonets! Having to explain, in triplicate, every lack or loss, with the replacement cost held over each unfortunate respondent's head until a plausible compromise could be reached!

Every lack was Lewrie's final responsibility as captain after all, every loss or condemnation of rotten stores. Department heads were liable for lack of accountability, certainly, but in the end there were some things *he* could be dunned for. After a final, prissy, and un-satisfied *harumph!* that no outright fraud had occurred, no sin of omission or commission which might lead to pay stoppage or court-martial, the senior clerk had written Lewrie a form which deducted from the pay due him, a copy of said form to

be forwarded to Admiralty for the clerks there, who could tally up his pay for
three years' service, another to go into his personnel file, one for the Portsmouth records, and one to be handed over to Lewrie for his own keeping.

With another huge sigh, Lewrie turned his back on those great-cabins and
went out the forrud passageway 'twixt the sadly empty dining coach and
the still-usable chart space, to the gun-deck to face his crew.

He had never de-commissioned a ship in wartime. *Shrike*, back in '83,
after the American Revolution was over; as a junior officer into *Telesto* in
'86; or sweet little *Alacrity*, a converted bomb-ketch he'd had, his first
official lieutenant's command, when she'd come home from the Bahamas
in '89. Those were all done in time of peace and were relatively joyous
occasions, for the hands had mostly been freed from the Navy, going off
to civilian pursuits and the pleasures of their homes, their families, with
the Fleet much reduced. Now, though . . .

The Royal Navy was gigantic, with nearly one hundred line-of-battle
ships and another hundred frigates, even more lesser ships in commission
out fighting their foes, worldwide. Nearly half the hands were impressed
or culled from debtors' prisons to man those fleets, and there would be no
freedom, even a brief tantalising spree, for most of his Jesters. At that
moment she lay far offshore to prevent desertions, daunted by the many
guard-boats which rowed Portsmouth's inner harbour with armed Marines
aboard with orders to shoot or apprehend; with truncheon-bearing Press
Gangs patrolling the docks to deter anyone who'd swum ashore in spite
of the guard-boats; or the vigilance of a ship's own Marines, who stood
harbour-watch with loaded muskets.

With the Navy so hungry for trained, experienced men who could hand,
reef, and steer, this well-shaken-down crew of his could end up scattered
in a heartbeat, sent off in dribs and drabs as need dictated to the foul
receiving ships to idle for weeks 'til a sufficient number was mustered to
draught aboard another ship newly commissioning, or one come in with
casualities, desertions, and deaths from battle, accidents, or sickness in need
of quick re-manning.

With any luck at all—though Lewrie rather doubted his Jesters would
find any; he'd seen lips smacking, greedy hands clapped together from other

ships' bulwarks, or the Impress Service—they *might* allow the crew to turn over, entire, into a new ship. With a *great* deal of luck, they might be allowed to remain aboard, intact, under the newest captain! Yet *Jester* would be going alongside at Gun Wharf to remove her artillery, along a stone quay to empty her of every last movable item to lighten her, including her very last ballast-stone, her masts and spars taken away, perhaps the lower masts drawn out like bad teeth. And she'd be weeks, perhaps as much as three months, in the hands of the dockyards being partially rebuilt. Except for those choice few holding Admiralty Warrant who were pretty-much assigned to her for life, the Fleet could not let valuable seamen sit idle.

What to say *to them?* Lewrie puzzled sadly.

He'd most hopefully made himself a list, assuming that some word might come down from London before this moment arrived offering him future employment. As a confirmed Commander he might go into another sloop of war like *Jester,* and the Admiralty would then allow him some few of his most trusted hands to ease his transition. Should they actually *promote* him (pray Jesus!) and make him "post" into a 5th or 6th Rate frigate, then they'd allow him even more of his favorites along to form the nucleus of a new and unfamiliar crew. Less than a dozen all told, even as a Post-Captain, but aboard that wished-for frigate, confronted with a sea of nigh two hundred strange faces, he'd need every salt he knew by sight or smell.

But there had *been* no word from the Lords Commissioners, from the new First Secretary, Mr. Evan Nepean; no word of future employment or promotion. He'd been "required and directed" to dot the last *i* and cross the last *t* . . . unlooked for and unloved (or so it seemed).

He smiled a sad, grim-lipped smile for the seamen and inferior petty officers gathered on the gun-deck, nodding and acknowledging the shy, lost, and inarticulate expressions from the ship's "people," whilst on his way to the quarterdeck. *God help 'em,* he thought; *they're just as hung on tenterhooks as I! And with a perfect right too!* Lewrie thought, clapping a few on the arm on his way. Many ratings aboard a warship were the whims of her captain, those informal positions aloft as yard-captains, top-mast captains, forecastle captains, the quarter gunners, and such . . . places of trust and seniority, marks of personal merit and authority which got them but a few more pence per month . . . Yeoman of the Powder, Yeomen of the Sheets, Bosun's Mate, Carpenter's Mate, members of a captain's boat-crew . . .

In a new ship, their qualities unknown to a new captain and his officers—who already had their coterie of favorites or *protégés*—they'd lose their preferential rates, their pride and esteem, and the slim pay which went with them. A valued man, elevated to petty officer in one ship, would be just another Able Seaman in another. Even if they stayed aboard *Jester,* her new captain would be bringing along his own tight little clique, and would demote and replace according to his own lights.

Lewrie went up the starboard gangway ladder to say his goodbyes to his waiting officers, to share a last, quick remembrance or two with them. They, at least, were officially looked after and would be going off to finer things. Though, considering the capricious whims of Admiralty, it'd be just as stressful and worrisome to see where each might alight.

Lieutenant Ralph Knolles, such an elegant, able, and cheerful young officer, sure to rise even higher and do great things. Mr. Edward Buchanon, the Sailing Master, that young-old seer and West Country mystic ... Midshipmen Martin Hyde and Clarence Spendlove, who'd turned into salt-stained, tarry-handed young men in their late teens; Spendlove, whose voice had broken and gone deep this commission—almost ready to face examining boards and earn their own lieutenants' commissions had they any fortune, patronage beyond his own, or "interest" with senior men.

Almost pleasurable it was, the first time this commission, Lewrie thought, to say his goodbyes to the gloomy, sarcastically bitter Mr. Howse, their Surgeon, that laconic critic who'd set his teeth on edge with his eternal disgust with the world in general and Lewrie's place in it in specific. And his built-in chorus of one, his mate LeGoff.

Peter Giles, the Purser—'twas relief Lewrie felt when taking leave of him; that he hadn't yet been caught, and Lewrie implicated as well, in guilt by association in some vaulting scheme which exceeded even the jaded tolerance of a corrupt Victualling Board. *Was ever a dog born t'be hung sooner or later . . . !* Lewrie thought, glad to see the back of him!

Giles, though, and his Jack-In-The-Breadroom, were as safe as houses, for he held Warrant and would continue on in her should he wish it. Mr. Crewe, her Master Gunner; Mr. Reese, her Carpenter; Mr. Paschal, the Sailmaker; Mr. Meggs, *Jester*'s Armourer; her Cooper; and a few such others would remain aboard in the yards right into her next commission.

As would Will Cony, unfortunately. Making this day even worse, making him wish he'd never tried to promote Will to Bosun. Cony had been his "man" since '81, back in the days of the siege of Yorktown, with him throughout all his adventures. . . .

"Well, then," Lewrie said at last, from his familiar "pulpit" by the middle of the quarterdeck rail overlooking the waist. "Damned if we haven't had a rare run of luck aboard, right, lads? Seen wonders . . . *done* wonders! Met some right bastards too, but we fought 'em and beat 'em all hollow too. And now come home . . . the most of us . . . safe and sound. You oldest hands, off *Cockerel*, you who came from *Windsor Castle*, *Agamemnon*, since Toulon . . . those who come aboard in early '94, right here in Portsmouth . . . all thrown together in the pot and stewed, 'til you became—shipmates. Bitter and the sweet, spicy and bland—and you'd know best which you are, hey?"

That got him a semblance of a laugh, which made it easier.

"A ship's company . . . *and* a damn' good'un! God bless you all for there'll never be another like you. Not for me! Where'er I go in the Fleet, I'll always have my Jesters . . . as the ring-measure for any other crew to fit through, to try and equal. I'm . . ."

Damme, I am not *goin'ta tear up and blub!* he told himself; *give me one more minute o' manhood! Besides, there's surely an Article of War against it!*

He looked to the side, where stood a party of clerks from Vice-Admiral Sir Peter Parker's staff, eager to get down to their business of paying off the hands. Beyond, there lurked a suspicious, hovering tender which he imagined must contain the Impress Service, ready with a list of ships needing hands. So part of his farewell speech seemed to be right out, that bit about taking joy of being home!

"Well, then . . ." he reiterated. "You know what they say 'bout changing ships. The best men you serve with once, honour them as examples the rest of yer life, and never see again. The dross show up like creditors . . . one commission after the other. I'd be proud to be with you, every last man-jack o' you! I'm as proud o' you as a captain can be! So *you* take pride, wherever you light! In what you did together . . . proud of *her*, our ship. Proud that for a wondrous three years, you were Jesters! Goodbye, you rogues. G . . . goodbye, Jesters. Now give us three cheers for the best ship in the Fleet! And the best *crew* in the Fleet! A ship and crew any captain'd be glad to command!" He added, for the benefit of that impatient spectre waiting overside, "Hip, hip . . . !"

A quick bustle, a final shake of hands, a last formal "leg" to the senior officers who had had enough human decency to *not* peer at their watch-faces to spur him to hurry (and who were most-like familiar with the pain he was experiencing in losing a ship), and he was at the gangway entry-port, while cheers still resounded from the crew.

He doffed his hat in salute, shared a nod with Marine Sergeant Bootheby and his elegantly turned out side-party, then turned to go . . . down those fresh-sanded and tarred boarding battens, gripping virgin-white new man-ropes strung through the battens' outer ends, so brightly served with ornate Turk's-Head knots and bound with colourful red spun-yarn trim. Then into the waiting barge and step aft to take a seat on a thwart near the tillerman, among all his chests, kegs, crated cabin furnishings, and canvas-bound goodies.

A matching barge stood nearby, idling "off-and-on" under oars in slack water, also piled high with possessions; a barge in which stood a young man in a Commander's uniform, his boat-cloak thrown back to show his epaulet. Glowering at Lewrie for taking so long, making him wait to claim his new ship; a grim "thanks for nothing, you bastard," grimace on his phyz for making his leave-taking too personal, poisoning his arrival in the afterglow of that intensely emotional farewell. *A purse-mouthed, mean-lookin' "git,"* Lewrie thought, resenting the hell out of him for replacing him. For "stealing" *Jester* from him!

Were you smart, you'd have waited 'til this evening after I was long gone, Lewrie glowered back just as stonily, as his Coxswain, Andrews, and his servant, Aspinall, clambered into the barge.

"Shove off then," Lewrie pronounced. And the new captain was strok-ing forward to take his barge's place below the entry-port in an eyeblink. As he drew close though, as they passed, Lewrie thought he saw the new man begin to beam in appreciation, his face turned upwards, bearing that ineffable look of a man gone "arse over tit" in love . . . that wide-eyed crinkle of joy that all sailors bestow upon only those loveliest of vessels. The new man, most likely less-senior, had the presence of mind to doff

Lewrie a cautious salute with his hat before clawing eagerly at the man-ropes.

Eager to claim the hands, Lewrie smirked to himself; *lay hold of 'em before the vultures from the dockyard did!* With the new captain in his barge were a half-dozen seamen, just as eager to board her and continue their favouritism and seniority under their patron.

"Portsmouth Point, sir?" the tillerman enquired.

"Aye, Portsmouth Point," Lewrie glumly agreed, facing the town, un-able to bear the tweetle of bosun's calls welcoming her new captain.

"Ain't gonna like dot new cap'um, sah," Andrews commented. " 'E didn't give 'em time t'give ya yer presents proper-like."

"What presents?" Lewrie gloomed as the barge turned, the older wa-terman by her mast beginning to hoist her single lugsail.

"Dere's a letter, sah," Andrews told him, untying a canvas packet and handing it over. "Model o' de ship . . . and d'is, sah."

Lewrie read the letter quickly, coughing to cover his chagrin. Every man-jack had signed it or X'd his mark (except for Mr. Howse and LeGoff, of course), thanking him for being a tolerant, firm-but-fair captain; vowing, should they have the chance, they'd be glad to ship with him again; wishing that he didn't have to leave *Jester.* . . .

Lewrie squinted over that, feeling his eyes mist up as the barge sailed out of *Jester*'s shadow into bright sunlight. "Ah, hummm!" was all he could manage to say, clearing a prodigious lump in his throat.

"Ain' often po' sailormen *git* a good cap'um, sah," Andrews told him, showing him the ship model. It was about two feet long, as fine a rendering as any Admiralty model run up to present to the King himself, with *Jester*'s every detail precisely and meticulously reproduced, every line, brace, clew, slab, or buntline strung spider-thin aloft. *Months, it'd taken,* he thought . . . *started* before *Lisbon and his glad news?*

"Dey's 'is too, sah," Andrews offered.

A coin-silver tankard, pint-sized, engraved with a scroll of seashells and chain round its base and upper lip, with a profile sail-plan of a sloop of war in all her bounding glory, and a scroll-board claiming her to be HMS *Jester* engraved below her. There was a suggestion of the waves, a bois-terously erose dash at her waterline, inverted Vees about one side . . . and a pair of leaping dolphins, the enigmatic heads of two smiling seals, and a forearm stretched forth from the deeps ahead of her bows, wielding a sword as if pointing her way onward. Seals and a sea-god—a cryptic meaning known only to one who'd been there, 'board *that* ship, in *that* crew, and only during *that* commission.

"My, God, it's beautiful, it's . . ." Lewrie mumbled in appreciation.

"T'other side, sir." Aspinall winked. "Read *t'other* side."

He turned the tankard, so the handle was to the drinker's right, discovering a dedication which would ever face the drinker:

Presented To Commander Alan Lewrie, R.N.
Lucky Captain of a Lucky Ship
From a Grateful & Appreciative Ship's Crew
of HMS *Jester* 1794–1797

"Model got done aboard, sir," Aspinall revealed eagerly. "Cup, well . . .'member Bosun Cony's runs ashore once we anchored? Took up a donation from ev'ry hand, he did."

"And I spoiled the moment for 'em," Lewrie groaned. "Too hot t'flee 'fore I . . ."

He'd vowed he'd not look back, but he did, even while the other new man was reading himself in, shouting his orders so everyone would hear and understand, from taffrail to jib-boom tip.

". . . directly charging and commanding the officers and company belonging to the said sloop of war subordinate to you to behave themselves jointly and severally in their respective employments with all due respect and obedience unto you, their said captain . . . !"

The crew's attention was bound inboard, yet he stood, his head bare, raised the letter high in one hand, the silver tankard high in the other. A few men upon the starboard gangway spotted him, nudged each other, and attracted the surreptitious attention of more. They waved hats and hands below the bulwark, smiling fit to bust, so the new captain would not spot them.

And when the new man finished reading himself in, there came a thunderous—undeserved—cheer.

Ruined it for him, Lewrie thought, a silly ass's smile plastered on his phyz, but with tears coursing down his cheeks at last; *well, what of it? Just bugger him! And he'd better treat 'em right!*

CHAPTER TWO

*T*here came a second hard leave-taking for a sailor; standing atop Portsdown Hill as the overloaded diligence coach toiled up to the crest and the passengers, as usual, got down to walk the muddy track to ease the horse teams . . . to gaze back and down at the wide sweep of Spithead and the Solent, past the Isle of Wight, outwards to the flood of the Channel as the tide turned. The harbours, so full of warships, a *forest* of masts . . . and savouring his last noseful of kelp, fish, and salt breezes . . . as if saying farewell forever to a dying lover!

Andrews and his clerk, Padgett, went one direction for Anglesgreen aboard a stout dray laden with his possessions. Lewrie and his manservant, Aspinall, went another, for London in the thrice-daily "dilly" . . . for Admiralty and word of future employment. The wind, now a *land* breeze, heavy with springtime growth, with nurturing rains and turned-earth smells, stole the sea-scent and whistled cool over the crest of the hill . . . almost foreboding, he could conjure?

Lewrie marvelled, though, how much England had changed during his absence; roads, where before there had been foot paths, branching from the main London route and teeming with waggon traffic. The main road now become a congested highway, with cottages, row-houses, shops, and inns lining the sides, where cows or sheep had grazed before! Mysterious, fuming, bustling manufactures crammed with workers, amidst the clank and hiss of new-fangled steam machines that drove belts, pumped water and spun looms and lathes, reeking of burning coal and the musty wet-laundry odour of the steam itself!

Tiny crossroads hamlets had blossomed into villages, villages into towns, and London had sprawled even further afield, absorbing a host of settlements and farmland into its industrial, residential conurbations as though it had *leapt* southward, almost to Guildford, in the span of a single Dog Watch! Like an oil stain, progress had spread.

They passed through new suburbs of London, looking just as seedy as the old ones, Lewrie took wry note. Bricks and windowpanes were already soot-blackened, the gutters filled with cast-off trash, horse droppings, and the scurrying carters and street vendors, artificers or mechanics, children or housewives, looked pinched and off their feed; careworn, driven urgent to their business. Or, a tad vexed, Lewrie wondered? As good and warm as the people were dressed, there was little colour to them, as if the gods of war-driven industry were just a tad *too* demanding. And despite the evident signs of wealth, London proper struck him as dowdy, fretful, and gloomy. Even the ornate gardens and parks were tinged, the swans no-ticeably off-white, for all the fume of coal smoke, which he had not thought quite so thick the last time he had come up to the city of his birth in '93.

And once alit from the "rumble-tumble" coach, it began to rain, of course, a sooty, pelting drizzle that brought the garbage-middens to life, as redolent as the old Fleet Ditch before it had been paved over and filled, ages before. The rain only whipped the crowds to greater speed, not in-doors, and he and Aspinall had almost been run over half a dozen times by carts or coaches, by trotting vendors shouting cursory " 'Ave care, sir!" or "By yer leave . . . damn ye!" as Lewrie tried to regain his "land legs," his former canny knack for city navigation, and to stay *somewhat* clean whilst they searched for lodgings for himself, his servant, and the wicker-caged Toulon.

"No rooms, sir," the inn-keeper at Willis's Rooms, his favourite lodgings, told him sadly, "not even for an old customer."

"Nothing lavish, sir," Lewrie wheedled, after spending the last two hours of a late, wet afternoon plodding from one inn to another. This was the most expensive place he could recall, but it set a good table, and it was growing dark. "My man could even sleep rough on a settee if we have to." No matter what Aspinall had to say about it!

"Well, there is a second-floor chamber, sir, but . . ." The owner frowned, raising his eyebrows at the thought of a gentleman *and* a common body-servant sharing that chamber. He gave Aspinall a once-over, frowning even deeper. "Dear Lord, sir. Is that a *cat* you have with you? Bless me, sir . . . never take animals, no, sir. It's not . . ."

"Sir Whosis, back in '93, sir," Lewrie countered, "brought his favourite hounds . . . kept 'em in his rooms. Fed 'em at-table too, as I recall. No fuss, then. What would that single room be worth, sir?"

Lewrie set his purse on the counter of the bar in the public rooms, aching for an excuse to get off his feet, to sidle over to the cheery fire and dry off a bit, over a mulled rum or a brandy. That purse gave off a promising *chinking* sound of solid coin.

"Coin, sir?" the inn-keeper gasped of a sudden, his brows going skyward. "But *course*, sir . . . just paid off your ship, did ye tell me? Well . . . that'd be silver . . . or guineas, sir? Not merchant-issue shoddy?"

"Fortunate in prize-money, sir," Lewrie boasted, loosening the drawstrings and spilling out an assortment. "Austrian Maria Theresas . . . silver dollars. Some Italian 'tin.' Looks insubstantial, but it's silver. Shillings . . . and aye, gold guineas."

"Bless me, sir. You should see what I'm offered these days." The inn-keeper smiled. "Like this'un, sir. Spanish piece of eight . . . but with the King's profile over-stamped. Four shillings, nine pence, or five shillings tuppence, no one knows exactly. They *say*, sir"—the inn-keeper dropped into a very confidential whisper—"that 'the Bank of England, to make its dollars pass, stamped the head of a fool 'pon the neck of an ass,' ha, ha! Good silver and gold, well, it's a rare commodity these days, I assure you. Be the ruin of commerce."

Sure enough, the piece of eight he'd produced had over-struck a portly George III over the latest slack-jawed Bourbon King of the Dons! To speak that way 'bout the King, though . . . !

"Now, sir . . . shall we say, uhm . . . guinea the day for you and your man . . . *and,* uhmm, your cat yonder, sir?" the inn-keeper proposed. "Lodgings *and* food all found, Commander Lewrie."

Yikes, Lewrie thought, *it's bald-faced rape!*

"*Decent* room, is it?" Lewrie sighed, laying out two guineas for two days. "I've hopes to complete my business with Admiralty by Saturday . . . and depart for home, so we can be there for Easter Sunday services at the least."

"First-floor front, with a good fireplace and a window, sir," the inn-keeper assured him, now jovial as anything as he swept those precious gold guineas off the counter and into a pocket. "Bedchamber and small parlour in one, but there's a screen I could put up . . . and a cot I could fetch down from the garret for your man."

"That'd right fine, thankee, sir," Lewrie told him.

"I'll see your things up to the room, Commander Lewrie, and once you've settled in, do avail yourself of the public rooms, a drink or two before mealtime. And would puss there like a dish o' cream?"

Sponged clean of most of the street smuts, feet up in one chair and slouched in another, Lewrie did avail himself of the public rooms, near enough to the roaring fire to take the chill off, as the lodgers came back from their rounds of the city for the night. A large glass of warmed brandy lay between his paws, from which he sipped, pleased as all get-out that he'd found shelter. Right down to "heel-taps," at last, and waving for the serving girl to fetch him another.

"Here ye go, sir . . . four pence," she said, dropping him a wee curtsy and scraping up a shilling from the table-top. She returned a few coppers. *Four pence? For a lone glass o' brandy . . . ?*

"Wait a bit . . . what in Hades are these?" Lewrie puzzled. They were no copper coins *he'd* ever seen. Better made, actually, than most pennies, truer-round, and with sharp-milled edges. But claiming to be from an assortment of private firms.

"Merchant shoddy, sir . . ." the girl explained. "Tokens, really, is wot they calls 'em, but any sort o' coins is so dear these days . . . most folk accept 'em. I've half me wages in 'em, an' there's nought turn up their noses. Honest, sir. Willis's does th' best 'e can, but times is hard."

"She speaks true, sir . . . no fraud," an older gentleman informed him from closer to the fire. "This bloody war's the fault. The Chinee trade, and all our silver going to India and China?" He sneered.

"Very well," Lewrie nodded to the girl, accepting the imitations for real currency and slipping her a true ha'penny for service rendered.

"Been away too long, sir," Lewrie commented, cocking a brow at his interlocutor. "*Fightin'* this . . . bloody war."

"No business of ours, sir, what happens on the Continent, or what happens to Frogs, Dons, and Dagoes. Mean t'say, sir, what's our good English Channel for, hmm?"

"Long as those Frogs, Dons—perhaps even some of those Dagoes— have *navies*, sir"—Lewrie bristled—"it *is* our business! What do you think we did at Saint Vincent? Broke up one part of a combination with an eye for our invasion, sir. If not of England, then of Ireland. . . ."

"Ah, to defend ourselves, aye, sir!" the older fellow chirped most happily. "Ain't that right, Douglas?" he asked his partner at their table, a cherubic old country squire–ish sort. "I'd not be averse to a *million* pounds being spent on our *defence*, sir. But not a groat more should go to Austria, Prussia. . . . It's their problem, isn't it? So they should spend *their* treasure if they think they need a war against the French. Blockade the French, keep their navy reined back. Keep their armies from overseas adventure, aye, sir. But . . . that's as far as we ought go before the country's bankrupt. Emulate the words of Washington . . . first president of the United States, sir . . . when he warned, 'Beware of foreign entanglements.' "

"All very fine, sir"—Lewrie sniffed archly—"for a powerless and isolated nation 'cross the seas . . . too impoverished to *aspire* to an empire. But lookee here, sir . . . no matter which government France has, they've always hated us; we've always hated them. Give 'em licence to conquer the rest of Europe? Dragoon all Europe into their fold and they'll be across that Channel of ours and at our throats. And what's the eventual cost of that, hey?"

Damme, never heard *the like, and from an Englishman too!* Lewrie fumed. Was the man a bloody Quaker, too meek to raise a hand to guard his *own* throat? Or one of those "Rights of Man" Levellers?

"You're new-come, sir, I'll warrant," the cherubic-looking old fellow who went by Douglas pooh-poohed. "Back from our most expensive 'wooden walls,' hmm? You've not seen the suffering, sir. Nor felt it your-self. Thousands more Enclosure Acts, farmers thrown out of work or off the land . . . *industry*," he sneered, "dragooning thousands into the mines and mills, sir. High wages, aye, but high taxes too, so that no one may make the living one made three years past. Price of grains gone through the roof, yet farmers such as myself barely breaking even e'en in a bumper year! Taxed to death, we are. . . ."

"Hear, hear!" several other gentlemen growled in agreement.

"You'd trust to a French occupation . . . to lower your *taxes!*" Lewrie sneered aloud and was gratified to hear an even larger, more vociferous chorus of "Hear! Hears!" from those of the opposing camp.

"You malign me, sir!" the angelically white-maned Douglas said, rear-ing back and suddenly looking as fierce as an old but game Viking Ber-serker. "Never the French! Rather, a reforming of our . . ."

The first older gentleman laid a restraining, cautioning hand on his friend's coat sleeve. "You mistake our motive, sir."

"Nay, sir," Lewrie snickered. "I *meant* to malign you actually."

Which won him a rowdy round of cheers, the thumping of tankards or fists on the tables from the more patriotic topers. Lewrie had himself a deep draught from his fresh brandy in celebration, knowing that the old fellow could glare fierce but would never press to cross steel with him or "blaze" with pistols. He could be as nasty as he wished to be! It looked to be hellish-good sport to berate the pair of them as un-patriotic.

I'm off duty—an half-pay "civilian," for the nonce, he reminded himself; *no more "firm but fair"! Damme, I ain't been free to be me malicious old self in a month of Sundays!*

"You have your opinion, sir," the first man said, much subdued. "We have ours. Do you spend time ashore, you may change yours."

"I very much doubt it," Lewrie began. But they were leaving, the first gentleman almost shaking "Douglas" to force him to keep mum. They gathered their capes and hats from the "Abigail" by the door and departed for cheerier taverns.

His shot at amusement over, Lewrie took another sip, heaved up a shrug, and reached over to their table to snag the newspaper they'd aban-doned in their haste to depart.

Now this'll be a rare treat, he thought; *reading a newspaper which hadn't been smudged nigh-illegible by an hundred previous hands, one which wasn't water-stained, rat-gnawed, folded and crinkled to the fragility of a yellow onion peel. And containing information newer than a month past!*

"Ahem, gentlemen," one of the inn-keeper's assistants announced from the double-doors to the dining room. "We are now serving." Those doors were thrown open, and a heady steam wafted out, so tempting that Lewrie's mouth began to water. A first shot at home-cooking, a proper English meal—course after course of his old favourites, he hoped as he rose quickly. A glutton's delight to welcome him back to all which he'd fought for—a glad repast worthy of the Prodigal Son's return!

He crammed the newspaper into a side pocket of his coat, sprang into action, and beat several slower feeders into the dining room! At the first sight of that groaning sideboard, laden with roasts, steaks, chops, savoury fowl—and a pudding the size of a capstan head—Alan consigned the pleasures of political nattering quite out of his mind!

CHAPTER THREE

*W*artime hadn't thinned the Waiting Room, Lewrie noticed, once he had left his cloak with an attendant. No matter those hundred ships of the line, those hundred frigates, sloops, brigs, and such which required every officer still sound in wind and limb . . . there were *indeed* a horde of others waiting. Rear-Admirals and Commodores . . . rather old fellows no higher in seniority than the Blue Squadron, he imagined, though some might have slowly clambered up the seniority list to the Red . . . because they'd outlived their contemporaries. Some positively doddered! There were Post-Captains blessed with both epaulets, denoting more than three years had passed since their promotion and at least one active commission at sea. They . . . the most of 'em . . . looked healthy enough to sail on the King's business, including junior captains with only one epaulet worn on the right shoulder. A mixed bag, that lot; some spry, healthy, and young, pacing impatiently. Others who looked old enough to be their fathers, plucked by dire need from a sea of lieutenants at long last, those men who'd had no hope of command, of promotion, for they were the unfortunates who were ever at the wrong place at the wrong time, had no patronage or "interest," and had never been chosen to serve aboard ships where they could shine in the eyes of an influential man of flag rank.

The same could pretty much be said for men of his own grade, with the epaulet on the left shoulder—the Commanders in the room. They either were too young to be so fortunate or looked too old and worn-out for the rank, the ones who'd go down on their knees and thank God for a "bloody war or a sickly season," as the old mess-toast went.

He had no eye for the many hopeful lieutenants and midshipmen in the Waiting Room. *The Devil with 'em*, he thought, *competition!* A lap or two about the room, looking for a seat, revealed no officer of his personal acquaintance.

Either the good, he thought sourly, or *the twit-like!*

The twits he'd served, or served *with*, he suspected, were well-connected twits and would be at sea that instant. The good men he'd known *should* be. He took that as a hopeful omen; that either way he was regarded by Admiralty—twit or good'un—he'd soon receive one more active-duty commission and not end up cooling his heels in here with the hopeless!

"Ah, Commander Lewrie, do come in, sir," the strange new secretary offered. *Not too cheerful, considering*, Lewrie thought; but he'd not sounded threatening either. "Evan Nepean, sir, First Secretary."

"Your servant, Mister Nepean," Lewrie cooed, as the door was shut behind him. Nepean waved him to a wing-back chair before a desk, then took a seat behind it, spreading his coat-tails carefully before he sat down. He was a much younger man than either old Phillip Stephens, or his deputy, Jackson, had been. Cultured, slim, and rapier-like, and togged out most nattily in the latest civilian style. Something about him, though, that arch look perhaps, that wryly observant glare, made Lewrie think he wasn't a man he'd exactly put his trust in.

"Well, well, sir," Nepean drawled, in a lofty, nasal accent of the titled and powerful. "So *you* are the infamous Lewrie." He smiled, looking at Lewrie intently over steepled fingers.

"Depending on which 'infamous' you had in mind, Mister Nepean," Lewrie most carefully replied, shifting from one buttock to the other, crossing his legs to guard his "nutmegs." *Damme, what'd he heard?*

"Why, 'the Ram-Cat,' sir," Nepean simpered, "the successful and 'lucky' Lewrie. Toulon, Genoa . . . of the recently promoted Rear-Admiral Nelson's squadron. The one well-known of—and dare I say it, sir, as highly commended by—a certain ah . . . audacious and unconventional gentleman from the Foreign Office? The Far East 'tween the wars. A certain Frenchman by name of Choundas? There and, of late, ashore near Genoa? I speak of *that* Commander Lewrie, sir."

"Ah!" Lewrie gawped. "Well, that!" He pretended to preen with at least a shred of becoming modesty. Thankful they didn't keep files on the *other* part of "infamous." "Nothing, really . . . just . . ."

"Some rather, uhm . . . *sub rosa* activities this past year in the Adriatic?" Nepean interrupted. "I've letters on file, hmmm . . ." Nepean thumbed through a short stack of correspondence. "Sir Malcom Shockley the M.P. . . . the millionaire. Lord, what a horrid word, do you not believe? Thankfully, a firm supporter of our faction and of the Prime Minister. One from Lord Peter Rushton *in* Lords. Though not known for anything much . . . still, full of praise for your nautical quality. At least his first address to the House of Lords could be construed as actually making sense—which is more than one may expect from one of that august body, so . . ."

Politics, again! Lewrie groaned to himself; *damme.* It had even crept into Admiralty, with this new man Evan Nepean thinking him brave because he was Tory and was spoken for by ones who were Tory! *Allied with William Pitt the Younger, am I? Wouldn't know him from Adam if he crawled up and bit me on the ankle! Nor the old Whig, Fox, either!*

Well, call this old dog any good name ye wish 'long as it puts me in command of a new ship! he decided, nodding sagaciously yet committing himself to nothing.

"More to the point, though, Commander Lewrie," Nepean sobered from his bout of hero-worship, becoming all business-like, "are your good 'characters' from Captain Thomas Charlton. And from Lord Saint Vincent . . . a new investiture; you wouldn't have heard of it yet. From Admiral Sir John Jervis, now made Earl."

"Good for him, sir," Lewrie crowed suddenly. "His ennoblement, rather." Yet wondering; *When the blazes did he ever take time to think good o' me?*

"Rather a furor in the Fleet, after The Glorious First of June, Commander Lewrie," Nepean scowled. "Admiral Howe allowing his flag captain, Sir Roger Curtis, to, ah . . . 'anoint' by mentioning only those few captains of line-of-battle ships present for honours whom he himself thought worthy . . . those who'd closed yardarm-to-yardarm to take their foe as prizes. For the rest who fought well, nothing. A medal struck, but given only to those fortunate few."

"Excuse me, sir, but . . . ?" Lewrie puzzled. "Whilst in Lisbon, in the careenage, I read a London paper and Admiral Jervis's report made no mention of anyone at all. So you're saying . . . ?"

"A taciturn man is the new Earl Saint Vincent, Commander, as I'm mortal certain you've already discovered." Nepean chuckled, shuffling one pile of papers aside and drawing out a single slim folder to open. "Yet he would not ever make the same mistake. Would never create even more jealousies among his officers. He sent Captain Robert Calder home with his dispatches . . . which glad arrival soon after resulted in Captain Calder being knighted and promoted. No, 'Old Jarvy,' as I believe the men of the Fleet are wont to call him, waited to write a more complete list and report of the action to the First Lord Earl Spencer, *after* he'd had time to assess things, to sort them out. This time, every captain of every ship-of-the-line present is to be honoured. Given a medal commemorating the battle too."

"I see, sir." Lewrie nodded again, still striving for "sagacity" but more than a little puzzled by this long, prosing prologue. "Then, again . . . good for 'Old Jarvy,' the Earl Saint Vincent, that is."

"*You,* sir, more to the point at hand, were cited in that letter to the First Lord," Nepean said with a smirk, very much like "I know something *you* don't know!"

"Ah? Sir?" Lewrie gulped, expectations rising.

"For rushing . . . let me see, how did he phrase it? Ah! 'For his intrepidity and alacrity at rushing to support HMS *Captain,* his fear-nought daring in engaging the enemy battle-line in complete disregard for the custom and usage of repeating frigates, at such hopeless odds in those minutes before he could hope for reinforcement or succour, I most respectfully request of your Lordship that Commander Alan Lewrie of the *Jester* sloop be included in the list of those to be honoured.' "

"Ah?" Lewrie gargled. "Mean t'say . . . *ah,* sir! Well . . . !"

"The only officer below 'post' rank to be so named, Commander Lewrie. Breaking away from the line as you did, in trusty and loyal . . . and dare I say, *heroic* fashion in support of your old squadron commander,

Horatio Nelson! 'Spite of all the rules to the contrary, the risk of court martial and infamy, well, sir! Well, well!" Nepean cried, sounding for a moment almost fawning in his appreciation.

"Well, sir, it was . . ." Lewrie began, fighting the urge to bark like a pack of seals at such an absurd characterisation.

Pushed *me out o' line, he did!* Ordered . . . *kickin' an' screamin'!*

"In spite of the volume of work still waiting, you will do me the honour of coming with me, Commander Lewrie," Nepean bade, motioning towards the door in the far wall, the one that led to the Board Room!

A discreet knock, a muffled bidding to enter, and they were in the presence of the First Lord of The Admiralty, George John, the Earl Spencer, a fairly tall and distinguished-looking fellow of middling, uncertain age. There followed some cooing remarks which Lewrie could never quite recall for the heady rush of blood in his ears. He would recall, however, the moment the medal was slipped over his head. Long and broad white satin riband, edged in blue, which passed through the oval of a large-ish gold medal—finely milled and rope-chained about its diameter, a scene of Victory standing on the prow of a galley and placing a laurel wreath on the brow of a triumphant Britannia.

". . . under the coat collar, over the waist-coat, so the medal will hang just above the pit of your stomach, sir," Alan thought he heard the Earl Spencer instruct. "First, Sir Robert Calder, now you, Commander Lewrie . . . the only ones I will have the honour to personally bestow. The rest are to be sent on to the Fleet, now blockading Cadiz, so that the Earl Saint Vincent may award them."

"Then I'm doubly honoured, milord," Lewrie murmured, still not quite featuring this was happening. This was fame! This was *glory* . . . beyond his wildest fantasies! Within a quim-hair of being knighted!

God, he thought; *I can dine out on this*, free, *for years!*

". . . suitable period of leave, then . . . will there be something open, Mister Nepean?" Earl Spencer enquired, as Lewrie swam his way back to the here-and-now.

"Several vessels will, I am certain, be coming open, milord," Nepean purred back. "Though none for several weeks, as I recall."

"There you are, then, good sir. Your few weeks of shore leave, Commander Lewrie." Earl Spencer beamed. "You reside where, sir?"

"A . . . Anglesgreen, milord. Just down the road past Guildford, in Surrey," he replied, his mind gibbering. *Bloody Hell, they goin' t'*promote *me into the bargain?*

"Family estates, sir?"

"Oh, *erm* . . . milord. Near my wife's relations," he admitted.

"Good huntin' country, Surrey," Spencer prosed on. "Wide open and rolling. Lovely riding. Which hunt do you follow, sir?"

"Only the local, sir. Sir Romney Embleton . . . baronet," Lewrie related, glad he could elide his way 'round how often he'd been invited to ride with them since he and Caroline had wed in '86. Sum total of zero, it was, since he'd shamed Sir Romney's otter-jawed, lack-wit son, Harry. Damn' near broke his nose, in point of fact! He could at the least *sound* like he still "Yoicks, tally-hoed" after foxes!

"Well, my regards to your wife and family, Commander Lewrie," the First Lord chuckled. "And do you take joy of a few weeks ashore. Mind, now . . . don't fall off anything and lame yourself. We expect a great deal of you once you're back in Navy harness, ha!"

"I shan't, and thankee most kindly, milord! *Most* kindly!" he babbled on his way out, with Evan Nepean taking hold of his elbow to steer him away before he said something lunatick.

"My Lord, that was . . . !" Lewrie marvelled, back in the privacy of Nepean's adjoining offices.

"Quite," Nepean said, with a firm nod, though sounding much less appreciative than he had before. "Well then, sir . . . I will turn all the official correspondence from your commission over to the junior clerks, though I don't imagine . . . after a thorough 'scouring' by Vice-Admiral Sir Peter Parker's staff at Portsmouth, that there's anything serious amiss to quibble over. My congratulations again, Commander Lewrie," he said, extending his hand for a quick shake. "I note that you *are* owing eleven pounds, two shillings, six pence. And there is the matter of your official certificate for your medal. That will be another two shillings, six pence. Do you prefer we may deduct the total from the pay certificate owing you, sir. Or you may deposit the sum with my under-clerk, then see the Pay Office superintendent, get your chit, and be on your way home."

Nepean was looking at his mantel clock whilst he said all that, no matter his hearty *bonhomie;* he'd done his duty, and it was time for him to take up others, and Lewrie's presence was a time-waster. Which made Lewrie all but snort with cynical amusement.

"I'll just pay your clerk, Mister Nepean," he drawled, with one brow up and a quirky smile on his face. "And damme if it ain't one o' the cheapest ways ever I heard of to get a medal. Stap me . . . I should have thought o' this sooner."

"Erm . . . yayss," Nepean purred back, just as chary of Lewrie of a sudden as Lewrie was of him. "Well, goodbye, Commander Lewrie. We will be in touch by post, hmmm . . . ?" And he chivvied Lewrie out of his offices into the care of an underling before Lewrie could utter another sound. The underling led him without a word to the aforementioned clerk, far down the hallway.

Lewrie felt like stopping dead in his tracks, or going back into Nepean's office, concerned about the sheaf of penny tracts which had been hidden in his borrowed newspaper the previous evening. All sorts of rabble-rousing Republican cant: no more King, annually elected Parliaments, votes for the Common Man. What rot! But given his unfortunate penchant for shooting off his mouth, as he just had, of indulging his smarmy wit . . . he didn't think he'd get another welcome. Or a bit more of Nepean's time of day.

He dug into his purse and paid on the nail, then waited for his slowly penned receipt for the sum owing. The clerk then opened a tin cash-box, and proceeded to begin counting out a stack of ornately made papers, muttering to himself and referring to a thick ledger.

"Damme, what are those, then?" Lewrie was forced to ask.

"This is the balance of your pay owing you, sir," the prim old fellow intoned most officiously. "Less advances previously paid out . . ."

"Looks like bum-fodder," Lewrie carped.

"Bank notes, sir"—the clerk tensed—"issued by the Bank of England are *hardly*, uhm . . . that which you just described, sir! They are perfectly good, legal tender throughout the realm, sir! There *is* the shortage of specie to consider, after all! They come in various denominations, you should note, sir . . . differing colours and such for a one- or two-pound note, the five, ten, and twenty. You *will* come across the odd fraud, issued by forgers or private or provincial banks . . . those which have not gone under the past two years, sir. Only these notes are legitimate, so you should give any received in exchange the closest inspection. And, of course, there are none *smaller* than a one pound."

"And I'm to be paid in these, am I? My crew, too, when it comes their due? 'Twill be a wonder do they not riot over 'em!"

"I fear so, Commander. But times are so terribly hard."

"Christ, what's the country comin' to?" he griped, stuffing the neat pile of bills into his coat pockets—they surely wouldn't go in a proper coin-purse!—and wondering how he'd get to Coutts's Bank to deposit them without losing half to a brisk breeze.

"One may only wonder, Commander . . . wonder, indeed!" that clerk lowed, like a mournful bovine.

CHAPTER FOUR

*W**hat a reassuring sameness and familiarity*, Lewrie thought, all but squirming with anticipation as his hired coach swept past the stone ruins of the Norman or Saxon castle at the edge of Sir Romney Embleton's lands, mossy old St. George's Church hard by the eastern bridge, then Anglesgreen itself. "Damme, more change!" he grumbled to himself, as he beheld a whole new row of houses on the south side of the stream, the clutch of new buildings 'round the Red Swan Inn, how the ancient Old Ploughman tavern had taken down a row-house to make a side garden for casual drinkers or bowlers. There was a *third* bridge . . . ! He clattered past quickly, 'round the curve of the Red Swan, onto the newly graveled road which forked off north, alongside Chiswick lands—taking the turning, he shouted to the coachman—onto a primeval, rutted goat track.

Trust Uncle Phineas Chiswick not to waste a single farthing for pea gravel on his private lane; just like the miserly old fart!

Lewrie sat up straighter, shifting from the larboard window to the starboard, for a first, tantalizing glimpse of his own home! "God!" he breathed in expectation.

There was a last turning between two (new) grey-brick pillars, onto his own lane, which *was* proper-gravelled and drained, wide enough for two coaches to pass, and lined with far set back sapling oaks. In twenty-five years, he'd have the makings of a drive found only on regal estates, he marvelled, beaming at Caroline's handiwork and forethought.

There was the house . . . !

The lane became a circular drive about an immense informal garden, tall and lush with flowers . . . what sort Lewrie wasn't quite sure, but they were blue, pink, white, pale yellow, rather pretty, uhm . . . *somethings,* he thought, a real English country garden that would bloom colourful from March 'til November. Caroline's work, that, and her green thumb.

There had been time for ivy (he was *fairly* sure he knew ivy when he saw it) to lay tentative creepers on the house front, about the imitation Palladian stucco central portal, and the homey grey brick. New white urns sat on either side of the portal as . . . *jardinieres,* he puzzled? Big as wash-tubs! Some yews and hollies to frame them between the windows—aye, definitely recognisable yews and hollies.

His hollies, his house, his house . . . *his* door! It was a glossy dark-blue, with his silvery Venetian–brass lion door-knocker prominent at its cen-tre . . . and that door was opening . . .

He was out of the coach before the postillion could get down to lower the metal step for him, knocking his hat off in the process, and galloping to enfold the brood which erupted from the house.

"Good God, Hugh!" he cried. "My, boy, my boy!" he whooped, as he lifted him off his feet. "I'm home! Gad, yer gettin' heavy as any man. Sewallis!" he said, lowering the wildly exuberant and squirming Hugh, to fling his arms about his eldest, who, for once, came into his arms with something akin to enthusiasm to embrace him. Ten, he was by then, and sprouted like a weed, already as tall as Lewrie's chin!

"God, you're a sight for sore eyes, Sewallis. Grown so . . . !"

"Welcome home, Father," Sewallis said, teared up and with his lower lip trembling, but clinging to some shred of his sober stoicism. "We've missed you so."

"Yay, you're back, you're back!" Hugh crowed, so excited that he was capering sidewise like a cross-gaited pony. "Did you kill lots of Frenchmen? Did you sink a lot of ships? What'd you bring us? Ooh, what's this . . . a *medal!* Hurrah, did you get it from the *King?*"

"Boys . . . my God!" He shuddered, hugging them close to either side of him. "And little Charlotte?" He knelt down, tears in his eyes, as he beheld a perfectly adorable wee girl-child, no longer a squawling chub, but a miniature young lady so like her mother, with her mother's radiant amber-hazel eyes and spider-web fine, light-brown hair, long and bound into a loose tail beneath a missish little mob-cap. "When I left, you were still in swaddles. Lord, is it you, Charlotte?"

She hung back, a tad leery of him, a coy finger tugging at one corner of her pert little mouth . . . staring at him wide-eyed, like at a bad bargain. She came within grasping range only at his coaxing.

"Are you *really* my daddy?" she asked of a sudden, sounding just a bit cross and hiding her pudgy little hands in the folds of her fully flounced little sack gown.

"Well, o' *course* I am, Charlotte," he assured her, a tad put off. "Just been away too long, that's all. Of course I am."

As if to say, "Well, that's alright then," she relented, rushed to reward him with such a radiant and flirtatious smile, and flung her arms 'round his neck. He picked her up and stood, not knowing quite what to do with such a delicate packet, as she at last giggled aloud and gave him a peck on the cheek.

Daughters, he thought ruefully, as he returned the favour upon both her cheeks; *boys, now . . . them I can understand! Hell, I was one!*

"Did you like the doll I sent you from Venice?" he asked her, as he paced about in a circle to admire her—now that she was satisfied that they were kin. "Did you get it . . . all safe and sound?"

"Ooh, Daddy, *yess!*" she squealed with delight. "Did you bring me another?"

"Alan!" From the doorway.

He spun about to face her. Caroline! He roared her name in joy. It *had* been three long years; so long he'd almost forgotten what she looked like, even with a miniature portrait hanging in his cabins, almost forgotten what she sounded like.

Hugh was prancing about, wearing his gold-laced hat. Sewallis was being his ever-helpful self, dragging a heavy valise towards the entry. Yet there was his wife, and he could have trampled them all in the dust in his haste to hold her.

She came to him with the same haste, and charming little Charlotte had to fend for herself as Lewrie lowered her to the ground, instantly forgotten, to free his arms for Caroline.

Fierce as a lioness, her arms were about his neck as he lifted her from her toes. Fierce and needy as a starving lion was he, were both of them, as their lips met. She was beaming, weeping, her tears hot on his cheeks and his neck as he held her, pressing her to him and re-discovering her taut, slim firmness, and the sweetly softer curves of her hips, her belly against his, the press of her breasts . . . !

"God, it's so *good* to be home!" Lewrie crowed at the skies as he lowered her, slid his hands down to grasp hers, and leaned back to re-gard her. Her hair was down, like Charlotte's, long, lustrous, and so fine-spun and loosely bound back in an almost girlish welcome, instead of a proper "goody" housewife's starched mob-cap. Clean, bright-shining . . . and sweet-smelling of her trademark citrony, flowery Hungary Water. Her eyes, her *merry* eyes! With the riant folds below them which waxed when she was happy . . . her mouth and lips, so widely spread in joy. . . .

Damme, a touch o' grey? he puzzled at the sight of her temples; *she ain't . . . I ain't . . . mean t'say, we ain't that old yet, surely . . . ?*

Crow's feet! *Merry*-lookin' crow's feet, he corrected himself instantly. He felt her hands, so spare and slim, looked at her from head-to-toe (smiling all the while, mind), and took in how spare her forearms were below the lacy froth trim at her elbows—a definite softening of her formerly firm flesh, a falling away from the bone beneath. . . .

Ah, but she did have the damn' fever, couple o' years ago, now didn't she? he assured himself; *that'd put a few years on anybody!*

He let go her hands and stepped forward to hold her close once more, to nuzzle at her neck, drink deep of her aroma, and stroke her back. "So damn' good t'be home! With such a lovely wife t'greet me! Swear t'Christ, Caroline . . . you're even lovelier than before!" Lewrie almost (but not quite) lied.

"Alan, I've missed you so!" she whispered in his ear. "Three *long* years! I'm sorry, I was abovestairs . . . hoping you'd come today. Preparing, should you . . . ?" She laughed softly.

"And a fine piece o' preparin' you've done, my dear," he told her. "Turned out like Sunday Divisions. Fair as morning . . ."

Here now, don't trowel *it on,* he chid himself; *well—hang it—do! She's a woman, ain't she? You* can't *pay enough compliments!*

They stood back from each other again, gazing fondly.

"Been dyin' t'be away from Portsmouth, London . . . achin'!"—Alan chuckled—"t'be with you . . . see your sweet, angel's face."

She teared up again. But she was smiling fit to bust.

"Love what you've done with the house, the drive, and all. And this fine round garden! What a splendid sight," he prated on. "I'd wager it's a fine thing to clap eyes on first thing of a morning . . . from our chambers, hmm? Or watch the dusk gather . . . ?" He leered.

"Mummy, see Daddy's medal!" Hugh prompted. "For killing ever so many Frogs!"

"Frenchmen, Hugh dear," Caroline automatically corrected.

"For killing Frenchmen then," Hugh amended.

"Not so polite to say 'round dear Sophie though, is it, Hugh?" Caroline instructed. "You must think of what might hurt people by the words you say . . . or the topics you mention, hmm?"

"It's alright, Hugh. I got this for fighting Spaniards." Alan winked. "The one for Frogs is to come by post."

"Hurray!" Hugh piped, and even Sewallis sounded glad.

"Let's go inside, shall we?" Lewrie suggested. "I'm fair dry, *and* a tad peckish. That coach ride . . . let me but park my fundament in my favorite wing-chair. See if it awakens! Oh, Caroline, this is my steward, Aspinall. And his burden . . . that's Toulon."

"Ma'am," Aspinall said, doffing his hat and making a shy "leg."

"Mister Aspinall," Caroline replied, with a regal incline of her head and a warm smile of welcome. "My husband has written of you so often. It will be quite the sailors' rendezvous here; you, Mister Padgett, and Andrews, for a time. I hope you take joy of your stay here."

"Lordy, I hope not, Mistress," Aspinall said, making a jape in his slow, shy way, "but . . . a sailors' rendezvous is where the Impress Gang gathers 'fore they goes out t'kidnap unwary sailormen."

"Let's call it 'Fiddler's Green,' then." Lewrie laughed out loud. "Free-flowin' rum, beer, and wine; music 'round the clock; and never a groat does the publican demand."

"Amen to that, Cap'um Lewrie." Aspinall smiled. "I'll be yer burden just 'til Monday, though, ma'am. Me and Padgett . . . we thought t'go back up t'London for a piece. Me mum an' dad's there . . . and Ma's doin' poorly. 'Til Cap'um Lewrie gets a new ship, ma'am."

"A new ship, yes . . . I see." Caroline frowned, turning to Alan for confirmation with a vexed, worrisome look. Complete with that vertical exclamation point wrinkled 'twixt her brows. "Do they say . . . ?"

"Oh, not for weeks, I'm bound, dearest," Lewrie hastened to assure her. "Nigh on a month, perhaps. The First Lord, Earl Spencer, to my face told me I was due a spell of shore leave."

"Daddy's new kitty?" Charlotte exclaimed, going to peer close into the wicker cage. "Ooh, I want to hold him!"

"I wouldn't, young miss," Aspinall cautioned. "He's a terror when he's upset. An' the coach ride didn't set him well."

"Aye, Charlotte, leave him be, for a while, there's a good chub."

"But, Daddy . . . !" the wee'un said, stamping an imperious foot.

"Let's go in," Lewrie said again. "I'm dying to see what you've done with the place. All those improvements you wrote of. . . ."

The formal salon was now furnished in light, airy fabrics, homey cherry or walnut settees, and such; the larger dining room was furnished as well. In the entry hall, those red-lacquered Venetian *bombe* commodes that Clotworthy Chute had "obtained" (how, he'd prefer never to know!) flanked the carpeted stairs, bearing coin-silver candelabras.

"Gawd, it's magnificent, Caroline!" He breathed in awe, as she preened proudly; a visitor might think the Lewries settled and financially secure for ages. More to the point, possessed of good taste all that age, which was more than could be said for even titled households, who equated cost with instant elegance, no matter how garish.

Toulon was making unsettled rumbling, hissing noises as Aspinall set his cage down in the entry hall beside the luggage. Wee Charlotte was down on her knees, poking and peeking.

"Best we feed him quick so he doesn't get it in his head to run outside and get lost," Lewrie suggested. " 'Fore he runs afoul of those setters Sewallis is so proud of, hey, Sewallis?"

He looked at his eldest son, remembering that Sewallis had been half terrified of his old cat, William Pitt, before he'd passed over.

Well, chary *of him* Lewrie amended to himself, being charitable.

Sewallis shared a look with him, glad that he'd remembered his dogs—

though he looked more than cool to the idea of a new cat about the place. He shrugged as if it were no matter, yet . . .

Aspinall gently moved Charlotte out of the way and opened the cage. Toulon bounded out, uttering a wary, confused trill, then leapt for the parlour, where he immediately slunk under a settee to fuss.

"Oh, come and see the morning room!" Caroline enthused, as she took Lewrie by the hand to lead him from one wonder to the next. "That particoloured fabric you sent me, darling . . . two bolts were just enough. See? *Much* too sheer for dress material, not in England at any rate. Heavens, do Venetian ladies strut about *that* undressed?"

Aye, they do, Lewrie secretly smirked; *an' a damn' fine show they were too!*

". . . drape this one large window. What do you think?"

He was a bit disappointed. He'd intended that she run up a gown from the fabric—or, as he'd most lasciviously hinted in his letter which had accompanied it, a sheer bed-gown and dressing robe? In his heart-of-hearts fantasy, he'd have loved to *see* her through both thin layers, every sweet inch of her flame-draped by the subtle, marbley waves of umber, peach, ochre, and burgundy, like one of Lady Emma Hamilton's most pornographic "Attitudes"!

Now that cloth made bright, cheerful drapes for the window in their smaller dining room, where they usually ate *en famille*, without houseguests. Caroline had coordinated plush, ochre velvet overdrapes, using the sheer material as gauzy inner drapes, and had tablecloth and napery of peach, with the other colours picked out here and there in the paintings' frames, some fresh paint on the chair rail, but . . . It wasn't the use he'd wished.

"Here, kitty-kitty!" He could hear Charlotte still coaxing in the salon, and a faint carp from Toulon as he was chivvied from pillar to post in search of a new hidey-hole in a strange, threatening house.

"Charlotte, leave the cat be!" Lewrie called over his shoulder, wearing a supposedly pleased smile of appreciation on his phyz for the drapes. "He's not used to you, and he wants to be left in peace!"

He said it in an exasperated, out-of-his-depth semblance of his best quarterdeck voice, the one he'd use on slow brace-tenders. Which brought forth a whine from Charlotte as she began to blub up, to be so loudly chastised.

"Alan, really . . ." Caroline gently chid.

"Don't want her eat' half-alive, that's all, dearest," Lewrie tried to quibble. "Aye, they're fetchin' as Hell, aren't they, these drapes? Whatever was I thinkin' . . . that you'd make a gown of it, in Anglesgreen, and all . . ."

"Oh, do come out, kitty . . . *Owwww!* Mummy!" was the shriek.

Rrrrowww! It could have been fright; it could have been a glad victory cry. Lewrie could see, once he'd turned his head, his cat making a dash for the stairs, a black-white streak nigh flat to the floor and his legs churning like a Naples centipede. There went another streak in pale blue moire satin and white lace, as Caroline tore off to comfort her "precious little girl." Left with the boys, Lewrie looked over to see Hugh pursing his mouth to blow a fart-like sound with his lips and rolling his eyes. Evidently, Charlotte's curiosity, and the teary result, wasn't exactly a new thing in their house. And Sewallis surprised him with a world-weary, almost adult sigh of exasperation. And a high-pitched "Hmmpph!" or "Tittch!"

"Girls," Lewrie agreed, hands behind his back, and tipping them both a conspiratorial wink. "They *do* take a power o' gettin' used to."

Lewrie figured he'd done enough damage indoors for the nonce. It was time to trot, 'til domestic "bliss" was re-established.

"How's your pony farin', lads? And, Sewallis, where're those dogs? Does your mother ever let 'em in the house?"

"Uhm, no . . . only when they were pups." Sewallis brightened. "We leave them part of the old coach-house. Do you want to see them? Now?"

"Aye, I do. You give your brother, Hugh, one too?" Lewrie joshed, leading them out through the kitchens.

"We share," Sewallis replied most primly.

"No, we don't. They're all his. Don't want a dog anyway. Want a fox kit. Or an otter!" Hugh grumped.

"No you don't, Hugh, not 'round my dogs. Why, they'd tear an otter or a fox to pieces," Sewallis harshly countered as they emerged in the sunshine to walk the old brick path between the kitchen garden and the flower garden. Bustling, careless of where they put their feet, three "men" striving to walk side-by-side . . . or lead and dominate.

"You'd sic them on 'em," Hugh groused.

"They're beastly . . . pests and nuisances," Sewallis snapped back. "Would *not*, but . . . they're ratty . . . ugly!"

"They're not; they're not!" Hugh shouted, in full cry by then. "They're pretty! So red and fluffy . . . or so sleek. An otter could be a playmate, slide into the creek with me . . ."

"Oh, wager yer mother'd love you slidin' down mud into creeks," Lewrie scoffed, ruffling Hugh's hair.

"He does already, and Mummy *doesn't* like it. He *knows*, but . . ."

"Boys," Lewrie cautioned. Away so long, he hadn't known they *could* be at each other's throats. And within a quarter-hour of his return too! And where'd prim little Sewallis, within a quim-hair of being dour as a parson, find bottom enough to boss Hugh about? Or try to anyway. Though Hugh was only eight, he was more than ready for a scrap to the knife-hilt! "Lookee here, lads . . . let's not you quarrel . . . my first day home, at any rate. Christ, you two go at each other like this *all* the time?"

"I'm sorry, Father," Sewallis muttered, much abashed.

"Well, he started it . . ."

"Ahem?" Lewrie barked, glaring.

"I know where there's an earth, where there's a mother fox, Daddy," Hugh wheedled. "And I've seen otters in the creek, up on Grandfather's new land. By the old tower? We could ride up . . . oh, once I show you them, *you'd* let me have a . . ."

There came a clatter of hooves from the farm lane which straggled off between the new brick barn and the old wattle-and-daub one they had turned into a coach-house. Coming into the stableyard, past their white-railed paddock where the children's pony trotted in excitement . . .

"*Grandfather* said I could have one, so . . ." Hugh prattled on.

Lewrie sighed. Rather heavily, it must be noted.

For here came two riders, back from a morning canter over their modest acreage, drawing the pony to extend his head over the railings and whicker at them, drawing a pack of spotted setters from the older barn, jog-trotting and yipping, with their tails lashing most gaily.

In the lead was a female . . . his ward since Toulon fell in '93, the Vicomtesse Sophie de Maubeuge, last of her noble line. No longer a frail, tremulous waif, he noted. She rode with an easy confidence, beaming a smile at him . . . at the world in general . . . and over her back to the second rider. No longer a delicate little fifteen-year-old, new-come from a convent, Sophie had turned into a spritely eighteen-year-old beauty, with rich red-auburn hair glowing in the spring sunshine, her green eyes alight with an impatient, girlish delight.

Astern, though . . . in the full fig of his regimentals from the old 19th Native Infantry of the East India Company army, was his own father, . . . Sir Hugo Saint George Willoughby. *Brigadier* Sir Hugo!

"Haw, the house! Haw, the new-come!" his father cried, waving his egret-feathered, heavily gold-laced cocked hat in the air. "Alan, my boy! Home at last! Give ye joy!"

"Mademeoiselle Sophie . . . *enchanté!*" Lewrie called out as she rode up to him.

"Commander Lewrie, *enchanté, aussi.*" She laughed, as he offered to take her reins and a hand to steady her. She swung off of her side-saddle, slipped her stirrup-foot, to jump-slide to the ground as graceful as a landing dove, almost squealing with glee. "You are home at last, *m'sieur. La,* the house has been on the pins and needles for the first sign of your coming. Welcome home, good sir! Welcome home!"

He embraced her, accepted a chaste peck on his cheek.

Three years has done her wonders, he thought. When he'd left, there'd been a girl bereft of fortune, title, family, her intended, and his own family, so sunk in grief that she could barely raise her voice above a mournful whisper, and possessed of the most fractured English. Now, though . . . but for a lilt, a turn of phrase, there was a girl who had the confidence, the poise and grace, and the easy, unaffected joy of any country-raised young English lady of the squirearchy who never had known any other style of living, or country.

The groomsman, a new face to Lewrie after the old one, Bodkins, was taking the reins from him, reaching out for the reins of the other horse. Then down sprang his father.

Shorter than he'd remembered from the Far East. *How odd,* Lewrie thought. White-haired now, thinner on top. Liver-spotted, by a dissolute youth. Damme, a dissolute bloody *life!* Yet still erect as a gun's ramrod, with the Damme-Boy twinkle of old in his eyes.

"My boy! My dearest boy!" Sir Hugo crowded, offering his arms for a paternal hug. "Ten damn' years it's been! Come ye here!"

And a very merry hello t'you too, Lewrie thought, with a weary sigh; *you wicked old fart!* He plastered a glad grin on his countenance and suffered to be embraced. Embraced his father in return, wondering all the while if Sir Hugo's elation to see him was a ruse . . . that he secretly was poor as a church-mouse, and this was the last port of refuge for a scoundrel.

Damme, never knew him t'be gladsome . . .'cept when he was needy o' something! Lewrie thought, as he was pounded on the back most heartily.

"Good to see you too, Father. Damn' glad," he lied, *rather well,* he thought. But he'd had a lifetime of practice by then.

CHAPTER FIVE

*T*he next few days were heaven, Lewrie thought. For starters, he got introduced to the dogs so they would not think of him as an entree whenever he wished to walk outside about his own lands. He re-met the pony (without getting nipped), remade acquaintance with his favourite horse, Anson, which whickered in glee to see him once again. They ate in the new, large dining room that night, in the light of those dolphin-and-trident, silvery-brass candelabras he'd bought in Venice before the hurried evacuation of the Adriatic, then spent a lively evening in the salon, opening the latest gifts for the children, for Caroline and Sophie, from Lisbon. Sipping on a fruity, nutty sherry he'd found in-cask from Oporto too. They'd played some tunes, Caroline to her flute, Sophie to the harpsichord, and he on his "tin-whistle" flageolet, and finally getting a compliment or two on how much he'd improved—though anything better than bird-squawks *could* be considered an improvement after all those years of practice.

After a tad too much wine, they'd at last retired, were lit up to bed, to a real, soft, and welcoming—unswaying—bedstead crisp and sweet-smelling of scrupulously clean linens, still redolent of a faint floral sachet and the soap in which they'd been boiled. Toulon had found a refuge at last, in their bedchamber, and had crept out of hiding for a frantic quarter-hour of reassuring "wubbies," much to Caroline's amusement.

"So much like the early days, my love," she whispered fondly, slid into

bed with him and lying close at last, after brushing out her hair. Toulon
was fair-taken with her too. "You . . . me, so completely alone and private." She chuckled, scrubbing Toulon under his chin and chops. "And
old William Pitt to pat and purr us to our rest. Or . . ." she added in a
huskier voice, "sull up on the fireplace bench whilst . . ."

"Sull up, Toulon, there's a good puss," Lewrie growled.

And once the last bed-side candle had been snuffed dark, it was much
like their first, nervous "honeymoon" night at the coaching inn on the way
to Portsmouth, as Caroline could finally welcome him home, in her own,
inimitable fashion, which fashion left him damned near purring—drained
and dreamless.

The next day, they'd coached to St. George's Church for Easter Sunday
services, turned out almost regal in their springtime best; and most dignified, Lewrie had thought. Caroline had worn her new gown and bonnet,
which had been most fetching; Sophie de Maubeuge too, looking ethereally
lovely and being ogled by the young men of the parish; the children
adorable, clean and unruffled (for a rare hour or three), and Lewrie and
his father tricked out in their best uniforms—Lewrie with that gold St.
Vincent medal clapping on his waistcoat buttons and a spanking-new gold-
bullion epaulet on his left shoulder, his dark-blue coat stiff with gold lace
which hadn't gone verdigris-green from salt air, yet. The whole family,
primly a-row in the same rented pew box.

It had been a joy afterwards to greet his brother-in-law, Governour
Chiswick, and his lovely dark-haired wife, Millicent. They'd had an heir
at last, and Millicent bade fair to present him with a second by late summer.
Serene, settled country squire was Brother Governour by then—stout and
getting stouter, halfway towards resembling the satirical artist Cruikshank's
depictions of John Bull. And where had the panther-lean, rope-muscled
side of North Carolina colonist beef Lewrie had known at Yorktown gone,
he wondered?

Mother Charlotte Chiswick was there, now living with Governour and
Millicent as a doting granny, a bit stooped and myopic, with hair gone
white as lamb's wool. And Uncle Phineas Chiswick himself, got up in his
best—though he looked as if he'd shopped for clothing in William Pitt

the *Elder's* last term in office. Lewrie had been struck dumb to see the miserly old bastard chortle and whinny with *bonhomie,* clap Brigadier Sir Hugo on the back, and he almost pleasant for once!

Emily, the vicar's spinster-daughter—traipsing hopefully in a new *ensemble* of her own, in her father's wake, still single and becoming just the *slightest* bit long-in-tooth.

And the Embletons and their coterie were there of course. It was damn' near their church, their vicar, their village, their parish, maybe even their half of the county. Dignified old Sir Romney Embleton, now master of the hunt; his slack-jawed, half-wit son, Harry, sporting *his* Yeoman Cavalry uniform, spurs ajingling, and preening amidst the same pack of rogues and rousters who had always surrounded him—looking a bit put out that no one made notice of his lieutenant-colonelcy of militia—this Sunday, at least.

"Master of hounds now . . . Harry," Sir Hugo had muttered to his son. "Think he's given up on civilian suitings for the duration of the war, hey? An M.P. . . . oh, very patriotic is Harry Embleton."

"God . . . pity the poor dogs then," Lewrie had whispered back, which had made his father snigger.

"The sort of man *born* t'be . . . cavalry," Sir Hugo sneered, and turned to translate that comment to his valet, a thoroughly ugly, one-eyed, old *havildar,* Trilochan Singh, of uncertain caste, from Sir Hugo's regiment in India. Had Lewrie run into him in a Calcutta *bazaar* back in the '80s, he'd have run for his life, for Trilochan Singh was raffish, bearded, and mustachioed, and looked the part of a swaggering *badmash,* a hill bandit who'd cut a man's heart out just 'cause it was a slow afternoon!

And no wonder Caroline doesn't know what to do with Father or his "man," Lewrie wondered to himself; *aren't Sikhs supposed to carry five knives all the time, or is it one? No matter . . . God, I'll wager there're more'n one of our maids sportin' more than pinch marks!*

"Sir Hugo . . ." Sir Romney said in passing, doffing his hat, cool but politely punctilious. "Vicomtess Sophie, *enchanté* . . . Mister and Mistress Lewrie . . ."

"Your servant, Sir Romney. And a lovely Easter Day it is, sir," Sir Hugo replied just as formally as they made their way to their waiting coach.

Galling as it was, Lewrie was forced by courtesy to doff a hat and make a "leg" to Sir Romney as well, as Caroline and Sophie dipped the baronet their own polite curtsies. Hugh and Sewallis emulated them, doffing hats, with Sewallis well on his way to a clumsy boy's "leg," as his mother had schooled him.

"Brigadier," Harry Embleton said, trailing his father.

"Ah, Colonel Embleton, sir." Sir Hugo fair-beamed.

"Leftenant Lewrie," Harry added, barely audible and stiff.

"Commander, actually," Lewrie gleefully corrected, turning on the "smarm," "and a good day to you, Colonel Embleton."

"Uhm, ah . . . yayss," Harry drawled, his gaze riveted upon that gold medal for a startled (or envious!) second or two before gaining his aplomb once more and greeting Caroline and Sophie.

Still *cool with Caroline,* Lewrie noted; *and for good reason, if he knows what's good for him—so she don't take her horsewhip to him a second time!* Pleasingly, Caroline gave as good as she got, as coolly pleasant yet formal—for the neighbours' sakes. *Hello,* though . . . !

He's practically slobberin'! Lewrie thought, as poor Harry had a word with Sophie; *poor chit, she can't know any better, surely, to simper back at him! Surely, Caroline's filled her in by now, if the servants hadn't, the new neighbours' daughters her age hadn't. Polite is one thing, but, for God's sake . . . she don't have to play coy at him!*

A glance over his shoulder at his impatient sire, already at the coach door, stirred Harry to motion; and he doffed and bowed a parting before making all the haste that "genteel" and "aristocratic languid" would allow to catch his daddy up.

"Well, at last he spoke to you, Alan," Caroline had breathed in wonder, once the Embletons had departed. "The beginning of a thaw, do you not think?"

"Perhaps, my dear," Lewrie allowed, "but he still fair gives me the shivers. Or the 'collywobbles,' " he added, with a sarcastic grin.

"Alan, on church grounds . . . before the children!" Caroline admonished, all but poking him in the ribs. "May you not moderate your . . . saltiness?"

"My pardon, my dear."

"Well then, let us be on our way," Caroline decided, "shooing" the children towards their own coach. "Easter dinner will be at . . . Uncle Phineas's in his role as *paterfamilias*"—she sighed at the necessity—"where we may break our fast with the bounty of the season and celebrate our Lord's ascension."

"Oh, joy," Lewrie had snickered, "fresh-grown bounty . . . all those ground nuts, tree bark, and mud. Nothing but the best for *his* kin, hey?"

That set the children to tittering wildly.

"Bark and mud!" Hugh contemplated rather *loudly*. "Ugghh!"

"Mud pies, with caramel sauce," Lewrie abetted.

"Pig slop soup!" Hugh dreamt up. "With cracklings!"

"Mud pie an' caramel!" Charlotte all but *shrieked*. "Yahahaha!"

"Children!" Caroline snapped, "do consider where you are, making such a row on God's ground! And of *who* you are . . . and comport yourselves according. Alan, really . . . !" she cautioned, swiveling her gaze upon him, nostrils pinched and like to breathe fire.

"Slip o' th' tongue, mizzuz," he replied, a'grovel, tugging at his forelock like a day labourer and crouching from the waist. " 'Twas drink an' bad companions, ma'am . . . won't 'appen agin, ma'am, beggin' yer pardon. Oh, don't flog me, ma'am . . . !"

"Hhmmph!" was her nose-high comment for *that*, on public view . . . though there was a forgiving, amused sparkle to her eyes; and her vertical exclamation point of vexation between her brows wasn't *that* deep, now was it?

CHAPTER SIX

*I*t was a splendid morning for a ride. The faint mists had gone away, the sun was well up, and the dew was barely dried. Birds chirped and fluttered over their newly hatched, young rabbits bounded ahead of them as they flushed them out, not so much a fearful scurrying as it was a playful, cat-like clearing of the ground in exaggerated and exuberant high-heeled hops. The aromas of new shoots, budding fruit-tree blossoms, of virginal, fresh-washed tree leaves commingled with the loamy scents of recently turned, slightly damp earth from planted fields . . . and the green-sap sweetness of hay, barley, wheat, hops, and rye sprouting in them; turned earth and a faint hint of manure turned in with it, came from the fallow fields which had been left for live-stock to graze over the past autumn, now broken for spring planting.

Skies of pale blue, brush-stroked and wisped with clouds, vivid greens of leaves, and even weeds, the paler greens of acres where crops had begun to venture forth, like a thin water-colour wash over a deep umber. Shin-high grasses waved as breezes took them on every cut-over hill, and the valleys between the woodlots, stark-stippled white with new lambs; and the darker, almost smoky blue-green of forests, copses, and woodlots, with here and there the faint skein of blue-white haze from brush-fires burning off piles of winter deadfall on such a safe, cool, moist day. And, as they topped one of the tumbling, sea-wave hills for a wider miles-long vista, even the faint sour reek from the fires seemed more the shades of living things than the spirits of the greyed, dessicated dead of winter.

Hugh, ever the adventurer, was further on ahead, urging his pony up another swelling hillock. Sewallis, now mounted on a proper horse (though a gentle runt of a twelve-hander), stayed closer to them, with his ears as a'cock as his mount's to an adult conversation, listening with sober interest. Or perhaps rueing that they hadn't taken any of his dogs along this morning—for fear of spooking Hugh's quest.

Or, Lewrie thought, giving him a glance; *sulking that it's Hugh we're indulging, not him. Thought, bein' so priggish, Sewallis would be more tolerant of Hugh, his watchdog, not his rival. When did this rivalry start?* he wondered, regretting being gone as they grew up.

"Won't you have the Devil's own time constructing yer lane?" Lewrie asked. "Up an' down, up an' down, all the way from our place to yours."

"Not if you come up Governour's lane first, Alan, me dear." His father smiled softly.

"Whatever possessed Uncle Phineas to sell you one square yard, I still have yet to fathom," Lewrie confessed, getting used to swaying and adjusting to Anson's gait over the hills.

"Money, my dear boy," Sir Hugo replied, smiling again. But it looked like a cadaverous leer of a practiced "Captain Sharp." "Oodles of money. Oh, I must admit he was loath, in the beginning, hoping it would confer to Governour entire after he was gone. Didn't wish to split it up. Not in *his* lifetime at least."

"Not after he spent most of his life scheming to shove it together." Lewrie snickered.

"Point taken, Alan," Sir Hugo grumphed. "Tolerate you as one of his tenants perhaps. Expect Governour to treat his brother, Burgess, the same when he returns from India. Pray God he does. Damned good soldier, is your younger brother-in-law. Would have got the regiment had I had anything to say about it, but . . . he was not the senior major. And money again . . . the new fool who got the colonelcy is a third son to one of the *nabobs* of 'John Company's' Governing Board."

"Ah . . . the same old story." Lewrie sighed philosophically. *He* had never prospered from *family* "interest"—or money, either—with this caddish old rakehell at his side to thank for both. At least in the Royal Navy, connexions could only advance the idiots just so far. Talent and seamanship counted in the long run. Though there *were* the admirals on foreign stations who'd made Post-Captains out of their sixteen-year-old sons, and . . . !

"Yes, and thank God for't," Sir Hugo hoorawed. "Else I'd have not gone a captain in a distinguished regiment like the Fourth. Been some tag-rag-and-bobtail ensign in a *kutch pultan* in the Fever Isles . . . or at John O' Groats! Well, no matter. Does Burgess not get a colonelcy from John Company, I'll have him back in England . . . on my staff . . .'fore he can turn his head to spit."

"*Your* staff?" Lewrie half-scoffed, swaying sidewise in his saddle to peer at his father, wondering who in his right mind would give him command of *British* troops again! "What bloody staff?"

"Why, I'm t'be military aide to the Lord Lieutenant of Surrey, Alan, me dear!" Sir Hugo hooted. "No matter the next-to-London counties are almost completely run by the Home Office; they still allow the token twits the office. And a dev'lish profitable office it is too! Yeomanry . . . militia forces . . . do I not make major-general by this time next year, I've either gone tits-up . . . or wasn't really tryin'!

"Another reason your Phineas Chiswick would sell me land, Alan," Sir Hugo confided, leaning a bit closer as they passed under some overhanging boughs at a sedate walk. "For the prestige o' havin' *me* for a neighbour! And for a word in his ear, now and again, as to profitable doin's . . . which I pick up from the *gora-logs*. Reason your Sir Romney is so affable, too . . . given the bile betwixt you and his son. Toad-eatin' ain't limited to the lower classes, Alan, me son. Oh, they're high and mighty men, Phineas and Sir Romney. Must confess, I care a power more for Sir Romney than ever I could for that . . . well. A decent, sporting gentleman he is. Dignified, of the old school. Now I'm a land-*owner*, and not a wealthy tenant, he's invited me to join the local hunt this winter. Committee decided I'm worthy."

"You!" Lewrie howled, feeling abused. Didn't they know what they were getting? he puzzled. Here *he* was, a long-time neighbour, affable as the day was long . . . well, to all but Harry. A bloody war hero, due to be a Post-Captain, equal rank to Harry, and he'd *still* be suckin' hoof-dust by the side of the road whilst his father would be garglin' claret stirrup-cups. This "fly" rogue, this . . . !

"Ride on, Sewallis. See what your brother's up to," Lewrie bade.

"But, Father . . ."

"Spur on now. He's out of sight and just like Goodyer's Pig, sure t'be in mischief."

"Oh, alright . . ." Sewallis grumbled.

"You'll blow it, you know," Lewrie told Sir Hugo, once Sewallis was out of earshot. "Sooner or later, that base nature of yours will . . ."

"Ours, me lad." Sir Hugo twinkled. *"Ours."*

"There'll be someone's unmarried daughter, a fit of temper, or something . . ." Lewrie stammered. "Grope yer host's maids, guesting . . ."

"Nothin' of the sort, lad." Sir Hugo dismissed him, waving a hand like shooing flies. Shooing horseflies for *real,* in point of fact. "For one, I ain't so spry these days that I can rantipole like a young buck-o'-the-first-head. I'm older and . . . pray God . . . wiser. Too wise t'be *caught,* do ye get my *meanin'?* For a second, I'll be off half the time to Guildford, London, or Glandon Park, where I may indulge those few penchants o' mine *discreetly* . . . with the better sort o' whores. I am a man o' simple tastes . . . ," Sir Hugo modestly declaimed.

"Like I'm First Lord o' the Admiralty," Lewrie groused back.

"Import me a sportin' sort o' doxy, t'pose as my housekeeper," Sir Hugo speculated. "Done all the time and well you know it. Just the one woman, though . . . brrrr!" He shivered at the thought of anything *close* to "domestic bliss." Or a lack of variety. "Well, mayhap I'll just stick to the buffet assortment o' courtesans. I can *hold* my wine. There's never been anyone said I couldn't. I've drunk some ragin' sponges under the table in me time too; and that's sayin' something for a man who's spent his life at mess-night in royal regiments like the Fourth! Where d'ye think our good English peerage *hide* their drunks but in the Army, hey? Or . . . the clergy. Gad, do I slosh down a *pint* less than most vicars and bishops, I'm ready for beatification! *Saint* bloody Hugo . . . the Temperate, haw!"

"The Chaste," Lewrie offered, tongue most firmly planted in his cheek, laughing at the image. At the bloody statue! Or in going to a "Saint Hugo's" and kneeling for communion.

"Do I dissemble well enough, well . . . perhaps even that, me boy." Sir Hugo nodded, as mischievous as ever. "Perhaps even that. There. There's the beginnings," he said, perking up like a gun dog on scent, as they topped a bald rise.

It was the tower, the broken-fanged, topless tower where he and Caroline had first kissed, declared their love. Atop a small, flat-top hill, with a view that went on for miles to the North and West. A rill ran South below it, almost lost in a thick stand of timber to its left. Another lay to the South, meandering the bottom of the last swale they had left, where they'd first dined *alfresco*. A long sweep and another rise, and there was the hill with the lone oak where he'd . . . and further beyond to the East, the sight of his own home farm, with Embleton estates beyond that. Just barely visible, sandwiched between, was the gloomy old red-brick pile which Phineas owned, off to the Nor'east.

The tower was being re-constructed, he could see. The rectangular, ancient stones had been gathered from where they'd fallen an age or more before and reset. New stones to match, from one of the nearby quarries, had been fetched in to raise it and provide the base of a new house which adjoined it. A basement had been dug out, lined with matching stones or brick.

"It's going to be huge!" Lewrie gasped at the expanse of the foundation, framed by the first courses of the outer, load-bearing walls.

"Not a bit of it," Sir Hugo replied. "It'll be one-level, so I don't gasp my way up and down stairs in my dotage. Like an old Roman-British villa . . . or an officer's *bungalow* out in India." His father kneed his horse into motion so they could ride over for a closer look. "Be in by August, they assure me . . . out from under Caroline's feet. I expect she'll appreciate that," he said, with a wry smirk.

"That quickly? Must cost a bundle, all that haste . . . ?" Lewrie probed, to discover just how *much* pelf his father had absconded with.

"Five thousand pounds, the land . . . two thousand for the house, before furnishin's," Sir Hugo off-handedly admitted, as if those sums were mere pittances.

"Dear Lord." Lewrie felt the need to gawp; who *had* Sir Hugo robbed . . . ?

"Be yours . . . when I'm gone," Sir Hugo informed him, "my son."

"Ah . . . ?" Lewrie realised, of a sudden. Rather hopefully.

"Three-hundred-sixty acres, all told. Cheek-by-jowl, you note, with yer hundred sixty rented from Phineas. But this'll be a paid-for freehold, free and clear, time I'm passed over. So I expect Phineas'll be too. Then Governour's yer landlord for the smaller parcel, and you and he can work out the details. This for Sewallis, eventually. He's eldest. Specify in yer will that he's t'rent the smaller to Hugh, for less than market value. Don't expect Hugh'll be home much to enjoy it though. Down for the Navy, I s'pose?"

"That was our intention," Lewrie admitted, "where I have a bit of influence. Find him a good first ship and captain."

"Pity. He's a natural-born horseman. Exuberant child. Daring. And a leader, e'en now. That's magic with troops. Now I've paid off all my creditors, made my pile, I'm a lot more welcome at Horse Guards than ever I was previous. An Army commission is a possibility. In a *bukshi* regiment too. Needs a bit o' polish though. A good boarding school, 'round the better sort. We could fund that together, Son . . ."

"Which did you have in mind, Father?" Lewrie grimaced at the memories of how many of the good ones *he'd* been tossed out of. "We tried that with me, remember? I doubt they're forgotten *me*, so . . ."

"Yayyss, well, there is that," Sir Hugo allowed, with a rueful smile of reverie. "Harrow, especially, hey? Boom! You were ever the rebellious young dog. Once Hugh's eighteen though . . . we could buy an Army commission. Captaincy first . . . then a majority, as he seasons."

"There's Sewallis to think of first. Two more years and he'll be due for a proper school. When he's twelve. Mature enough to stand up to the bullies he'll meet, sure as Fate."

"We'll see him right," Sir Hugo offered. "Damme, what's money for if not t'see yer children well-placed, well-educated? And ease the first few hurdles? Money *and* influence. Grandchildren, rather. I will put up half his tuition and such . . . a modest allowance too, for both the boys. Charlotte, too, when it's her time to be shipped off to be 'finished.' "

"Why, that's . . . that's magnanimous of you, Father. I . . ."

"Told you long ago, Son. Would've bought you a bloody pony and cart, was that what you wished." Sir Hugo sighed, drawing a plaid kerchief from his sleeve for a blow of his drink-veined nose. "Wasted my youth, me best middle years. I'll probably waste my dotage too, do I not look sharp about it. Wasn't much of a father to *you*, and that's a God's honest truth, hey?"

"A-bloody-men," Lewrie snorted back.

"Made up for't, after me own fashion . . . in India."

An orgy with the three girls of his private *bibikhana*, as Lewrie recalled it; a cut of the best loot from the Mindanao pirates' hoard, after they'd slaughtered 'em at Balabac; and aye, some of Caroline's most impressive jewelry from that. . . .

"Ah, but yer too old an' jaded to spoil now, Alan, me dear," Sir Hugo scoffed, playfully tipping his son's cocked hat half over his nose.

No, *I'm not!* Lewrie thought; *have a stab at it!*

"Sewallis and Hugh, now . . . second chances?" Sir Hugo went on, sounding regretful, but hopeful too. "Reason I bought land here, do you see. Might have been a horrid father . . . and a shite-arsed husband a time'r two. But! I might just make a hellish-good grandfather . . . do you not mind. Be around when you can't be. Take a tad of the wind out of Master Hugh's sails . . . that the way you tarry sorts express it? *But* a tad. Sewallis, well . . . impart of a dab o' backbone, a pinch of confidence now and again. With an heroic sailor for a father, and . . . dare I say it . . . an heroic soldier for a grandfather, that might inspire him. When you're at sea . . . I could stand in your stead . . . ? Nought to undermine Caroline, o' course, but . . . ?"

"You'll not turn 'em into Corinthians, swear," Lewrie dithered, torn between acceptance of the peace offering (and the largesse which went with it) or in shouting, "No way in Hell!" for what deviltry Sir Hugo still had fermenting in his breast, no matter his high-flown sentiments.

Look how I turned out! he pointed out to himself; *and that with him being there but a* tenth *of the time! Now,* "watch-and-watch" . . .

"Like I did with you, d'ye mean?" Sir Hugo scoffed. "God, was yer own doin', that. I merely set you the example . . ."

"A bad'un," Lewrie reminded him, smirking, even so.

"Good God, most tykes don't get even that, so sing small and be grateful!" his father japed in mock-seriousness. "Half that due to no mother in the house t'moderate. Your own mother, then old Alice . . . up and dyin' too."

"Well . . ."

"Aye, 'tis a rakehellish life I've led, Alan. Not that it was not the grandest fun, mind. I've one true son I *know* I sired, turned out decent. One step-daughter a ten-guinea whore now . . . and Gerald. Wherever *he's* got to, he's most-like but one step away from swallowin' frogs at fairs for tuppence. But here you are with a fine wife and three fine, healthy children, who'll be raised *decent*. I've no livin' relations, no wife, no one to leave a farthing to, and a bit too old t'be startin' a new family for myself, d'ye see. Christ, money! All I've to show for my life is the bit o' 'tin' I gathered soldierin'. Like muckin' out abattoirs, though the pay's better, sometimes. Well, a *slew* o' 'tin,' to be frank about it. 'Cause I was ever fortunate t'be in the right places and light-fingered t'boot! Should have written first 'bout my intentions . . . should you've said 'no,' then I would never have come here, but . . ."

How much *"tin"*? Lewrie wondered; *you a "chicken* nabob"?

"Odd way t'get a ready-made family, though . . . for what, nine or ten thousand pounds?" Lewrie asked, one brow up. Gently probing.

"Nearer to twelve, all told." Sir Hugo shrugged. "Drop in the bucket. Balabac . . . rebel *rajas*'s palaces . . . good fortune in the opium trade to China? I could have bought Phineas's estate entire . . . lock, stock, and barrel . . . and still have had plenty left," he boasted.

"Christ!" Lewrie exclaimed, with a low whistle. All his prize-money—should it ever be adjudged and sent to him, mind!—and he'd still be a beggar compared to . . . "Well, then . . . I 'spose . . . you'll *not* turn Hugh towards cavalry, hear me? He's much too clever for that."

"No, I'll leave that to the likes of Harry Embleton, Son." Sir Hugo laughed, much relieved that he *had*, in essence, "bought" himself a ready-made family after all. And assuaged his conscience, Lewrie surmised; though he was never quite sure if Sir Hugo truly *had* one or was merely hymn-singing from memory of how proper folk did things!

"Damme'f I don't like Sir Romney toppin' fine, but . . . there's a good chance the best part o' Harry ran down the footman's leg. Sort o' dim bastard that turns up in the mess as a Cornet o' Cavalry—so stupid that even the *others* notice." Sir Hugo guffawed.

"Well, then . . ." Lewrie summed up, reaching for his reins. "I s'pose we should be going. 'Fore they maim each other, hmm? See those otters of yours at play? Boys? Saddle up!" he called.

"Erm . . . thankee, Alan," Sir Hugo said, offering his hand.

"Not much I could do about it now you've already bought land, is there?" Lewrie sighed, as he swung up atop Anson. "Sorry. Didn't quite come out right, did it? Force of habit . . . t'be on tenterhooks around you. Wary. It'll take gettin' used to, Father," Lewrie replied, offering his hand. "Mind now, Hugh's not to *have* an otter pup. Not take one home. Just 'adopt' one . . . up here at his grandfather's. You'll not encourage him, will you?"

"Son!" Sir Hugo shied, acting much maligned. *"Moi?"*

CHAPTER SEVEN

*L*ewrie went over the farm's books the next morning in his study. The entries were in Caroline's neat, copper-plate script—or in their overseer's awkward scrawl. Receipts for seed and such were arranged in one pile and receipts for the sale of sheep, cattle, hogs, wool, corn, and such were in another. Caroline sat by the open double-doors facing the gardens by the side of the house on the west side, knitting and playing games with Toulon, who was mellowing to house-life, and farm-life, quickly.

Keepin' her eyes on me? Lewrie wondered, *T'see do I smile or do I glower? And glower over what?* He almost shivered, recalling their first "post-honeymoon" spat in the Bahamas, when he'd come home from three months amidst the "down islands" and hadn't appreciated what-all she'd accomplished to turn a rented coach-house into a showplace, had erred by jibing her over the odd pastel the house had been re-painted, as if he were an uncaring cad and she too hen-headed to run their house, present him with a going concern that anyone would be proud of.

"Does something particular trouble you, dear?" she asked, one brow up and her voice a bit hesitant. Not so hesitant, though, that she didn't sound . . . resentful that he might have found something amiss.

"Just as Governour said," Lewrie admitted, tossing away the newest ledger and leaning back in his chair to puff his lips, frustrated. "Taxes, labour costs. Damme, do we double our profits . . . as you have done, my dear," he complimented her, and meant it, which eased her greatly. "With the prices we got, at pre-war tax rates and pre-war wages for workers, we should've cleared over £300 . . . not £200 this past year. Head above water yet . . . and all that, but . . . Damme, I wish workin' for a naval hero'd be worth *something!*"

"Even Maggie Cony, Alan," Caroline said, putting aside all her knitting to cross to the desk and stand behind him, one arm caressing his neck and shoulder. "They offered her work in the kitchens of the Red Swan, and I couldn't match it. With the baby and their cottage in the village to keep up . . . closer to home *and* more money, you see. I was sorry to see her go, she was such a treasure, but little I could do to keep her, no matter how friendly we were."

And hadn't replaced her, Lewrie noted, saving nearly eight pounds *per annum*. With the boys old enough, their private tutor had been sent away after the last term just ended. Besides, the new village school was just as good, though nowhere near as uppercrust—and cost a good deal less. No more need of a proper governess, just an older, widowed maid-of-all-work to tend Charlotte. No, grand as it looked, a Lewrie household didn't seem like it'd be awash in footmen, butlers, serving-girls, and such—not anytime soon, at any rate.

"Besides, your name'd not draw workers, Alan," Caroline imparted, sweeping her skirts aside to first sit on the arm of his chair . . . then lean back and snuggle into his lap. "Mind, *we* think the world of you, but . . ."

He interrupted her to steal a gentle, teasing, wifely kiss.

"Unless there's a grand victory like Saint Vincent, most folk could care less about the war," she told him as she nestled in. "And they forget that a week later. Why, last year, the London Mob stoned the King's carriage! Shouting, 'No more King, no more war, and no more Pitt'!"

"They *what?*" Lewrie stiffened in outrage. "Why, I never heard the like! Be stormin' the Tower of London next! Buildin' guillotines and loppin' off heads! Didn't see *that* in any papers come by me."

Hold on, yes, I have heard the like, Lewrie reminded himself; *back in London, that packet o' penny tracts . . . those men at Willis's Rooms!*

"Higher taxes, price of feeding themselves gone right through the roof, feeding their families," Caroline mused sadly. "And all the men away, in the Army or the Navy. And, believe it or not, even these high wages they're getting, even with a scarcity of able-bodied hands, can't keep up. Levies on everything needful, Alan. Soap, beer, boots, clothing, on candles. Taxes on sugar, salt, coffee, and tea . . . not that you can still *find* tea for sale, 'less it's been smuggled across from France, mind," Caroline complained. "Bricks, tobacco, rum, windowpane glass, windows themselves . . . four pence, mind you, on a copy of a newspaper! I've heard some mine or mill workers earn eighteen pounds per annum and ten of that goes out in taxes or necessities! The same for *our* necessities . . . as I'm sure you saw in my ledgers."

"Aye, I did." Lewrie winced at the year-end sum.

"There have been rumours of riots," she confided, nestling closer to him with a worried look. "Labouring groups organising to stop work for higher pay . . . though they've been outlawed. Along with all of that *Rights of Man*, Thomas Paine, croaking."

"Never thought I'd hear such tripe, in England of all places," Lewrie sighed, sliding a protective arm about her. "Damme, don't they know, do they stop working, they starve our defences? Don't they know the Frogs are ready to come conquer us? Ungrateful curs! They wish to *parlez-vous* and bow to a Liberty Tree, see all the churches boarded up and turned into 'Temples of Reason'?"

There came a knock from the entry hall on the double-doors.

"Beggin' yah pahdon, sah," Andrews's voice came soft and melodious as he filled in for a proper butler. "But 'tis Bosun Cony's wife come callin', sah. Missuz Maggie? Say she got t'speak t'ya, sah. It be urgent, she say."

"Um, ahh . . ." Lewrie grunted, disentangling himself, helping Caroline up from their compromising position, so she could push her gown and her hair straight, and he could reset his waist-coat, shoot cuffs, and appear "respectable." "Very well, Andrews, I'll be out directly. I do declare, Caroline. Speak of the Devil, hmmm?"

"Hardly the Devil, darling," Caroline chuckled. "Maggie's too dear to us to be calling her that. More-like . . . seeing a red-bird as sign someone'll come unexpected. Like we believed in the Carolinas."

Lewrie opened the doors and stepped out into the entry-hall, to espy a worried-looking Maggie Cony, the flaxen-haired helpmeet to his old friend and compatriot. While not a classic beauty, for a country woman she was usually most fetching, in a strong, no-nonsense way . . . and more than a match for her absent husband.

"Mistress Cony!" He beamed. "And *young* Will too! Bless me . . . nothing's gone amiss since we saw you at church, has it? Something urgent, I heard?"

Will had been detained at Portsmouth for a few days longer, just until the ship could be properly housed in a stone dry dock. Lewrie had issued leave-tickets for the senior hands, and Will should be on his way home, unless the new captain had decided not to honour them. He'd sent a thick packet of sea-letters on with Andrews and Padgett too, as they'd come on to Anglesgreen with his goods. Everything had been just fine, he'd thought. . . .

"Somethin' awful happenin' down t'Portsmouth, Captain Lewrie, sir," Maggie blurted out. "Coach just came with a note from Will . . . fetched it me at the Red Swan. He'll not be coming home, sir!"

"Well, damme, he shall!" Lewrie declared, "if I have to coach down to Portsmouth myself and set his new captain straight. I give you my word on *that*, Mistress."

"Worse'n that, sir. Will got his leave-ticket, aye, and his new captain said 'twas alright him comin' on, but . . . Now he writes he can't leave the ship nor the dockyards. Can't leave Portsmouth a'*tall*, sir! None o' the sailors can. There's been *mutiny* in Portsmouth . . . nigh on the whole Channel Fleet, sir! Navy won't take any orders t'sail, won't stir, 'til their . . . demands have been met! Oh Lord, Captain Lewrie, sir!" Maggie Cony said, one hand for her son, and wringing the other in her apron. "*Mutiny*, sir! They'll fetch soldiers t'put it down, an' my Will right in the middle of it. There'll be hundreds kilt a'fightin' . . . hundreds *hanged*, 'fore 'tis done!"

"Mutiny!" Lewrie gasped. "What, the whole bloody *Fleet*? It . . . that just can't *be!* They've . . . mean t'say . . . !" He sputtered, turning to Caroline for assurance this wasn't a nightmare.

One ship, aye, with an ogre for a captain. Lewrie shivered, wincing as he recalled how close HMS *Cockerel* was to mutiny with that batch of slave-driving fiends in her gunroom and midshipmen's berths.

He saw Caroline shudder, but seem to shrug too, as if this was merely

one more threatening event in a whole year of earth-shaking, and unbe-
lievable, events. With all the anger and want in the land she had just
spoken of, all the unrest he'd seen in those penny tracts, those Republican,
rebellious screeds . . . !

Labourers rioting, aye . . . civilians'd *do such*—he groped for a thread
of understanding—*but never the tars! Not* my *jacks!* Irish, maybe—but the
best part of the Navy—*his* Navy? And where might it spread?

"Have you Will's letter, ma'am? Good. Let me *see* that!"

BOOK TWO

Tamen aspera regum perpetimur iuga,
nec melior parere recuso.

Yet we endure the cruel yoke of kings,
nor though the better man do I refuse obedience.
—*ARGONAUTICA*, BOOK V, 487–89
VALERIUS FLACCUS

CHAPTER EIGHT

*T*hey took the shorter road down from Portsdown Hill this time beneath
the furiously whirling signal telegraph station, to the slightly inland town
of Portsea. It was a clear day, so Lewrie, Maggie Cony, and young Will
could espy far beyond Gosport, Haslar Hospital, several forts including
the one opposite Portsmouth Point—manned, the forts were. Above the
walls of fortifications circling Portsmouth itself, framed 'twixt Portsmouth
and Southsea Castle—pent atop the golden-galleon-spire of the Church of
St. Thomas A' Becket—lay the Fleet.

Proud three-decker 1st- and 2nd-Rate flagships, two-decker 3rd and 4th
Rates, slim frigates and sloops of war, brigs, schooners, and cutters, bulky
transports converted from men-o'-war to carry troops and stores for a
world-wide war; sheer-hulks and receiving ships reduced to a gantline and
lower-most masts, where new-caught lubbers and seamen languished 'til a
warship had need of them.

All of them flying battle-flags, the stark, unadorned blood-red flags
without the British canton! Commission pendants still streamed, but none
of the flagships wore broad pendants denoting the presence of an admiral
or commodore—only the battle colours, nothing national!

Militia paraded in Portsea as their coach slowed, shunted aside to make
room for soldiery and idling onlookers. There were hardly any sailors to
be seen, naval or civilian. Marines in full kit stood here and there in full

squads, their bayonets unsheathed and fixed under the muzzles of their muskets. Usually, a parade of troops brought out the spectators, raised cheers, the fluttering of handkerchiefs by the town women, and the tittery delight of youngsters. But not this time, Lewrie noted; now, the doleful beats of drums, the clomp of crude-made boots, the clop of his coach's horses, and the funereal rumbles from its iron-shod wheels seemed the only sounds.

Right—into the main gate of the dockyard, and several minutes in argument with a Marine Captain, no matter Lewrie was wearing uniform; then at last proceeding past the Hard, Gun Wharf, the mast-pool, and the small Royal Naval Academy, and the Commissioner's House, the Rope Walk—and a few more aggressively curious roving marine patrols!—until they could alight hard by one of the stone graving docks, where HMS *Jester* stood propped and stranded, looking like a scrofulous, dead whale. With her bottom exposed, all the sheet copper, paper, and felt ripped off, and a good third of her underwater planking stripped away for replacing, she looked more a ship*wreck* than a ship of war. She did not fly any flags, since she was officially out of commission, in the hands of the yards. And, Lewrie was grateful to see, she did not sport that rebellious red banner either.

"I'd go aboard," he told an idling yard worker by her brow, eyeing that shaky-looking gangplank which led from the lip of the dock to her starboard entry-port, perched rather high-ish above the floor of the graving dock and all its accumulated trash, muck, and filth, in about a foot of verminous-looking harbour water. A few rare workmen pretended to do something constructive beneath her.

"You her cap'um, sir?" The dock worker yawned.

"Her last captain," Lewrie explained.

" 'Ey ain't too fond o' awficers come callin', sir. But ye c'n try." The man shrugged.

"Hoy, *Jester!*" Lewrie shouted, about halfway across that brow.

Several heads popped up over the sail-tending gangway bulwarks, where a harbour-watch party evidently had been loafing. A few sailors mounted to the quarterdeck, hands in their pockets and their hats far back on their heads.

Damme! Lewrie fumed; no warrant or petty officer standing deck-watch? And common seamen, walking the *quarterdeck* without leave?

"Permission to come aboard, to visit . . ." Lewrie called over.

"Denied, sir . . . sorry," a strange voice rasped back. "Beggin' yer pardon, sir, but . . . there'll be no officers return aboard 'til all our grievances been settled."

Lewrie went colt-eyed at that reply, his eyebrows up to his hat brim in shock at being spoken to so by a common seaman. *Damme!* Lewrie gawped again, taking a closer look; *that saucy bugger's armed!* He had himself a closer peer at the sailors who'd been lazing on deck before, and those who'd come up to see the commotion. Wide baldrics were hung over their shoulders, supporting scabbarded cutlasses. Pistols poked from their waistbands, most piratical; and those who served as watch or side-party held muskets and sported cartouche boxes!

"None of your officers are aboard then?" Lewrie puzzled aloud. "And they *gave* you the keys to the arms chests? Not even a midshipman left?"

"Nary a one, sir," the strange seaman shouted back. "All sent ashore, just after the delegates of the Fleet decided. Bosun an' the Master Gunner'z in charge, sir. Charge o' th' arms too, sir. And . . . beggin' yer pardon again, sir, but . . . we vowed no Commission Officer's to come aboard 'til . . ."

"I am Commander Lewrie . . . *Jester's* last captain," Lewrie stated, moving forward a few feet along that rickety gangplank. "I've come to *see* your Bosun, Mister Cony. I've brought his wife and child along . . . there they are, yonder."

"Oh, a social call then, sir!" The leading sailor brightened. "In 'at case, aye, sir . . . come aboard. Passin' th' word for th' Bosun!"

Several of the mutinous hands relayed that shout to summon the Bosun on deck, as Lewrie waved Maggie and little Will forward to join him. "Side-party . . . ! Present . . . !"

They would offer him a proper salute then, though the muskets were most-like loaded, if not primed, as well! Lewrie took it, doffing his hat to the quarterdeck and side-party as if *Jester* was still a ship in proper hands . . . and everything was normal!

"Maggie, darlin'!" Will Cony shouted, as soon as he had gained the deck. He rushed up to help her the last few steps inboard through the entry-port. Maggie swept him into a fierce, protective hug just as quickly, with little Will clinging to his father's leg like a limpet to a rock. The armed sailors, their duties done, lowered their muskets to lean on, and cooed and chuckled softly, breaking into fond smiles!

"Cap'um, sir!" Will exclaimed, after he'd scooped his child up to eye-level, still with one arm about his wife. "God o' Mercy, sir . . . 'twas 'opin' yew'd come. An' thankee f'r bringin' Maggie an' little Will. Didn' know when I'd see 'em again, f'r all this . . ."

"Will, damme . . . just what in Hell *is* all . . . this?" Lewrie asked.

"Will ya be 'avin' a seat, sir? Th' explainin'll take a piece. Hoy, this's Mister Tuggle . . . new Master Gunner. Mister Tuggle, could we fetch up table an' chairs . . . any sort o' seats? This is my old cap'um, Commander Lewrie, Mister Tuggle."

"Sir," the Master Gunner intoned, straightening himself like a "piss and gaiters" sergeant of marines. "Pleasure t'meet ye, sir. We know ye for a fair-minded man, sir. Of yer old warrants and petty officers . . . name in the Fleet, sir?"

As a table from the officer's gunroom, some chairs or kegs were fetched, there came a parade up from below: Mr. Reese, Mr. Paschal, and Mr. Meggs—Hogge the Gunner's Mate, the "Dutchie" Mr. Rahl, some of the hands who'd served this ship since the very first—all smiling in welcome and in pleasure of the *rencontre*—though a tad sheepish, Lewrie noted as he took a seat at the table, after acknowledging their helloes.

"Small beer, sir?" Cony offered. "Ah, 'ere we go, sir. Need a 'wet,' I s'pose. Mind 'at keg, Maggie. 'Tis tarry, but 'twill 'ave t'serve f'r yer seat . . . an' sure t'be bad f'r yer 'andsome new gown, me love. Will, do ye climb up on yer daddy's lap, whilst we 'ave ourselves a yarnin'? Do ye not mind me sitting, 'at is, sir . . . ?"

"Aye, seat yourself, Will. This isn't official. And after so many years together . . ." he said with a shrug and a smile. "I'm not here in any capacity 'cept to see you away for home like your leave-ticket allows. Not to meet with any, uhm . . . what-you-call-'ems."

"Delegates, sir." Cony fidgeted a bit, his eyes going cutty as a bag of nails. "Fleet Delegates an' . . . ship delegates."

"Right." Lewrie nodded, taking a sip of the beer before him. "Delegates. I'm not representing anyone, so . . . this is personal."

"Well, sir . . ." Will sighed, scratching his head. He took himself a deepish quaff before continuing. "This'z a tad, uhm . . . well . . ."

"Well?" Lewrie joshed. "A *deep* subject, that."

"Aye, sir . . . aye." Will nodded sagely, mustering up a chuckle of his own for a second. "But, uhm . . . d'ye see, Cap'um. Me . . . an' Mister Tuggle, uhm . . . Mister Reese, an' Sadler, sir . . . we *are* th' delegates. Got elected, like, by the rest o' th' 'ands."

"Oh, Will, my God, what's t'become o' ya?" Maggie gasped aloud, hands to her mouth. "*Tell* me they don't know it yet!"

"Signed our names, Maggie . . . right out in th' open, like. Same as th' rest." Cony winced, taking another duck-and-cover sip of beer.

"Well, I'll be damned." Lewrie groaned. "Why in Hell?"

"Day'r two after ya left th' ship, sir." Will wriggled about as he began to explain, wiping his mouth with the back of his hand. "See, these petitions come aboard from th' line-o'-battle ships, all signed by ev'ry liner in Channel Fleet. Boats visitin' back an' forth, folks lookin' up ol' shipmates . . . ya know how 'at is, don't ya, Cap'um, why a body'd not think o' thing of h'it. First off, they waz about pay . . . Mister Tuggle, show th' cap'um 'at first 'un we got."

"Uhm, er . . . here, sir." Tuggle complied, rather warily. "D'ye see, sir, ah . . . Commander Lewrie? Hands haven't been paid, Lord knows how long, nor how far in arrears, not the six months usual. And with the redcoats gettin' a rise in pay two years ago too, well . . ."

He handed over a document. Lewrie scanned it, feeling like he should be using tongs, not fingers. This could surely burn up a Navy career like a fireplace ember would consume a carpet! He did smirk at it though; for it was Admiralty paper, water-marked with "GR"—the monogram for Georgius Rex!

To the Right Honourable the Lords Commissioners of the Admiralty. THE HUMBLE PETITION of the seamen aboard His Majesty's Ship _____ in behalf of themselves and all others serving in His Majesty's fleets

Humbly Sheweth

THAT your petitioners must humbly intreat your Lordships will take the hardships of which they complain into your consideration, not in the least doubting that Wisdom and Goodness will induce your Lordships to grant them a speedy Redress.

It is now upwards of two years since your Lordships' petitioners observed with Pleasure the Increase of Pay which has been granted the Army and Militia, and the separate provision for their wives and families—naturally expecting that they should in turn experience the same Munificence, but alas, no notice has been taken of Them, nor the smallest provision . . .

The petition went on to state most assuredly that the seamen of the Royal Navy were His Majesty's most loyal and most courageous men, especially in such trying times, when their country called them to . . . "so pressingly advance once more to face her foes . . ." With what additional vigour and happy minds they would *fly* to their duty should they know that they'd be paid more money, in line with the increases the Army (and the idle Militia) got—and pointed out that the Navy hadn't gotten a rise in pay since the times of Charles I!

"Well, hmmm . . ." Lewrie commented, ducking-and-covering behind a quaff of his beer for a moment of thought; *damme, anything I say will be misconstrued as encouraging a mutiny . . . mine own arse nailed to the mainmast. But . . . ? Could I cosset 'em out of it?* he wondered. *Save a ship for the loyalist side; that would be another favour Admiralty owes me!*

"Oh, for God's sake, Mister Tuggle, you look half-strangled," Lewrie said with a faint smile. " 'Long as Will's taking his ease, why do you not, yourself, sir? Mind now . . . , as I said, I have no brief to negotiate, nothing official, but . . ."

"Aye, thankee, sir, thankee right kindly." Tuggle relented with a whoof of expelled breath. He pulled up a tarry keg and bobbed his head as he poured himself a piggin of beer, after bobbing his head to seem to beg even more permission. Sailors had been flogged half-dead in the Fleet who'd even dared *begin* a conversation with some officers! Or take any liberties of familiarity with them. Tuggle was treading on very shaky ground, and he knew it.

"I must say, this petition was quite respectful. And handsomely done. A *small* pay rise, and a more timely paying *of* it, well . . . your officers, I assure you, experience just such frustration. I don't see how that this letter led to . . . *this!*" Lewrie cried, holding the damning document aloft to sweep over his head to encompass the whole rebellious harbour. "And compared to the liners anchored out there, you're in shoal waters. Guns landed ashore, trapped in the graving dock . . . why, it's a wonder the Port Admiral hasn't sent Marines here already to root you out. A mutiny for this piddlin' . . . ?"

" 'Scuse me, Cap'um Lewrie, but"—Cony interjected—"this'd been sent weeks afore, an' nary an answer did t'others get. Sent up t'Admiralty, sir . . . sent t'Lord Howe too, we 'eard tell. Might even o' been sent t'that fellow Fox up in Parliament . . ."

"Aye, the Great Patriot, for certain, sir . . . bein' so liberal an' all?" Tuggle added, sounding a trifle more enthused. Whether he admired Charles James Fox, the new champion of the Common Man, or the beer more—well, Lewrie was uncertain. "But like Mister Cony says . . . no reply, sir. So this time the committees determined they'd not put back t'sea 'thout we get *some* answer. Orders come down Easter morn t'sail. Lord Bridport ordered Vice-Admiral Gardner t'drop eight ships down t'Saint Helen's Patch and await a wind, sir? Well, they didn't . . . not a man moved. Obeyed orders, sir, all orders but that 'un. Afore then, well, sir . . ." Tuggle related, more chummily. "Lord Bridport, he knew what was goin' on, or had an inklin' at last. He asked for the ships t'send him more specific complaints and . . ."

"He bloody *what?*" Lewrie barked, half-strangled on his beer.

Open the floodgates to the lower deck? Lewrie marvelled to himself; *oh, try and lance it 'fore it festers, but, my God! The wrong damn' way! Why, every man-jack had something that rankled him about being in the Navy, pressed or volunteered!*

"Said he couldn't deal with anonymous petitions, sir," Cony admitted. "Why we ended up signin' our names. Valentine Joyce, in *Royal George* . . . th' speaker for all, sir . . . he signed first o' th' list. Sorry, Maggie, but I had t'do h'it. Wot those Yankee Doodles said durin' th' war . . . 'we hang t'gither, or we all hang sep'rate'?"

"You were coerced, Cony," Lewrie objected, offering him a way out. "The people looked to you, and . . ."

"Most o' th' old crew's gone, sir," Cony cut him off gently. "Turned over t'other ships . . . promoted up an' out. Wot 'ands we got, they're new-come. Cap'um Mallard's lot, he brought with 'im? Even them agreed, sir."

"Oh, 'twas a sore patch for him, that, sir! Been with him for years, they had." Tuggle grunted with a dab of humour, but even more sympathy for the new fool who'd seen his "pets" turn on him. "Voted for me an' Will, they did, sir, same'z the old hands remainin'. Then we swore, sir."

"Took a Bible-oath, Cap'um," Cony stated, chin up in a noble, bright-eyed conviction. "Swore t'be true t'th' cause, we did. There were *Marines* took the oath, sir. Stap me, did they not!"

"An' swore t'keep proper order, sir . . . e'en without Commission Officers aboard," Tuggle chimed in. "Ye look sharp with a glass out yonder, sir. They've rove yard ropes from the yardarm tips."

"A threat against . . . ?"

"No, sir!" Tuggle objected. "No threat 'gainst officers, sir! A threat t'any bully-bucks who get out o' line. Officers and wimmen t'be turned out, sir . . . no spirits t'be smuggled aboard, and no folder-ol, no debauch. Repairs, store-keepin', watch-standin', same'z . . ."

"An' 'ard 'nough 'at is, Cap'um Lewrie," Cony smiled wryly. "Why, th' Fleet's workin' alive with Yew-nited Irish, sworn t'ruin it, so France c'n sail over an' help 'em do they 'ave another risin' . . ."

"Quota Men, sir." Tuggle sneered. "We've a few. Worst lot o' drunks, rowdies, back-stabbers . . . *thieves*, sir!" Tuggle growled, and several of the new-come men, and most of the old Jesters still aboard, chimed in with a like growl of disgust.

"No matter, they're no sort o' sailormen, nor watermen either, sir," Cony stuck in. "Ev'ry county, ev'ry borough, an' town'z down t' supply so many men each Assizes f'r th' Navy . . . their quota."

"So they muck out their gaols and loonie bins, and pass 'em on to the Fleet?" Lewrie scowled.

"Bloody right, sir . . . beggin' yer pardon, Maggie darlin'," Will Cony rejoined, most heartily. " 'Ere, Maggie, you take young Will for a piece. 'E's 'z squirmy'z a worm in hot ashes. Oh, they're scamps, idlers, back-talkers an' sea-lawyers, Cap'um. Won't none of 'em make Ord'nary Seamen do ya give 'em a month o' Sundays. No idea o' what it means t'be a proper shipmate. Drunks, hen-heads, cut-throats . . . why, we'd all be better off were they transported f'r life t'that New South Wales! Man's possessions . . ."

"Man's tools, sir!" Mr. Reese, the Carpenter, shouted.

"Ain't safe from 'e, do ya 'ide 'em in th' powder magazines!" Cony barked, which raised another agreeing rumble of discontent from the true seamen and petty officers gathered 'round them.

Lewrie forced himself to scowl more deeply, though he felt like breaking out in laughter. For here was the same plaint he'd heard for years in midshipmen's cockpits, officer's gunrooms, and many a captain's great-cabins—about the sailors they *already* had! And for it to come from men 'afore the mast *too*, well . . . !

"Anyways, sir . . . refusin' t'sail, that got their Lordship attention, right smart." Tuggle sighed, once the hands had calmed down. Lewrie noticed that a few of the new-comes were blushing or scowling—some of those Quota Men here, among real sailors?

"I would imagine that would," Lewrie japed, deadpan.

"Anyway, sir," Tuggle went on, "we, the Fleet Delegates, that is, come up with our list o' grievances Lord Bridport asked us for. Written up proper and signed this time. Reasonable demands, sir, I am mortal-certain you'd call 'em too, Commander Lewrie, bein' a long-time officer, an' all. You've seen how things're done, how the hands are treated. Oh, there's some private grievances from some ships . . . 'bout removin' th' real death-floggers an' th' truly cruel officers'n mates . . . men so cruel it'd make yer eyes water, sir. Nought like you, I've heard, nossir."

"An' we're holdin' out for a gen'ral pardon too, sir," Sadler chimed in from one side. "In writin', so we don't end up like the lads 'board *Culloden* a few years back. . . ."

Culloden, the same two-decker Troubridge had fought so well just recently at St. Vincent, with pretty much the same crew. Aye, Lewrie recalled that she'd staged a brief mutiny. Captain Troubridge had been saddled with a perfect whore of a warship, barely in any condition to put to sea, and her people had demanded that they turn over into some other, safer ship or have *Culloden* into the yards for a proper refit. Surprisingly, the Admiralty had given into their demands, though they needed every ship at sea, and they'd sworn to her crew that they'd be forgiven. Yet as soon as they'd returned to duty, Troubridge and the Marines had rushed them and seized the ten ringleaders. Five of them had ended up being hanged by the neck until dead, then their corpses tarred and chained and displayed 'til their bones fell apart.

"Admiral Gardner called aboard his flagship, *Queen Charlotte*, sir," Cony grunted, sour from the memory. "Urged 'em t'give way an' return t'duty. Said they could swear loyalty, sign a tribute to th' Admiralty, an' it'd all be forgiven. 'Ey wouldn't, though, sir . . . not 'thout a pardon, not 'thout their demands. So he cursed 'em . . . called 'em *cowards*, sir! Swore ev'ry fifth man'd be hanged . . . swore they *all* deserved hangin'. Just'z good'z spittin' on 'em, sir. An' them some o' th' best sailors in th' Fleet. His own *crew*, sir!"

"So what *were* these, uhm . . . grievances?" Lewrie asked.

"Well, the wages, that's still first, sir," Tuggle announced. He produced a folded copy of the document which had been copied for every ship and laid it on the table. Lewrie put one hand in his lap and the other on his beer; no way was he going to touch that!

"Ahem . . ." Tuggle began to read, " ' . . . that our provisions be raised to the weight of sixteen ounces to the pound, and of a better quality; and that our measures may be the same as those used in the commercial code of this country . . .' "

Well, God help the pursers, Lewrie thought; *that'd put 'em out of business in a Dog Watch! No profit for 'em in* that!

"Uhm . . . 'that there be no flour served while we are in harbour, in any port whatsoever under the command of the British flag; and also that there might be granted a sufficiency of vegetables of such kind as may be most plentiful in the ports to which we go; which we grievously complain and lay under the want of.' "

"So we gets the fresh meat from them dockyard thieves the regulations says we should, sir," Sadler groused. "Pound o' bread, even freshbaked 'Tommy,' won't *never* be the match of a pound o' beef, sir! And the flour's so cheap, they *claim* t'issue the beeves or hogs then pocket the diff'rence!"

"Sick care, sir," Tuggle added, tapping a marlin-spike finger on the document. "Man gets sick or injured, he might as well turn up his toes an' die, for all the care most surgeons give. Cram 'em deep below where there's no fresh air, cram 'em in the orlop, some do . . . and the surgeons and mates responsible for buyin' their *own* medicines, sir? Well, you know how cheese-parin' they are 'bout that. Like we say in the grievances here, sir . . . 'that these necessities be not on any account *embezzled*.' "

"Then I may presume, Mister Tuggle, that Surgeon Mister Howse and his mate left the ship soon after?" Lewrie chuckled.

"Sure t'God did, sir," Cony supplied, most cheerfully. "First warrant-holders off, in fact. Called us ungrateful curs, sir, after all they'd . . . *done* fer us!"

Lewrie winced to himself; too much use o' that term "ungrateful curs," hmm?

"Now, sir . . ." Tuggle went on, stern-faced as an instructor at his first morning class—and sure to be disappointed by his scholars. "The fourth thing we want is liberty. Real shore-liberty, for those of the hands deservin'. Like *Jester*, sir . . . three years in foreign waters, and what'd she get, sir? Anchored out, combed for the Press. At best, put Out of Discipline, and all the hands, wives, children, and the hired drabs amingle . . . that's not respectful at all, sir. No privacy, and in me last ship, sir . . . there were these midshipmen who loved t'wander in, watch proper married folk at their *couplin'* . . . beggin' yer pardon, Mrs. Cony. Leave-tickets for trusted men, long-time married men, sir. And holders of warrant, so they could go home, outside the port town, when back in England. Liberty o' th seaport for the younger and unmarried. Now, mayhap there'll be some . . . like these new Quota Men and such . . . who have t'stay aboard 'cause you can't trust 'em, and mayhap ya ferry the doxies out for *them*, but . . ."

You haven't a bloody hope, Lewrie sadly thought; *you stay stubborn over that 'un, and you'll still be mutineers 'til next Epiphany! Navy can't take the risk, can't send a third of a crew ashore, not if there's a French fleet just 'cross Channel and the wind shifts of a sudden. And, Lord . . . how many'd ever come* back? *No, impossible. . . .*

"Last thing, sir," Cony said, drawing Lewrie back from a pose of half-focused inattention. "Well, almost . . . right now, any man is wounded in action or sick . . .'is pay's docked 'til he's back on 'is pins an' discharged from sick-berth. We figger 'e oughta get all 'is pay straight through. Does 'e land at Haslar or Greenwich Hospital, ends up Discharged, then 'e's pensioned off; but for God's sake, sir . . . don't dock 'is *last* bit o' money, then turn 'im out t'starve in civilian life where 'e can't earn 'alf th' livin' 'e coulda made as a sailor. Broke up, crippled, missin' legs an' arms and such . . ."

"Our pay goes up, sir . . . so does the pay for Greenwich Pensioners," Tuggle said, as though it was already decided. "But that's a pittance. And for a man grown up at sea, what sort o' life would it be t'end a beggar ashore!" Tuggle drew out "ashore!" as if it were a biblical curse. "An' never tread a deck again, sir? Never see a foreign port, nor have pride in a voyage done, a storm weathered, nor a watch shared with real sailor-men . . ."

"A sunrise, a sunset," Lewrie sighed wistfully, wondering if there'd be a Navy, another deck for him to tread, if this mutiny went on much longer. What would *he* do as a . . . civilian? "Uh . . . ahem!"

"Now, 'sides the pardon, sir"—Tuggle said, clearing his throat with a tutorly whinny—"here's the last bit, so their Lordships know we're reasonable men, askin' no more'n our due. Ahem . . ."

It is also unanimously agreed by the Fleet, that, from this day, no grievance shall be received, in order to convince the nation at large that we know when to cease to ask, as well as to begin, and that we ask nothing but what is moderate, and may be granted without detriment to the Nation, or the injury of the Service.

Given on board the *Queen Charlotte,* by the delegates of the Fleet, the 18th day of April 1797

"Now that ain't askin' so much, is it, sir?" one of the older hands enquired. "Not like we're askin' for th' moon."

Isn't it? Lewrie wondered sadly.

"Last we heard, sir"—Tuggle told him as Lewrie got his feet to pace, hands in the small of his back—"they'd agreed to the rise in pay. Nothin' official yet, but . . . do they give us better wages, then surely they're considerin' the rest."

"Wouldn't that be enough then?" Lewrie asked. "To end this?"

"Well, nossir." Tuggle sighed, after a long thought. "We wrote back thankin' 'em for the pay rise, but . . .'til we get the fresh meat back an' the flour removed . . . the vegetables . . . the pensions *and* the signed pardon from the King, we don't stir, sir. We'll maintain discipline and order, keep the ships up proper . . . but we won't stir from Portsmouth, sir."

"Even do the French come out from Brest or the Dutch from the Texel?" Lewrie scoffed quickly. "You'd sit idle if they invade us?"

"Well, sir . . . uhm"—Will Cony wheedled for a moment as he got to his own feet to look his old captain and compatriot eye-to-eye—"might be best then . . . does Whitehall worry 'bout such . . . that we come to an agreement soon'z they can, sir."

Stone-faced, and cold as Christmas, Will Cony, of all people in the Navy telling him he'd not sail to his country's defence? It was inconceivable! Could an easy-going, loyal old tar like Will Cony put his back up and refuse to yield a single point, then what in Hell was the world coming to?

"Sail over t'France . . . give 'e Froggies th' fleet," some faceless voice at the back of the pack crowed. "Be swimmin' in gold, fer that!"

"Here, none o' that now!" Tuggle barked, wheeling to confront such sentiments. "Who said that? Own up, man!"

No one did, though no one glared back too angrily or reddened with embarrassment to betray himself.

"Aye, beware of talk like that!" Lewrie roared, like he still had the right to roar on these beloved decks. "That's not mutiny . . . that's treason 'gainst King and Country. Levelling, Republican poisoning talk! London Corresponding Society talk, same as annual Parliaments, no King . . ." he trailed off, a tad limply.

He wasn't sure what else the London Corresponding Society wanted, couldn't recall their other points in those tracts he'd discovered!

"Any man talks of stealing the fleet and sailing off for France isn't a true Englishman, lads. He's a viper in your breast, planted on you by schemers who plot treason. Besides, *Jester* ain't exactly *fit* for sailin' to France at the moment, now is she? Damme, if we do not get what we want, and they try to take us, why I just might steal me a row-boat for spite . . . and sell it to the Frogs, hah? Will any of ya be swimmin' in gold for that, hey?" he mimicked.

There was a certain, sardonic logic to it that made them laugh, at least the slightest bit.

"Whoever said that, you lads watch him close . . . make sure that you take whatever else he suggests with a *handful* of salt!" Lewrie told them. "Damme, not three weeks ago, I told the old hands among you I was as proud of you as a captain could be, and now look at what you've gotten yourselves talked into! Come on, men! Settle for better wages and a few concessions. You're in no spot to sail away from a graving dock, and you're in no spot to resist, without artillery."

"Took an oath, sir," Tuggle insisted. "Beggin' yer pardon, sir, but our minds're made up . . . same as yours, by the sound of it. Said yerself, sir . . . you didn't come to negotiate. Don't have an ear with Admiralty to help or hinder, sir. Beggin' yer pardon, sir, but . . . it might be best did ya go ashore. Like t'other officers, sir."

"Will, I came for you," Lewrie snapped, after having himself a long, incredulous gawp at Tuggle. He hadn't been ordered about like that since he was a midshipman! "I'm asking, as a friend, leave it. There's still your leave-ticket. *You'd* let him off, wouldn't you, Mister Tuggle? Lads? Here's his wife and child begging . . . damn you all! Here's *me* begging!" he demanded. "Will you come *away*, Mister Cony?"

"Nossir, I s'pose not." Cony grimaced, after heaving a long, deep sigh of regret. "A'ready signed me name as a delegate. Leave-ticket'd not mean much do h'it go again' us."

"Will, for God's sake, *noooo!*" Maggie wailed. "Come away!"

Cony went to her, to take her hands and lead her a little off to one side, gently trying to explain. "Swore me a Bible-oath, dear Maggie. Can't rightly say I ever did afore. Man who'd break faith with 'at, well . . . ain't much of a man atall."

"They'll hang you, sure as Fate . . . !" his wife shrilled, pale as death and like to faint with fear.

"Can't slide off an' let th' lads down neither, darlin' . . . not after 'ey made me one o' their rep—Gawd, ain't h'it a break-teeth word though—rep-re-sent-atives?"

"Then I'll stay with you, Will . . . me and the boy!" Mrs. Cony shuddered, reaching down and finding a firm Country-English spunk to draw on. "God help us, Will, but no matter the folly you've got in, if yer that determined . . . then you must think yerself right. And if you think you're right, then I'll stand by you through thick an' thin, same as we vowed . . . at our *marryin'* Bible-oath!"

"Ah, ya can't, Maggie," Cony muttered sadly. "Committee said t'put all women ashore, out o' harm's way, so we could keep good order, proper Ship's Discipline . . . so they don' think us nothin' but drunks an' debauchers. Can't make no exceptions, dear as I'd wish . . . Maggie, come 'ere a minute. Give me leave, Cap'um? 'fore ya takes 'em back 'ome for me?"

Lewrie saw it was no use and gravely nodded. Will and Maggie went aft towards the taffrails for a last few words of parting, while Lewrie retrieved his hat, then paced away towards the entry-port. And little Will, tears running down his face, aware his dad'd not be with him anytime soon—saw himself being cosseted and dandled on old Mr. Paschal's knee, surrounded by some older petty officers and seamen who had children of their own, making a fuss over him, cooing, making faces to amuse him, though Will wailed inconsolably.

Lewrie felt a presence near him and turned to meet the sheepish gaze of *Jester*'s new Master Gunner, Mister Tuggle.

"You're a hopeless pack of bloody fools, you know," Lewrie said accusingly. "And do you get Will Cony court-martialed and hung aside you, then I swear t'Christ, I'll dance on your grave!"

"I s'pose you may be right, sir," Tuggle confessed, looking a bit lost and hopeless at that moment. "But the fat's in the fire for sure, sir. There's always a chance they'll give us better'n half what we asked. Be satisfied with that . . . a bit more'n half, sir."

"Is there much to this . . . from that London Corresponding Society?" Lewrie simply had to know. "Saw some tracts. Priestley, Place . . . some of that lot. Did they stir this up or did it . . . ?"

"You forgot Mister Thelwall and Mister Binns, sir, a heap of others," Tuggle said, with a brief, weary smile. "I'd reckon 'least a quarter o' the new hands—those Quota Men and United Irishmen . . . pressed Americans—have Thom Paine's *Rights of Man, Part the Second,* damn'-near memorised by now, sir. No King, sir? No House of Lords, just Commons . . . annual Parliaments . . . fair wages, pensions, decent working hours, and conditions, sir? Right t'vote for any man making £6 a year, not £100, any who pay 'scot and lot'? Lord, sir! Even gone so far as to preach on giving *wimmen* the vote, sir! Did ya ever hear such tripe, Commander Lewrie? Has nought t'do with the Fleet; 'tis nothing we wish! As to yer question, sir . . . though I 'spect we've a few LCS men aboard . . . wasn't them started this. Seen none o' their tracts. No one *ashore* stirred the fleet t'mutiny, either, sir. This come from the sailors themselves, sir; and did some of the wild-eyed, radical shite . . . beggin' yer pardon, sir . . . come up, 'twas rejected by the delegates early on. We're loyal men, sir," Tuggle insisted. "Just want better rations . . . pay, a tad better treatment, sir . . . that's all we demand. T'be treated like *men,* sir. We aren't all drunken, brainless animals, sir, like most officers and th' Admiralty think. We'll do our duty for King and Country should we be called to . . . we're still True Blue Hearts o' Oak at bottom, sir."

Lewrie opened his mouth to make a reply, but decided against a rebuttal; it could only come out an exasperated sneer, he suspected.

"I trust, Mister Tuggle, that *you* are sincere 'bout doing your duty should it come—should the French come," Lewrie said, instead. "And with Will Cony so stubborn over this, I trust you're all as sincere in your grievances too. I *cannot* wish you good fortune, you know it. Yet . . . for Will's sake, if nothing else . . . I wish that I could."

"For Will Cony's sake then, Commander Lewrie, sir. For Will's sake." Mr. Tuggle grimly nodded, with only a tiny crinkle at the corners of his eyes.

All Lewrie could do after that was to go aft, to take charge of Bosun Cony's family, and escort them off the ship, back to their carriage—and take them home, their quest a failure.

CHAPTER NINE

Lewrie was feeling particularly helpless, and hapless, after a few more days. No letter had come from Admiralty to offer employment, as he had smugly expected; it was spring planting season, about which he knew absolutely *nothing*, no matter his few idle half-pay years as a gentleman—tenant farmer before the war—that was Caroline's bailiwick and none of his. He had been known to raise his hat, but nothing green!

His civilian suitings were once more hopelessly out of style as well, and to waste money updating his shore wardrobe at a time when the farm needed every pence in these tight times could appear selfish and "hen-headed" spendthrift, showing disloyalty to Caroline. Besides, he half-dreaded, to invest in civilian togs might signal a surrender or a willingness to *remain* ashore on half-pay for the rest of his life! The Fates, he superstitiously feared, took note of such accommodations.

Practically in a Dog Watch, he had been reduced from a powerful warship captain to a mere centurion, mouthing repetitions of his tribune-wife's dictates to their hired labourers, without even half a clue to what they portended or a decent idea of what proper work such orders involved, or how such labour was to be carried out!

On top of that, the household was also feverishly engaged with the dreaded spring cleaning; and did he not wish to be "press-ganged" into moving furniture or emptying pantry shelves, a man still possessed of his higher faculties would make himself scarce, perhaps oversee the boiling of water, as one did for childbirth at best, and leaving the womenfolk to their "pagan" rites, rituals, and mysteries.

Simpler societies, such as the South Sea Islanders or the Seminole and Muskogee Indians he had dealt with in '82, had solutions for menfolk and warriors in situations such as these, Lewrie recalled—the Long-House, where women were barred. London had its clubs. Lewrie, and Anglesgreen, had the public houses.

After a horseback tour of his acres, a word or two with the new foreman and his mates, Lewrie betook himself to the Old Ploughman tavern.

The pub was uncrowded in the morning hours of course; the *real* farmers who knew what they were about were out busily doing it. Even the more-gentlemanly Red Swan Inn that he rode past, where he was anathema as long as *any* Embleton still drew breath, only had a coach or two, a saddle horse or two, out front.

Lewrie handed his reins to the Ploughman's newest boyish "daisy-kicker," said hello to old Mr. Beakman and his spinster daughter (whom Will Cony had jilted years before, Lewrie recalled with a newfound sadness for his missing Bosun), ordered up a mug of light, sprightly new spring ale to steel himself for a look at the even more troubling world beyond, and called for the newspapers.

Mr. Beakman's own *Publican's Advertiser* was warmly supportive of the mutiny, and the seamen's cause, but wisely shied away from seeming too "political"—unless it wished to be suppressed by the government, of course! Last evening's London *Courier*, and the fresh-come morning *Chronicle*, were Whig papers and Fox-ite; they hardly even said that the mutiny was even a mutiny yet! Just the "disturbance at Spithead" or . . . *oh, Christ,* Lewrie groaned! The *Chronicle* bore the disturbing tidings that the mutiny had now spread to the dozen line-of-battle ships based at Plymouth too! A list of ships that had raised the red flags was included. *Hmmm,* he puzzled; very few of the frigates were listed . . . yet. But that made sense; pay didn't matter aboard frigates. It was all prize-money they were after, and frigates were more comfortable ships, with more room per hand, not so crowded . . . and a lot less dull a life than plodding aboard a "liner" or swinging at anchor waiting for the foe to come out and challenge them.

For a brief, hopeful time, the mutiny had appeared to be ended, just after he'd come back from Portsmouth. Parliament had been rumoured to be meeting, the House of Commons to debate a bill for supplementary funds that the Prime Minister and Councillor of The Exchequer—William Pitt the Younger—were drawing up to add to the annual Admiralty expenditures. "His Nobs," King George, had been rumoured to have left off dunking and gambling at Bath and had *seemed* amenable to the general pardon the mutineers requested. Tory, pro-government dailies had hinted that crews were returning to full discipline, taking their exiled officers back aboard. . . .

A few days later though . . .

Pitt *had* spoken to the Commons, rambling through a speech that notably omitted any mention of Navy, Mutiny, Seamen, Pay, or even Water! The Whigs and Fox-ite factions had been on him like dogs on a butcher's castoffs; questions had been raised, enquiries into the matter threatened. Elderly Admiral Lord Howe had had to rise to defend himself.

Howe had admitted that he *had* gotten anonymous copies of their demands *weeks* before but had been reassured by Sir Hugh Seymour, the Admiralty's senior man at Portsmouth, that he'd seen no signs of mutinous assemblies, seen any grievance letters, and had thought that the copies Howe had gotten were the work of a malicious individual. Pitt and his First Lord of The Admiralty had been forced to admit that they had had inklings of mutiny—and had sat on it!

Following Pitt's dreadful speech, the sailors had put officers ashore once more, re-hoisted the red flags, and re-rove the yard-ropes, sure they were being set up with false promises for another betrayal, soon to be winnowed and hung as *Culloden*'s ringleaders had been.

To make things worse, the Earl Spencer had told Commons that he had ordered completely new sets of weights and measures to be used for sailors' rations—Admiralty could not redress that grievance until the new weights were available.

That, Lewrie scoffed, was a bald-faced admission that corruption and graft went from bottom to top, from ships' pursers to the dockyard warehouses, from jobbers to the Victualling Board itself! That even civilian purveyors were being cheated when they put their goods on the Admiralty scales!

Panicked by the resurgence of the mutiny, Commons had elected to scrounge up an extra £900,000 for the Navy Estimate, and the King signed a pardon, but by then it was too little, too late!

"Not over yet, sir?" Beakman's daughter enquired as she fetched him a top-up of spring ale.

"No, and God knows when it ever will be . . . thankee," Lewrie told her.

"Poor Mizzuz Cony, not knowin' . . ." the daughter said, with a tiny cluck of her tongue, before returning to the long, oak bar counter.

Never married after Will took up with Maggie, Lewrie speculated; *gettin' long-in-tooth and haggard. God, a publican's daughter not taken yet, even did she look like the arse-end of a sheep?* He rather doubted that Mistress Beakman had much real sympathy in her soul for Maggie Cony; spite and glee for a long-awaited comeuppance was more like it!

He turned to the Tory papers. Both *The Times* and the *Gazette* were incensed that the mutineers were demanding relief from tyrannical officers and mates too. How dare "common" seamen hope to dictate to the aristocracy, the squirearchy, their "betters" to decide who was capable, or suitable, to command them! Never in Hell, both papers were firm in saying, should HM government, Admiralty, or the landed gentry surrender their rights as honourable gentlemen; why, it violated that sacred principle of the gentleman-officer, the dignity of the Navy—the dignity of the monarch himself! Why, with times so parlous, and revolution run riot on the Continent, in America . . . !

Lewrie shoved *The Times* away in disgust. Right here, on this very village commons the day before, the local Yeomanry and Militia had drilled. As his father had said, to prepare them should they be called out to march to Portsmouth—just in case.

Would the mutineers turn their artillery on the shore, fire upon British troops, if their demands were not met? Would British soldiers fire upon British tars? Lewrie wondered with a frown; that was even a more disturbing question. For if that happened, all bets were off, and England might go the way of France, with blood in the streets and the aristocracy, the King and Queen—and serving officers! Lewrie queasily imagined—thrown out, thrown in gaol, even guillotined, just like it had come to the port of Toulon and his now-dead French Royalist compatriots in '93. Would he and Caroline and the children end up as refugees in foreign lands as those

Royalists had? Or dead, like Charles Auguste, Baron de Crillart, and all his kin but Sophie de Maubeuge?

Caroline had kin—Rebel kin—in the Cape Fear country, back in North Carolina. And Caroline and her parents and brothers had fled them too, become refugees in England. Had the American Chiwicks mellowed enough for a welcome, he wondered? But what joy was there in that— the United States had practically scrapped their navy once the Revolution was over, and what could he do, except . . . *farm!* Jesus!

There came a hellish din from abovestairs, the scrape and clang of something heavy and metallic, the "sloosh" of water, followed not a moment later by a trickle of water off the smoky overhead oak beams of the low-ceilinged public house's common rooms.

"What the Devil?" Lewrie griped aloud, standing quickly to flee a positive flood of sudsy water leaking through the ancient floorboards above.

"Oh, so *sorry,* Squire Lewrie, but we're doin' spring cleaning," Mistress Beakman gasped. "Per'aps you'd be safer on the side garden."

"Thought I'd *escaped* spring cleaning," he groused, rescuing his pile of newspapers and his wide-brimmed felt hat. "Might as well go home at this rate."

"*Sor*-ry, Mizzus!" a woman wailed from abovestairs. "The kettle o' wash water spilled. But it's bringin' up a *power* o' grime! Will ya wish us t'start on the public rooms then?"

"Aye," Mistress Beakman called aloft. "Will you not stay for the mail coach, then, Squire Lewrie Won't be a half-hour, with every road dry so far this week, sir," she prattled on. "Should've done the cleanin' and moppin' before the Muster Day, but . . . and wasn't that the grand sight, sir. Your good wife and wee daughter turned out so fine and your ward, Miz Sophie, lookin' so fresh and fetchin' in that pale green chiffony gown, her new straw bonnet, and all . . . Aye, she's rare wondrous t'see, sir . . . poor, motherless lass, bein' French and so far from home. Still, Muster Day seemed t'cheer her . . . Squire Harry and his cavalry lads especial"—she breezed on, fanning her face, as if overcome with lust or excitement herself—"bouncin' on her toes and clappin' and cheerin' so . . ."

Something was being said beyond idle chatter and "gush," Lewrie suspected, and he raised a brow over it. As cattily delighted as she was over Will Cony's "comeuppance," and her rival Maggie's sufferings for it at long last, Lewrie suspected that he was being slyly baited.

Will had been *his* "man"; and he was the interloper from rakish London who had shamed Harry, stolen his "intended" Caroline. Did she blame *him* for being jilted, and was she now suggesting that he would be getting a well-deserved "comeuppance" too?

"Fetch you a fresh mug in the side garden whilst ya wait for the mail coach t'come then, shall I, sir?" she chirped.

"Uhm, aye . . . I s'pose," Lewrie allowed.

"Lord, as if I don't have enough worries on my plate as it is!" Lewrie grumbled to himself as he betook himself out to the open-sided, covered garden porch and took a dry seat at a newish oak-slab table.

World's goin' t'Hell in a hand-basket, and even domesticity has its pitfalls, he decided. Oh, there'd been signs, right from Easter Church services. "Women!" he muttered under his breath.

They just *won't* do the sensible thing. Offer sugar or salt and they'll take salt, every time . . .'cause it's sharper tasting. *Bad* man, oh, a *baddd* man—stay away, he wished he could simply order her. Or don't, you silly chit; *be* a fool, if you wish.

He supposed Sophie was bored to tears by the poor choice of eligible bachelors in the neighbourhood. She was eighteen now, and her sap was rising; and girls that age began to think of which tree a nest could be built in . . . and how best to feather it. Sophie was penniless, without dowry or "dot" to offer, without personal paraphernalia to take with her, beyond what Caroline had sewed with her, and if she thought the Lewries would stand her marriage portion, she'd best have another think coming . . . especially if her choice was as abysmally unfortunate as the Honourable Harry Embleton!

"Maybe it's simple youthful rebellion," he grumbled. The 'tween years' headstrong urge to kick over the traces, no matter how gentle or kind the traces? "Or maybe it's because she's French!" He smirked.

Oh, they were a perverse race, the Frogs. He could not imagine that she found Harry attractive—only another otter could be attracted to such a profile. He was an idiot . . . therefore controllable? Bosh!

Lewrie could not feature Sophie as being so guileful, so mercenary, so . . . scheming! Yet for no discernible reason, she suddenly had not seemed *averse* to being fawned at by that feckless fool, Harry. She had few opportunities outside Caroline's sharp notice, but that didn't signify. Caroline was sure that *something* was going on behind their backs, yet he feared speaking to her about it; speak too often and disparagingly about a swain, and young chits would—perversely!—run with glee to the very thing or person one warned them against!

And God knows, I did . . . gladly! Alan told himself; *not that anyone in charge of me ever took the time to give me fair warnings.*

Yet just yesterday, amid all the pomp and pageantry that little Anglesgreen could produce, the stamp and slap of musket drill and marching, the clatter of cavalry hooves, the tootles of "The Bowld Soldier Boy" that his father, as the senior officer hereabouts had chosen from his Indian army days as one of his very favourites . . . there Sophie had been, making sheep's eyes and hooded glances, mostly at Harry.

Oh, she'd bantered prettily with Richard Oakes too; and if Alan had his druthers, of all the rakehellish local lads, Richard Oakes was his choice, should she deign to swoon over *anyone!* Nowhere near rich, but his family owned their own land; he was handsome, well-knit, rode well, sang well . . . the best of a bad lot, frankly, for being a member of Harry's roistering, hell-for-leather coterie. Educated, was known to *not* move his lips when he read . . . didn't look like a sack of cast-off clothes in his finery . . . and, most especially, did *not* resemble an otter with dysentery!

Perhaps I should at least try to solve this one small problem, Lewrie thought with a fresh frown; *there's damn-all I can do about the rest. If I'm fated to stay "beached" 'til the mutiny ends, pray God it does . . . soon! or . . .*

There came a clatter from the East, the sight of a coach rising over the hill by the old ruins, threading the overhanging, road-spanning boughs of centuries-old oaks. Shopkeepers emerged from the doors of their establishments, housewives popped from their homes. The mail coach brought them out to see something new, hear something new, see a strange face in their staid village life.

Lewrie rose too, ignoring his mug of ale, to stand by the kerb in front of the pub where the coach usually stopped. The wee "daisy-kicker" sprang to seize the reins. A mail sack was flung down. There were no passengers alighting this morning; then the coachee whipped up and clattered the swaying "dilly" on its way to Petersfield.

"Why, 'tis a good thing you waited, Squire Lewrie, for there's a whole packet for ya," Miss Beakman tittered. "Oh, and by-the-by, the milliner, Mistress Clowes, left this note here for you, but it clean fled my mind with all the scrubbin' we . . ."

"Ah, thankee, Mistress," Lewrie replied, adding that letter to the pile bound with a hank of twine. "Bills, bills, bills . . . ah, ha!"

A larger letter, of much finer paper, watermarked with the GR for Georgius Rex for King George III . . . sealed with a dark-blue wax, stamped with crown and anchors . . . Admiralty!

It appeared that domesticity, any worries anent young Sophie de Maubeuge, the spring planting . . . it could all go hang of a sudden.

And feeling the perversity of being delighted, Lewrie *was* delighted! But not guilty enough to stifle a broad grin of relief!

Flinging coins on the table, he drained his mug and called out, "Boy, my horse!"

CHAPTER TEN

*O*h, *m'sieur*, you are back so early!" Sophie de Maubeuge said in surprise as he practically burst through the front door. She might have been the belle of yesterday's Militia parade and drills, but Caroline—sprung from more frugal, practical Colonial stock—had engrained real work into her. Sophie was dressed in one of her oldest sack gowns, and a maid's apron and mob-cap. With a cloth-wrapped broom, she had been sweeping for cobwebs in the entry hall. Not very energetically, Lewrie suspected; she *had* been raised as a French aristocrat since birth.

"The tavern was not *amusant?*" Sophie enquired, obviously eager for an excuse to leave off servants' work and twinkling with wit.

"Informative, but not amusing, no, Sophie," Lewrie answered, in a rush still. "Where is Caroline?"

"In 'er *boudoir*, up . . ."

"Excuse me then," he said, bounding for the staircase.

"Ze post 'ave arriv-ed? You wish zat I, uhm . . . *classer, non* . . . sort it for *vous, m'sieur?*" she offered, stepping forward and eyeing that loose bundle with what Lewrie could only feel was . . . alarm.

"Thank you, no, Sophie, it's only bloody bills!" Lewrie shouted down from the landing on his way up the second pair-of-stairs. "I'll sort 'em later. Caroline?"

Helpful little chuck, he thought, but no *wonder* if she wishes a way out with Harry—or anyone—to avoid Caroline's housewifery work!

"Why, what is it, Alan?" his wife asked, with an amused chuckle in her throat as he stepped into their bedroom. She had been sorting out bed-linens, stowing away home-sewn winter quilts and blankets.

Slaying the triumphant smile he had worn since first breaking the seal on his Admiralty letter, he held it up in mute statement, now unfolded to the full, with its official seals of office in view.

Caroline wrapped one arm about a bedpost to support herself, while her other hand flew to cover her stricken mouth with trembling fingers. "Oh, no . . . oh, God, no!" she quavered. "You're barely home two weeks; they *promised* you it could be weeks more before . . . !"

"I'm to have a frigate, dearest," he told her, "that means I'll be made 'post'! With this mutiny still on, they simply must get ships to sea, un-tainted ships, otherwise . . ."

She positively glowered at him, despite her shock and grief!

Damme, wrong tack, Alan thought, *got things out of order!*

"Caroline, I truly am sorry; I thought we'd have more time too . . . peaceful weeks with you and the children, but . . ." he attempted saying to cosset her, tossing the bundle of unopened letters and bills to the foot of the bed so that he could go and embrace her. "But as long as this war lasts—'growl ye may, but go ye must.' I can't . . ."

"I *know*, Alan!" she gravelled back, arms crossed over her bosom; tears and betrayal-glints in her eyes. "Dear Lord, how *well* I know by now. I wish you'd never even *seen* a warship all your born days!"

"Well . . ." he stammered, surprised and spurned by her vehemence, "there've been times I'd wish the same, my love, believe me. *Cockerel*. My first ship, *Ariadne* . . . loony Treghues's *Desperate* . . ."

"But you're a *Navy* man," she jeered back, refusing his offered em-braces, back-pedaling towards her cedar chests, "off like a flash at their first . . . their *every* beck and call. *Eager* to dash away for your glory and honour . . . while those who love you must remain, abandoned . . . worry-ing and fretting, a-and . . . !"

"Caroline," he whispered, taking a tentative step forward, but she would have none of it, retreating towards the windows with a swish of her skirts. "Dear?" he lamely begged to her turned back.

"How little time we've really had, Alan," she accused. "Those three years in the Bahamas . . . a mere four *more* here, in our own home. Making a life so sweet and filled with every delight a man could imagine. Heirs, and land, friends and community, family, and . . . !"

"And then a war came, which threatens them all," Lewrie reminded her, more sternly than he meant to. "You know I had to respond to our country's call, dear. I don't know what else I could've . . ."

"You could have *stayed*, Alan!" she accused, whirling to face him again, that vertical furrow in her brows. "If I, if we, meant anything at all to you . . ."

They'd had arguments before, but Lewrie felt that this one would be memorable. So surprised was he, so betrayed by his usually supportive and admiring wife, he felt that he could only blush with shame; for she was right on the nail-head with her accusations!

"Four years on the land, you could have at least made an *effort* to learn the farm's ways . . . to uphold and aid me," she fumed, now looking bleak and haggard in her quiet rage. She stomped past him to shut the door so the servants or children couldn't hear. "But you didn't. You *played* at it! And as soon as Admiralty sounds their bosun's pipes, why off you scuttle to wear King's Coat, again, so you can stalk about your quarterdeck, *relishing* it!"

He would have told her that they were rightly termed the bosun's "calls," but thought better of it immediately.

"It's what I *am*, Caroline," Lewrie said with a sigh. "It's who you married, mind . . . a Sea Officer of the King and . . ."

"Yes, you are," she sighed in turn, leaning on the door as if exhausted past all contemplation of future improvement. "And a glad one . . . you know you are. Glad to sail away to who knows where; glad to be free of your familial responsibilities. Glad to wallow in gore and shot, expose yourself to danger, 'til it catches up with you some day . . . so long as you can chase after . . . *glory!* Gone so long, so far, thinking a letter every rare now and then, a pack of 'pretties' from a foreign port, atones for your absence!" she hissed.

"Dearest . . ."

"No thought for the ones you leave behind," she continued, hands to her face to daub her tears. "Now your war isn't the short one you thought when *last* you left us . . . *is* it, Alan?" Caroline jeered. "God knows, another year or two perhaps. God save us, another five, *ten?* Another three-year commission, before we see you for a bare month, or less, before the next one, and the next one . . . and . . . ! Damn you, and damn the Royal Navy, just . . . !"

Her anger broke in a flood of weeping, wrenching sobs that shook her frame, made her shoulders shudder. She lifted her apron's hem to swab her inflamed face, and Lewrie at last could step forward to scoop her into his arms, offer mute comfort and sympathy. He rocked her, as if dancing from one foot to the other, laid her head on his shoulder, and stroked her long, lean back—afraid to say a word more for now.

At last she made a sniffle, drew a deep breath, and sighed in resignation. "How soon then?" she asked, in a wee girlish voice into his shirt collar.

"My reply off by afternoon post," Lewrie speculated—gently. "Depart by first light tomorrow, I fear. I really *am* sorry, dear'un. You don't know *how* sorry. Our joys together . . . us and the children . . . you're not the only one who misses peace and normalcy. Tranquility."

"Do they say where you're to go?" she asked, clenching back at him, her face cooler against his at last.

"I rather doubt Portsmouth or Plymouth are in any mood for new ships to commission at the moment," he dared to scoff. "First, up to London . . . then perhaps the Nore or Great Yarmouth. Some port close to home, I'd suspect, with the French *and* Dutch fleets threatening us. I doubt it's to be a foreign station, not for a year or better most-like," he told her, leaning back a bit, emboldened by her resignation to meet her eyes once more.

"So . . . not too far, or long, a separation?" Caroline softened, leaning back herself, for a tiny crumb of promise.

"Perhaps even close enough to get home every month or so," he said with a shrug. "Can't count on it, but . . . when winter comes down, if I'm still home-ported, the weather'll bind me in harbour for weeks at a time. We could have you and the children down to visit. School can go hang for a bit, or fetch their tutor along . . ."

Aye, that's the way, m'girl, he thought; *perk up game, as you always do! Put the best face on it.*

"Care to lay a wager with me, dearest?" he joshed, feeling he was now on safer ground. "*Lay* odds with me, hmm? I win, and I get you . . . with no tykes underfoot . . . just the two of us, for hotel weekends."

"And what do I win if you're wrong, Alan?" she queried, still dubious, but much closer to an amused grin than she had been.

"Why, you get *me*, m'dear!" he promised, "a joyous romp, so you may do what you will with me, have your beastly way with me!"

"Oh, you're incorrigible," she sighed. But, Lewrie noted, this time it was a teasing sigh. "I s'pose we should begin packing you."

"Let's both pack . . . Hell's Bells, let's *all* pack, Caroline," he insisted, all come over with inspiration. "The overseer can deal with the farm for a few days. We'll *all* go up to London, perhaps beyond to my new ship, 'til I'm settled aboard."

"Alan, I can't abandon the farm work, not now, not . . ." Caroline balked, but with a pensive, almost eager sound, as if considering it.

" *'Course* you can!" he rejoined quickly. "Extend the times we have together by a fortnight at least! The boys are out of school; you'll be free of my pesky father for a while . . . and when was the last time Sophie saw London? Do her good to see more of the world. Other likely young lads, hmm? Turn her head? Gawd, that'd be four birds or more with one stone, hah? Let's do, love! I'm to be made 'post,' so we deserve to celebrate!"

"Well . . ." She hesitated, head cocked to one side, and swishing her long tail of hair under her mob-cap. A sly smile sprang to life. "Whyever not, then? Yes, let's!" And she sprang to her wardrobe to open it for likely gowns suitable to impress.

And thank bloody Christ that *mellowed her!* Lewrie thought.

He sat on the foot of the bed to sort the rest of the mail, as she measured a dress against her. Bills, mostly tiny sums, he noted; and thank God for that, else they'd not be able to afford a diverting jaunt to the city. More prize-money deposited in his Coutts's account by his solicitor, Mr. Mountjoy, aha! But a tithe of what he'd really reaped so far, but more than enough to offset their sudden lunatick excursion *and* tide the farm over for the rest of the year's needs.

"Bloody Hell!" he barked, of a sudden.

"Yes, it's much too plain," Caroline agreed, misunderstanding his meaning and hanging the last gown she'd tried back in the wardrobe. "Though you needn't take such a harsh tone as to . . ."

"No, Caroline, look!" he insisted, bounding from the bed. "The scales are gone from our eyes, as it were. This bill from a milliner, a Mistress Cowles . . ."

"Quite cunning, dearest, and not really that expensive really," Caroline continued to apologise. "Sophie, Charlotte, and I only ordered one apiece for spring."

"Ah, but it's not a bill, love . . .'tis a *billet-doux!*" Lewrie cried, waving it at her. "*Wondered* why a local bill needed wax seals. It's really from Harry Embleton . . . suggesting an actual assignation."

"Let me see that!" Caroline demanded, fresh fury in her voice; thankfully for Lewrie, none directed at him for a change. "Why, the conniving . . . hmph! See if she has our trade in future! I know she's been at her shop quite often lately, but . . . I hardly expected Sophie to exhibit such back-alley guile. The thoughtless, headstrong chit!"

"Like that Frog novel, *Les Liaisons Dangereuses,*" Lewrie scoffed, more than glad for Caroline to be on other ground. "Lovers passed letters easier than . . . gas!"

"And what would *you* know of such scandalous scribbling . . . Alan?"

"Well, I heard tell . . ." he waffled, turtling his neck into his collar once more. "Men talk, don't ye know . . . in the gunroom," Lewrie gruffly, *most* off-handedly, added.

"I shall speak harshly with her about this," Caroline promised. "All this time I thought her sweet and naive, but now . . . ! Warn that young miss I'll have no lies or dangerous folderol in my household! Surely she must have sense enough to see that he's so bad for her, or any true Christian young lady! I really *must* put my foot down in this instance . . . bring her up short before she . . ."

Uh-oh! Lewrie thought in sudden panic; *and when cornered like a rat, accused of foolishness, she'll turn and bite back and blab about Phoebe Aretino and me . . . for jingle-brained spite! There's an end to Domestic Bliss, by God!*

"Caroline, she's but a child still," he cooed instead, going to embrace his wife to cosset her out of another pet. "Besides, do we accuse her, act as if we don't trust her, we will lose all the affection she's developed with us, and she'll practically *run* to Harry. Or the first human-lookin' substitute. All the way to Gretna Green, hey? The first hedge-priest or false-justice that'd wed her to a charming rogue? No, dear, that's not the way! I must . . . insist!"

Beg, would be more like it! he told himself in a fret.

"Use my father. Sophie finds him amusing, calls him *Granpere.* Some of his rough, uhm . . . sagacity about men might be of more avail," he urged. "God knows, he must be good for something! She needs soft, insistent, and loving . . . motherly, paterfamilial . . . advice. Guidance."

She stared at him for a long moment, her hands and that damned *billet-doux* limply hung together on her belly. He felt a need to see to his fly-buttons, his neck-stock, under such close inspection.

"Alan, you continually amaze me," she said at last, forming her fondest grin, that furrow disappearing, and the riant folds below her eyes acrinkle. "You're right, of course. Harsh words and accusations . . . once hurled . . . can never be recovered—or forgiven."

" 'Least said, soonest mended,' " Lewrie dared breathe in relief.

"Where *do* you get your insight, being so much in the company of sailors, my dear?" She actually snickered, coming to give him a grateful hug and a peck on the lips. "I'd feared her head being turned by Harry . . . he is rich, and she is not . . . *we* are not."

"Un-used to household drudgery, though she tries to accommodate your wishes . . . from love and gratitude, m'dear," he tacked on, "with sisterly, dare I even say, uhm . . . daughter-ly obedience? She's come to love you . . . us, after all."

"That's true, too, love," Caroline gently chuckled. "Sophie is never going to be a 'goodie' housewife. A magnificent hostess, wife, or house-*mistress,* but . . . yes. Soft words and sage advice, drop by gentle drop, will be more suitable. *And,* your father's cautions given her during their rides and card games. A stiff warning to that colluding Mistress Cowles . . . a word to Harry. Or should I merely take down my horsewhip, do you think, dearest? Might he get the hint?"

"Perfect, my dear. Well, off to London, all of us?"

"Yes. By first light tomorrow. You write your letters, whilst I pack." She kissed him once more, deeper, with more meaning, before going to the door. "And be sure to reserve us a separate room at Willis's, will you? I mean to hold you to your wager . . . dear Alan!"

Whew! he thought in relief; *can I finesse 'em or not?*

"Children . . . boys! Sophie? Guess what?" Caroline announced.

CHAPTER ELEVEN

*L*ike a presaging omen of his new-found prospects, the coach ride up to London had been a cool but sunny delight. The weather had turned off splendid, the roads dried out, but not so dusty they couldn't lower the sash windows of their coach and savour the aromas and sounds of a marvelous springtime, though travelling with children aboard wasn't a thing Lewrie was quite used to. There were times he envied Andrews—up on the driver's seat with their coachee to make room in-board and free of the nonsense. "London!" Charlotte would scream, whenever a new village or town loomed up before them. "Are we *there* yet?" Hugh would demand . . . at about every tenth milepost. Sewallis, thankfully, kept his own counsel for the most part, and his lip buttoned, decrying only the most marvelous sights which flickered by as their coach reeled off a goodly clip, almost as fast as one of the new "balloon coaches" which bore the Royal Mails. No mud—well, not much, anyway—flew up to daub them, no herds of geese, sheep, beeves, or turkeys blocked the road so completely they'd have to come to a complete stop . . .

No, the delays they suffered were for nourishment, for sweets or fruits hawked by pedlars at the kerbs of the towns they passed. And, of course, the inevitable ". . . Mummy, I have to, uhm . . . *now!*" bawled by Charlotte, sometimes by Hugh. "But, darling, you just, uhm . . . not a mile back." "I know, but Mummy . . . !" Hugh, at least, could be taken behind a hedge by the side of the road, whilst the horses got a rest; Charlotte, though . . . well, that required a proper inn, a proper jakes, a proper escort from Caroline or Sophie with the family's travelling "necessary" bundle. Followed by a sweet, perhaps . . . ?

"Commander Lewrie?" the tiler gawked. "Back again, are we, sir? Aye, sir . . . on th' list, sir. Workin' ya like a dray-horse, ain't they, sir? In an' out, in an' out. Go-on-in, sir, there's-a-horde-o'-others waitin' . . ."

And again in a promising omen, his heels had barely cooled in the infamous Waiting Room before his name was called and he was abovestairs to see Nepean once more. And it was personally gratifying for Lewrie to have so many contemporaries in the Waiting Room that day, even some of the renowned fighting captains, peer from their corner coteries of admirers and well-wishers to wonder who he was or why he had the gold St. Vincent medal clattering on his chest as he made his way to the stairs.

"Commander Lewrie, aha," Evan Nepean commented, allowing himself a stab at "glad" welcome. "Do take a seat, sir. You've quite enjoyed a *few* weeks ashore, I take it?"

"Oh quite, Mister Nepean," Lewrie replied, hat in his lap and his legs crossed. *Damme, this is goin' main-well,* he allowed himself to imagine. "Though I did take a trip down to Portsmouth to visit my old ship . . . try to talk the hands remaining out of their nonsense. Wasn't to be, sorry to say."

"Aha," Nepean barked, looking cross. "Portsmouth, did you? I see. And whilst there, sir . . . did you happen to come across any tracts amongst your former crew, sir? Of a radical, rebellious nature, which might be to blame for this mutiny?" Nepean suddenly demanded.

"None, sir," Lewrie replied, guardedly. "And on that head, sir, I did enquire. But I was assured by my old Bosun that he'd seen none, and that the, uhm, disturbance was spontaneous—within the Fleet—with no prompting from shore. Though with so many Quota Men, these United

Irishmen being 'pressed lately, well . . . there's sure to be radicals in each draught from the receiving ships. Spirit of the times, more-like, sir. Known him since '81, sir, and he's truthful as the day is . . ."

"Hmmm . . . odd." Nepean sighed, looking disappointed. "We were *sure* . . . the Duke of Portland . . . responsible for hunting down utterers of treason and mutinous, rebellious assemblages. He's agents afoot in Portsmouth, looking into the matter. Done a magnificent job of hounding our Republican schemers. Break up every meeting place, drive them from pillar to post. We'd hopes that the plucking . . . or the arrest and silencing of a few ranters might de-fuse this . . . take away their leadership, d'ye see. Can't expect lack-wit, drunken sailors to hold out for long once the instigators are cast into prison, hmm?"

"Beg pardon, Mister Nepean," Lewrie countered. "But it was my impression that the sailors did their own scheming . . . crosspatch or no. I'll grant you, the petitions my old hands showed me were written rather well, which might seem suspiciously like someone wrote 'em for them, but . . . our tars ain't *that* child-like, the bulk of 'em. Oh, the total lubbers, the failed 'prentices, and clerks with grudges . . ."

"You do not *side* with the sailors' demands, do you, sir?" the secretary posed. "Surely," he purred, come over all suspicious.

Shit! Lewrie sighed; *and it was goin' so bloody well! I'll be hauled out o' here in chains, next!*

"Of course *not,* sir!" he barked back, laying a thick scowl 'pon his phyz. "And I was most distressed to find my counsel wasted, even with men I'd sailed with for years. Trusted . . . !"

He almost thought of throwing in a petulant *"ungrateful curs!"* which seemed to be the common coin lately, but forebade.

"I am gratified to hear that, Commander Lewrie," Nepean said, seeming to relent. He got that quirky "I know something you don't" smirk on his face, thumbed a folder to his right, and drew out a sheet of paper. He held it up to the light to read over just once more, to prolong the suspense. He let out a satisfied wee sniff.

Bastard! Lewrie thought in heat, though posing "just waiting."

"It is my honour to tell you, Commander Lewrie, that our Lords Commissioners have seen fit to offer you the *Proteus* Frigate."

"And it is my honour to accept, sir . . . gladly!" Lewrie breathed in relief. "Where is she, sir?"

"At Chatham Dockyard, Lewrie." Nepean deigned to grin, holding out that precious document 'twixt thumb and forefinger. Florid scrollwork in the penmanship, yet legible as block-printing and suitable to the solemnity of the occasion; a square stamp in the upper left-hand corner bearing the seal of Admiralty embossed into the thick paper . . . and a tax stamp half-way down the left side.

By the Commifsioners for executing the Office of Lord. High. Admiral of Great Britain, and. Ireland &c and all of his Majesty's Plantations &c.

To Captain <u>Alan Lewrie</u>, hereby appointed Captain of his Majesty's <u>Ship</u> the <u>Proteus.</u>

"Dear Lord." Alan grinned in awe. "What is she, sir?"

Nepean chuckled with amusement at his surprise, "A 32-gun of the 5th Rate . . . which requires a Post-Captain into her."

God, they've been building those for years, Alan thought quickly; *lying at Chatham . . . sure to be a total refit and old as the hills, but no matter!* He was now to make £15 8s. per lunar month, have an honest-to-God *frigate* to command! And he'd made the long leap to "post" at last! There it was in black-and-white, down in the left-hand bottom corner—his date of seniority. Newest of the new—again it was no matter! Junior-most captain in the Fleet that morning to be certain. Yet . . . who in Hell gave a tinker's damn for that?

"*Proteus,*" he muttered, savouring her name. "The divine oracle of Greek myth, as I recall . . . the so-called 'Shepherd of the Sea'?"

"Uhm, more like the Roman, Captain Lewrie," Nepean corrected, pulling at his nose. "B'lieve *Nereus* was the Greek. Fathered all the Naiads . . . ?"

Are we there yet? Lewrie wondered, hiding his smile; *wonder if old Nereus, or Proteus, got asked that? Well, I was close, hey?*

". . . one could assume so many shapes when he was cornered, before revealing the truth of the matter, a proper oracle." Nepean smirked.

Damn useful social skill, Lewrie thought; *sounds like me . . . and sounds like we'll get on together.*

"Well, then . . ." Nepean drawled.

"I'll take my leave then, sir"—Lewrie cried, leaping to his feet and knowing an exit cue when he heard one—"and coach down to Chatham instanter."

"Just left the graving dock, I believe she has, sir," Mr. Nepean informed him, already digging at a pile of more pressing letters. "A partial crew aboard. Time enough, though, for a slight celebration . . . and for you to go well stocked in cabin stores, hmm?"

"Aye, sir, I s'pose," Lewrie allowed, wishing he could shift his epaulet to his right shoulder that instant, so he could descend to the Waiting Room and put a nose or two out of joint. "My thanks, sir . . . my undying thanks. Good morning to you, Mister Nepean."

"And a good morning to you, Captain Lewrie," Nepean had grace enough to say. "Do you remember to see my under-clerk on your way, sir. There is the slight matter of the tax . . . ?"

"Ah, yes," Lewrie soured a bit, taking a look at the stamp upon that precious document. They were dunning him for another two shillings and six pence! "Right, then . . ."

"How *did* you put it last time, Captain Lewrie?" Nepean drawled, tweaking him a trifle sardonically. " 'Damme, had I known it was this cheap, I'd have done it long before'?"

"Uhm . . . aye, sir," Lewrie cringed. "Quite."

He turned to go, then stopped himself, reminded of a vital point which had not been mentioned, but should have been.

"Uhm, Mister Nepean, sir . . ."

"Uhmm?" Nepean replied, looking up from his papers with a brow cocked in the beginnings of petulant impatience, though not stretched *quite* so thin as to bark or bare his teeth . . . yet.

"The matter of my retinue, so to speak, sir. Usually a captain is allowed some of his old hands to accompany him into a new ship."

"Ah, yes." Nepean sighed, abandoning his work, faced with what amounted to a real problem and not a time-waster. He steepled fingers below the vane of his nose, brow creased in thought.

"I've my Cox'n, my clerk, and cabin-steward with me, sir, that's the

lot. Perhaps some hands off *Jester* could be called away to Chatham?
There's my old Bosun, a damned good gunner named Rahl . . . Yeoman
of The Powder now, but a keen-eyed shot as Quarter-Gunner should he
take the re-rating. There are some Able Seamen been with me since Toulon . . ."

"But, Captain Lewrie," Nepean frowned, opening his hands and closing
one to a fist, so he could shake an admonitory finger at him, "your last
ship now lies at Portsmouth and is reputed to be actively supportive of
the sailors' cause. We simply cannot have men such as those spread
throughout the rest of the Navy, which is so far free of the taint of mutiny.
I know it is the custom and usage that captains have reliable, personally
spoken-for men from their last ships, but . . . given the fragile nature of
these current circumstances, I do not see how we may oblige you. 'Pon
my life, I can't."

"I see, sir," Lewrie sighed, crestfallen, and pondering how he would
fare, recruiting at Chatham, in a strange town, without a single old hand
ashore at any "rondy" to vouch for him. Did he not gather a proper crew
in a set period of time, his precious commission document would be so
much bum-fodder—they'd assign another new Post-Captain to take his
place, and he'd revert to being a Commander, waiting his turn at another
sloop of war, if he was lucky. Or stuck at home back in Anglesgreen with
all its distasteful, civilian, and domestic doings, fretting crops and Sophie
and Harry Embleton, were he not!

"Once aboard at Chatham, you may forward to me a list of names you
might recall from previous commissions, Captain Lewrie," Nepean suggested—tossed out like a sop he didn't have to spend much on. "Then,
are they still in the Navy, and *are* they presently aboard ship in an untainted
port, we may be able to accommodate you, but . . ." Mr. Nepean lifted his
hands palms up and gave him one of those hopeless and powerless shrugs
more commonly seen on rug merchants who'd failed to strike a compromise on price.

"I see, sir," Lewrie sighed, much abashed.

"Ah, but you're such a knacky and resourceful fellow, Lewrie," Nepean
said with a purr, which meant he wouldn't lift a finger more to help him
in this regard, "and you've taken command of vessels before, where you
were too junior a lieutenant to fetch aboard your favourites. I'm sure, once

you explain your plight to the Regulating Captain of the Impress Service at Chatham, he will send you such trustworthy hands and petty officers as he has. I will write him at once, and send a copy on to Vice-Admiral Charles Buckner, flag officer commanding at the Nore. 'Twixt the two of them, I am certain you will find proper redress."

"That's satisfactory, sir . . . thankee," Lewrie told him, though it wasn't in the least satisfactory—in normal times.

"Well then, Captain Lewrie," Nepean said, "allow me to wish success to His Majesty's Ship *Proteus* . . . and to her new captain then. May all good fortune attend you, and her, sir."

'Long as I just go! Lewrie snickered to himself.

"I'll see what I can 'bout success, sir. Good day."

CHAPTER TWELVE

*T*hey'd stayed in London that whole day and the next, for there was so much to see to: visit his solicitor Mr. Matthew Mountjoy to arrange funds and inform him of his new situation; hunt up Aspinall and Padgett; shop for cabin-stores as Nepean had suggested; attend to getting his epaulets shifted. New stockings in both cotton and silk, a new stock or two, a new dress shirt or two; cases and small kegs of wine, brandy, and such, and other foodstuffs specially prepared for a Sea Officer's life at Fortnum & Mason's, shopping at Frybourg And Treyer's in the Haymarket. And shopping with the children, shopping with Caroline and Sophie . . . it was a hellish sudden outlay. But fun. Mountjoy had been happy to inform him that another £900 had come in from the Mediterranean prize-courts, less taxes and deductions, less prize-court fees, and his own; a tidy sum to be sure, and half of it gone in a twinkling, but the rest enough to keep his family with real style for at least another five years!

They'd taken in a military parade in Hyde Park, listened to the bands and cheered, attended the theatres in Covent Garden and in Drury Lane, eaten out both evenings, gotten a spell of decent weather on the first night and strolled Covent Gardens, and danced. The second night there'd been a subscription ball to celebrate the up-coming nuptials of King George's daughter Charlotte, the Princess-Royal, to the German Prince of Wurttemburg. Caroline had been glowing in a spanking new gown, with some of Grannie Lewrie's jewelry and some of that loot which Alan had brought back from the Far East in '86; some of it they loaned to Sophie for the two evenings. Both were as be-gemmed as *any* royal, and Lewrie had nigh worn out his shoes in dancing almost every dance with them.

Though after her second turn 'round the chalked floors of that huge salon, Sophie had had all the male company she might have wished, all eager to make the acquaintance of the intriguing young woman who had danced with the naval officer with the medal on his breast. She'd been coyly ecstatic, hiding her eye-rolling and her little chirps of glee behind her fan when on the sidelines, yet archly imperious and seemingly uncaring for even the handsomest partner upon the floor.

There'd not been much sleep that evening to be sure, what with dancing 'til nearly one, a cold collation with champagne after, then a coach-ride back to Willis's, and Sophie simply had to laugh out loud, purr, or titter (and damn' near shriek! at times) over her success with Society, with her and Caroline chortling over the night 'til all hours.

Lewrie awoke after a brief four hours of sleep a tad dry-mouthed from all the champagne and wines he'd taken aboard, woke to a bustling as loud (it seemed) as a 12-pounder being hauled 'cross the deck to run-out position, as their household went about packing up for the coach trip to Chatham. Everything in a rush, a search for mis-placed shoes, hats, and last night's fineries which had been flung "will-he, nill-he," the slamming of chest lids and the patter of children's feet at a scamper, too excited to be shoved into proper clothing. Andrews was there with the sea-going stores stowed away aboard a hired cart, and Padgett was there, shyly avoiding being trampled. Aspinall was back and eager to re-prove his worth, whetting Lewrie's razor on a strop, frothing up shaving soap, proffering a towel, a bowl, and pitcher of hot water on the wash-hand stand . . . babbling away a mile-a-minute as he got out that fresh shirt and stock, blacked Lewrie's best shore-going boots, and stood ready to shove him into order once he'd sluiced his admittedly thick head, face, and neck, shaved himself half-raw, and slugged down a single cup of chocolate.

Then down to a boisterous breakfast in the common rooms, everyone chattering and nattering, and the place filled with commercial travelers and chapmen, all eager to chew up something and swallow it, then be out and doing. Pay the establishment the final reckoning. "Mummy, I have to, uhm . . . !" Into the coach, and they were off by half-past nine. Down to the Thames and across to the south bank. "Mummy, I have to . . . !" for another stop by the semaphore telegraph station at New Cross and Dept-ford Dockyards. "Are we there, *already?*" from Hugh, who'd prefer to take a walking tour to look at all the ships under construction.

Greenwich Naval Hospital went flying by, then the Royal Arsenal at Woolwich, and the testing of an artillery piece—a rather heavy-caliber and *loud* piece—set them to howling with delight. Putting Lewrie's teeth on edge, it should be noted. He really did need a nap about as bad as any man born by then, but the excitement of the day kept him alert, to point out Gallons Reach and Barking Reach in the Thames to their left-hand side. Halfway Reach and Purfleet, the Long Reach—"Why do they call 'em reaches, Daddy?"—"What ship is that, Daddy?"—"Why do they call it Fiddler's Road, when it's not a road at all?"—"Is that your new ship then?"—"Uhm, Mummy, I have to . . . !"

Greenhithe and Swanscombe went by, Gravesend loomed up, little Charlotte thinking they'd come back to London by some conjurement and disgusted with the idea of a Grave's End—"What a horrid name!"

Forty miles of it, with a stop for a midday meal at a coaching tavern—and many, *many* more "necessary" stops, it goes without saying. The hired cart had no trouble keeping up with the bowling coach, for it very seldom had the *chance* to bowl along, not more than a quarter of an hour, at the most, before there was another call to halt.

Just as the scent of the Medway came to his nostrils, signifying nearly an end to their journey, Lewrie was most heartily sick of the lot of them and wondered why he'd ever suggested they *all* come along, this *far* along—

Could o' left 'em in London. He sighed taut-lipped; *could've had a good nap by now. Deed done. Sophie rescued—head turned and sure t'be entranced by other young men by now. Caroline just'z pleased with things had we parted after breakfast. Though we didn't get a goodbye tumble, for all the sky-larkin' . . . Fatherhood, Christ! What man of a right mind'd abide it, did he know goin' in . . . !*

"Are we there yet?" Hugh bellowed, leaning far out the coach windows for a first sight of the river 'round a bend in the road of the close-by conurbation of Rochester and Chatham just across the way and the steamy, smoky, coal-grate fug of civilisation.

"Aye, by God . . . we *are!*" Lewrie roared back. Half in exasperation, having about all he could stand of "family closeness"; half in joy that, by the sight of spires in town and the soaring erectness of mast tips at the dockyard just downriver, they *were,* finally, there!

"Dear, must you be so short with him?" Caroline chid, clucking her tongue like she was calling pullets to the food-pail. "He was but enquiring."

"Does he not *just,* my dear," Lewrie rejoined, feeling a bile rise as he was forced to swallow what he *really* had wished to say. Scream, rather! He threw in a sickly smile to show his good intentions.

"Uhm, I must own . . ." Caroline whispered, allowing a tiny smile to play at the corners of her lips in spite of her statement.

"Quite." Lewrie nodded, just as Hugh came lumbering back from the coach window to tumble into his lap, step on his right foot, and reach across to draw Sewallis's notice to the sight he had out of his window. "Ow, God . . . !"

"Mummy, look!" Charlotte piped, ashiver with bliss. "London!"

CHAPTER THIRTEEN

C ommissioner Proby, in charge of Chatham Dockyards and uncrowned king of the Medway all the way downriver to Sheerness, allowed him in for a preparatory meeting. He was, for a very busy man, all affability and hospitality. "Always happy to greet an officer come to take charge of one of our ships, Captain Lewrie." He beamed quite cordially.

"*Proteus* was refitted here, sir?" Lewrie asked, over a very good cup of coffee. "Or, built here originally, d'ye mean?"

"Just completed," Proby told him, pleased to enlighten him.

"My pardons, Commissioner Proby, I thought no more 5th Rate, 32-gun frigates were to be built . . . especially the 12-pounder 32s. Most of the Fleet prefer the 18-pounder 36s now. So she's *new*? Brand-new? Oh, my word!" Lewrie beamed back, most beatifically, soon as he saw how fortunate he was.

"One of the very last to be ordered, and one of the last of her sort constructed." Proby chuckled. "A variation on the *Thames* class, with but some minor alterations to her forefoot and entry . . . borrowed from the French. The Nicholson shipyards built her on speculation for a new class of light frigate, later purchased as a one-off under private contract with the Navy Board, sir. Just 'cross the river they are, at Frindsbury."

"A private yard then . . ." Lewrie sobered.

"Nought to fear, sir," Proby boomed in good humour. "They are completely competent. Nothing done 'at the back o' the beach,' like most new-come builders these days. They built 'Billy Ruff'n', one of the finest 3rd Rate 74s in the Fleet."

"The *Bellerophon*, indeed!" Lewrie brightened.

"Well-constructed . . . if I do say so myself, sir," Proby went on, pouring them a top-up of coffee. "Saw to that. Nothing but good Hamburg or Baltic oak for scantlings, inner plankings, or riders. And Hamburg oak for second and third futtocks—English oak for her keel, first futtocks, decks, knees, and deadwood. 'Tis gettin' devilish-hard to find enough English oak for complete construction, what with the demand for warships in such numbers. No, just launched one month ago and straight into the drydock for coppering and her masts. She's afloat now. And I expect you're afire to see her, hey?" He winked.

"Most thoroughly aflame, sir," Lewrie agreed.

Over the last of their coffee, Proby filled him in on her specifications: that *Proteus* was 105 feet on her keel, and 125 feet on the range of her gun-deck, about 150 feet overall from taffrail to the tip of her jib-boom. She was three inches shy of 35 feet in beam, at her widest midship span, and would draw three inches shy of 15 feet when fully armed, stored, and laden—or so Mr. Nicholson predicted. She would weigh around 740 tons, when on her proper waterline, and carry twenty-six 12-pounder carriage-guns of the new Blomefield pattern on her gun-deck, thirteen to either beam broadside. She was allotted six 6-pounders for her forecastle and quarterdeck as chase guns, and six 24-pounder carronades for close action.

"Part of her crew is already aboard, all her officers," Proby remarked, as they gathered hats and cloaks to go down to his coach for the short ride to the waterfront. "Short of crew, naturally, but . . ."

"And her masts are already stepped, Mr. Proby?" Lewrie asked, creasing his brow in thought. "I thought that was a captain's prerogative . . . to set her rigging up to his own tastes."

"Masts set up, top-masts standing, and lower yards crossed, sir," Proby said to him as they settled into the leather seats of his coach. "Her previous captain had seen to it . . . 'fore he departed, poor fellow."

"Sorry, sir, but I was not aware there had *been* a previous captain," Lewrie said carefully. "He left recent, then, did he? Why?"

"Not a week past, sir," Proby replied, turning sombre, shifting uncomfortably on his seat, the fine leather giving out a squeaking as he did so. He leant forward a bit to speak more softly—guardedly.

"You're getting command of a fine frigate, Captain Lewrie. Oh, a wondrous-fine new ship!" Proby assured him. "But..." he muttered, "there *are* some things about her a tad ... queer-like, e'en so."

"Such as, sir?" Lewrie enquired, crossing his legs for luck—to protect his "nutmegs" against the eerie chill which took him.

Damme, Jester *an' her doin's was queer enough!* he thought.

"At her launching day"—Proby squinted as if pained—"a fine day, sir. Sunshine *and* the high tide ... a rare event on the Medway, as I'm certain you'll agree. A retired admiral, come down from London, him and his good lady, to do the actual naming."

"His *lady* did her naming?" Lewrie puzzled, nigh to gaping. It was rarely allowed—it was bad luck! He constricted his thighs for more protection against such an odd event.

"As good as, in essence, Captain Lewrie. As good as," Proby sighed. "The admiral ... a most distinguished fellow; he did the actual honours with the port bottle ... his lady by his side, no real role in things, as it should be, no. But she was one of those er, what-you-call-'ems ... the romantic, literary sorts. Quite taken with this fellow Ossian, d'ye see ..."

"And who's *he*, when he's up and dressed?" Lewried scowled, in wonder where this was all going.

"Some deuced scribbler ... translated a batch of Irish sagas and such ... Gaelic myths and legends set to poetry," Proby quibbled, not sounding too impressed himself. "The romantic rage of the moment. So I'm told. Elves and brownies, dancing fairies and magic circles, sword-wielding heroes and Druid magicians conjuring up all manner of spells and potions. Singing swords, so please you! Have you ever *heard* the like? Irish! *They* probably take it as history ... Gospel!"

"And so this Ossian ...?" Lewrie prompted.

"The lady's enthusiasms for all this bilge water got the better of her— and she did strike me, right from the first time I clapped eye on her, that she was the forbidding sort o' mort who'd run her household her way, and Heaven help the husband who gainsayed her—well, it was obvious she'd put a flea in his ear, and him a bloody Rear-Admiral and should have *known* better. Comes the moment to name her ..."

Tell me before I throttle you, you lame twit! Lewrie groaned.

"... stands up there on the platform 'neath her bows, thousands of folk from Hoo, Rochester, Chalk, and Sheerness watching. Band from the Chatham Marines ready to play her into the water. Officials down from London—Navy Board and all. Bishop of Rochester there too ... and that was the worst part."

Lean a tad closer, just *a tad, and* ... Lewrie thought, furious. And his fingers twitching for the leap from his lap to the throat.

"Adrape with flags from bow-to-stern, cradle all that's holding her, and all but the dog-shores removed ..." Proby whispered, acting as if, were he a Catholic, he'd be flying over his rosary beads like some Chinee merchant at his abacus. "Should have suspected. *Had* him a nose on at breakfast, 'fore we rowed over to Frindsbury, and her nudging at him like a fishwife all that time, whispering in his ear ..."

Right, you're for it! Lewrie thought, raising one hand, staring at how strong his fingers flexed.

"Stood up there, 'fore one and all, and called out, 'Success to His Majesty's Ship' ... came all over queer he did and waited, with a smirk on his face." Proby all but groaned and wrung his hands. "At last he says ... *Merlin*"

Uhmhmm, Lewrie thought, feeling an urge to shrug; *what's so bad 'bout that? Old King Arthur's pet conjurer. So ... ?*

"Well, the crowd went dead-silent, and the Bishop of Rochester damn' near swooned away, sir." Proby grunted. "Mean t'say, Captain Lewrie, a *pagan* religious figure, a Celt Druid! And there right in front of his *nose* was one of the Chicheley brother's best figureheads of the sea-god, driving his chariot drawn by dolphins and seals ...!"

Seals, oh Christ!" Lewrie chilled, dropping his hands to his lap for more protection, all thought of mayhem quite flown his head.

"Well, sir, she slipped away right after," Proby told him, in awe of it still himself. "Dog-shores just gave *way,* with no one at the saws to free 'em! Everyone whey-faced, and the Admiralty representative steps up and takes the bottle and glass from the admiral. He *had* drunk off the glass of port but hadn't thrown the bottle to break on her bows, so it wasn't *quite* done, d'ye see, and could still be salvaged. And the Admiralty man takes a quick slug from the neck, throws the bottle, it breaks on her bow-timbers, and he calls out, 'Success to His Majesty's Ship *Proteus*, the name they'd already picked. Then the band starts up, and the people start cheering . . . and . . ."

"And?" Lewrie pressed, crossing his fingers for good measure.

"She *stuck*, sir! Stuck dead on the ways, still cradled. Tons of tallow, so slick a rat couldn't crawl up the slipway, but there she was . . . stuck firm as anything," Proby whispered. "And the cradle, it usually starts to fall apart once a launched ship gets way on her on the skids . . . designed to break up once she's afloat. Held like it's *bolted* together. Not cocked a bit off-centre, not hung up on anything beneath her, Captain Lewrie, but . . . she just . . . won't . . . *move!*"

"Dear, Lord," Lewrie sighed. Very softly and circumspectly, it should here be noted. "A bad-luck ship . . . a 'Jonah'?"

"Who's to say, sir?" Proby groaned, sounding a tad miserable. "But here's a stranger part. Good sawyer in Nicholson's yards, he's out on the slipway with his little boy . . . to cut the dog-shores. Comes 'round afore her bows, trying to think of what to do. She misses that high tide, and it's days more before she's depth enough to launch proper, without damaging her quick-work. Everybody watching, and he just walks up to her forefoot, lays a hand on her cutwater—it appeared that he *said* something—then . . . one shove of his little *boy's* hand and she gives out the most hideous groan, like the cradle is about to give way and break up. But instead . . . away she goes, smooth as any launch as ever I did see."

"Ah, well!" Lewrie felt reason to say with a relieved chuckle, yet a bit of a shiver. "And here I thought you were about to say how she crushed him and his boy . . . drew blood on her naming day. Wheew!"

"Ah, but the sawyer and his son, sir . . . they're *Irish!*" Proby most ominously pointed out, hunched up in his cloak as if he was fearful of sitting too erect. "Irish, d'ye see. Seen many an odd thing in my time concerning the launching of ships. Most go smooth as silk and no problem, 'cause they're just a 'thing' at that moment and don't get their soul 'til after they've been in saltwater for a spell. Now and then, though, there are the blood-drinkers. A sloop of war once mashed three men when she veered off the straight-and-narrow on her way in, and God help every man-jack who served aboard her, 'til she ran aground five years later and drowned her entire crew off the Hebrides. There's a two-decker 64 from

this dockyard that's cost the careers of four captains by now, and she's . . .
I'll not call down bad luck by naming her . . . had more strange accidents
and deaths among her crew than any other of her type. Man-a-month
dying, last I heard of her. Even *Bellerophon*, sir . . . blowing a perfect gale
the night before her launching. Came to see if the shores would hold 'til
morning, and there she was *afloat*. . . . Launched *herself*, d'ye see? Chris-
tened her myself, after the fact. I think she was so eager to swim, Captain
Lewrie, that she wouldn't wait. Aye, the 'Billy Ruff'n' had an odd birthing,
sir. But for the life o' me I cannot recall an event stranger than *Proteus*,
not in years!"

"Well, that's coincidence, surely . . ." Lewrie objected. "That she came
from the same yard. And the matter of the sawyer . . ."

"Like *she* approved of *Merlin*, though the Church wouldn't, then balked
at being *Proteus*," Proby rhapsodised, as if in awe of the odd. "And only
a Gaelic blessing made her accept it . . . groaning over it but going in, at
last . . . at the touch of a mere lad."

"Well, since then at least there's been no sign . . ." Lewrie said. He
thought *sign* too close to *portent*, and after a slight cough, amended that
to, "There's been no troubles in her or with her?"

Proby shrugged, as if forced to say it, like a reluctant witness giving
damning testimony against a friend.

"There *is* the matter of her previous captain."

"Aye?" Lewrie posed, wondering if his leg was being pulled.

"Captain The Honourable William Churchwell. Man in his earliest four-
ties, as best I could judge, sir," Proby went on. "A bit of the Tartar, or
so I gathered from others, a real taut-hand. But a most experienced officer.
Dined with him several times, once he'd come down to read himself in
command—Just after she went into the graving dock for her coppering.
A most righteous man too, Captain Lewrie, brought up strict in the
Church, and . . . for a Sea Officer . . . a very proper and sober Christian.
Would have the hide off a seaman did he hear even a slight blasphemy or
profane oath. Rare in the Navy, his sort."

Bloody right they are, Lewrie thought, keeping a non-committal glaze
to his features; *a sea-goin' parson. Damn' rare breed those . . . thankfully!*

"Abstemious too, sir. Rarely touched more than a single glass of wine
an entire meal, sir, and could only be pressed by the convivial folk to a

rare second. Seen it myself," Proby related. And they both shook their heads in wonder at Captain Churchwell's contrary nature; it was a rare gentleman who'd put away fewer than two *bottles* of wine a day—it was the expected thing, part of a gentleman's *ton*.

The coach slowed, rocking on its leather straps as it came to a stop just by the King's Stairs, which led to a boat-landing. They alit, which activity delayed the rest of Proby's tale. Below the stairs lay a gaily painted ten-oared barge, Commissioner Proby's own, flying his personal flag; and hard by, a more plebeian hired cutter occupied by Aspinall, Andrews, and Padgett, laden with cabin-stores and furnishings, and Toulon in his wicker travelling basket.

"Ah, there she is, Captain Lewrie," Proby said, filled with pride of his latest creation for the Royal Navy. "A beauty, is she not?"

"All ships are, sir . . . but aye! This 'un . . . !" Lewrie swore, at his first sight of her. "She's lovely!"

Tall, erect, trig, and proud, glistening with newness, her tarred and painted sides shining and reflecting back the prismatic light flash of river water, HMS *Proteus* was indeed a lovely, new-cut precious gem of the shipbuilders' arcane science. Her bowsprit and jib-boom were steeved slightly lower than most frigates he'd seen, the way he liked 'em, for that meant larger heads'ls with more draw, closer to the deck, and more ability to go like a witch to windward. Her entry was not an apple-cheeked bulb from the waterline up, but angled slimmer and tapering narrower, to merge far before her cutwater in an aggressive, out-thrust extension of her sprit and head timbers, her cut-water angled a few degrees more astern than was customary to give her grace. Even at a quarter-mile's distance, without a glass, Lewrie could discern Frenchness in her pedigree, with a touch of stocky English usage aft, where she widened and flared for accommodation space and storage as far forrud as possible. He knew, just from looking at her, that her forecastle could be burdened by a pair of 6-pounder chase-guns *and* a pair of 24-pounder carronades, and *still* have the buoyancy and form to her front third to ride up and over even the tallest storm-wave without ploughing under, like a ship with a *too*-fine entry might.

Tumble-home inward from the chain-wale and gunwale, narrowing to save top-weight, all neatly proportioned like a surface-basking whale, broken by the row of gun-ports and the upper gunwale, which was painted a rather pretty buff tan. There was the glitter of gilt paint 'round her larboard entry-port, which at that angle as she lay bows upriver, streaming from a permanent moor, faced them; gilt glitters too, further aft where the quarter galleries jutted out from her curved sides and nearly upright stern timbers. A commissioning pendant swirled and curled high aloft, a small ensign in the eyes of her bows—a harbour jack—and the Red Ensign of a ship yet to be assigned to a particular squadron or fleet, an "independent ship," now and then outfurled to a lazy breeze. And all as pristine-new as the ship herself.

"I thought you would not mind did we use my barge to take you out to her 'stead of requesting of her to send over your gig," Mr. Proby said, after taking a long, satisfying gander of his own.

"Thankee, Mister Proby, that's most accommodating of you, and I would be honoured," Lewrie said, unable to tear his gaze from her, in a lust to be abroad and too impatient to wait for a boat to row shoreward to fetch him . . . like a parcel.

My frigate! he exulted, even if she was accursed; *my frigate, my first frigate! The freedom, the power . . . those guns of hers! God help me, but I do love 'em. Ships and guns . . . and the reek o' both!*

"Andrews?" he called over to the hired boat. "I'll go in the barge. Do you see my dunnage to the larboard port?"

"Aye, aye, Cap'um!" his Cox'n shouted back.

They descended the King's Stairs, got into the barge, and were shoved off. It was after Proby's Cox'n had a way on her, and steering clear of shore, before Proby continued his tale.

"Ah, Captain Churchwell," Proby sighed, toying with the lapels of his cloak. "He and his chaplain came ashore to dine with me that last evening. And as sober a lot as ever you could wish for, Captain Lewrie."

"The *last* evening? You don't mean t'say . . . ?"

"Saw him to his gig, just there at the King's Stairs, as we did just now in my coach," Proby gloomed, turning a weathered face downriver to keep an eye on the ships in his charge, the refits and all of the new construction still skeleton-like on the slipways; and to get a whiff of ocean, Lewrie suspected.

"And not a half-hour later, his chaplain was dead. Drowned." Proby sighed.

Well, a chaplain, that's no loss, Lewrie thought most sourly; *a reverend on a ship's a bit gloomy-makin' anyway. Haven't seen one of 'em worth a tuppenny shit, and most vessels sail without 'em.*

"How terrible!" he felt compelled to gasp though.

"Dead calm, just at slack water it was, sir," Proby said, with another dis-believing shake of his head. "Not a breath of wind stirring, and no cause for *Proteus* to roll or toss. Side-party up on her gangway ready to render honours.

"It *might* have been someone on the main deck took a poke with something through the scuppers, but no one could recall seeing hands on deck that late at night, other than the side-party up above the gun-ports on the starboard gangway. But . . ."

"But, sir?" Lewrie pressed, feeling his hands twitch once more with impatience, as Proby turned the tale into a two-volume novel.

"For no apparent *cause,* sir . . . she heaved a slow roll starb'd," Proby whispered, leaning close to Lewrie on the thwart they shared near the sternsheets. "The chaplain, Reverend Talmidge, was halfway aloft, and Captain Churchwell was just by the lip of the entry-port, when she did her roll. And then, sir!—Captain Churchwell gave out a yelp, like he was stung by a wasp, he told me later—and lost his grasp on the man-ropes. He slipped and fell backwards, slid down into Reverend Talmidge and knocked him loose as well, and they both hit the water and went under. Right 'twixt ship and boat, without touching either, sir . . . not a mark on the gig, as there would have been had the Reverend Talmidge struck his head on her gunn'ls and knocked himself out. Captain Churchwell came to the surface a moment later, and his boat-crew pulled him out. But the chaplain never did. Now both men were strong swimmers, I was told, since boyhood; and Captain Churchwell thought that the chaplain might be beneath the gig, trapped and unconscious, and he dove under, searching for him, but never found him. He was *never* found, Captain Lewrie."

"That's odd," Lewrie had to admit aloud. "Usually a drowned man comes up, sooner or later. Downriver, perhaps . . . ?"

"We searched, sir, indeed we did. Captain Churchwell had boats on the river not a half-hour later," Proby told him. "He sent news to me, requesting everything that'd float to search, as far as Gillingham Reach, the first morning and for several days after; but nary a sign of him did anyone see. And even did a man strike his noggin and put himself out, well . . . being 'round ships, ports, and rivers the most part of my life, Captain Lewrie, I've seen men fall overside, seen drownings aplenty, God save me. And the most of 'em *do* come up, right after they fall in. 'Fore their clothes get soaked, they've enough buoyancy for at least a *single* surfacing, if they've a scrap of air in their lungs."

"Well, perhaps he drew in a breath, but underwater . . ." Lewrie surmised. So far it was a tragic tale, *perhaps* indicative of his new ship's— perverse nature? he shivered—Gaelic, Druidic, and Celtic soul. Certainly there was a frigate near her like, HMS *Druid*, built back in the early '80s, and there'd been a spot of bother at first over her name, with the Established Church's Ecclesiastical Court upset by an allusion to the old pagan ways and the necromancing Druids. He had never heard, though, that she'd been trouble. Made into a trooper, last he'd heard . . . with guns removed, *en flute*, so she could transport a whole battalion at once.

But the way Proby was glooming and ticking the side of his nose, as if in sage warning, he wondered when the other shoe might drop.

"It could be as you say, sir, for I've seen that happen also," Proby confessed. " 'Mongst the drunk-as-lords, the ones who did strike their heads. But, sir . . . Reverend Talmidge was stone-cold sober when he entered that gig. And no one could recall him striking his head . . . no dented wood, no smear of blood or hair . . . ?" Proby shrugged. "And may I remind you, noted to be a strong swimmer. I sometimes wish our Lords Commissioners might follow the example of the Dutch Navy. They require every man-jack sent to sea to learn how to swim, or know how before joining. And their surgeons and surgeon's mates can revive a drowned man in almost miraculous fashion by laying him out face-down over a large keg laid on its side. Roll him back and forth and, more than half the time, he begins to cough and sputter and spew up what he swallowed or breathed in. And is returned to the living, Captain Lewrie, like Lazarus called out from his grave by Our Dear Saviour. I have seen that done too, sir, in my time."

"So he lost his chaplain, sir. But you said he was her *previous* captain?" Lewrie urged. "What *made* Captain Churchwell . . . 'previous'?"

"Oh, sir," Proby groaned, looking appalled. "Close as brothers they were to each other . . . cater-cousins from the same county, the same social set. Captain Churchwell was as heartbroken as a man who'd just lost all his brothers and sisters at a single stroke!"

"He threw over his commission due to grief, Mister Proby?" Lewrie frowned. Well, it did take all kinds, he felt like saying.

"I'll warrant there was a certain amount of grief, the cause." Proby nodded, looking seaward once more, towards HMS *Proteus,* to judge how near she was. "And guilt, for he was the one who'd jostled Talmidge when he slipped and fell. And that was an odd thing too, in addition to her strange roll. The man-ropes were spanking-new manila, hairy as so many badgers and dry as dust. The batten steps had been fresh-tarred, with sand scattered for a good foothold. No cause for him to slip at all. No linseed oil anywhere in sight for him to slip on with hand *or* foot."

"Prickly strands of manila . . . that might have been what he said stung him, sir," Lewrie suggested, turning to eye his new ship also.

"Sting a lubber, sir," Proby grunted most querulously. "Or sting a lady's soft hands. But never a tarry-handed sailor like him. Had a bear's grip, he did . . . and all over rope-handling callouses."

"So?" Lewrie shrugged. "Why *that* night then?"

"I recall most vividly him saying that it felt like he'd gotten stung by several wasps at once, Captain Lewrie," Proby told him. "At the tail end of winter, when they're still a'nest? No, he claimed the ship . . . *bit* him!"

"Beg pardon?" Lewrie gawped. "Bit him, did y'say?"

"Claimed she hated him and was out to kill him too," Proby told him, shrugging. "Not five days later, he wrote Admiralty asking for immediate relief. Aged ten years, he appeared, as haggard as a dog's dinner. Unkempt, his hair turned grey almost overnight, I tell you. And falling-down *drunk,* sir! Him, so abstemious before, but in his cups right 'round the clock afterwards. Running on deck at all hours, claiming he heard voices warning him to leave or die? Mister Ludlow claims he smelled sober in the beginning, even when he told the most horrendous fantasies and saw things no one else on deck saw, sir. Turned out the Marines to search his cabins more than a few times and claimed there was someone there, but nary a sign of an intruder there was. He began drinking soon after that. After the first two days, I think it was. Babbling to himself, weeping before the

hands . . . 'twas a sorry spectacle Captain Churchwell was when he took
the coach back to London. Never seen a man so shattered in body and
soul."

"Perhaps he was one of those secret topers, Mister Proby," Lewrie
wondered, "who hold it well and hide it well. Does a man play a role well
enough in public . . . and don't most people . . . ?"

"Seen more than my share of those too, in my time, sir"—Proby chuckled—"claiming to be the strictest abstainers . . . but experience gives the
lie to their lies. Didn't look the sort. That sort of lust for drink will show
in a man his age. In Sea Officers more than most, as I'm certain you've
noted. No, sir, I may attest to you that this demonic craving for spirits
was sudden. And the poor devil was quite capsized."

"Well, perhaps she bit him after all, sir. In a way? Bottle-bit?" Lewrie
could not help saying, with a quirky smirk.

Proteus was near now—not a musket-shot off—and the barge was steering to pass under her out-thrust bowsprit and jib-boom, about ten yards
in front of her bows to gain her starboard side. There was a thunder of
feet as her partial crew was mustered, the shrill of bosun's calls to summon
a side-party.

"Boat ahoy!" came a shout from her larboard cat-head, from the strange
midshipman of the harbour watch.

"*Proteus!*" Proby's midshipman in the sternsheets cried back, to warn
them that their caller was not just any officer, but her new captain. The
bow-man thrust four fingers in the air, showing the number of side-men
to be mustered.

"Perhaps she did, Captain Lewrie," Proby snipped, sounding as if he
was put off by Lewrie's cynical comment. "Perhaps she did, at that. And
the very oddest thing was, sir, the poor Captain Churchwell and the Reverend Talmidge both, sir . . . were Anglo-Irish. Son of an Irish peer,
Churchwell was, from near Drogheda. And Talmidge the younger son
of another, gone into the ministry. Both families were land-owning in the
large way," Proby drawled. "The most extensive estates, equal to whole
counties, with hundreds, if not thousands, of poor Irish tenants. Absentee
landowners, most of the time, with them living well-off in Dublin or
London most of the year. Anglo . . . *Irish*, sir! Protestant folk. Now were
a ship to find her soul and resent her name, it just might be that, does

she prefer something Gaelic or Celtic—like some of this fellow Ossian's romancings—she might have resented a Protestant English churchman and a taut-handed Tartar of a captain? Hmmm?"

"Murder, perhaps, sir," Lewrie said, after he'd gotten his jaw re-hinged. "But by someone in the *crew*. One of those United Irish I'm certain you've heard about. A sea-lawyer Quota Man who'd gotten what he thought was an unfair portion of the 'cat'? Half o' that lot are better off in prison or swingin' from a gibbet at Tyburn. One or more of their poorest tenants come into the Fleet to find him over them and couldn't resist takin' revenge for bein' turfed off their little plots?"

"All those possibilities were considered, Captain Lewrie, but so far, there is no plausible explanation. Oh, but she's a wondrous ship, sir. As lovely as a swan, do you not think? But who ever knows how a ship will turn out? Even more unpredictable than children, sir. And heartbreaking to see them turn off evil, to see them fail to be the sort you'd wished them to be. Ships, sir." Mr. Proby sighed, a bit wistfully philosophical. "I do believe, Captain Lewrie, that ships live, after a fashion. Call it heretical, or pagan . . . or simple-minded superstition, but being 'round 'em so many years, I've come to believe it. Mariners suspect it, merchant or Navy. As I'm certain you do."

"They're more than oak and iron, Mister Proby, aye," Lewrie was forced to confess. "My last ship, well . . . there was a spirit to her too. A kindly one. Gad, you make my skin crawl, sir."

"I did not intend to daunt you, sir," Proby insisted, as the barge coasted towards the main-chains, those suspect boarding battens and man-ropes. "There *could* be a most prosaic explanation for all of the oddities surrounding her. . . ."

Aye, and it could be Lir*'s work, Lewrie silently scoffed; elves and leprechauns skitterin' about with drawn daggers too! Eeriness, just waitn' for the next . . . her next victim! Has he turned on me?*

". . . either way, sir. This ship has, I must avow, discovered her spirit early. She may be mettlesome, but never dull. And does she have a will of her own, well . . . it's the most-willful stallions make the best chargers. You'd not take a mare to sea, sir . . . a dim gelding! No, you'd prefer a fighter!"

Is he tryin' t'sell me a haunted house? Lewrie felt like sneering. *Oh, don't mind the old spook by the fire; he's no bother!* Ghastly *hole in the roof,* *but I'm sure you're the sort* appreciates *fresh air!*

"And I'm certain you will have the most splendid fortune with her, Captain Lewrie," Proby concluded, as the barge's bow thumped on her timbers, and the bow-man lanced out with his boat-hook to grab at the chain platform. "And here we are!"

She plan t'murder me too? Lewrie wondered, as he swung his sword to the back of his left leg, stood up, and flung back his cloak to show off his epaulet. *I ain't an Anglo-Irish landowner, so she can forget* that *score! Callin'* me *well-churched'd be a real amusement, so that's out. Is she upset with bein'* an English frigate, well too damn' bad! Maybe we'll get on together . . . ?

He eyed the battens: dry as anything, fresh-tarred, sprinkled with grit. The man-ropes rove through the eyes of the battens were as white as snow, served with red spun-yarn, just waiting . . .

Hell, maybe I'm just as much a pagan as any she could wish! he told himself as he stepped on the barge's gunn'l to step over; *I mean, God knows, most people who know me well already think so!*

CHAPTER FOURTEEN

Such a sea of faces, he thought, even with her just partly manned. Seamen, lubbers, idlers, and waisters, petty officers and their mates on the gun-deck below him, a double file of Marines lined up to either hand just aft of them. A scurrilous lot, the most of 'em though, he took time to note: ill-clad, pasty-faced, and filthy, in the "long-clothing" they'd worn in gaols or debtors' prisons, what the seamen among them had used for disguises so they wouldn't be chased by the Impress gangs.

" ' . . . by virtue of the Power and Authority to us given, we do hereby constitute and appoint you Captain of His Majesty's Ship' "—he read off, speaking in an authoritative semi-bellow; he paused for one anxious second— " *'Proteus,'* " he declared.

And took a breath before continuing, waiting to see if top-masts might come crashing down on him for insulting her. He'd made his way up her side without harm, been saluted on the gangway from the instant his hat's vane loomed over the lip of the entry-port. So far, so good!

" 'Willing and requiring you forthwith to go on board and take upon you the Charge and Command of Captain in her accordingly. Strictly charging all the Officers and Company belonging to the said Ship subordinate to you to behave themselves jointly and severally in their respective Employments with all due Respect and Obedience unto you their said Captain, and you likewise . . .' "

An odd lot, those officers he'd just barely met too; not quite the most promising at first appearance. But then, who ever was, Lewrie sarcastically wondered?

Then here came the phrase he hated the most. Army commissions were almost like love-letters, replete with "Greetings," and spoke of the recipients as "trusty and beloved," in whom the Sovereign reposed "especial Trust and Confidence in your Loyalty, Courage, and Good Conduct." The Fleet, however . . .

" ' . . . superior Officers for His Majesty's Service. Hereof nor you nor any of you may fail as you will answer the contrary at your peril. And for so doing this shall be your Warrant. Given under our hands and the Seal of the Office of Admiralty this ninth day of May, 1797 in the thirty-seventh year of His Majesty's Reign.' "

Lewrie carefully slipped his precious commission document into a folio of other papers and handed it to his Cox'n, Andrews, then turned to peer once more into that sea of strange new faces, that ear-cocked, shuffling pack.

"Not many get this chance," he carefully began, weighing words' meanings. "A spanking-new ship to serve in, not a month from the slipways, a ship still in search of her heart, her soul, as young and callow as a spring hatchling."

And we'll just hope she's not found a spiteful *heart*, he wished to himself, feeling the urge to cross his fingers behind his back, for luck. He noted the grave nods from the older hands, the long-serving petty officers who knew the nature of ships; from those horny-handed men already clad in slop clothing whom he wished he could mistake for experienced Ordinary or Able Seamen upon whom he could rely.

"A spanking-new captain, too," he allowed himself to say, with no shame in confessing, "from command of one of the sweetest sloops of war ever you did see. You older men . . . you know better than any what makes a new ship come alive. From your old ships, where you came of age and rate . . . gladsome ships, for the most part, I trust. Do you miss them, well . . . you just bring our *Proteus* that spirit, and we'll get on well. Did you come from ships you're glad to see the back of, did you fetch along bad habits and bad feelings, well . . . overside with 'em, For I will tell you all that I'm firm . . . but I do trust that I'm fair, as well. Did some turn-

over as bad bargains . . . then *Proteus* is your place to start over with a
clean slate. Do you serve her . . . and me . . . chearly, then all that's gone
before is so much jetsam. Is that a fair bargain, lads?"

Men cleared their throats and coughed, shuffled their feet, and cut their
eyes left or right; but they also nodded and gave voice to a grudging
assent, with a chorus of "Aye, sir."

"You new-comes"—Lewrie continued, allowing himself to smile again
and shaking his head at them—"outright volunteers . . .'pressed . . . drug
off drunk or bashed senseless." He waited and heard moans or suppressed
titters of bleak amusement from some at their predicament, a few louder
guffaws from the true sailors at the plight of their new shipmates.

"For the Joining Bounty, or to serve your King and Country"—Lewrie
sobered—"to clear off of trouble or to get out of gaol, I could care less
either. There's an old saw in the Fleet that says, 'You shouldna joined if
ya can't take a joke.' And, perhaps, now you have had a tiny taste o' Navy
life, you're wondering what in God's name you got yourselves into, hey?
But . . . no matter where you came from, or where the Navy found you,
you start with a clean slate too. Every man present—the others we'll recruit
or bring aboard in the coming weeks before we sail—will become . . .
sailors," he stressed. "Seamen . . . Royal Navy seamen. Oh yes, we'll make
sailors of you, you mark my words! *Fighting* sailors, who could look the
Devil in the eye and tell him to go piss himself! Sailors who can swagger into
any tavern the wide world 'round and be respected . . . no matter where you
set out in life; no matter what you did before. You new-comes . . . is that a
fair bargain for *you* then?"

Pathetic, really. Some of them purse-lipped and too proud, too shattered
by their comedown; some so hangdog morose, who stared down at their
feet so that it appeared they hadn't heard a word he'd said; some cutty-
eyed and cynical, all but ready to spit on the decks in sullen truculence at
such a promise, when every promise made to them had been broken, time
and again. Most, though, Lewrie was happy to see, did respond with a
whipped puppy eagerness, wary but hopeful.

"And as we make you sailors . . . teach you the hard things which you
have to know to serve this ship properly"—Lewrie promised them—"and
I'll tell you now; it'll be hard learning; ships and the sea are the hardest
task-mistresses of any calling, and we'll not have time to be always gentle

or as patient as you'd probably like . . . we'll make you something even finer . . . we'll make *shipmates*. Make you seamen . . . so proud of serving in *Proteus* . . . of being *known* as Proteuses"—*or should we call 'em Proteans?* he pondered, unable to resist the urge to stick his tongue firmly in his cheek—"that this strange new horde of names and faces will become as familiar to you—perhaps as close to you—as your own families. That's bein' shipmates. *For* each other, when no one else is. *For* each other, when things are bleakest. *With* each other in danger's hour. Or with each other, in the good times. Shipmates. Sailors . . . and warriors. A fine calling to aspire to. No finer name, nor sentiment to admire. And we'll do it together. Me . . . you new-come lads, and our experienced hands. Startin' fresh . . . together. In this marvelous new ship of ours. Starting today. That's all, for now. Mister Ludlow, dismiss the people and carry on."

"Aye, aye, sir," Lieutenant Ludlow piped up in a gravely *basso*.

Lewrie turned his head to look at him, sensing something sardonic in his First Officer's tone of voice; a weary amusement, from having heard such inspiriting "guff" once too often from a new captain, was it?

He was a man of about Lewrie's age, or perhaps a year or two older; wide-shouldered and thickset, with a sea-browned, sea-whipped visage half gone to well-worn leather. His features were regular enough to be unremarkable, but for a sour, down-turned mouth, and a pervading stolidity of manner. As if he'd seen it all long before, heard it all, been there and back. . . .

Lewrie could pretty-well sense that Lt. Simon Ludlow would never be one of those shipmates *he'd* recall with much fondness in later years. Competent, humourless, perhaps a bit resentful to be serving a younger man? Or wary and guarded in their first days of association? 'Long as he did a thorough job though, it didn't signify.

His other two lieutenants were a rosier prospect, as he got an introduction to them. Second Officer Anthony Langlie was in his midtwenties and, again, a fellow of regular-enough features to be unremarkable—the sort found in an hundred gunrooms in the Navy; about as tall as Lewrie was, long and lean and rangy, with romantically curly hair in the newfangled style which had set half the London chick-a-biddies in a swoon; dark, curly hair; smallish brown eyes set rather far apart under a beetling brow. He was all affable and cheery though and seemed the type who'd retained a devil-may-care streak beneath his professionalism.

The Third Lieutenant, Lewis Wyman, was much younger, just about as "fresh-hatched" as Lewrie had deemed the ship and crew; for *Proteus* was his first ship as a Commission Officer. He was a gracious, puckish lad of twenty-one or twenty-two; fair-complected and ginger-haired, with blue eyes, and a "my goodness gracious" callowness about him, as if seeing the sea for the very first time. He was half a minnikin, at least three inches shorter than Lewrie's five-foot-nine, and looked fair to being blown away like swan's down by their first good gale. His handshake, though, was vise-like, proper-calloused, and rope-toughened.

"Delighted to be here, sir . . . quite," Lt. Wyman assured him as he bobbed and grinned, unabashedly cheerful.

Lewrie turned to the next fellow, his new Sailing Master.

"Mister Winwood, sir . . ." Ludlow supplied in a polit-ish rasp.

"Your servant, sir," Winwood intoned carefully, doffing his hat to him. He was youngish for a Master, perhaps a bit beyond mid-thirties . . . primmer and of a soberer mien than most of Lewrie's experience, with an accent more like squirearchy Kentish, Lewrie assumed at first hearing.

"Do we sail waters with which I'm unfamiliar, I'd expect it to be me, *your* servant, Mister Winwood," Lewrie allowed with an easy grin.

"Oh." Winwood took time to ponder, as if to remind himself that people *did,* now and then, make jests. "Of course, Captain. I see your point."

"In falling down the Medway to the Nore of a certainty." Lewrie nodded back. "Only done it the once . . . thankee, Jesus."

Winwood seemed to wince a bit. *At the blasphemy,* Lewrie asked himself, *or was it me blabbin' how new-come I am? God, take hold o' yer bloody errant tongue and act like a proper captain ought! Solemn, all-wise . . . and dyspeptic!*

"We'll see her safe, Captain, sir," Winwood declared, devoutly earnest. "Rest assured of it."

"With your able guidance, Mister Winwood, I harbour no qualms whatsoever," Lewrie glibly replied more forthrightly and looking him straight in the eye. "The same able guidance you'd have given Captain Churchwell," he added, hoping for an inkling into *Proteus*'s mystery.

"A sorrowful pity, sir." Winwood nodded. "Him and his chaplain both. You'd not, uhm . . . pardon me for asking, sir, but . . . will you be carrying a chaplain on ship's books as well?"

"Hadn't planned on it, Mister Winwood," Lewrie answered, keeping a straight face. "More room for 'em aboard a ship of the line."

"Ah, I see, sir." Winwood gloomed, sounding a bit crestfallen.

'Twas the blasphemy, Lewrie decided, as he turned away to greet another stranger; *Hell, p'raps me soundin' cunny-thumbed too. Has to be another o' Churchwell's sort . . . a proper Bible-thumper.*

"Leftenant Devereux, sir," Ludlow supplied, putting stress to the "Lef-," as the Army and Marines pronounced it. "In charge of our marine contingent." And once more sounding almost taunting with that slight oddity of stress. It obviously irked Devereux, for that young officer suffered a tic in one cheek as he was introduced.

"First *Lef*-tenant Blase Devereux, Captain Lewrie, sir," that immaculate worthy added, as he doffed his hat. "M'sergeant, Skipwith, down yonder. Corp'rals O'Neil—he's the one puddin'-faced brawler from Limerick, sir; Plympton, sir, our Devonian. Full complement of Marines, sir . . . forty privates all told," Devereux offered, with a stiff-backed professional air, though still managing to sound miffed. He was in his late-twenties, as elegant and lint-less a paragon of marine "spit-and-polish" as any. A gentleman, Lewrie decided at once, with a private income in addition to his pay. And a grudge 'gainst Ludlow?

"Lieutenant Devereux, sir," Lewrie said, with a faint smile on his face and offering his hand. "Don't mind your Marines gettin' yer hands dirty now and again, do you, sir?"

"Uhm . . . in what manner, sir?" Devereux blinked, suspicious of common pulley-hauley duties. The enforced separation between sailors and Marines, put aboard to guard against mutiny and disorders, was an ever touchy subject; the marine complement's disdain for ship-work was not to be violated—or the two communities allowed to mingle too freely.

"I've found aboard my previous ships, sir, that the Marines were some of the best shots with the carriage-guns," Lewrie told him. "Did we fight short-handed, sir, I'd admire did the Marines practice at artillery drill. The quarterdeck carronades, 6-pounders, swivels . . . ?"

"Uhm, well . . . of course, sir," Devereux cautiously allowed, not finding any traps in such usage. They'd not have to mix with the crew in the waist on the 12-pounder great-guns, be allowed to trod a sacred quarter-deck. . . . "A most sensible suggestion, sir."

"And I thank you for your cooperation, sir." Lewrie beamed.

"Purser, sir . . . Mister Coote," Ludlow rumbled.

"Your humble servant, sir," *Proteus*'s "Nip-Cheese" stated, all agreeable and welcoming. Coote was a man in his forties, togged out in a plain blue coat and breeches, with a red waist-coat, and an unadorned black cocked hat. He seemed very anxious to please. Given Lewrie's long suspicion of "pussers," he wondered what sins that anxiety covered.

"Pleased t'make your acquaintance, Mister Coote," Lewrie said. "I wonder, though, sir . . ."

Rock him back on his heels right off, Lewrie told himself; *works wonders, do they think you're onto 'em from the very first.*

"The hands, Mister Coote." Lewrie frowned, all but making "tsk-tsk" cluckings. "Your slop-clothing is not aboard yet, is it? That's why the new-comes are still in filthy civilian rags?"

"Why, nossir!" Coote gawped back, looking as if he wished he'd be able to wring his paws in distress. "No orders to release anything yet, Captain Lewrie. The First Lieutenant said to . . ."

"Told him to wait, sir," Ludlow snapped, " 'til the new captain had come aboard. Might not've cared for Captain Churchwell's choices, sir. Hammocks and such've been issued, but we were waiting to see how you wished 'em dressed, sir."

"And you now have aboard, Mister Coote . . . ?" Lewrie prompted his purser. *Damme, it sounds a reasonable decision after all*, he thought. Some captains had odd preferences for their men's appearance. There was no regulated uniform for people "before the mast" yet.

"Red chequered calico shirts, sir," Coote informed him, with a wary glance towards Ludlow. "White duck trousers, blue duck . . . blue round jackets, black tarred hats, sir . . ."

"Issue blue slop-trousers then," Lewrie decided quickly. "A single pair o' white for Sunday Divisions. Two pair o' blue for sea-duty. Shows less dirt and tar, and they won't be spending half their 'Rope-Yarn Sundays' tryin' to scrub the white'uns clean."

"Aye, sir." Coote brightened. "And, sir, save on soap issue too. Trying to do their washing with salt water? Or a wee bucket of fresh, now and then?"

A pint a man, per day, for cleanliness—that was what was allowed for shaving, bathing (did any of them actually believe in such an activity!), or scrubbing.

"Exactly, Mister Coote," Lewrie chuckled. "Neckerchiefs? Oh, see what you may do 'bout finding some red'uns . . . for a distinguishing splash o' colour. Black hats . . . all of a piece, mind. So the people are as much alike in dress as we can make 'em, right from the first. A blue round jacket per man too. Brass buttons for rated men."

"I've black horn buttons for the rest, sir!" Coote enthused.

"Very well, then, Mister Coote, see to it," Lewrie ordered him. "And, Mister Ludlow, rig the wash-deck pumps and make sure the people are sluiced clean o' vermin an' such . . . have you not already? As the slop-clothing is issued."

"Aye, aye, sir," Ludlow agreed. Or at least it sounded as if he agreed; grudgingly, did he, though?

Then Lewrie met the ship's Surgeon, a Mr. Thomas Shirley, a gangly fellow in his mid-twenties, and his Surgeon's Mates; one was named Hodson, even younger and greener than Shirley, little better (he himself admitted) than an apothecary, in training as it were. Mr. Durant, though, was much older and boasted more experience. Had he been English-born, he might have held Shirley's berth. But Mr. Durant was emigré French. Landed like a gaffed fish on a strange shore, he'd wheedled a position from the Sick & Hurt Board after two years of effort, the only way he had in a leery England to support his family, he sketched out for Lewrie's information, after trying the charity hospitals and private practice.

"You escaped, sir?"

"From Toulon, *Capitaine*," Durant admitted. "*Quel tragique . . .*"

"Ah, I was there. Aye, it was, sir," Lewrie gloomed along with him. "We left at the same time, I should think. Night before . . . ?"

"*Oui*, Capitaine. An' I know of you," Durant said. "What you did for so many Royalists you sail away from zere. *Merci, Capitaine*. I promise you grateful service, *oui!*"

"I count on it, sir," Lewrie replied.

"You'll be going to your cabins now, sir?" Ludlow supposed. "Get settled in, sir?"

"No." Lewrie frowned. "Might as well make the acquaintance of as many warrants as I can. Have the Bosun, his mate, the Master Gunner . . . the department heads, gather in the waist, Mister Ludlow."

"Aye, aye, sir," Ludlow answered, sounding aggrieved? Lewrie had to think, again. What *was* the man's problem? *Bit more o' that, and I will* really *give him a problem t'fret over!*

So while Andrews, Padgett, and Aspinall turned-to aft to erect his furnishings and possessions in the great-cabins, Lewrie descended to the gun-deck, admiring his lovely new artillery pieces. A crowd of older hands gathered 'round him. The Bosun was a Mr. Arthur Pendarves, a hawk-billed, sere fellow from Cornwall, who looked as if he'd spent most of his life squinting at wind and weather. As did his mate, Mr. Towpenny, a shorter, spritelier version from Bristol. Mr. Handcocks, the Master Gunner, a tall, lean, and balding fellow in his middle forties; and his mate, Mr. Morley, who was, again, younger. Mr. Garraway, their Carpenter; Mr. Reyne, the Sailmaker; Offley, the Armourer; the Yeomen of the Sheets, who served on the sail-trimming gangways, Betts and Robbins; the Yeoman of The Powder, who served in the magazine; a man named Kever, who looked as pasty as if he hadn't left the magazine since his teens; the three Quartermasters: Motte, Austen, and O'Leary; Hickey, a young apprentice Sailmaker's Mate; a whole slew of Quarter Gunners—*Proteus* was rated a full eight petty-officer gunners; Dowe, O'Hare, and Magee, who were the Quartermaster's Mates on the helm; the gloomy Mr. Neale, who was their Master At Arms and had probably been *born* gloomy; and a brace of Ship's Corporals—Burton and Ragster. And, of course, they all made the lame jape that that poor fellow was "Ragster-riches"!

Nugent and Shoemake, the Master's Mates, Nugent being another Irishman. Lewrie was beginning to notice that they had more than their fair share of hands aboard from that unhappy and rebellious isle! And finally, the midshipmen—all bloody six of them.

There were the young'uns—Midshipmen Elwes and Nicholas, both about fourteen or fifteen and seemingly sweet-natured and a tad shy. There was a Midshipman Sevier, who looked to be around eighteen, the sort who would bob and choke on even polite conversation. A slightly older, and very quick-witted, Mr. Adair, but, being a Scot, and well-educated in comparison to his English contemporaries, he *would* seem to be witty; a Mr. Catterall, who was now twenty-one, a blond-haired wag Lewrie could deduce at once—he was most notably from Lancs, for all his local accent; and finally, Mr. Midshipman Peacham, a tad older in his mid-twenties, a very tarry customer, but one unfortunate in "interest" or patronage so far. He was curtly polite, horny-handed; the type of senior midshipman Lewrie thought he could depend on from his first impression. Peacham looked the perfect image of a real tarpaulin man, of the most knowledgeable sort, and overdue for a lieutenancy.

He shared a few words with them all, taking over an hour or more to do so. Though he doubted he'd be able to recall all those names by 4:00 A.M. when they rose to scrub decks and begin the ship's day, he was of the opinion that making the effort to reach out was the main thing. Not so chearly with them as to be taken for a "Popularity Jack," but it never hurt to try and size people up and make them realise that he was not a tacit, tyrannical Tartar either.

"Well, gentlemen . . ." He shrugged at last. "I hope you will not take it to heart if I have to ask your names again over the next week. Too long aboard a smaller ship, where after a time one'd *wish* to see just one unfamiliar face. Until the morrow. Oh, Mister Pendarves?"

"Aye, sir," the Bosun replied, perking up, yet looking guarded.

"Once the hands have eat tomorrow, we'll look her over," Lewrie warned him. "Keel to trucks, and me in my worst slop-clothing. Then you may tell me what you lack, before we fall downriver."

"Well, sir . . . hands for work'd be my mainest plaint, sir," Mr. Pendarves told him bluntly. "Recruit or press more hands, sir. We are in fair shape for stores and such, else. A tad light on rations . . . keep her draught light for the trip to the Nore, sir, where we'll stock, at Sheerness."

"But given fair recruiting here at Chatham, a few more Able or Ordinary Seamen . . . and a week's 'River Discipline,' we could let slip, Mister Pendarves?" Lewrie pressed him for his opinion.

"Aye, sir. Could." The Bosun shrugged, almost wincing.

"But . . ." Lewrie queried closer, getting a bit fed up with all the tiptoe-y responses he'd gotten since he'd stepped aboard. "Might you think there's a reason not?"

"Recruitin', sir," Pendarves muttered in a gruff voice, taking off his hat to stand like a supplicant labourer at the rear door of his master. "Warrants an' petty officers, some of their mates, an' friends . . . a first draught off th' receivin' ship. An' Cap'um Churchwell's men . . . that's all we have, sir. Doubt we find many more willin'; not here in Chatham, Captain. Cause o' . . ." Pendarves winced again at being on the spot, of being the one to bring bad news.

"Oh, I see." Lewrie nodded, cocking his head to one side. "There is her . . . reputation to deal with."

"Aye, sir . . . that'd be it, mainly." Pendarves flushed.

"Many aboard wish they could turn over into a new ship, Bosun?"

"Well, sir . . . there's more than a few Irish aboard . . . hands outa the West Country too, sir. An' I *know* it sounds daft, but . . ."

"West Country yourself, I'd guess, Mister Pendarves?" Lewrie interjected and received a bob of the Bosun's head. "Welsh, Devonian, Cornish . . . men who think her cursed. Men who wish off her?"

"Some, like I say, sir," Pendarves confessed.

"Hmmm . . . how well did Captain Churchwell do at recruiting then?" Lewrie wondered.

"Well . . . right awful, Captain." Pendarves grimaced for bearing even more bad news. "Onliest *volunteers*, d'ye see, were shipmates come aboard t'sail with old friends, sir. 'Pressed men, a few hands turned over from the hulks . . . Quota Men'n such. Cap'um Churchwell only tried but a few days 'fore he was, uhm . . . when the chaplain drowned. Give it up, I s'pose, right after, sir."

"And the First Officer, Mister Ludlow?" Lewrie frowned. "Went ashore and tried too, did he? Afterwards? After Captain Churchwell departed?"

"A day or two, sir, but . . . jacks see him comin', they'd scamper off 'fore he could trot out an ale!" Bosun Pendarves marvelled that British tars would refuse even free drinks, no matter could they sign up, or refuse to, at a 'rondy.' "Come back two days, since, an' . . ."

Pendarves bit off any trace of criticism of an officer.

"I see." Lewrie sighed, pacing about the deck, over to larboard to lay a hand on one of his new Blomefield Pattern 12-pounders, to lean a hip against the gun's cascabel and the swell of the breech. "Short of real sailors, and too many landsmen lubbers. Can't crew her with a pack of know-nothings right out of gaol. Unless . . . unless *Proteus* is really a very lucky ship after all, Mister Pendarves."

"Lucky, sir?" The Bosun came near to openly scoffing.

"You're quite right, Bosun." Lewrie grinned, shoving off from his resting spot. "It sounds daft, doesn't it. Superstition or not, sailors believe in good and bad luck, don't they."

"Well . . . aye, sir."

"You and me, Bosun," Lewrie intimated, "we're seamen. We've seen things, heard things . . . odd, strange, unexplainable things . . ."

And ain't it smug o' me, Lewrie chid himself, *t'put us both on the same footing. He's more experience in his least finger than* I'll *ever . . . !*

"What's her *name*, Mister Pendarves?"

"*P . . . Proteus,* sir," the Bosun answered with a slight pause, as if afraid to say it aloud.

"Her figurehead, sir. . . ." Lewrie all but winked. "Proteus, the Roman shepherd of the sea . . . Greeks called him Nereus, but either name meant the same sea-god. A divine oracle, he was. And there he is . . . in his chariot he drove 'cross the wide world's oceans, drawn by dolphins and . . . *seals,* Mister Pendarves. Seals!"

"Like *L* . . . uhm, ah . . . ," Bosun Pendarves flummoxed, afraid to say that fearsome name from his boyhood tales either.

"Funny thing about Proteus, or Nereus, or *whatever* he went by. A man wished his prophecies, he had to find him first. Then he had to wrestle him, hold him so he couldn't get away. Proteus changed his shape . . . he could become any living thing in the sea, d'ye see, sir?" Lewrie intimated further, almost crooning as he spun his tale. "Turned into little things so he could swim out of your grasp. Turned into whales and sharks or ferocious sea-dragons to frighten you into letting go. You had to let him run through his gamut of creatures . . . last of all, he was a seal . . . and then a man, sir," Lewrie elaborated, not sure from his ancient readings, not sure if he wasn't spinning a huge lie he'd be caught in by Pendarves and the others later for lack of lore.

"Like a, uhm . . ." Pendarves goggled, eyes blared in wonder by then, to hear the ancient tales retold in a slightly different version, to hear an *officer* relate them, as if he too believed! "Like he was a . . . *selkie,* sir?"

"Very *like* a selkie, Mister Pendarves." Lewrie beamed, as his Bosun caught on, feeling a dread, eldritch chill ascend his spine, no matter if he was lying and manipulating or not! "So . . . how close do you think they really came . . . when they chose her name? *Merlin,* that would've suited her, hey? But then Admiralty changed things at the last second and took that back. But that Celtic or Gaelic sawyer and his wee lad . . . what'd he *say* to her, Bosun?"

Lewrie leaned close, hissing his words in a harsh whisper, for security against being *too* manipulative; after all, he'd seen enough aboard *Jester* of a pagan sea-god's ways to tread more than a touch wary. And he never wished his beliefs . . . or his *seeming* beliefs . . . to be bandied about.

"And then . . . the touch of that lad's merest hand and . . . down the ways she went, groaning over it . . . but going," Lewrie purred seductively. "Did they bless her . . . the right way? The old, *lost* way? Did she accept the name *Proteus* as a huge jape on everyone, in spite of them? Take water and swim the world's oceans and bedamned to 'em, Mister Pendarves? Knowing that Proteus, Nereus, or . . . *Lir,* it makes no diff'rence, for they're all the same long-lost, forgotten sea-god?"

There, he'd invoked it, feeling another shiver of awe—fear!

But his tarry-handed, stout-thewed Bosun had wavered away to the thick base of the main-mast, hard by the break of the quarterdeck. Pendarves laid a hand on the mast's anti-boarding pike beckets (*never* the mast itself, for that was bad luck!) almost reverently. He gazed up its height, the convoluted maze of rigging and spars, then down at the white-planed and sanded deck planks—and began a crafty smile.

"It could be as you say, sir," Pendarves said at last, swallowing as if he had a massive lump in his throat. "That'd mean she *ain't* a cursed ship."

"Nothing we could print on the recruiting handbills," Lewrie agreed, "but could say on the sly at the 'rondys' . . . you and some of the other respected senior hands. West Country men, hmm?"

"Aye, sir." Pendarves grinned wider, brightened by the prospect of a "run" ashore in the pubs.

"I'll see you in the early-early then, Mister Pendarves," Lewrie said in dismissal. "We'll give this new ship of ours a thorough inspection. Warn the others so they'll not show too badly. But not so much warning they think they can pull the wool over my eyes . . . hmm?"

A good beginning, Lewrie rather smugly deemed it, after doffing his hat and ascending the larboard ladder to his quarterdeck for a moment of reflection before taking a look at his new great-cabins.

As long as I've not gone and doomed my arse, he thought; *being too damned boastful or . . . sacrilegious?*

CHAPTER FIFTEEN

Proteus rounded up, coaxed, (or flat-out lied to) another fourteen seamen or lubbers from Chatham, volunteers who were of a mind to take to the sea. It was a pitiful result, for all of Lewrie's, Ludlows's, and Pendarves's efforts at recruiting ashore. They were still shy of the ninety-one seamen allotted, about a dozen shy of the twenty-two servants (who could quickly learn the seamen's trade) recommended for a vessel of their size and gunpower. Then the pool of possibles had dried up, turning further recruiting work into frustrating futility.

It didn't help their cause, Lewrie most-sourly thought, that the mutinies at Portsmouth and Plymouth were still going on. News had come that retired Admiral Lord Howe—"Black Dick, the Seaman's Friend"—would be coaching down to Portsmouth and Spithead to negotiate an end to it, giving hopes of a final settlement. But desperate as England was for closure, most men of a mind to volunteer were holding out 'til the settlement had been *reached* and what demands the illegal working-men's guilds and underground organisations and the penny-tract writers were making to tack onto the settlement with the Fleet were inciting even more truculence and resistance to taking the Joining Bounty, when it might be worth more in a fortnight, when shipboard conditions and rations might be better!

There was nothing for it but to work what few they had into the basic stages of "River Discipline" and hope for the best. The Impress Service

could not help them, and Lewrie's old captain, Lilycrop, wasn't the Regulating Captain of the Deptford recruiting district any longer, so Lewrie
was reduced to shaking the staleness off his few experienced hands and
drilling a semblance of nautical lore into his wooly-headed new-comers so
they could get downriver to Sheerness in one piece.

Sheerness and the Nore was where they'd find sailors; at least more
warm bodies who could be driven or bullied into something nigh to sailors.
The receiving hulks and out-dated, line-of-battle ships there were crammed
full of them. Admiral Buckner, the officer commanding at the Nore, had
written back claiming that his static flagship, *Sandwich*, had a crew of nine
hundred with an additional five hundred "volunteers" aboard. As soon as
Proteus arrived, he'd be *more* than happy to ease his over-crowding.

Getting there to lay hold of them though . . . !

Proteus would have to work her way down the crowded, teeming, bendy
Medway, a river simply heaving with brisk tidal flows, cross-swept by
perverse winds from over marshes and lowlands, flanked by reeking mudflats and shoals, and the navigable channel reduced to a cart-path by the
rapid ebbs, which narrow navigable channel was then even more crowded
by a myriad of sailing barges, scows, fishing boats and coasters, tenders,
merchant vessels, and other warships, all seeking the same precious, safe,
and scant ribbon of deep water.

Proteus could run ashore, take the ground and be stuck for days on the
shoals or mudflats, or half-wreck herself in collision with some other vessel,
most especially one of those bastardly civilian captains of a towing scow
with a long string of barges astern of him, who seemed to derive their sole
pleasure in life from making things difficult for everybody else. Or col-
lecting high damages from the smash-ups!

Lewrie dreaded the necessity, but finally had to admit that he had no
other choice. It was sail—and risk his ship and career upon the vagaries
of the river and its traffic—or admit defeat.

He had his Sailing Master in and swotted up every text he possessed
which might offer a clue as to how he might pull this off without that
career-ending disaster he feared so much.

"Nought to fear, sir," Mr. Winwood assured him, though looking a
trifle askance at just how tarry-handed his new captain really was . . .

"Know the Nore like the back o' me hand. And the river pilots'll see us safe, sir."

A last supper aboard; with his officers invited to dine in the great-cabins with his wife, children, and ward; he'd borrowed furniture from the officers' gunroom to seat everyone.

And for a man nigh to sweating pistol-balls (or at least fine buckshot by then!) it had turned off quite convivial and a most musical evening. He'd learned by then in his life how to disguise his trepidations and sure-to-God knew how to be witty and amusing. With Caroline and her flute, he and his more-modest flageolet, they had had a round of tunes with their after-supper brandy, and Lieutenant Wyman had produced his violin, at which he was better than passing-fair. Lieutenant Langlie of the romantic locks also proved himself to be a vocalist of some ability. And while Sophie was deprived of her harpsichord, she had sung along in an angelically high voice. With her eyes ashine in admiration of someone other than the beastly Harry Embleton for once, for several, in point of fact. Young Lieutenant Wyman's musical ability and his infectiously amusing air; Lieutenant Langlie's voice and his bronzed features—even a brace of the older midshipmen! For their last time together, it had really been quite gay, and Lewrie and Caroline had shared pleased glances that things had gone so well regarding Sophie and her brief exposure to a wider world and the variety of young men her age in it! Sewallis, Hugh, and Charlotte had even (mostly) behaved well!

Though, Lewrie felt like gritting his teeth and at times allowing himself a snarl or two, it was mostly pleasant. Even with all his professional concerns weighing on him, the new ship and crew so demanding of his time and interest, Lewrie had reached that moment he always reached, the one which always made him feel so inhuman, so dis-connected from what real people should feel . . . and so guilty for his lack.

The children, no matter how delightful or loving, had grown to be irksome, and he wished for a respite from them and their ados. His lovely, accomplished wife, so graceful and gracious, so loving, sensible, and affectionate—a woman most men would kill for as a mate!—was becoming

an intrusion into his thoughts, his fretting over manoeuvring *Proteus* seaward, of stocking her, manning her, readying her . . . ! 'Twas *her* needs,
her desires took precedence; and her faults and lacks—and her foreboding
reputation!—which filled his waking thoughts and made him squirm with
desperation to be off and free!

It didn't help that Caroline sensed this, as she did so many of his moods
by then, and could feel the stand-offish apartness of a driven man beneath
his cheerful exterior sham. He was becoming that feckless, uncaring, and
ungrateful boor she'd wept about back in Anglesgreen, the one who'd
throw off every tie to land and family to dash off at the slightest whiff of
tar and salt!

And it *really* didn't help his feelings of inhuman boorishness that she
was so *very* bloody . . . *good* about it! Not so much accepting their separation, or his eagerness for it, really, as she was "bearing up"—like a
Christian martyr whose immolation depended on the timely arrival of a
waggon-load of kindling. Saintly! She was long suffering, sweet-natured,
temperate, and patient to the very end, and not letting her true feelings
show even for an instant—for the children's sake, for *his* sake, and his
career's. Though she *could* put more import into a faint sigh than most
people could cram down the muzzle of a 42-pounder fortress gun . . . !

Her silent patience irked him by then about as much as the antics of
the children. "Go on," she as much as said to him, "*be* a heartless monster.
I'll grin and bear it, no matter how sore you hurt me . . . us. But don't
you feel the slightest pangs of guilt?"

Aye, he did, which only made him wish that he could fly away—even
sooner or quicker!

Marriages, Lewrie thought, most melancholic, as he waved shoreward at
them as they stood forlorn but brave atop the King's Stairs to watch his
departure. *Christ, who thought them up? Had to've been some hermit in a
hair shirt . . . his little joke on the rest o' mankind! Or God's more a cynic
than we think Him!*

The night before, they'd said their goodbyes in a final hour of privacy
in his quarters. He'd hugged them all, cajoled them all, and dried more

than one set of tears. Now, once *Proteus* was well on her way downriver, Caroline would take them all back to London for a last round of sights, shows, and shopping before returning to Anglesgreen, their adventures over. His, however, were just beginning. And in a most perilous way too.

The high tide had just begun to ebb, and turn from slackwater. Even though it was an ungodly hour to be up and stirring, he had to make the most of that tide. It was nippy and cool, and the faint hint of sunrise promised a bleak, overcast day, with a whiff of rain on the light breezes, breezes which, unfortunately, stood from out of the Nor'east. The hands stood at sail-handling posts or about the capstan head, their few ship's boys and boy servants ready with the nippers to serve the messenger cable to the thigh-thick mooring hawser. A Medway river pilot stood by the quartermasters on the wheel, clapping his hands for warmth and chatting quite gaily with Mr. Winwood. With impatience, Lewrie could imagine, as he listened to those mittened paws slapping together now and again.

Proteus tried to stream downriver with the turning tidal flow, her stern pointing something near to Nor'east; the direction the Medway ran from Chatham until it got to Gillingham Reach and the sharp bend to the Sou'east. The wind, however, had just enough force to it to shove her down, even under bare poles, so that her bows pointed about due West. Directly against the tide, that wind. It promised to be an eventful morning!

Dear Lord in Heaven, Lewrie thought, deciding that prayers might not go *too* far amiss; *let me get her down to Sheerness . . . safe. Lady, do you have a soul, remember I ain't yer enemy? You're a ship, born and bred, and yer proper place is the sea . . . so let's get down there. Be perverse as ya wish once there, but . . . it's me or ya get a* real *bastard for a captain next time! Christ, I'm daft . . .*

"Very well, sirs," he announced in a voice he thought much too chipper and loud, as he turned away from the bulwarks and the sight of his family and wished Royal Navy captains could cross their fingers for luck in public. "Let us be going, even if it is a windward tide."

They stiffened, ceased their whispered morning chatters, and the tin mugs of coffee were stashed away so they could be about the demanding business. Everyone looked *so* bloody keen and earnest, masking the fears they felt. Lewrie could almost (but not quite) sympathise.

"Would you recommend we tack or wear off the mooring, sir?" he asked of the river pilot. "Bows to windward or alee?"

"Either'd suit just as well, Captain Lewrie," the pilot replied, with a long, lazy yawn, as if it were no matter to him. "Bows alee'd save a spot o' labour when we get to the bend. But there's bags of sea room alee, sir. Bows a'weather, you'd have to tack at the bend . . . and do you end up 'in-stays,' well . . ."

There was that, Lewrie thought; *trying to tack in the narrow confines of the river bend, most-like with a dozen contrary vessels coming upriver and vying for sea room.* Should they not get her bow 'round, she'd drift on the tidal current, right onto the far shore's mudflats! He'd been reading accounts of how to weather the Medway, had tried to recall his one-and-only down-river passage from so long before. That had been with a helpful beam wind from the West-Nor'west. He'd lain awake and schemed, played a tiny paper boat model down the river chart (when Toulon wasn't swatting it halfway to France or Peterborough!) in all imaginable weather conditions. This one, though, was the one he'd feared worst, almost as bad as a leeward tide, with wind and current flowing the same direction, which would have had them dragging anchors astern at the "trip" to keep from being hared along quite out of all control and at a prodigious rate of knots!

No, this crew's not well-drilled enough for a proper tack. Alan sighed, feeling his innards shriveling. *We'd muck it, sure'z Fate!* It was bows alee for them, and all the sail-handling and helm commands he would give— arse backwards!

"Back and fill, then . . . bows alee," Lewrie decided aloud.

"Nought t'fear, sir." The pilot yawned again.

Easy for him t'say. Lewrie glowered. *Think I'm fearful, do . . . ?*

"Larboard bower's a'cock-bill by the ring-painter, sir," Ludlow supplied, sounding much more agreeable and cooperative this day, now he had something nautical and challenging to do. Or delighting in goading his new captain into folly, Lewrie could also conjure! Taking joy from his dithering and delay. "Shank-painter's free, and we've a stream-anchor prepared astern, as you ordered, sir. Just in case."

"Very well, Mister Ludlow," Lewrie snapped, steeling himself, and for a dread, blank moment trying to recall what commands to issue and in what order. He cast a glance aloft at the commissioning pendant to see how strong the wind was and whether it was steady or not. It was firmly out of the Nor'east, dead foul of the tide and river.

"We'll sheer her 'round first, gentlemen," he pronounced with a nip to his voice. "Helm hard-over to larboard . . . hard alee, Quartermasters."

Streaming back from her mooring buoy by a single cable, *Proteus* already had steerageway, with that tide sluicing past her rudder and down her sides. With the helm hard-over to leeward, the tide forced her to turn, still tethered, bringing her stern up into the wind and her bows down towards the lee shores to the South.

She was held to the permanent mooring buoy by a single hawser up forrud, doubled from the starboard hawse hole to the metal ring atop the buoy and back to a belay, at fairly middling-stays. He'd placed Mr. Midshipman Adair, his best and brightest so far, all the way forrud in charge of letting slip.

"Mister Peacham," Lewrie barked, wheeling to face his eldest of the middies, who stood with the afterguard in charge of the mizzenmast. "Stand by to hoist spanker to get her stern 'round. Mister Ludlow . . . stand ready with the tops'ls and inner jib."

Up her stern came, *Proteus* angling more across the tideway with her stern almost directly into the wind. Any further and she'd snub on that mooring cable, Lewrie knew, fail to wheel far enough Sutherly to set sail, yet . . . for good or ill . . . they had to let go, to trust in the wind and tide to take her and let her get a touch of way on so they could sail her off and not trip over the buoy—or drift helplessly to strand her on the south bank!

Soon . . . wait, she'll snub . . . now! Lewrie thought, drawing in a preparatory breath. "Mister Adair . . . let slip!" he almost screamed. The wind . . . had it come almost due aft yet? A touch of veering on his left cheek? "Man the captsan! Haul in! Smartly, now!"

She was free, untethered. Horny bare feet pounded the deck as the hands on the capstan thundered about in a circle, breasting to the bars, the pawls ratcheting as fast as a trotting horse's hooves, winding the messenger cable inboard about its drum, with the heavier hawser "nippered" to it. That heavy cable groaned and grated through the eye of the hawse hole.

With no sails aloft, *Proteus* was taken by the out-flowing tide, adrift slowly astern, still so slowly turning with her helm hard-over, and her 740 tons of deadweight too much for the wind on her tall sides, her masts, and the maze of her rigging. There, the wind, a tiny touch on her larboard quarters!

"Hoist away aft, Mister Peacham! Sheet the spanker hard a'starboard! Mister Ludlow . . . let's begin with the foretops'l."

"Aye, aye, sir," Ludlow piped back, all enthusiasm, yet sounding dubious in spite of it. "Hoy, there! Let fall the foretops'l! Brace starboard! Clews . . . halliards . . . jears, an' haul away!"

Up the yard went from its rest upon the foretop, with topmen out on the foot-ropes freeing the brails, the clews singing in the blocks to haul the lower corners down to bare them to the wind, the canvas rustling and shivering as it began to belly in fits and starts, loose-footed.

Proteus was now swinging, not quite under control yet, drifting and driven by the tideway, the spanker forcing her stern down and her bows up, so she lay Sou'easterly, almost abeam the river, and angling more and more windward.

"Mister Adair! Bare the inner jib, larboard tack!"

Just enough pressure on her bows to keep her from swinging up too far into the wind, and getting her foretops'l laid aback on the mast! And that muddy, dangerous lee shore about as far away as Lewrie could spit, it seemed!

"Main tops'l, Mister Ludlow, hoist away!" Lewrie pressed for more sail and more control. "Mizzen tops'l too . . . but brace her all aback!"

Christ, he gloomed, just about ready to drop the larboard bower and surrender, admit he was a fraud, give up this nonsense, and slink off! She was now athwart the tideway, beam-onto the wind, hauled off by that shred of the inner jib's tack for the moment, but still making way mostly East, which would drift her onto the shore any second, did the tops'ls not fill and . . . !

Come on, lady, you can do it! he groaned to himself; *God knows I'm not sure if I can, but you . . . !*

Hmm, though . . .

The tops'ls were now fully alive, almost thundering as they were set wind-full. Slackly wind-full, but bellied out and drawing, braced 'round to be brushed by the wind, to shape it and cup it for an instant before it soughed past at an acute angle.

And *Proteus* began to steady, broadside to the wind, sailing *into* the wind, and making an awkward course to the Nor'east, still a bit too near that lee shore than Lewrie cared for, but . . . ! She was going downriver with the tide, her fore and main tops'ls giving her lift, and the mizzen tops'l all aback to act as a brake as if she was cocked up to windward, fetched to! Turning a bit too *much* to windward, so . . .

"Mister Peacham, brail up the spanker to the gaff for a bit," Lewrie called, after a *long* moment of thought. "Mister Adair, douse the inner jib . . . for a bit!" he shouted forrud.

And without the wind's pressure on the spanker to act directly opposite of the usual effect, which would normally have swung her bow off, she steadied once more, a bit more broadside to the wind and the river. *Got it now, I think!* he told himself; *bows get too high, I re-hoist the inner jib up for-rud and that'll push her bows back down. Does she trend too far off the wind, I re-hoist the spanker aft, makin' her stern-heavy. Rudder . . . well, hmm. What rudder? We're sailin' as fast as the tide, so we've no rudder control at all 'til we reach the river bend and try to haul our wind and sail Large to the Sou'east . . .*

And if it all goes to shit, he assured himself, though still a bit more than a tad shuddery; *we just douse sail and drop anchors. Do we meet a string o' barges, or get goin' too fast, we brace the tops'ls aback to slow down. Balance wind 'gainst tide . . . just sit in one spot for a bit . . . ?* As long as the wind complied and continued out of the Nor'east, it was—quite illogically and most disconcertingly—what was known as "smooth sailing"!

"Neatly done, sir," the river pilot drawled, with a beamish eye. "In-credible, ain't it . . . what you can do with a ship, do you set your mind to it? Short handed you may be, Captain Lewrie, but you've a talented batch of officers and mates. Includin' yerself, sir. Goes without sayin'."

"Ah . . . hmm, well," Lewrie cautiously allowed, wondering if he was being twitted. There was still plenty of river left in which he could come a spectacular cropper. *Don't know what the blazes I'm about,* he chid himself. *Never done this in me life; don't know . . . damn' fraud!*

"This'll be the worst stretch, sir," the pilot went on, rocking on the balls of his feet, looking as if he'd be inclined to sing or hum in another minute. "No traffic this early it seems. Once to the bend Sou'east into Gillingham Reach, we'll be off the wind on larboard tack. Inner, outer jibs, an' foretopmast stays'l to get her bows down, then we'll fly for a spell. Tricky bit there, sir, oh mercy!" the pilot enthused. "Tricky as anything."

"Indeed!" Lewrie snapped, feeling more reason for misery.

"Traffic, for certain, in Gillingham Reach, sir," the man went on, most blithe. "Upriver boats huggin' the weather shore, and us to cross the Reach and hug it too . . . beam-reachin' the wind for the main channel. Nasty shoals t'loo'rd, I can tell ye, so ye won't wish to be forced down on 'em. Where the channel narrows, 'fore it opens up once more? Sutherly pass below the shoals is possible, but 'tis fearsome narrow, and this tide'll be ebbin' too quick to trust to it by the time we get there. Short, sharp, beat t'weather into the northern channel where there's more room, I'd suggest, Captain Lewrie. Barring the odd lighters and ignorant barge captains, hey? Or some brute of a 'liner' comin' upriver for a refit, ha, ha? No worry though, sir. We'll be right as rain. Right . . . as . . . rain, ha, ha!"

If I didn't need him so damn' much, Lewrie grimly told himself, *I think I could most cheerfully kill him!*

"Uhm . . . Mister Ludlow. Sheet home the spanker," he instructed instead, bleakly taking in their progress, taking notice of what lay outboard, again. "We're stern-high."

"Aye, aye, sir!"

He looked aft. Amazingly, Chathman and Rochester's spires were already far astern, the King's Stairs unable to be seen. He'd sailed his family "under the horizon" and hadn't had the time to give them a final backward glance, even a last wave of his hat. *Proteus,* according to the small-scale chart tacked to the traverse board by the binnacle cabinet, was already nearly two miles downriver, within a mile of the bend into Gillingham Reach and making a goodly way on the strengthening tide. He'd been too busy to notice, would *still* be busy . . . about as busy as a one-armed tavern wench, 'til they got into the estuary by Queenborough, within sight of Sheerness and the wider mouth of the rivers in the Nore anchorage, where they could drop anchor at last between the Isle of Sheppey and the Isle of Grain.

He felt a surge of remorse, which rose to dominate his worries of handling this strange new ship, for ignoring his family so completely. Yet beneath his qualms from imagining the disaster which still could happen . . . he felt a sense of relief. Loved and cherished as they were, he was free of them, freed from their concerns, their domestic . . .

God, yer such a callous bastard, he sighed to himself!

Across the lowlands, marshes, and mudflats, the Nor'east winds brought a faint hint of deeper waters, of ocean beyond. He *was* free, almost asea once more, in a spanking-new frigate. With a bit more luck to this short passage, he'd be at the edge of the sea, almost ready for anything . . .

Whack! Quickly followed by an outraged yelp.

Lewrie turned to see one of the new-comes in the afterguard on his knees by the weather braces for that backed mizzen tops'l. Mr. Peacham stood over him, with a petty officer close by, whacking at his palm with a rope "starter."

"Gittup, ya stewpid git!" the petty officer snarled. "You'll learn t'keep yer hands off that brace 'til I tells ya t'tail on!"

"Worn't gonna *free* it," the lubber carped, getting back to his feet, " 'twoz just seein' 'ow ya tie h'it proper . . . ow!"

Midshipman Peacham cuffed the volunteer on the side of his head, sending him sprawling again. "None of your civilian sauce, damn you! No back talking to your betters!" He held out a hand to demand of the petty officer his starter, as if he planned to lash the unfortunate to the deck until he learned. The other new-comes stood aghast, and even the few experienced men of the afterguard looked cutty-eyed over it.

"Mister Peacham, sir!" Lewrie barked. "A word with you. Sir."

Peacham put on a bland expression and came to his side, dutiful and obedient.

"Mister Peacham," Lewrie muttered, leaning close so others could not hear. "We're short-handed and barely a herd, much less a crew yet. I *will* allow the Bosun and his mates to 'touch up' crewmen when necessary, but damme if my midshipmen will lay hands on our people. You will not indulge in such again, sir. Do I make my meaning clear to you?"

"Uh, aye, sir. Perfectly clear, sir," Peacham managed to choke out, still striving for blandness, though seeming appalled by the idea that physical force would be denied him.

"Officers are not allowed such," Lewrie expanded with a growl of displeasure. "You, sir, are an officer in training. You must learn to enforce discipline and obedience without resorting to violence on your own part. That's what the senior hands are for."

"Aye, aye, Captain." Peacham nodded.

"And you will caution your petty officer to save his starter, and his fists, for worse reasons than a new-come's curiosity," Lewrie concluded. "Storm, battle, imminent shipwreck, a *real* cause for haste, sir! *Not* to preface a warning about accidentally slacking the mizzen weather brace. Can he not instruct and lead without his starter, then I'll find myself a likely lad who can. You will put him on notice on that head, Mister Peacham. Firmly and forcefully. Lead . . . not drive!"

"Aye, aye, Captain." Peacham nodded again, sounding grave, but looking a touch wary of his new commanding officer's ways. He doffed his hat and departed.

Lewrie whirled about to see if *Proteus* had gone out of control during his intimate tirade, but found her drifting along rather nicely, still broadside-on to the river and the wind, and nearing the bend into Gillingham Reach. There was a small two-master anchored on the weather shore, unable to stem the tide with her sails on that light wind. She was far out of the main channel and would present no threat. Over the waving marsh grasses and stunted trees, he could see what he took for a large sailing barge 'round the bend. It was going to get exciting in a minute!

"When we bear up to windward, then haul off, sir?" he enquired of the river pilot. "How much depth is there, do we intend to shave the eastern lee shore and avoid yon barge, sir?"

"Bags o' water, sir, 'til you're within half a cable of shore," the pilot breezed off with a wave of his hand in the general direction. "Barge'll bear up, I'd expect, Captain. He already sees us, and he'll not wish to get any further down to loo'rd than he is at present," he said, then took a half-step closer to caution, "Were I you, sir, 'tis about time to bare the spanker and swing her bows windward, ready to haul off and fly once we're midchannel of the bend, sir."

"Mizzen tops'l?" Lewrie fretted in a whisper. "Spanish reef 'til we're round and clear of the barge?"

"I would, sir, aye."

"Very well. Mister Ludlow? Hoist the spanker and stand by to brail up the mizzen tops'l . . . Spanish reefed, and ease the weather brace. Stand by to hoist the inner jib once we're off the wind."

"Aye, aye, sir," Ludlow parroted, barking orders through a brass speaking trumpet so there'd be no confusion (well, as little as possible anyway) and no chore left undone for lack of hearing. That done, he turned inboard to look at Lewrie, waiting for a nod of acknowledgment that his orders were complete. And did he barely smirk, with one eye cast aft towards the afterguard and that recent incident?

It could have been innocent, Lewrie fumed; *wryness over a newly gettin' whomped. Or was it wryness over me bein' soft?*

Peacham and Ludlow, so he'd learned in the few days he'd had to familiarise himself with ship and crew, had served together before; and Peacham had come aboard on Ludlow's recommendation. The younger gentlemen volunteers were of the previous captain's choosing, allowed berths to foster support and "interest" with patrons.

Damme, Lewrie fretted; *is* Proteus *t'be* Cockerel *all over again? A pack o' brutes I'll have to watch like a hawk 'fore they ruin this ship with starters an' the lash? Beat an' cuff this crew right from the start an' poison her? Damme, there's mutiny enough in the Fleet already for that shitten sort! Won't they ever . . . ?*

"Brail up mizzen tops'l, bare the inner jib tack!" Lewrie shouted. *Proteus* swung up bows to windward a bit too far for his liking, tops'ls rustling and unable to draw enough wind. The tide would carry her about, but . . .

"Better . . . wait for it . . ." he counseled, as his frigate wafted on, angled for the centre of the river bend, pointed right at that unfortunate barge which was now seen to be towing two empty lighters, each with a scrap of lugsail aloft on short masts to help out. An eye for the lee shore, judging drift to leeward once they turned, and . . .

"Helm over, Quartermasters," he cried. "Lee tops'l braces, lee jib sheets! Hoist the inner jib, hoist spanker!"

Proteus began to swing to the right, taking the faint breeze on her larboard side, the tops'ls wheeling about and filling once more as the winds found them, the mizzen tops'l creaking as it pivoted, and the spanker filling and whooshing from left to right above the quarterdeck. There was a chuckle of water 'neath her stern, 'round her transom post and her rudder, as she began to gather way, faster than the tide could draw her.

Missed you by a bloody mile! Lewrie crowed to himself, seeing the barge captain waving a fist (and making some *very* English gestures) in his direction as *Proteus* bore off and began to rumble downriver . . . at least two musket-shots clear of collision with barge or lighters.

"Quartermasters, a full point to weather . . . mid-channel," Lewrie instructed. "Once abeam the wind, allow nothing to loo'rd."

"Aye, aye, sir . . . nothin' t'loo'rd," Mr. Motte the senior said.

There's one tricky bit over, Lewrie congratulated himself; *now . . . only four or five more t'go 'til we're safe as houses.* He gave his First Officer, Ludlow, another searching glance; but he was huddled in his coat, round-shouldered and enigmatic once more. Lewrie turned to spy aft at Peacham and the afterguard, but could find nothing amiss in that direction either. Some hurt feelings, a touch of sulkiness . . . ?

Well, do I have potential trouble aboard, he assured himself, *I have time to get it sorted out at the Nore. Cure some newlies' ignorance 'fore sailing further, sort out the truly stupid, and . . .*

"Three-master in the main channel, sir!" Mr. Winwood hailed with some urgency. "Breastin' the tide under all plain sail."

"Making leeway of course?" Lewrie winced, leaning over the larboard bulwarks to peer out.

"Afraid so, sir."

"Well, we'll *try* to pass alee of her," Lewrie said, hands firm in the small of his back as he strode back towards the wheel, with more confidence in his voice than his innards. "She's the pilot's so-called bags of room to weather. Quartermaster, maintain course, but give us a point alee when I call for it. No more than a single point, mind."

Brace up, you bastard, he thought, *else! Make leeway like a wood chip, and we'll surely collide, you . . . !*

Shit! Just, shit!

BOOK THREE

Fit fragor, aetheris ceu Iuppiter arduus arces
impulerit, imas manus aut Neptunia terras.

There is a crash, as though Jupiter had risen in might
and overthrown the citadels of heaven,
or Neptune's arm had rocked the foundations
of the world.

—ARGONAUTICA, BOOK V, 168–64
VALERIUS FLACCUS

CHAPTER SIXTEEN

Gloomy damn' place, Lewrie sighed to himself, as he emerged on the quarterdeck by his private after-companionway ladder, abaft of the great-cabin's coach-top. It had rained during the night, after they'd dropped anchor, and though it was now mid-May, the wind had a bite to it. He'd allowed himself a full bottle of burgundy with his solitary supper, a stout brandy before, and two glasses of a good aged port out of that ten-gallon barricoe he'd bought at Fortnum & Mason's . . . to celebrate a safe arrival off Sheerness. To settle his nerves. In point of fact, his nerves had gotten so steady—somewhere following cheese and sweet biscuits—that he'd been temporarily immobilised! Aspinall and Andrews had had to pour him into his hanging bed-cot! But he felt he'd more than earned his over-imbibing.

Proteus lay safely anchored just off Garrison Point, her heaviest "best-bower" down, with a stream-anchor astern to keep her from fouling another ship should the wind or tide take her. Before going aft to his lone celebration, he'd summoned the crew to gather 'round the break of the quarterdeck, had congratulated them for a safe passage downriver, had joshed them gently on things that had gone wrong, and had pointed out how to improve. Then, he had ordered a bullock slaughtered for their supper and had ordered "Splice The Main-Brace," to make an extra issue of rum. "Won't always be thus," he'd cautioned them; "once at sea, we won't make such jolly distinctions. Proper performance of duty will be

167

expected as commonplace. Then we'll only celebrate surviving a storm, the taking of a rich prize . . . or beating the Be-Jesus out of the French!"

Depressin', he griped to himself, wringing the already thick sheaf of official paperwork between his hands—meaning both his "head" from taking aboard his load of spirits the previous evening and the sight of Sheerness and the tossing Nore besides. They were about equal for depressing.

Low, muddy, shoaling, and windswept, and even a bright day of sunshine probably couldn't make Sheerness any fairer a prospect. It was a garrison town, a warehousing and dockyard town, ringed with forts which usually fell early to any foe who tried to enter the Thames or Medway. Stopping them was the job of the more-substantial forts at the many tight bends in the Thames or Medway further upriver. The ships assembled here were not organised in a proper fleet, flotilla, or squadron. They were just *here*, because the Nore and Sheerness were at the mouth of the Thames and Medway, near enough to London and the many shipbuilding and armaments industries in the capital's environs to supply them at little cost in shipping.

Dozens of ships, he noted, taking a deep breath of clean air, as he waited for his gig to be reported ready; dozens of warships, he corrected himself. There were night on an hundred or more merchantmen close at hand waiting for a suitable wind and tide to proceed up the Thames to the Pool of London and the thousands of cargo-handling docks. Or waiting for a wind-shift to carry them seaward, to join a convoy forming in the Downs. Full-rigged ships, ocean-going vessels deep-laden with treasures, the lofty Indiamen or packets from the Caribbean. Coasters and colliers filled with fish, coal, timber, pig iron, tin, wool, bales of manufactured clothing, or shoes from other small ports in the British Isles. And trading smacks loaded with oysters or poultry, eager to be first to market for a hungry city—they were all here or off on the horizon, streaming dense as poured treacle from night anchorages off the Leigh Sands, the Warp, and the Maplin Sands, up the Queen's Channel along the Yantlet Flats . . . even the short way 'round from the Whitstable oyster beds, up the shallow, narrow Oaze to the Swale, from Faversham behind the Medway Boom, to Queenborough.

He'd prefer (had he his indolent druthers!) to sleep in, nurse his in-
dulgent "head," and curl up with a good book and a warm cat, but there
were "duty calls" he must make this dreary, nippy morning; upon Vice-
Admiral Charles Buckner, for one, the "Officer In Command of HM Ships
and Vessels in the River Medway and At The Buoy of The Nore," to give
his full title—who had promised to solve his manpower shortage. And
upon the Commissioner of HM Dockyards at Sheerness, Captain Francis
John Hartwell, to arrange the lading of the tons upon tons of supplies due
Proteus to put her in full fig: bags of biscuit, kegs of salt-meats, waxed
cheeses, dried peas, ground flour by the boatload, the powder and shot
and cartridge cloth to fill her magazines . . . and whatever his Purser, Mr.
Coote, might wish to stow below for later. She was even short of rum,
wine, and small beer at the moment, and afloat above her load waterline.

"De boat be ready, sah," Andrews reported at last.

"Very well, let's be going." Lewrie sighed, stuffing his paperwork into
a sewn sailcloth haversack slung over his shoulder beneath his boat-cloak
and wishing he'd had time for another restoring *pot* of coffee!

Things went well ashore. Buckner was an old fellow, welcoming as could
be asked for, though seeming troubled. Lewrie put that down to his being
in charge of everything, and nothing, for he had no command over the
warships gathered in the Nore, only with an eye to fitting them, manning
them, making repairs, and passing them on to other units.

He'd had some good news, even so. The semaphore telegraph had
wagged the news that Admiral Howe's negotiations with the mutineers at
Spithead were going well, and a final solution now looked very likely.

"One which, I trust," Admiral Buckner had sighed, "will settle the
grievances once and for all. Not only for Channel Fleet, but with the
mutineers at Plymouth too, Captain Lewrie. And . . . uhm, a close-run
thing. There was some fighting at Spithead aboard a *few* ships . . . nothing
too drastic, but . . . the sort of thing which might have caused a violent
rebellion had it spread. Spread *much* wider, d'ye see."

"Something akin to the *Culloden* business, sir?" Lewrie had asked, feeling a tad more perceptive by then; Vice-Admiral Buckner had had a large
coffee pot at hand and had been most liberal in sharing.

"Captains acting a bit too forcefully . . . engaging in perfidious, two-faced dealings, aye." Buckner had nodded. "Captains were forced to . . . uhm, back down in the face of resistance. Sensibly, I must allow. The retention of a single ship . . . the return of a vessel or two to proper order . . . could never balance against the rancour incited—among vessels *beyond* Portsmouth." Buckner had most mystifyingly hinted.

"D'ye mean *here*, at the Nore, sir? Or at Great Yarmouth too?"

"There have been, uhm . . . letters of grievances sent me, Lewrie—so far from individual ships—requesting shore-leave, back pay, food issues much *like* the demands of the Spithead mutineers. The removal of certain officers and mates they deem tyrannical or overly harsh, aye." Buckner had gloomed, and Lewrie had realised that his troubled mien was due to more than his usual travails. "Nothing organised so far. And pray Jesus when word of settlement arrives . . . as I am mortal-certain we will receive in a few more days . . . the terms and conditions will be mollifying throughout the Navy."

"A sloop of war named *Jester* was not cited as one of the ships where violence erupted, was she, sir?"

"Ah, no, Captain Lewrie. I do not recall any mention of that ship. Your last command, I suspect, sir? Rest easy . . . on *that* head, at the least. Now, sir . . . *how* many men did you say you desired? My, my!"

The last task of his day's work away from *Proteus*. With a precious letter from Vice-Admiral Buckner and his Regulating Captain of the Impress Service safely in hand, he went aboard HMS *Sandwich* to pick up more seamen (hopefully!) and some more warm bodies to fill in the gaps in his watch-and-quarter bills. He stopped to pick up Lieutenant Ludlow to go along with him to aid him in the choosing.

Sandwich was crammed far beyond his most horrid imaginings. It reeked like an abattoir despite being scrubbed daily, the sickly, foetid reek of a hospital ward where hopelessly sick or wounded men were left to perish in their own good time.

As Buckner's flagship she was fully manned, ostensibly fit for sea at a day's notice, stocked and stored and armed for battle not one hour out to sea against any Dutch ships which might try the Thames and Medway again, as they had in wars of the previous century.

But she'd been saddled with hundreds more new-comes and recently impressed sailors, with all the other receiving ships already full with others. Buckner had been specific that they must choose from among the potential hands aboard *Sandwich,* not the other hulks. To reduce the odours, Lewrie suspected most cynically; when he made his rare appearances aboard her.

God, they were a villainous lot! He'd thought that the people who'd greeted him aboard *Proteus* had approached "villainous," but this crowd gave "villainous" a whole new aspect! Not only were they clad in rags and greasy civilian clothes, the most of them, but they shivered in bare feet, bare shins devoid of stockings, and even the ones who gave the appearance of nautical experience could barely boast of a single, thin shirt and a pair of torn, stained slop-trousers, a neck-kerchief, or a hat of any description. They smelled like a corpse's armpit, emitting a sour cloud of steam from being pent so close and thick below decks and freshly exposed to the cool open airs. Some were speckled with a host of rash-marks; fleas, lice-bites, saltwater boils, and ulcers that had grown large as the wens and buboes seen with the Black Death! Doddering oldsters, pitifully shivering children, barely in their teens. Long-haired, grey-haired, gap-toothed. As miserable an assortment of wretchedness as ever he'd imagined!

"This is Captain Lewrie . . . of the *Proteus* frigate," *Sandwich*'s officer shouted to the hundred or so gathered amidships. "He is come for willing hands. A frigate, lads! Now who'll step forward to volunteer for her? Anyone? Nought of you willing to serve your King and Country in a fine, tall frigate? Damme!"

Lewrie looked at the faces glaring back at him, most wearing an utter blankness, a weariness beyond all reckoning of the opportunity he offered. Here and there were younger, fitter faces, men with straight backs and clean limbs, a few who'd retained their clothing and tried to keep themselves in better order. He hoped some of them might step forward.

"God, what a pot-mess!" Ludlow sniped, ready to spit on deck and be done with the lot of them. "Not one of 'em better than what a crop-sick hound'd spew up!"

"Their issue slops, sir? Where are they?" Lewrie asked.

"Lord, sir"—*Sandwich*'s lieutenant sneered then, in a loud voice, to their faces—"gutter scum such as them? Improvident drunkards such as them, sir? Sold or gambled 'em away with no thought for the morrow, like all their lot do, 'thout you'd *beat* some sense into 'em. Weaker'uns . . . well, mayhap the tougher stole 'em blind, Captain Lewrie. Be the first to admit such happens." The officer shrugged, as if it was of no matter to him what these "recruits" did amongst themselves. "*Real* sailors are so rare now, sir . . . we have to settle for the hopeless shit, such as these! Who'd rob shipmates, hey, you lot? No more dawdling . . . let's have some of you step forward and volunteer 'fore we choose you by throwin' rocks."

"A moment, sir . . ." Lewrie snapped, his neck burning with anger at the lieutenant's choice of words, of being such a cruel bastard. "I would like to address them. Your surgeon has cleared them, I trust?"

"Aye, sir . . . I s'pose," the lieutenant allowed.

He'd not thought to fetch his own surgeon, Mr. Shirley, along. He had not expected, however, to be presented with a spectacle such as these poor wretches.

"You men . . ." he began, "those sailors among you. Far back in the rear there . . . suspicious, I'd imagine." He chuckled. "*Proteus* is a frigate, and you know what that means. She's fast, well-armed, and has more deck space and mess space than other ships. So you won't be living with two other bastards' elbows in your eyes, off-watch. And a frigate means prize-money. To the Devil with ships-of-the-line like *Sandwich*. She'll never catch anything, but a frigate will. I've been lucky with prize-money in my last ship, and so my people've been too! There's frigate-men come home so rich they bought new pocket watches, then *fried* 'em in lard in public just for the Hell of it! *Proteus* is a spanking-new frigate too! Just come down from the Chatham yard. Not a month in commission. You lubbers, you know what that means, do you? She doesn't *stink!* Fresh, clean paint and tar, sweet-smelling timbers, nothing rotting in the bilges . . . and as pretty as a brand-new house. A fast ship, a *proud* ship . . ."

"I will, sir!" someone in the back called out, though several sneered at him for sounding so eager. He came forward, a slim, young man with a nervous smile that showed he had most of his teeth. "Mash, sir. Topman, sir. I'll volunteer for her."

"Very well, Mash." Lewrie beamed. "Any mates of yours able to hand, reef, and steer . . . serve a gun, back yonder? Any others wish to ship with Mash, then?" he called out.

He saw a pair of likely men shrug and pick up their seabags to shuffle through the press of men and also volunteer.

"Martyn, sir," one husky brute said. "Ord'n'ry Seaman, sir."

"Lucas, sir," said a blond-haired teen. "Topman, sir."

"Bannister, sir," claimed a whip-thin, dark, ferrety lad. "I done a voyage'r two, but ain't rated Ord'nary yet."

"Good, though, we can use you, and thankee, Bannister," Lewrie said, clapping him on the shoulder as he passed to stand to one side. "Any other sailors or watermen of a mind to get out of this hell-ship? Get clean again? Eat decent rations again?"

"Me, sir!" A wee lad about Sewallis's age and size piped up in a falsetto. "Come on, Da!" he said to the man who stood behind him with his hands on his shoulders. "Be t'gether?"

"What's your name, lad?" Lewrie grinned. The boy didn't look like much of a sailor, but at least he was enthusiastic, and he hoped that enthusiasm might spread.

"Grace, s'please ye, sir." The boy tentatively smiled back.

"You're kin?" Lewrie asked the elder man behind him, hoping that the lad wasn't the grownup's "plaything."

"Grace, sir," the man said. He was withered, ropy, and wiry, and looked as if he'd spent his life on the water somewhere. "Had us our own fishin' smack outa Whitstable; but she went down back durin' the winter, an' . . ."

All they'd owned, most-like, Lewrie surmised; and once lost, they had laboured for others, for a tenth of the income they'd made on their own bottom. For friends, neighbors, or no!

" 'Tis me grandson, Cap'um, sir," the elder admitted with pride. He was grey-haired, missing some teeth, but appeared sound in wind and limb. "Never sailed 'board a *big* ship all me born days, sir. Me an' me son too, here," he said, indicating a third possibility. "But . . ."

"Young Grace . . . Middle Grace, and . . . Elder Grace, aye." Lewrie nodded. "Three pay certificates for the one household then, men?"

"Aye, reckon it'd help, sir. We'll volunteer f'r yer frigate," the middle one allowed, as he gathered up his few pitiful possessions.

More began to come forward, though some Lewrie and Ludlow had to turn away. They were too spindly, too weak and hacking with coughs, or covered with sores, some just too shifty and cutty-eyed—too old, too *young*, even for ship's servants. And how the Impress Service had hoped to justify dredging *them* up, Lewrie couldn't begin to fathom.

"Bennett, sir." Then, Peacock and Thornton, Humphries and Inman and Slocombe and Sugden, Grainger and Brough. Only half were sailors, or could even charitably admit they were on a first-name basis with a *basin* of water . . . but every sound man was more than welcome.

Spooner signed aboard, then Richard, then Brahms . . .

"German, are you, Brahms?" Lewrie asked.

"Crikey, me a Dutchie, sir?" The East End Londoner guffawed.

Two older fellows came up, both with hard hands of common labourers now fallen on hard times, drink, or a faint brush with the law.

"Smyth, sir," one said, cloaked in a blanket and little else. "With a 'wye,' sir. Ess-Emm-Wye-Tee-H'aich."

"Rumbold, sir," the other announced, this one almost bald with but a monkish fringe of white-ish hair above his prominent jug ears. "I was a waggoner, sir. Know some 'bout ropes an' such . . ."

"Better than those who don't know ropes or knots, Rumbold," Lewrie assured him, steering him towards the growing clutch of men by the lower entry-port.

Some smaller, younger lads just into their teens volunteered; fit for servants now; later they could train them aloft as budding topmen. Soon as they fed them back to where their ribs didn't show, that is, and hosed them down under a wash-deck pump so they would no longer resemble a pack of chimney-sweep's apprentices.

"A frigate, d'ye say, sor?" a man dared to ask from the middle of the remaining horde. "Them as go swift as th' very birds, sor?"

"A frigate, aye," Lewrie responded, put a bit on his guard by the man's deep Irish brogue. As if he didn't already have enough of those on his books already. He'd hoped, in the far east of England, to scrape up mostly English sailors.

"Lord!" Ludlow sneered in harsh voice, "Paddies! All brawn and no wits. Can we not be a little choosier, Captain, sir?"

"Furfy, I am, sir, and that proud I'd be t'get off this prison-barge, Yer Honour . . . me an' me mates too," Furfy boasted, elbowing at some others near him. "We ain't sailors, nossir, but we're strong, as yer officer says, and fit, sir . . . eager t'learn?"

"Of a mind to join your mate, Furfy, are you, men?" Lewne asked.

"Kavanaugh, sor. Aye, that I be," one piped up quickly.

"Cahill, sir." Then, "Ahern, sir. Aye, I'll stick wi' Mick."

"Sir, ya feed Mother Desmond's boy Liam three meals a day, and I'm yours f'r life, so I am!" another chortled, doffing a ragged, and shapeless, farm hat, a Black Irishman, with ebon hair and blue eyes.

"Mind your manners, you boggish cur!" Ludlow snapped. "Not him, sir, beggin' yer pardon. Too much the sky-larkin' sea-lawyer to me."

"Any skills, Desmond?" Lewrie enquired, despite the caution.

"I read some, write some . . . taught others some, sir. Fiddler, play *uillean* pipes . . . songs an' stories. Figure cyphers an' numbers. And a strong back, when all else fails me, sir. Bit o' th' auld harp?"

"A sea-lawyer, as I said, sir," Ludlow sneered. "One step shy of the gallows, I'll warrant. A hopeless drunkard too, most-like."

"Faith, sir," Deamond began to protest, with a smile on his face, "but what man alive'd say 'no' to a drop o' th' . . ."

"I'll go into her, sir!" someone from the far side announced as he clambered up from below, dragging his possessions in a hammock-roll and a seabag. He stepped forward to doff a tarred, round, flat-brim sailor's hat. This one, at least, had kept the bulk of his issue kit and was dressed in worn, faded, mended, but clean seaman's clothes, and looked to be a real tarpaulin hand in his middle thirties. He wore a full beard and mustache, despite the fashion for being smooth-shaven—perhaps to conceal the hint of a dark red scar which sketched his left cheek and the tinge of blue-blackness which stained his face—a flare-up from a powder charge or a burst from a gun's barrel as the fellow had sponged out in a previous battle.

"Bales, sir," the bearded fellow reported crisply, standing at an easy attention with his head up, quite unlike the remaining volunteers' hunched, hopeless shiverings. "Able Seaman, sir. And a middling good gunner, sir."

"Bales, hey?" Lewrie grinned in pleasure. "Had an old captain named Bales. How'd the other recruiters miss you, Bales?"

"Just come aboard last evening, sir, is why," the man replied. "Turned over from *Hussar*—28, sir—paid off at Deptford."

"Good, we'll take you, Bales," Lewrie decided. "Join with the others yonder. Now, Desmond . . ." Lewrie said, turning back to the Irishman. "Any *useful* skills?"

"Strength for th' hard labour, sir," Desmond admitted, still chipper even under Ludlow's glare, "but wit enough *t'learn* a sailor's trade. A stout an' willin' heart, sir, an' ever a cheery disposition for any task ye put me. Fell in with Furfy an' th' lads, an' I'd hate t'part from 'em, sir. Be left behind, a'mournin'? Like th' auld song goes, Cap'um . . . 'one sword, at lea-est, thy right shall guard . . . o-one faithful har-up shall praise thee,' " Desmond actually sang out in a high, clear tenor.

"Which old song is that you cite, Desmond?" Lewrie chuckled.

"Why, 'tis th' auld 'Minstrel Boy,' sir!" Desmond replied.

"Well, 'Minstrel Boy,' you don't wish to part from your mates; then I'm not the one to turn my nose up at a real live volunteer. Go join 'em and be ready to transfer over to *Proteus*."

"I thankee from th' bottom o' me heart, sir, that I do!" volunteer Desmond boomed, doffing his hat once more and bowing from his waist. He plucked up his small bundle of belongings tied up in a thread-bare shirt and dashed to rejoin his friends before Lewrie could change his mind, despite Lt. Ludlow's grunts of disapproval.

They winnowed a few more and came within five hands of the full number of ninety-one seamen, or young teens who could be trained as seamen, and made up most of their lack in lubbers, waisters, and servants—those stout but stupid, too old to send aloft. They could use anyone who could serve on the gangways to haul in teams on halliards, braces, lift-lines, clews, buntlines, or jears; or serve the guns on the run-out tackles to drive them up a sloping deck to the gun-ports.

There were no others aboard *Sandwich* even remotely healthy, or suitable, and more than a few that even made Lewrie feel a twinge, now and then, of suspicion of a criminal background.

He'd done what he could to man his ship and get her ready for sea. Now, according to Captain Hartwell, he might have as long as two weeks before receiving orders to sail and join some squadron of ships, where *Proteus*, like all fast frigates, was all too rare and desperately needed. It would be up to his officers and petty officers from here on out to drive, lead, drag, or harangue them into a crew.

All three of his ship's boats were working, as were a brace from *Sandwich*, to ferry the new hands over to her. Lewrie stood by the rail with a faint smile on his face, thinking how discomfited his Purser, Mr. Coote, would be. He'd have to issue the most of the new-comes a fresh set of slop-clothing, plates, spoons, shoes, blankets . . . when they'd already lost, gambled away, or sold a first issue; and his books would be as badly out of joint as his nose, Lewrie was mortal-certain!

As he made his way to the entry-port to take a salute from HMS *Sandwich*'s side-party, he felt he had good reason for another celebratory indulgence with his supper that evening. For one, he'd missed his midday meal for all his errands; for a second, he'd succeeded at one more vital step in making *Proteus* a serviceable warship, safeguarding his precious commission into her; and third . . . he'd found a way to put a "pusser" in a bad mood!

Not bad, for a day's work! he decided.

CHAPTER SEVENTEEN

Bloody, gloomy damn' place, Lewrie thought even more grimly the next morning. It was overcast, a touch windy, and both seas and skies were fretfully grey. Sheerness hadn't blossomed overnight either—it was still the same low-lying pile of crowded warehouses, manufactures, and houses, crammed together any-old-how. Only the sea walls and the bulkheads which elevated it above the high tide made it look substantial and fortified.

And he already had a discipline problem.

He had barely shaved and scrubbed his face and neck in a liberal basin of shore water, sat down to his breakfast of fried eggs, a hash of bacon and shredded potatoes, and fresh-baked shore bread, when he heard a commotion without the gun-deck entry to his quarters. He slurped up a scalding portion of coffee, took a morsel of jammed and buttered toast and chewed quickly before the marine sentry's musket butt thundered on the deck planking.

"First off'cer . . . SAH!"

"Enter," Lewrie managed to mumble past his tasty quid, allowing himself as much bile into his voice as he wished for such an ill-timed interruption of his few moments of morning calm.

" 'Morning, sir," Ludlow grunted, ducking his head to clear the overhead deck beams, with his hat under his arm. "Beg t'report, Captain . . .

three men on charges. One for theft, sir ... T'other two for the fight that resulted."

"Who are they then?" Lewrie sighed, scowling over the rim of his cup.

"Thief was Landsman Haslip, sir. Caught dipping into Landsman Furfy's seabag. Landsman Desmond caught him at it, and they both lit into him, sir."

"God help the poor bastard then." Lewrie shrugged, remembering that this fellow Haslip was a puny, shifty runt with the air of a practiced gaol-bird, whilst the new-comes, Furfy and Desmond, were burlier, younger; and Furfy had fists the size of middling pot roasts! "Haslip still breathin', is he ... there's a wonder, Mister Ludlow?"

"Looks like a fresh-skinned rabbit, sir," Ludlow told him, but without a trace of humour which that remark might have drawn from him. "Ship's Corporals attempted to intervene, Captain. But those Paddies wouldn't have it and took a swing or two at Burton and Ragster, sir."

"Shit." Lewrie frowned, laying down his fork.

"*Told* you we should have been choosy, sir ...'bout taking those damned Irish aboard," Ludlow grumbled. "Nothing but trouble, the lot of 'em ... their whole bloody shiftless race."

Gloomy, he said it, but with a trace of glee for being proved to be correct; hiding it damned well, he must have thought to himself, but Lewrie glared back at him.

"Irish ... Yankee Doodles ... Cuffies ... or bloody tattooed savages, Mister Ludlow," Lewrie barked, "now they're ours, it doesn't signify. Discipline and punishment are the same. We'll treat them all the same too, no matter where a hand springs from."

"Aye, aye, sir." Ludlow nodded, with a trace of weariness.

"And, *sir*," Lewrie griped, "you may suggest all you wish, 'long as it's for the common good. *But*, sir ... you'll not take that doubtful tone with me. Or play 'I told you so.' Hear me, sir?"

"Aye, aye, sir," Ludlow cheeped, all obedient, though with his eyes slitting, either in surprise or distaste.

"We'll discuss this later, sir," Lewrie told him. "As for our offenders ... I'll hold 'mast' at Two Bells of the Forenoon. Warn your midshipmen or mates to be ready to testify about their behaviour ... good or ill, along with the Ship's Corporals."

"Very good, sir. I'll do it directly, sir," Ludlow said as he bowed his way out.

Lewrie picked up his knife and fork and began dining once more. Toulon jumped up on the table with a prefatory *"Ummph!"* to sniff, lift one paw as he sat, and fan the air as if begging, with his mournfully abused face on. *"Mew?"* he barely managed, as if too famished to ask.

"Aspinall, hasn't this cat had his breakfast yet?"

"Aye, 'e has, sir," his servant said, leaning out from the pantry, wiping his hands on a stained dish-clout. "Three strips o' bacon all by hisself. An' thought well o' th' tatty-hash too, sir."

"Well, damme . . . fetch his plate, Aspinall." Lewrie sighed. "I think another dab'd do him. Mister Padgett?"

"Aye, sir," his clerk replied from aft in his day-cabin.

"Look up Landsman Haslip in ship's books. See if he's a Quota Man or how he was recruited," Lewrie directed, as Aspinall returned with the small bowl which Toulon usually ate from, with another heap of hash from the sideboard in it. "Hmmm . . . another dollop for me as well, Aspinall. It's main-tasty this morning," Lewrie said, taking a pleasureable moment to watch his ram-cat tuck in most daintily.

"Not a full day aboard and you're already in trouble, lads," Lewrie pretended to sneer at Furfy and Desmond, who stood hatless and hangdog before his desk. "Did they read the Articles of War to you aboard *Sandwich?* Or once you were in the Impress tender?"

"Yessir," they muttered, unable to look him in the eyes.

"Read us a power o' 'whereases,' aye, sir," Furfy expanded.

"Article the Twenty-third, lads . . ." Lewrie intoned, "says that 'no one shall quarrel or fight in the ship, nor use reproachful or provoking speeches tending to make any quarrel or disturbance, upon pain of imprisonment' . . . or whatever punishment I think fit. Now *Proteus* is still in port. This could, d'ye wish it, be sent ashore for court martial. But I don't think you'd like that much, would you?"

"Uh, nossir . . . no, Yer Honour, sir." They cringed.

The Court Martial Jack was already flying across the harbour, as a board of Post-Captains off some of the line-of-battle ships convened to deal with a whole raft of malefactors aboard HMS *Inflexible*, an old stores-ship, this morning.

"Formal charges'd put you in irons, cooped up in another ship's brig, 'mongst strangers," Lewrie informed them. "Might take days . . . before they got 'round to your case." He forced himself to glower hot. Furfy's use of "Yer Honour, sir," told him the bulky fellow had been in the dock before. "And your trial'd go 'bout as fast as havin' yerself a hedge-whore . . . 'in, out . . . repeat if necessary.' Now, do you *insist* on your rights then . . ."

"Nossir . . . no, so please, Yer Honour, sir!"

"Now, then." Lewrie sighed, leaning back in his chair. "Goin' for Has-lip, that I can understand. A thief caught red-handed by his shipmates *deserves* a thrashing! There's none worse to have aboard a ship than a thief who'd steal from his own kind. But once the Ship's Corporals came to break it up, you should have stopped right there . . . d'ye hear me? You *caught* him, well and good. They'd have taken over, brought him to me on charges, and you'd have been blameless, see? It would be up to ship's justice, my justice, from then on. Like you'd turned him over to the 'Char-lies' or the Bow Street Runners in London. You will *not* continue to thump him t'get your own back. You will *not* take a poke or two at Burton and Ragster, the 'captain' of your working party, a petty officer, or midship-man! Know why, you idiots? Allow me to point out Article the Twenty-first. 'None shall presume to quarrel with his superior officer upon pain of *severe* punishment . . . nor strike any such—upon *pain of death!* Or, oth-erwise, as a court martial shall find the matter to deserve.' Never will you lay hands on those above you. Or even back talk 'em. Now do you get it, my pretties?"

"Oh, arra!" Furfy groaned, turning pale.

"Lord save us, sir, we . . . !" Desmond wavered, looking like-about to faint in dread.

"They read it to you; you should have known," Lewrie cut him off. "There is no excuse for it, most especially ignorance. Landsman Furfy, Landsman Desmond, I find you guilty of refusing to cease fighting, of disobeying lawful orders to desist, and of quarrelling with a superior. Since, however, you are only a week in the Navy, and less than a day aboard *Proteus*, I will . . . this once, mind! . . . be lenient. Do you ever come before me again in violation of Article the Twenty-first, I will have you triced up and flogged bloody raw! As for now . . ."

They blanched, shared a worried look, then turned their gaze on him, all but quivering in their shoes.

"Ten days bread and water. Ten days deprived of rum, wine, or even small beer. Bread to be ship's biscuit, not 'Tommy.' No tobacco either. And you will both serve as hammockmen to the Ship's Corporals for those ten days, atop your other duties: fetchin', scrubbin', and scourin' their laundry and such."

No rum, no wine, no beer? No tobacco to ease their idle hours? It was a death blow! And to survive on water and biscuit, when every other man was eating shore-bread, fresh meat from shore . . . !

"Dismissed," Lewrie snapped. "Now, for Landsman Haslip, Mister Ludlow."

"Aye, aye, sir." Ludlow nodded. There it was again—another querulous note in his voice that hinted of disapproval of leniency for Furfy and Desmond; what he'd wished for was the maximum of two-dozen lashes. "Pass the word for Landsman Haslip to present himself!" he barked at the Marine inside the great-cabin.

"Passin' t'word fer Landsman Haslip!" the outer sentry echoed.

Then there came the sounds of cheering, a chorus of 'Hip, Hip, Hooray!' which made Lewrie turn up the corners of his mouth with wry amusement. The crew must have been on the Irishmen's side in the matter and were expressing satisfaction for his lenient sentence despite the risk they ran to dare approve or disapprove. A first sign of spirit in this new crew of his? he wondered.

No, he thought a moment later, as a scrubbed-up Haslip was led in from the gun-deck, past his dining-coach, chart-space, and pantry.

It wasn't coming from *Proteus*'s forecastle; it was too far off for that and sounded as if it was getting louder, as if it was coming from a great many ships at the same time. He furrowed his brows and rose from his desk to discover what holiday might elicit such cheers from every warship at the Nore, dissonant and un-organised.

"Mister Ludlow, we miss something? Restoration Day, perhaps?"

"Don't know, sir?" Ludlow puzzled. "Not Restoration Day, for certain. That's not for . . ."

"Off'cer th' Watch, Mister Wyman, *SAH!*" the outer gun-deck sentry cried, slamming his musket butt with the crash of an explosion, and the tone of his shout more urgent than "parade-ground."

"Captain . . . !" Lieutenant Wyman gasped as he burst in, almost wringing his hat in his hands, his complexion flushed. "It's *mutiny*, sir! The Nore too! *Every* ship, sir . . . hands cheering in the rigging . . . plain battle flags flying, and . . . yard ropes rove, sir!"

"Bloody . . . !" Lewrie yelped, as if stung. He dashed forrud to see for himself, careening off Haslip and his marine guards. Out upon the gun-deck, up a ladder to the quarterdeck to peer out hatless, and suddenly breathless from more than haste. He lunged for the binnacle rack for a telescope, then froze . . . for it really wasn't necessary.

Sandwich . . . Latona . . . Inflexible . . . Champion, a 20-gunner, the old stores-ship *Grampus . . .* every line-of-battle ship, every vessel in the Nore . . . ! And they all flew the red mutiny flags, sported damnable yard ropes from their course and tops'l spars! In fact, HMS *Proteus* was about the only Royal Navy vessel that *didn't!*

"Christ, not here too!" Lewrie felt like wailing.

"Lord, sir, what'll we do?" Lieutenant Wyman almost begged.

Now *there* was a good question, if Lewrie'd ever heard one!

CHAPTER EIGHTEEN

*H*is first instinct was to beat to Quarters, to load and run out his artillery, raise the anti-boarding nets, open the arms chests, and prepare his crew to defend the ship until they could get sail on her and escape the anchorage.

But so far *Proteus* had spent most of her time in "River Discipline" at the rawest basics—knots, tracing the rigging, the making or tending of sail, anchor and cable work, striking and raising top-masts, or hoisting boats off the cross-deck beams, lowering them overside, and then recovering them, along with some practical oar-work about the harbour or mooring. Until he had formed a full crew, he hadn't planned on telling-off gun crews, so only the seamen with previous experience were adept at gunnery practice. That would have been part of this *new* week's curriculum, he'd hoped. Now, though . . .

Short of rations, water, firewood, powder, and shot, *Proteus* had only one chance of beinging swept up in mutiny: flee at once, escape the Nore, and try to make good her lacks at another Royal dockyard!

"Mister Pendarves?" he shouted. "Mister Devereux?"

"Here, sir," the marine officer called back from the quarterdeck, already immaculately turned out in full kit.

"Turn out your Marines, sir, at once!" Lewrie snarled. "Armed, mind . . . to the teeth!"

"Captain?" the Bosun queried from below in the waist.

"Bosun, pipe 'All Hands.' Muster hands to man the capstan, then prepare to make sail!" Lewrie called down to him. "We're leaving harbour quick as we can. If you have to cut the bower and kedge away, so be it."

Pendarves's silver call began to peep and shrill, joined by the sounds from his junior, Towpenny's. Feet, shod or bare, began to drum on the oaken decks as the crew responded to their summons, racing from below to mill and bleat in confusion. Some knew the call and went to their proper stations at once. Others, the fresh-caught landsmen, had the civilian penchant for chattering about it before being collared by the yeomen or detail "captains"; berated, shoved, fisted, or "started" to their proper positions. Spry young topmen clambered aloft, up the rat-lines and out over the futtock shrouds to the fighting tops, beyond to the tops'l yards to scoot out precariously on the foot-ropes to loose harbour gaskets and brails to free sails.

Lewrie took time to have another gander round the anchorage. A cutter was stroking for *Proteus*'s larboard entry-port, filled with seamen from HMS *Sandwich*, whose rigging was filled with cheering sailors.

"Glass, Mister Nicholas," Lewrie demanded of the sweet-natured fourteen-year old midshipman who was near the binnacle cabinet darting eyes about in wide-eyed wonder, as Devereux's drummer began a long roll and a fife joined the urgent shrieks of the bosun's calls. The lad fetched him a telescope.

"Damme, not a night glass, Mister Nicholas!" Lewrie howled with impatience, after one look through the telescope, which, unlike the day glasses, turned everything upside-down and backwards.

"Here, sir?" Midshipman Elwes Fetched a substitute, having seen Nicholas's mistake and corrected it.

Better, Lewrie thought, taking a peek at the oncoming boat; *well, not really! Damme . . . no midshipman steerin' . . . eight oarsmen, nigh on a dozen more aboard . . . armed!*

He'd seen the spikey danger of erect musket barrels, the gleam of wan sunlight on fixed bayonets and bared cutlass blades.

"Mister Devereux! A file of your men to guard the entry-port!" Lewrie shouted. "No one from yonder cutter is t'be allowed aboard!"

"Aye, aye, sir. Corpr'l Plympton . . . ?"

"Shoot if you have to," Lewrie fretted in a loud voice. There was a sentiment in the Navy that officers, captains especially, should ever strive to maintain the disposition of a stoic, no matter how dire the circumstances; that they should present the world a calm, unruffled demeanour, reassuring those under them to behave properly. Should a tidal wave arise to swamp their ship and take them all down to Perdition, a *proper* captain should pull out his pocket watch, stare at it glumly, and announce, "Ah, right on time!"

Not Alan Lewrie, unfortunately.

"Andrews, fetch me my hat," he bade to his Cox'n, who stood by the top of the after-companionway ladder to his private quarters. "My sword, and the double-barrel pistols too!"

"Aye, aye, sah!" Andrews said, hustling below at once.

The cutter was about a single musket shot away from them, coming fast. Lewrie turned to look inboard, at his crew on the gangways and the capstan.

"Ready, sir," Pendarves reported. "Hands at Stations for Leavin' Harbour.' "

"Very well, Mister Pendarves. Mister Ludlow? Set a buoy on the kedge anchor and haul us in to short stays on the bower. Stand ready to make sail."

"Aye, sir!" Ludlow barked. "Mister Peacham, free the kedge . . . buoy the bitter end o' the cable. Forrud, there! Fleet the messenger to the capstan . . . nippermen, ready? Breast to the bars . . ."

The younger lads brought the lighter, dry messenger cable out, took three-and-a-half turns about the capstan drum, and fastened the nippers to the much thicker anchor cable, which could never be reeled in directly. Bars were dropped into the pigeon-holes, and three men to each bar faced-to, placed their hands in front and below the bars, with thumbs out and up to avoid pinching, shoved their chests against the bars, and stood poised to begin shoving to wind the messenger in.

But that was *all* they did. That was as far as they went.

"Sir!" Midshipman Peacham yawped from back aft.

Four men of the afterguard stood about the jear bitts, to which the light kedge cable was warped. Protecting it from being undone!

"Goddammit!" Lewrie growled. "Mister Langlie, go aft, assist Mister Peacham. Let go the kedge cable . . . buoy bedamned."

"Nossir," some loud naysayer shouted.

"*What?*" he screeched, in total, goggling disbelief.

"Nossir!" The Master Gunner, Mr. Handcocks, had dared to mount to the quarterdeck, with his mate, Mr. Morley, behind him, and the Yeoman of the Powder, that pale spook Kever, in tow. "We won't be sailin', sir."

"Damn you, Mister Handcocks, get your arse back on the gun-deck at once! There'll be no mutiny in this ship!"

"But there is, Captain," Handcocks disagreed, in almost a reasonable voice of amiable, idle disagreement. "We're decided. The Nore will support the grievances o' the Spithead lads."

"Mister Devereux, you will clear the quarterdeck," Lewrie said to his marine officer. "Place any hand who resists making sail under arrest. You can start with Mister Handcocks."

"Aye, sir," Devereux snapped, drawing his slim sword. "Corp'ral O'Neil, seize those men."

"Uh, wellsir . . . uh . . ." Corporal O'Neil waffled, still standing at attention with his musket by his side. "Don' reckon I kin do that, sir. Can't obey that order, sir."

"You . . . bloody . . . *what?*" It was Lieutenant Devereux's turn to yelp.

"Won't raise hands 'gainst no man, sir . . . not 'til terms're all agreed at Portsmouth. Maintain proper order, sir, but . . ." The Marine blushed, his tongue tangling over unfamiliar concepts, shrugging helplessly, looking to his squad of privates for eloquence.

" 'Hoy, the boat!" Corporal Plympton was shouting to the cutter as it came alongside, levelling his musket down at an extreme angle to aim at the men he thought were leaders. "Sheer off. You're not t'come aboard, d'ye hear me?"

"Sir, it'd be best were ya t'hand over the keys t'th' arms chests, 'fore someone gets hurt for no call, Captain, sir," Handcocks suggested, with his hand out, as if Lewrie had the precious keys on him.

"I'll be damned if I do, Mister Handcocks," Lewrie shot back at him. "Try and take 'em, and I'll make sure they hang you higher than Haman."

"Get below where you belong, you buggers!" Lt. Ludlow roared, stepping forward to cuff Mr. Morley and the wispy Kever, shoving them towards the larboard quarterdeck ladder. "Lay hands on me and you'll swing at Execution Dock. Don't!" he cautioned Handcocks, who had raised his fists and a belaying pin to defend his minions. "Do ye disobey, you're gallows-meat!" He lunged and shoved Handcocks back to join his followers, then drew his sword.

But there were other sailors dashing for the quarterdeck with belaying pins in their hands, boarding pikes stripped from the chained beckets about the base of the masts.

Some were surrounding the Marines by the entry-port, shouting in their ears, overbearing and daunting them, pressing so close they had no room in which to lower their muskets or draw their hangers.

"Andrews?" Lewrie bellowed, daring to glance aft to see if his Cox'n had fetched his weapons yet. "Damn!" He sagged.

Andrews was back on deck . . . so was Aspinall and his clerk, Mr. Padgett; all with their hands bound and clasped firmly in the grip of mutineers from the afterguard. Midshipman Peacham and Lt. Langlie were off to one side, closely surrounded by others, who still would not dare actually lay hands on them, but hemmed them in so snugly they had no room to defend themselves or take a single step either.

Pipes were shrilling urgently, panicky, and the gun-deck seethed with arguments pro and con, with the whines of the dazed and confused. And cheering, as the passengers from the cutter below the entry-port got aboard, despite Lewrie's orders, despite the musket-armed Marines, who were either dis-armed by now or firmly aligned with the mutiny to begin with! Mustering to a new leader!

"Man the yards, lads!" one of the new-comers was crying, waving a cutlass in the air. "Reeve yard ropes aloft, d'ye hear there? Break out the battle flags from the taffrail lockers, you lot! Declare for the cause . . . be quick about it! Huzzah for sailors' rights! Huzzah!"

"Please, sirs . . ." Handcocks interrupted. "Do ya sheathe them swords, Mister Ludlow. Lef'ten't Devereux, sir? Yer out-numbered . . . no call for violence. Ship's ours now, sirs, same'z t'others. Won't make no point. We've the artillery."

Handcocks gestured to the guns. One of those brutal 12-pounder carriage guns had been rolled back from its port, freed of its tackles, and secured to other deck ringbolts, aimed aft at the door to Lewrie's cabins. Lighter 2-pounder swivel guns sprouted from their stanchions along the gangways—pointed aft and inboard! Seamen stood by them, fondling car-

tridge bags of grape-shot and canister, which they had yet to ram down
the muzzles; grape-shot and canister which could scour the quarterdeck or
gun-deck cleaner than a billiards table was there any resistance or disrup-
tion. They didn't look particularly glad about it—but they were standing
ready, with flintlocks fitted and the trigger cords in their hands!

"Damn you all!" Lewrie snarled, whirling about to face the men nearest
him, the uneasy Marines who still held weapons, the sailors who sported
belaying pins, crow-levers, or rammers from the quarterdeck guns, boarding pikes, marling-spikes, tar-paying loggerheads, or clasp knives. "Admiral
Lord Howe is in Portsmouth to settle things. They may be settled as we
speak. Come *on*, lads . . . don't *do* this! Any man proved a mutineer . . .
in arms! . . . laying hands on superiors, threatening superiors, will *hang*
when this is over! Drop your weapons, go back to your stations, and
submit to orders."

"Sorry, sir . . . can't do that just yet." Handcocks disputed in a sad tone.
"Not 'til word comes from Portsmouth. Not 'til all grievances're satisfied.
What they demand, we want, too, Captain, sir. And we won't obey orders
t'sail. Do we not take hands with the other lads, well . . . there's a chance
we won't be included in the settlement, d'ye see? Like it only applies
t'them? Not us?"

"Oh, don't be a *complete* fool, Mister Handcocks!" Lewrie sneered.
"Portsmouth, Plymouth . . . that's half the Fleet in home waters. Don't you
think Admiralty needs this over, quick as dammit? All of it over? Of *course*
it'll be Navy-wide!"

If they've any bloody sense, he thought, hoping he wasn't lying.

"Wouldn't be so sure o' that, lads!" the well-armed stranger from the
cutter shouted, barging his way through the press to confront Lewrie, with
his drawn cutlass in his hand and a brace of pistols in his waistband.
"Cheese-parin' bastards'd starve us t'death 'fore we see a shillin' more'n
necessary. Congratulations, mates! You stood up an' took her like real
men, soon'z ya saw th' red banners, an' proved faithful t'th' cause!" he
orated, flinging his arms about to brandish his sword, bellowing to be
heard. "Huzzah, brother seamen! Cheer, now, lads! Hip—hip—hooray!"

They did, rather more lustily than Lewrie expected; though there were
an encouraging number who only went through the motions unwilling.

Sadly, though, he also noted more than a minority eagerly at the halliards, lowering the Red Ensign to replace it with the plain battle flag, or out on the course-yards' tips, reeving ropes . . . to which hanging nooses could quickly be bent!

"Now then, brothers . . . !" the squat stranger cajoled.

"Now then," Lewrie countered quickly, "you can get your arse off my bloody quarterdeck. And put that damn' cutlass away 'fore you hurt yourself."

"Oh, I'll sheathe, sir," the stranger rasped, looking sly. "Do these tyrant officers sheathe alike. I'll let 'em keep 'em, for now . . ."

"How bloody *gracious* of you!" Lewrie sneered, so adrip with acid that most within earshot were forced to laugh.

"Aye, 'long'z they stow 'em below in their cabins an' appear on deck unarmed, sir. You're the Captain, I take it, sir? Here, see me do it, sir; I'm sheatin' my cutlass now. An' I'm . . . requestin' . . . yer officers do the same?"

Lewrie looked at Ludlow and Devereux. They were glaring, panting with anger and outrage. Ludlow looked glazed-over, ready to lash out; Devereux's slyer eyes were calm, half-slitted, darting about for an opening or an advantage. He'd be the more scientific fighter, did that come, the more dangerous. Ludlow, though, was about to go off at half-cock, draw blood out of rage, and that'd . . . !

"Mister Ludlow," Lewrie said, in a captain's proper stoic tone, "in the face of overwhelming opposition, I request that you put your sword away. As the Master Gunner said, there is no call for you to perish without a chance to alter the situation. Or aggravate it?" he hinted. "Lieutenant Devereux, my pardons, sir, but I have to ask the same of you. I would not have you fall needlessly, sir."

"Very well, Captain." Devereux sighed, sounding disappointed, as he released the watch-spring tension of his body with an exhalation that sounded like a deflating pig-bladder, rose an inch or so from the taut crouch he'd held, and flourished his sword in a circle before he sheathed it, gaining a bit of his own back by making the nearer mutineers flinch from its wickedly sharp tip.

"Mister Ludlow?" Lewrie was forced to insist.

"Gahh!" Ludlow spat, making a chopping motion with his sword out of sheer frustration. "Damn you all! Yer scum . . . fuckin' scum! Damn' fools! I'll see you all in chains; I'll break the lot of you! Signed your death warrants, ya have, every last mother's son!"

But Ludlow raised his scabbard and clumsily stabbed at it, to jab his sword-tip into it and ram it home. He glared at Lewrie, with ultimate scorn and bloody murder on his phyz!

"Never thought I'd see the day a Royal Navy captain'd just give up his ship at the first whim o' cut-throats an' trash!" Ludlow snarled, as he turned away to stomp his way below, shoving the close press apart with his shoulders, glaring defiance, and muttering dire imprecations.

"See how th' proud're brought low, lads, an' tyrants banished!" the stranger hooted. " 'Least yer captain's sensible."

"Fuck you, too!" Lewrie hissed back with an evil grin.

"Thomas McCann, sir. Able Seaman. An' you're Captain Lewrie."

"I am. McCann," Lewrie grudgingly allowed, taut-lipped.

"Heard o' ye, we have," McCann leered. "Called 'the Ram-Cat' I heard-tell. *Fightin'* captain. Not so cruel an' high-nose proud'z some. Though, ye all *are*. Firm but fair, hah! Don't mean dis-respect, sir . . ."

"Do you not, McCann?" Alan scoffed. "Does *this* not?"

"Delegates've decided, sir," McCann ploughed on, oblivious to Lewrie's scorn. "Officers behave, they won't be discomfited. Ship's discipline t'be maintained. Officers, warrants, mates, an' midshipmen t'be obeyed 'long as it's run-o'-th'-mill duties. Barrin' th' last few minutes, sir, no man'll raise a hand 'gainst any superior nor show any signs o' dis-respect. Belongin's t'be safe, even personal pistols an' swords . . .'long as they're below an' unloaded. We give ye a promise on that. 'Cept, we'll turn out the man-killers an' tyrants as soon as we name 'em."

"*How* reassuring," Alan drawled, with one brow up.

"Just 'til word comes from Portsmouth that them bloodsuckers at Admiralty's declared all our demands're met, sir," McCann ranted, with an odd look to his eyes. "That all brother seamen been victorious, do ye see. As a caution, like . . . so none o' us're ordered t'fight brother sailors at Spithead or Plymouth an' we know for certain we're included in th' terms an' them bastards won't betray us. Our cause is *just*, I tell ye! Their grievances're ours too!" McCann all but raved.

Christ, I'm dealing with a bloody lunatick! Lewrie realised.

"So's we don't get betrayed like them Cullodens!" someone back in the crowd crowed. "Pay, more pay!" howled another. "Fairer share o' prize-money!" suggested another. "Proper rations an' honest weights . . . shore leave whene'er we wish . . . bigger rum ration!" they gabbled.

"Turn out th' villains put over us . . . like Ludlow!"

"Lash 'em bloody, *then* turn 'em out!"

It dissolved into a bedlam of things they wanted, their shouts blending into a brutish cacophony, even less musical then the baying of wolves, 'til their inchoate roars became a general, lusty cheering. It had to peter out, after a while, and it did, though McCann and several others pumped their arms like orchestra leaders to sustain it.

"Now, sir . . ." McCann leered. "I'll be havin' th' keys to th' arms chests."

Lewrie looked at him askance, cocking his head to one side. He looked aloft at those new flags flying from every mast, as if bemused. He took time to study the gloss of his boots, clasped his hands behind his back . . .

"No," he said at last. "I don't think so."

"Now, lookee here, sir, don't ye . . . !" McCann blustered.

"Didn't you just say that no violence would be offered, McCann?" Lewrie said, dead-level serious. "That means the crew has no *need* for weapons, doesn't it. Did you not say that proper order and discipline, and respect for officers, will be maintained? In normal usage, the arms chests would be locked anyway. Therefore . . . unless you break your word and lay hands on me, rifle my possessions, or put a knife to my throat, the keys will stay in my possession. You *claim* to hold *Proteus* already. Therefore you don't *need* weapons. No, sir, I refuse to hand the keys over to you. Totally."

"But . . ." McCann blubbered, his eyes almost crossed in concentration, sputtering and bending to mutter with his fellow mutineers, to try and find some loophole in the logic of Lewrie's statement, or make sense of such high-flown, "break-teeth" speech. Instead, he turned on Handcocks, Morley, and Kever, urging them to do something.

"Damme, was *I* in *Proteus*, *I'd* have th' arms chest keys!" McCann screeched, then stomped off towards the entry-port, dragging his coterie of fellow mutineers with him, glowering, cursing, and muttering much as Lt. Ludlow had just moments before!

"We're *allowed* to carry on with a normal ship's work day, Mister Handcocks?" Lewrie demanded of his chief mutineer.

"Well . . . aye, sir." Handcocks blushed, looking cutty-eyed.

"I take it *you* think you are now in command of *Proteus?*" Lewrie scoffed. "*You* will allow me to resume my hearing on Landsman Haslip? We may man the boats and ferry supplies from shore . . . sir?"

"Uhm . . . let me, ask, Captain, sir," Handcocks mumbled, slinking off to join the group of Sandwiches by the entry-port, who were still deep in a frustrated conversation over the keys.

"Mister Coote, you here, sir?" Lewrie asked, turning about.

"Aye, sir," a shaken Coote replied. "I s'pose."

"Stand ready to go ashore. Mister Langlie? With Lieutenant Ludlow off the quarterdeck, do you take charge of the Forenoon Watch. Tell-off men to assist the Purser ashore. Mister Pendarves?" Lewrie bellowed down to the gun-deck. "Assemble working parties to ferry stores offshore!"

"Aye, *aye,* sir!" Pendarves shouted back, looking about as forlorn as a landed trout and eager for a command from a proper authority.

"Now look here, sir . . . !" McCann snapped, returning, reinforced by his own followers from *Sandwich* and the *Proteus* mutineer leaders.

"*Proteus* must be stocked with four months' supplies for sea," Lewrie informed him soberly. "We're short of salt-meat, flour, biscuit, small beer, rum, wine, cheeses, dried peas, portable soup . . . presently she has but half the powder and shot required. Now, sir . . . do you say you're *loyal* Britons, mutinying for your *grievances* . . . and *not* traitorous rebels in the pay of foreign foes! Then readying this ship for sea, does the mutiny end and we're ordered out to fight the Dutch, or the French, is vital. A normal ship's routine, which you just said you would not interfere with? Surely, even you can see that."

"Gawd, I wish . . . !" McCann gargled, raising a fist. "Ye an' yer sort, yer all alike! Thinkin' yer so damn' clever an' smug! I . . . !"

"Short of rations, powder and shot, mate," Bales hinted, from the rear of the pack, elbowing and sidling forward to stand alongside McCann. "Do they cut us off from the warehouses in Sheerness, what'll we do then? Think on't. What'll we eat 'til it's settled?"

"Th' people're for us! Th' common folk'd not let 'em!" McCann countered, eyes bulging with fervour. "Th' high an' mighty'll tremble in their beds do they even try t'cut us off! The whole nation arise . . . !"

"Aye, though . . . we should stock her, gunn'l-deep." The Gunner sighed. "Just in case, like."

"Right, then!" McCann sneered, sensing another defeat within a five-minute span. "Go 'head an' stock her. But no midshipmen, none o' their brutal sort're t'work th' boats. Senior hands. *Loyal* men on th' tillers an' oars . . . brothers t'th' cause. No escape for th' weak, them as won't swear t'uphold th' cause neither."

"Very good then." Lewrie nodded, striving to *not* look as glad as he felt that he was dealing with a witless escapee from Bedlam. "I assume normal duties also encompasses my hearing for Landsman Haslip? Mister Pendarves! Muster boat-crews! We will go below . . ."

"Nossir, ye won't!" McCann barked. "*We'll* do it! Man's a thief! Stole from brother sailors, so he'll get *sailors'* justice! An' no boat-crews t'go ashore 'til ye've elected yer delegates, Handcocks . . . picked yer committee 'board ship for runnin' her, an' delegates t'th' committee 'board *Sandwich*." He nudged Handcocks under the ribs. "An' weed out them as'd cozen ye . . . Have ev'ry man-jack in an' make 'em swear on a Bible t'be loyal or else."

"No," Lewrie insisted once more, quite flatly, and pinching at the bridge of his nose as if wearied beyond endurance.

"Now, lookee . . . !" McCann threatened, going wild-eyed again.

"Justice is mine, McCann," Lewrie pointed out. "Determining the crime and punishment for it 'board this ship is the Captain's prerogative alone, and well you know it. You assure me and the others that this mutiny will end when the grievances are satisfactorily settled . . . and ships at the Nore are included in the terms. That's what you told my crew to get them to join you? That's what you profess?"

"It is!" McCann shouted back.

"Then once you return to subordination and discipline, you will once more be under a captain's supervision, which includes hearing any violations of the Articles of War, or Admiralty Regulations," Lewrie hammered home. "To unsurp my right to hear and judge Haslip will make any sentence you and the . . . delegates! . . . decide, illegal. Unless you . . . or some one of you . . ." he growled, searching the nearest faces for defiance, "wish to declare himself a Commission Officer and *presume* to issue orders . . . then the custom and usage of the Sea Service says that I, alone, can judge. You can go below and do all the . . . electing! . . . you wish to choose your delegates. But you will *not* usurp my power of command! Or my right to conduct 'captain's mast.' "

"Arrr!" McCann howled with frustration, "a pox on ye, an' th' Devil take *all* officers! I wish t'God we could just hang ye all an' be done! Choose new'uns an' start fresh, by God!"

Frightfully, there were more than one or two growls of agreement from the men mustered before him; thankfully though, they seemed to be Sandwiches, not Proteuses. Bales, the new-come mutineer, even went so far as to take McCann by the elbow and whisper in his ear, to warn him to temper his remarks or hide his true sentiments.

Mutiny was one thing, Lewrie thought, turning to match eyes with his remaining officers; mutiny with the threat of physical violence or the murder of superiors was different. Lewrie thought to compare the almost-dignified, sober-headed truculence of what he'd experienced at Portsmouth—a much more respectful and respectable plea for better conditions—with the very beginnings of this version, which was led, he suspected, by a whole baying *pack* of hotheads like this McCann! If so, it was a damn' narrow razor's edge he'd have to tread before this was over!

Oddly, Lt. Langlie was looking back at him with the tiniest of grins on his face, the one corner of his mouth turned up, all but tipping him a conspiratorial wink of encouragement! He shrugged back his perplexity—and his gratitude for Langlie's silent support.

"Right, then," McCann announced quite grudgingly, much taken down from his rant of the short minute before. "Yer a Commission Sea Officer . . . 'mast' on this Haslip bastard is yours. But we'll choose who we will for delegates; get yer whole crew firm b'hind us . . ."

"And what of those who *don't* wish to swear allegiance with you, McCann?" Lewrie asked, feeling suddenly pleased that he'd regained a tiny bit of authority in the midst of raving chaos, already scheming as to how he might undermine this particular mutiny aboard his ship. "Bligh over yonder," Alan said, gesturing towards HMS *Director*, a 64-gunner 'cross the harbour, "had his loyal hands who went in the longboat with him—even him!" He snorted in derision. "You can't just force everyone to be

loyal to you if they don't wish to. Or are too fearful of the consequences . . . as you *should* be." He stuck on, slyly.

Oh, God, yes! he thought. *Hull the buggers; make 'em sweat . . . !*

"Ah, but isn't that what *you* and the *Navy* do, sir?" Able Seaman Bales
just-as-slyly japed. "Make 'em loyal . . . without a chance to choose for
themselves?"

The nearby mutineers had themselves a real knee-slapping hoot at that
one and passed it on along the gangways, down into the waist, and aft to
the taffrails to their mates, where it elicited the same mirth.

Lewrie's face suffused with sudden anger, that he'd been bested by an
unexpected opponent, by an un-looked-for fount of wits. Whatever shred
of authority he'd wished to salvage, whatever doubts he'd wished to plant
in them, were ripped away in a twinkling, torn to atoms.

This is over, I'll see you swing in tar an' chains, you smarmy bastard!
Lewrie swore to himself; *you and McCann, most of all!*

"*We'll* let you know when we're done, sir," Bales smirked, with an air
as if he had already been elected leader and was taking charge. "When
we're ready to send boats to the storehouse wharves. Just'z soon as we've
chosen delegates, Captain."

"And I, for my part, Seaman Bales," Lewrie gritted back, "will expect
the crew to muster aft to witness punishment when *I* order them to . . . no
matter where you are in your . . . elections. Hear me?"

"Oh, aye, sir . . . we're looking forward to that." Bales grinned.

"Twelve men for th' ship, mind," McCann advised as he followed them,
remaining on the gangway so he could depart through the entry-port and
go off to cause even more mischief aboard other ships. "Two for th' fleet
committee, t'meet aboard *Sandwich*. An' one 'captain' . . . no matter his
high-an'-mightiness . . . right, brothers?"

McCann was departing, shouting a last set of encouraging words to the
crew in general and pumping Bales's hand quite vigourously.

"There's a viper in our breast, no error," Lewrie gravelled, in a bleak
mood. "And me that chose him, special! Damme, what a fool I was! He
must be one of the chief plotters . . . planted on us as a sham volunteer
just so he could stir 'em up to mischief . . ."

"Uh, sah . . ." Andrews suggested in a low voice, after a bashful cough into his fist. "Jus' one feller come aboard las' night, sah . . . 'E couldna stirred 'em up, much . . . not dot quick. Scheme musta been a-fest'rin' fo' some time. 'Mong some o' de lads we got at Chatham . . . even 'fore we got 'em, Cap'um."

"Aye, you're probably right, Andrews," Lewrie had to admit to his Cox'n. "Damme, what's the world coming to? What next? A total civilian rebellion too?"

There was no answer to that one.

Or nothing anyone would ever dare put into words!

He looked outboard, seeking salvation, like a marooned sailor on a desert isle might scan the horizon for a scrap of tops'ls which might mean rescue. But there was no cause for hope in sight.

Every ship at the Nore flew the plain red flags of rebellion . . . every ship now sported yard ropes. Boats full of senior officers were streaming from *Inflexible,* steered by their personal coxswains, rowed by their personal boat-crews, rushing too late to reclaim the commands they'd lost.

Signal flags flapped busily from the roof of the Dockard Commissioner's house, and from Vice-Admiral Buckner's shore residence.

The semaphore tower on Garrison Point was "talking" in a flurry of whirling arms. To the next station at Queenborough, thence across the low country to Gadshill or Beacon Hill, near Chatham. From there, the news would now be "flashed" in a matter of minutes to Swanscombe station near Greenhithe alerting the Tilbury river forts, then on to Shooter's Hill, about equidistant between the Royal Arsenal at Woolwich and Greenwich Naval Hospital—to New Cross, West Square on the south bank of the Thames, and at last across the river, to Admiralty.

Informing their Lords Commissioners that another entire bloody *ad hoc* fleet had been lost—to Mutiny!

CHAPTER NINETEEN

$\mathcal{P}$ermission to enter the gunroom, sir," Lewrie announced with a cough into his fist, as he stood by the berth-deck portal which led to his officers' quarters. Normally, the gunroom was a holy-of-holies, off-limits to all but those who lodged there, their personal hammockmen or body-servants, their cook or table-servants. Captains were included in the banned category, since they had their own great-cabins one deck above, equal in size to the hull space shared by eight or more men below them. The enforced separation allowed them a haven of peace and quiet from the tumult of a working vessel, from the wrath of a demanding captain, the sight of the common seamen . . . usually.

He waited, one brow up in demand, as Lt. Ludlow took his sweet time mulling over the heathenish idea of allowing him into their sanctuary, filling the doorway set into the insubstantial deal-and-canvas "bulkhead" partition, which was more a token of privacy than real.

"Aye, sir . . . come in, sir." Ludlow nodded at last, stepping to one side. He did not say that Lewrie was welcome though.

"Thankee, Mister Ludlow," Lewrie said, forcing himself to act pleasant as he stepped inside, his hat under his arm. "Ah. All here, I see, gentlemen . . . our middies too."

Langlie, Wyman, Mr. Winwood the Sailing Master, Surgeon Shirley, Purser Coote, and Marine Lieutenant Devereux filled the seats down both sides of their mess table. The chair at the head of the table was Ludlow's, now empty. There was an eighth chair available, but Lewrie would not go any further towards upsetting the gunroom's well-run order by taking it. Besides, it was at the vice-end of the table, below the salt—and a place for those inferior to Ludlow. Lewrie walked slowly aft, giving the midshipmen, who were perched on the sideboard or were forced to stand a'lean against the interior partitions, an encouraging smile or two.

"Might you do us the honour of partaking in a glass of brandy, sir?" Lt. Langlie offered. Lewrie could see that at least one bottle had already been rendered a "dead soldier," on its side atop the table, with a fresh one already half-drained beside it.

"Thankee, Mister Langlie, and I do appreciate the offer and the gunroom's hospitality, but . . . no," Lewrie told him pleasantly. "Bit early in the day for me, d'ye see. On a sensible day, mind. Proceed, though, yourselves . . . don't let my presence discourage your cheer."

"I thought it best, did we put our heads together . . . informally," he began to explain. "Summoning you to my cabins might have raised the suspicions of our so-called . . . committee. Might have made them refuse to allow it, and . . ."

"Damn 'em all, root and branch," Midshipman Peacham growled at that, with his glass halfway to his lips. "Ungrateful pigs!"

The committee had elected a dozen hands to run the ship, chosen the Master Gunner, Mr. Handcocks, and his mate, Morley, to represent her aboard the flagship of the mutiny, and had "requested" that watch-standing officers and midshipmen go below, off-duty, and remain out of sight unless there was an evolution to perform.

And had chosen that blackguard, Able Seaman Bales, to be their temporary "captain" in charge of *Proteus* until the seamen's grievances had been answered, and the mutiny was declared over! And Bales chose a day of "Rope Yarn Sunday" and celebration in place of those chores of lading ship he'd been so insistent upon two hours before.

Leaving the officers with nothing to do and no reason to stay on deck in the presence of their mutinous inferiors.

"Listen to 'em," Ludlow spat, reaching for the half-full bottle. "Caterwaulin' an' caperin' . . ."

Proteus thrummed to the stamp of feet as their mutineers danced their joy, clapped and sang rowdy songs to the music of the fiddle and the fife, and the songs echoed faintly as far as the gunroom, through those insubstantial screens.

"Quite clever of 'em," Lewrie snapped. "Take a day of rest to cajole the unconvinced. Like we do at a recruiting 'rondy,' to beguile 'em to join in the first place."

"Have 'em all in their pockets 'fore dark," Ludlow gloomed.

"I don't think so, Mister Ludlow," Lewrie disagreed. "That is the reason I'm here, so we may decide what to do tomorrow, when they begin to face reality. Hopefully, they are enough in league with Spithead to remain in a *form* of discipline, and . . ."

"Discipline! Bah!" Ludlow griped most sourly.

"I've seen it, sir. *You* have not," Lewrie snapped at his First Officer. Badly as he needed the support of all of his officers, Lewrie would most gladly have pitched Ludlow overboard. Being at-table, with a drink in his hand, in his own *sanctum sanctorum*, was making his First Lieutenant even less guarded with his opinions, he suspected.

"I beg your pardon, sir." Ludlow stiffened, eyeing him owlish and half-seas-over with brandy. "Do proceed, sir."

"We've a new crew," Lewrie ploughed on, trying to ignore that latest jape. "They haven't formed cliques yet. You saw how it was on deck. A middlin' pack of determined men, reinforced by the hands who came aboard from *Sandwich*. Christ Almighty, we only got our last thirty or so yesterday . . . and I doubt that Bales is the only one linked to the plot. Any of the others strike you as sea-lawyers? Dressed well . . . kept their kit, t'make themselves look more desirable as volunteers?"

"Some of the Irish, sir?" Midshipman Elwes suggested in a wary piping, surrounded by other nodding, sage heads too shy to speak up.

"United Irishmen, aye, Mister Elwes," Lewrie was quick to agree with the lad and reward him with a smile. "Sworn to drive us out of their island . . . waitin' for the bloody Frogs to land and arm them. We have to be wary of that lot. Not *all* of our Irishmen, I'd suspect. A half-dozen, at best. And the rest following along so far."

"Uhm . . ." Lt. Wyman said, raising his hand like a schoolboy. "Would there not be more than a few hands still loyal, sir? But out-numbered and cowed?"

"Exactly, Mister Wyman!" Lewrie congratulated him. "Now, *we've* not

been thrown together with our crew that long either, but I do trust
you have already discovered the characters of most in that short time. We
have to make up lists. Scribble down those in your watches or divisions
you suspect . . . a second list of those you think might be caught in the
middle—those who haven't thrown their lot in with the leaders and could
still be swayed. Those we might be able to work on."

"Do *they* ever give us the chance though, Captain," Lieutenant Ludlow
all but sneered. "At their pleasure, dammit all."

"This Bales fellow . . ." Lewrie said, pacing down the length of the
table towards Ludlow's end. Thinking again about sinewy fingers tightening about some rancourous bastard's throat—most specifically *this* cav-
illing bastard's windpipe, and *squeezing* . . . ! Glaring Ludlow to a
drink-sodden, blessedly cowed silence for a moment.

"*He* was the one suggested we have to be laden with rations and powder
and shot," Lewrie smirked, "for whatever ends he had in mind. And this
ship can't proceed to sea 'thout we have the opportunity to train the hands
further. Innocent evolutions and drills. Which give us the chance to make
out lists . . . three lists, gentlemen.

"One, of the true ringleaders we most suspect, and those people in
league with 'em." He ticked off on his fingers. "Second, a list of those still
loyal. The third . . . the sheep in the middle. A day or two of watchin'
close, takin' note of them like you were thinkin' of rating them for a
promotion will suffice. Take strolls on deck, for the air if nothing else.
Then put your heads together. And we'll convene meetings like this to go
over the lists. An invitation to some of you to dine in with me might seem
a plausible excuse. Some music?" He grinned slyly. And saw his officers
and midshipmen gather a bit of hope in the midst of what seemed a hopeless situation.

"And when we *do* organise working parties to lade stores, sir," Lt.
Langlie snickered, "we'll have even more opportunity to sift them out . . .
separate the sheep from the goats, as it were!"

"Once again, exactly, Mister Langlie!" Lewrie chuckled. "Chat them up.
Put on a pleased expression, no matter your personal thoughts. Firm, but
fair. Agreeable and affable, as if you hold no grudges over their betrayal."

"Seem to *agree* with 'em, sir?" Peacham gasped.

"Absolutely *not,* sir!" Lewrie snarled. "You are to do nothing to encourage or abet the mutiny. No winking at it. No, the best pose to strike, I should think, would be . . . tolerance and patience. As a father might towards wayward children. Tolerate no dis-respect, any threats. God, report 'em to this Bales character! Stand on your dignity and your rights! Because once this is over, they'll be under your discipline again, and they don't wish to do anything which may be . . . remembered, hmm? We're *somewhat* assured that they're going to show respect to officers and petty officers, or discipline those who break that rule themselves."

"Report them to *Bales*, sir?" Midshipman Nicholas gawped, eyes wide with astonishment and looking more than a little lost. Or, as Lewrie suspected, more than a little befuddled by the gunroom's booze.

"He's declared himself temporary 'captain,' Mister Nicholas," Lewrie sighed. "Whyever not? He's taken the responsibility for any infractions by the crew upon himself for the nonce. Like Spithead, I expect our mutineers will declare that they're loyal and True Blue Hearts of Oak . . . just waitin' for their demands to be met. Those at Spithead said they'd maintain sobriety and good order among themselves. The yard ropes weren't a threat to officers there, sirs. They hoisted 'em to keep their *own* kind in line, my old crew told me."

"I'd suspect, though, sir . . ." Langlie said most shrewdly, "we will be tested sore 'fore this is done. Deliberate taunts and japes. 'Twill demand a *power* of patience from us all, do you not believe?"

"Amen, Mister Langlie." Lewrie nodded. "From all of us, sirs," he said, trying to lock eyes with all of them in turn. Lt. Ludlow . . . *most* especially. But Ludlow was busy picking at lint on his cuffs. "Anger, I'm afraid, is forbidden us. Public threats, taunts, and gibes are denied us as well. We can't *curse* them back to obedience."

"But!" he cautioned. "A sly word, whispered in the right ear . . . once you've discovered the right ears . . . may sow seeds of doubt and fear in 'em. Reminders, that once this ends, *we're* back in charge . . . and we'll remember the names of those who were complete traitors and rogues. Encouragement for those who didn't join hands with 'em. And encouragement to those wavering . . ."

"So we can take the ship back, sir?" Sailing Master Winwood, at last, commented. He looked quite worried.

"If it comes to it, sir," Lewrie nodded, grim. "But Admiral Howe's gone to Portsmouth. It may be no more than a few days' turmoil here before we hear that Spithead and Plymouth have been settled, and the Nore will then have no grievances to complain of; and this mutiny will collapse of its own. The settlement will most-like apply Fleet-wide, Mister Winwood. Something else to remind 'em of, sirs, when we are back on deck, givin' orders, even temporarily. Remind 'em to wait 'til they hear the settlement before they do something they'd regret."

"If that's all they have in mind, sir," Mr. Coote sighed. "I truly do *hope* that's all they have in mind. United Irishmen, though . . . revolutionaries even amongst good Englishmen, who wish to emulate the French Republic . . ."

"I know, Mister Coote." Lewrie shrugged. "But for now we're assured it concerns rations, shore leave, pay, and such. Have to take that at face value. 'Til they prove us wrong, that is."

"Do we pray that is not the case, sir." The Surgeon, Mr. Shirley, groaned. "That they prove that supposition wrong, that is."

"Indeed," Lewrie said, hands in the small of his back, rocking on the balls of his feet. "Something else to 'smoak out,' gentleman . . . when you're allowed on deck. Keep your ears cocked for any talk among the hands that sounds rebellious. Dangerously rebellious. Republican cant . . . ? There's a *chance* there's more to this than the stated causes. We must hope that those who hold such traitorous views are distinctly in the minority."

"And the bulk of the hands are to be warned to guard themselves against being led to greater folly, sir," Lt. Devereux supposed aloud. "Anything that so much as smacks of Paris . . . or Thomas Paine. . . ."

"Most shrewdly noted, sir," Lewrie said, with a half bow to the wits of his marine officer. "They declare themselves loyal Englishmen asking for but a tuppence of their due. Anything else, though . . ."

"Hid it well-enough from us"—Ludlow countered, slurring his words by then—"the back-stabbin' bastards. Who's t'say what they're hidin' from us now, hey?"

"That's 'hey . . . *sir*,' Mister Ludlow," Lewrie hissed. "And I will thank you to remember it!"

Damn him! he thought. *I've just about had all I can take from this fool! Might as well be in league with the mutineers for all the good he is to me! Ruinin' the good mood I created . . . look at 'em now, cringin' like*

*whipped puppies when just a second ago they were eager to start cajolin' the
people!*

"We'll begin making preliminary lists, sir," Lt. Langlie said quickly.
"Right, lads? Who to approach first. And we'll keep our ears and eyes
open, sir, as you ordered. All of us, sir."

"Very good, Mister Langlie," Lewrie relented, forcing himself to grin
in gratitude. "I know I am a very fortunate captain to have a set of officers
on whom I may completely rely," he told them. With another "so there!"
glare at Ludlow as he sprawled at the table, insensible to almost everything
by then.

"Keep our own counsel," Marine Lt. Devereux added, glowering significantly first at Ludlow, then at some others. "And most especially our
tempers, in the doing, Captain, sir."

"Thankee, Mister Devereux. Thank you all," Lewrie said. "Now, I will
plague you no longer, and I am grateful for you allowing me to interrupt
your off-duty time. I will have my Cox'n send down written invitations
to dine with me tonight. Once you've made first stabs at winnowing our
chaff, hmm? Good day, gentlemen."

"Good day, sir," they chorused, rising as he departed. Ludlow even
managed to stagger to his feet. With a bit of help.

Lewrie emerged on the gun-deck, took a deep breath of air, and scowled
at his crew gathered in the waist beneath the boat-tier beams. They were
still dancing hornpipes, slapping time with their hands on their thighs,
beating time with stacks of spoons, as the fiddler and the marine fifers
supplied the tune. He saw the Black Irishman, Desmond, strangling what
looked to be a long-necked cat, making a reedy wailing over a flute-like
tube. That must be what he called *uillean* pipes, softer and mellower than
their blaring Scots cousins. Everyone seemed to be having a grand time,
except for Landsman Haslip, of course. He had been left where he'd fallen
and was still being studiously ignored by his "shipmates."

Lewrie climbed to the quarterdeck, feeling a bit smug about how he'd
handled that problem. He'd found him guilty of theft, doomed him to a
dozen lashes, and also broken up the elections of delegates by having "All
Hands Aft To Witness Punishment" piped.

A neat little homily he'd preached, about crime and sailors who were unworthy of being called "shipmates," the sort never to be trusted. He'd seen at least a dozen sets of teeth grinding in the mouths of the most dedicated mutineers—and had begun a short list of his own!

Then after Haslip had taken his dozen lashes from the "cat"—wielded most enthusiastically by Bosun Pendarves and his mates, in the place of authority—he'd turned Haslip over to the crew.

"I've given him *my* dozen," Lewrie had declared, "but a rogue of his . . . stripe . . . will only resent me, and authority, for it. Now he's yours. Prove that *you* won't tolerate a thief . . . form a gauntlet!"

They'd leapt to it, forming two lines facing each other, fists and rope-ends ready, and Haslip had been dragged from the hatch grating, back bloody and wailing in pain. Bosun Pendarves stood ahead of him with a cutlass leveled at Haslip's breast, so he'd be forced to a slow pace and not run down the gauntlet quickly, if he didn't want to be skewered. Haslip had been pummeled and bludgeoned, beaten senseless, shrieking and cowering from their blows. A dash of salt water to wash the cat-o'-nine-tail's cuts as he lay prostrate, a surgeon's mate with warm tar to daub his wounds . . . normally, once punishment was done, the malefactor's mates would help him below, sneak him a tot of rum, tell him how well he'd borne up. But not for Haslip.

Pray God, Lewrie thought, studying his cavorting crew; *they've no use for this mutiny, once news comes from Portsmouth either!*

He cocked his head as Desmond, on his odd pipes, and the fiddler, began a new tune. Lewrie smiled to realise it was the same one that his father Sir Hugo had marched his militia to . . . "The Bowld Soldier Boy"!

Some of his men looked up at him, as if "cocking a snook" at him with that Irish air, waiting for his reaction. They were disappointed if they thought he would mottle or glower with anger though, for his right hand began to beat the measure on the cap-rail of the quarterdeck nettings. Toulon, intrigued, leapt from out of nowhere to preen, arch, and pace the rolled hammocks stowed in the nettings, as Lewrie petted him with his other hand. And smiled, in spite of himself.

Desmond, Furfy, a few others, nodded back at him, even tentatively smiled. 'Twas a faint sign, but a hopeful one, Lewrie dared think.

CHAPTER TWENTY

*N*o, this'un wasn't the same sort of mutiny as the one he'd seen at Portsmouth, Lewrie decided early on. There was nothing orderly or even sane about it.

The frigate *San Fiorenzo* had come in, all tricked out in holiday best, to bear the newlywed Princess Charlotte and her princely German groom over to the Continent for their honeymoon. When *San Fiorenzo* had balked and attempted to sail free, she'd been *fired upon*, her rigging cut up by solid shot! Moments later, she'd reluctantly decided to enlist in the cause of their so-called "Brother Seamen."

The Fleet Delegates had also moved eight small gunboats from the Little Nore anchorage into the Great Nore, to secure their weaponry for their own use. On their way out, all of them had fired their artillery at the shore forts, again with solid round-shot. Perhaps it was to show the mutineers' resolve to the Admiralty and its local officials. Or a first round, Lewrie feared, to spur the beginning of a nationwide rebellion? Certainly, they weren't celebration shots, not with solid ball!

News—a mere rumor so far—had come from London that Admiral Lord Howe had succeeded in negotiating a settlement of the original Spithead mutiny. Working parties ferrying supplies from shore had come back, whooping and hollering with delight over the tidings. Portsmouth and Plymouth, the entire Channel Fleet, were said to be returned to discipline and duty. Word was, "Black Dick" and his lady-wife had gotten a *fete*, their carriage unhorsed and drawn through Portsmouth's streets to the town's largest inn by teams of grateful sailors; where Howe had dined-in the chief mutineers and drunk toasts with them—as "matey" as anyone could ask for!

Yet so far in Sheerness and the Nore, those rumored tidings hadn't done much to ease the fervour of the newest mutineers. If anything, news of a peaceful, agreeable settlement had only sparked a new wave of frolic, riotous street parading and shore drinking—but no hint of acceptance of a settlement here.

So for another morning, Lewrie studied the shore with a glass, so close off Garrison Point, he could all but taste the meat and drink. Sailors, done with meetings at Checquers Public House, their chosen shore rendezvous, paraded the streets, tricked out in red cockades and waving their infernal plain red flags of rebellion. Each large group had its hired band, and the sounds of competing melodies blended into an atonal jollity as one pack collided with another with a rival band and simply *had* to out-tootle, out-blare, or out-drum the others. Even atop the ramparts of the shore forts, drunken sailors could be seen—troublingly arm-in-arm with equally drunken *soldiers*, or hanging with arms round each other's necks, swaying and singing airs.

Respectable citizens of Sheerness, Lewrie didn't doubt, were all inside behind locked doors, huddled over their silver plate and valuables. Yet the streets were full of garish trulls and sharpers; poorer civilians out for a good time as long as it lasted; or secret traitors and rebels of Republican bent out to stir up even worse troubles?

Children and women also capered and danced with the sailors. There *was* a chance they were legitimate wives, come down to Sheerness to support their sailor menfolk. Or, as Lewrie also sourly surmised, whores out to make a killing off the myriad of sailors given liberal amounts of shore leave for a rare once.

Not that they had to go ashore for that, Lewrie sighed, as he lowered his telescope and collapsed its tubes; publicans' and pedlars' bumboats plied the harbour waters, ferrying cargoes of gew-gaws out to the ships, proffering the temporary "wives" to seamen who had coin enough to support and claim them. Without a strict watch set by the Bosun and harbour watches, he was mortal-certain every doxy bore small flasks of spirits under her gowns, inside her stockings or hat, to sell in spite of the Fleet Delegates' edict against private spirits.

Oh, *Proteus* was a merry ship! Music wafted up from the seamen's mess deck, from the forecastle too, for several bumboats lolled under her entry-ports, and real wives and children, and false wives, strolled the gun-deck or danced in drunken, half-clad abandon, groping at their men, being groped and pawed, before being led below for a quick fumble 'tween the mess tables with two blankets hung for privacy.

Caught staring down from the quarterdeck too long, one blowsy blonde bawd jerked down the top of her ragged sack gown and shimmied, flaunt-ing a brace of pendulous, but rather impressively sized teats at him, shriek-ing and calling him a "dirty ole awf'cer!" drawing the attention of several of his hands to her antics, to his staring.

God, what a dirty puzzle, he snorted in derision! Yet doffed his hat and, beaming, bowed her a courtly "leg."

She shrieked again, then blew him a kiss, before turning to have her dugs groped by her partner. The men had laughed—not *at him,* he sus-pected; it had sounded good-natured.

And Able Seaman Bales, seated atop a 12-pounder's breech, with his arms crossed over his chest, cast him a brow-raised glare, with a shrewd cast to his phyz after that brief antic.

Point for me, Alan told himself as he paced away, ignoring that glare; *now he's sure to think up something else new to undermine me and my authority. Has to!*

It was dev'lish-queer, Lewrie thought; *this confrontation 'twixt me and this Bales creature . . . he seems t'take it so damn' personal! Not just a scheming sea-lawyer* born *for mutiny an' damn all officers, but . . . like he hates officers in general, but me in the* most *particular!*

He fetched up at the traffrails and leaned on them, gazing out to sea, and wondered if there was an advantage to save *Proteus* in this fellow Bales's seething dislike; some way to use that against him, as a fatal weak-ness. But for the life of him, Lewrie could not recall a Seaman Bales in his past whom he had offended, from any former ship.

Kin to his old first captain, aboard HMS *Ariadne,* way back in 1780?

Surely not—kin would come into the Fleet a midshipman, in spite of Captain Bales being cashiered after his court martial at English Harbour, Antigua. That was the way of the world, and "interest," in the Royal Navy. Sons of fools weren't *quite* the fools that their fathers were . . . 'Til they *proved* it, of course! Lewrie snickered to himself!

Then—"Oh!" struck him.

What if this Bales *was* old Bales's kin, too penniless and without influence at Admiralty to get the usual "leg up"? Then he would have had to ship as a volunteer, go "before the mast," at first. But with a good education, surely he'd have advanced past his mostly illiterate fellow sailors, have made Master's Mate by now?

"Damme," Lewrie whispered to himself, "wasn't *me* cost old Bales his career. I spoke up *for* him, lauded him." *Even if I did lie like a rug,* he ruefully chid himself; *toadyin' for a good name of my own!* And no way to get to the bottom of it. . . . without asking *this* Bales!

"No, goddamn your eyes, no! And take your fool's face to Hell, you impudent gutter trash!"

Lewrie turned about, wincing at the tone and recognising that voice. It was Midshipman Peacham, railing at one of the hands from the afterguard—doing exactly what he'd warned them not to do days before!

Hands in the small of his back, reminding himself once more about being dignified, deliberate, and slow, he paced towards the altercation; but the seamen knuckled his forehead and sloped off before he could arrive, face suffused with what looked like murderous resentment.

"Mister Peacham, sir . . . something amiss?" he intoned.

"Captain, sir!" Peacham fumed. "These disputatious . . . hounds! I have never heard the like for Jack-Sauce, obstreperous . . . !"

"Such as?" Lewrie purred, keeping a solemn face.

" 'Ahem, sir,' he says to me, Captain, Sir"—Peacham stammered in a face-suffusing heat of his own—" 'beggin' yer pardon, sir,' he poses! 'Would you be so good as to advance me the "socket-fee" for a doxy of my own, sir?' the bastard asked! Purser to dispense funds for his rut . . . ?"

"As you say, Mister Peacham." Lewrie sniffed, striving to keep a straight face. "A bit of Jack-Sauce. Unless, of course, you thought he was *serious . . . ?*"

"I will not abide it, sir! Never!" Peacham declared stiffly.

"Oh, yes you will, sir . . . for the nonce, as I said below a few days ago? You do recall that, sir? Me, in the gunroom?" Lewrie posed. "Tolerant, paternal, unruffled, and patient 'til this is ended. Now, do you have wits remaining, sir . . . recall his name and rating, make a sharp note of it, and wait for that 'later.' To see if he was merely taking the chance to make a jest at an officer's expense, whether he was put up to it, or . . . whether there was something malicious about it."

"Malicious, of a certainty, Captain, sir!" Peacham averred.

"We'll see, once they're back in discipline, Mister Peacham," Lewrie told him. "Now go below and duck your head. Stay there 'til you've mastered yourself. So you won't explode the next time one of them twits you, hmm? Do they discover you're likely to rage at 'em, the more they'll try you on. For the fun of it," Lewrie cautioned. "And do they discover you're vulnerable, it might be one of the real ringleaders who'll try to get you to rise to their bait—and cause *real* trouble."

"Ahh . . ." Peacham sighed, sounding damn' close to an insubordinate cry of disagreement. He swallowed heavily, cringing as if rebuked.

"There, see how easy that is, Mister Peacham?" Lewrie snickered, instead of bellowing at the fool. "Practice, sir . . . practice."

"Aye, aye, sir," Peacham said, doffing his hat and departing.

Another thing to puzzle over, Lewrie frowned, as he paced back to the hammock nettings overlooking that boisterous waist of the ship and the "country-dance" revelry going on there. Ominously, Article the Fifth issued by the mutineers had specified that all ships were to keep their navigators aboard; as if, should their mutiny fail, they could sail off the ships they'd seized . . . to foreign, enemy ports?

But most ship's committees had put officers ashore. Captains had been sent packing, most willingly, and revolted by the betrayal of their crews. Committees had deemed some officers, midshipmen, and mates as "Soul Drivers" and cruel, abusive tyrants and had jeered them over the side right-chearly, vowing they'd never allow them to return. Not in this life-time, they wouldn't. And had Howe agreed to *that?*

But aboard *Proteus* . . . no one had been denounced or turned out, yet. Well, grumbled about, denounced in a fashion, but . . . ? That was a bit odd—something else for Lewrie to ponder; whyever *not?*

And can I goad 'em to put Peacham and Ludlow off? Lewrie speculated. *Christ, both of 'em two loads for the proverbial camel's back . . . !* Sooner or later, not being masters of themselves, they'd pop off, issue too great an insult to someone, and the crew would have another reason to resent authority, even after this was finished! *Proteus* might also be finished, and his command of her with it! The Admiralty might turn out the entire crew, captain and officers, and start fresh.

Three sailors mounted the larboard ladder to the quarterdeck, as if daring each other to do so. Lewrie steeled himself for a bit of Jack-Sauce, and saw Able Seaman Bales from the corner of his eye, still seated atop the breech of the 12-pounder gun, but watching most carefully, with his tongue in his cheek.

"Uhm . . . beggin' yer pardon, sir," one of them chortled, elbowed into speech by the ones flanking him and a bit behind for protection. "Permission t'speak, Cap'um, sir," he said, removing his hat.

"Go ahead." Lewrie sighed, already wearied.

"Would ya be so good, sir . . . as t'issue each man a bottle o' gin fer breakfast, Cap'um, sir?" the unfortunate managed to say, shivering with mirth. The others were blubbering their lips in strangled glee.

"Oh, for God's sake." Lewrie sighed again, pinching the bridge of his nose. "Is *that* all?"

"Wellsir, uhm . . . aye, sir. Thet is . . ."

"Me, I'd love to oblige you, frankly," Lewrie told them.

"Ah, sir? *Really,* sir?"

"But you know the rules, lads," Lewrie blathered on. "Naval regulations, and your own leaders, say there's to be no private liquor allowed, ever. So I'm afraid I can't. But . . . d'ye see your so-called temporary captain, Seaman Bales, there . . ." Lewrie smiled.

"Uhm . . ."

"Now, do you ask him, well . . . he might relent and allow you. I heard it said he has a private income beyond his Navy pay," Lewrie extemporised. "How else'd he come aboard with such a complete kit, hmmm? Do you ask him nicely, he might take you ashore with him and sport you to yer gin. Just ask him."

"Sir, ah . . ." they goggled at him, and at each other.

"Well, go on!" Lewrie urged, most "mately." "Ask him. 'Nothin' ventured, nothin' gained,' as they always say. And good luck!"

"Er, aye, aye, Cap'um, sir, we will!" the spokesman enthused with a hopeful sound. They trooped down the ladder to the waist, scampering to approach Bales, and put their outrageous demand to him.

Lord, Alan shrugged, *there's three simpler than yer average tars!*

Before Bales could begin to bark at them and disabuse them, he glared upwards at Lewrie with a look of pure rage.

And take that *you sly bastard!* Lewrie thought.

CHAPTER TWENTY-ONE

Alan was writing Caroline a letter, though when he could get it to her, he wasn't sure. Much like the fate of most letters written when at sea, to be held until they put into a foreign port, met a ship sailing for home, or rendezvoused with a squadron flagship, the delegates had decreed that no letters would be allowed to go ashore.

Writing was a difficult chore, for Toulon, when not striving to catch and kill the waving quill pen's end, had developed a fondness for stretching his sleek, furry length atop anything Lewrie attempted to write or even read. Desktop, dining table, or the chart-table, it made no difference. Did he make paper rattle, Toulon would be there in a heartbeat—and in a most playful, insistent mood, rolling over onto his side or back to bare his white belly, and push or pat with his paws until he got some petting. Or, brought labour (of which, Alan assumed, most cats highly disapproved!) to a grinding halt.

"Toulon, now . . . damn yer eyes!" Lewrie fretted, shifting pen and paper closer to him. But over the cat rolled, right onto his back and put all four paws in the air, his thick, hairy tail lazily lashing, and purring in idle, impish delight. Squarely in the middle of the letter.

"Aren't you supposed t'sleep or something?" Lewrie groaned, on the verge of surrender. "It's daytime, fer God's sake. It's what cats *do!* Eat, shit, sleep . . . eat, pee, sleep. Don't you know the drill?"

"Weow?" Toulon demanded, wriggling nearer the desk's edge with his pitiful face on.

There was a rap on the outer door.

"Captain, sir?"

"Enter," Alan snapped.

"Sir, there's a boat coming alongside," Mr. Midshipman Catterall informed him as he stepped inside.

"Gunn'l down with gin, is she?" Lewrie frowned. "That why the hands are cheerin' so lusty?"

"Uhm . . . I gather one of the key ringleaders has come to call on us, sir." Catterall blinked back. "But nary a bottle in sight, sir. Come empty-handed, Captain. A *very* poor house-warming guest."

"Bugger him, then," Lewrie said, forced to smile in spite of the interruption by Catterall's jest. He rose and made his way forrud to go on deck. "I s'pose we must see this apparition for ourselves . . . and if he wishes to wet his throat, he'd best have brought his own spirits. Lead on, Mister Catterall."

"Aye, aye, sir," Catterall said, with a sly grin. "I'd expect rabble-rousing is a *dry* endeavour sir."

Lewrie smiled again, as he clapped on his hat.

And let's just hope it's not that lunatick, McCann, again!

Well at least, thought Lewrie, it wasn't McCann the hands were cheering, though that idiot was in the party of visiting leaders of the mutiny, hanging back in the rear for once, like a spear-carrier in an Italian opera.

Lewrie thought to take his rightful place amidships by the nettings at the forward edge of the quarterdeck so he could study this new arrival, remember faces if not names for later, and remind his mutinous crew just who *should* be in charge. But the visitors usurped that post, marching directly from the starboard entry-port to the quarterdeck, and forced Lewrie, Catterall, and the few other midshipmen and officers who had come to answer their own curiosity to hang back far out of range of being tainted by appearing *too* curious—or tacitly supportive! They ended in a clump near the taffrail flag lockers, almost out of earshot, and mostly ignored by the enthusiastic sailors who were hoorawing what seemed an important visitor.

The stranger, Alan noted, was of middling height and build, and dressed much like a Commission Officer or Warrant Officer: gentlemanly white breeches, stockings and shirt, with a plain, dark blue, brass-buttoned coat over a yellowy, striped waist-coat. For shoes, he sported a pair of half-boots, another gentlemanly affection. On his head, the man wore a hairy beaver-fur hat, the sort with long and wide flaps that could be turned down over his ears and neck in bad weather.

The stranger waved his arms, crying out to *Proteus*'s crew, shaking hands here and there with the most forward, glad-handing his way to the nettings like a Member of Parliament on the hustings might work his borough's pubs for re-election. Though he was of such regular features as could be deemed handsome, he was of a swarthy or sun-baked complexion. And there was a half-focused, almost dreamy glint to his eyes—the eyes of a romantic. Lewrie scowled with distaste. Or was he just as daft as his compatriot, McCann? He took an instant dislike to him.

"Ah, sir," Marine Lieutenant Devereux said, doffing his hat in salute as he came up to see their raree-show. "Odd, do you not think, sir . . . he carries himself with the airs of a born gentleman. Surely, he cannot *be* an officer, Captain, in league with Republican rebels?"

"A rogue officer?" Lewrie puzzled. "Pray not! We've troubles enough from the common seamen and mates who organised this mutiny."

"Wearing a sword, sir," Devereux pointed out in a low mutter.

"What looks to be a good pistol in his belt too. An officer's accoutrements, damn his eyes."

"Hip-hip . . . hooray, lads!" their Seaman Bales and Gunner, Mr. Handcocks, were exulting. "Three cheers for Richard Parker . . . President o' the Floatin' Republic . . . an' Admiral o' *our* Fleet!"

"What gall!" Lt. Wyman gasped at the effrontery.

"Now, now . . . lads . . ." this Richard Parker was saying, come over all modest and self-deprecating, pushing his hands at the crew as if to hush them so he could speak. Or, more-likely, to hush such damning talk! To declare a rival government to the established one—and the Crown—to promote oneself from sailor or mate to the highest peak of the Commission

Officer list, a jealously guarded Admiralty right, could get anybody hanged in an eyeblink, even if the mutiny here at the Nore ended this instant!

"Hmmm . . .'tis a good sword at that," Lewrie had to admit once this Parker person had turned about a full circle to silence the crowd. It *was* an officer's long, slim smallsword; not the cutlass from some arms chest more suitable to a seaman.

"Pinched, most-like, sir," Midshipman Catterall sneered, from the off-hand side, "from the gunroom of his own ship."

"Right, lads . . . give me an ear now. Hush!" Parker demanded, and they finally left off all that raucous cheering.

There, that's better, Lewrie told himself; *'fore Toulon got so scared he had his own litter o' kittens!*

"We've heard from Spithead!" Parker dangled like a lure, making everyone lean forward and hold their breaths. "It's official. They've reached an agreement!"

Lewrie winced at the noise, even if it was joyful tidings.

"Lads, the terms . . . !" Parker screeched, to no avail.

"Brother Seamen!" McCann howled, stepping forward, and waving his cutlass aloft. "Hist, now! Hist t'th' president! Th' man-eatin' bastards give in t'us . . . th' common folk've triumphed over 'em! Give heed now!"

"They've won better rations"—Parker went on, once they had calmed at McCann's behest—"proper weights and measures . . . sick-berth pay, and proper medical care," he ticked off on his fingers. "They've gotten the rise in pay, for seamen, Marines, *and* pensioners . . ."

"Purged their ships o' tyrannical officers'n mates too!" That pop-eyed McCann felt thrilled to add. "And full pardons!"

"Fingers in yer ears . . ." Lewrie sighed to his assembled officers, before taking his own advice.

"Yyyyeeeaaahhhh!"

Well, thank God, Lewrie thought, as the cheering went on for a full minute or two more, turning to share relieved looks with his senior people and a few bold seamen who'd held themselves aloof from mutinous doings so far; *mutiny's over, and we can get back to work. No lastin' harm done 'mongst the people; I've still my command . . .*

"Listen, though, listen!" Parker shouted, as their cheers began to wane, wearing a somber face. "One thing they didn't get was the more liberal shore leave. Still limited to seaports or aboard ships, same as we have now. Still have to have our loved ones come out to us, 'stead of us going to them, and going ashore decided by individual captains' whims, still . . ."

"Damn 'em all, the soul-drivers!" someone cried.

"Well, that's all fine for Channel Fleet, lads!" Parked yelled, hands on his hips and looking about, taking a moment to peer aft at the ship's senior officers. "But there's a problem with it all. Listen . . . what Admiral Howe negotiated with the Spithead lads . . ."

"Our brother seamen, our fellow suff'rers!" McCann raved. And made Parker wince for a moment. "Tell 'em, brother Parker!"

". . . terms they agreed to was *not* an Act of Parliament! It was only an Order In Council! And *they're* only good for a year and a day, not permanent, like a proper Act!" Parker cautioned. "And so far it only applies to Spithead and Plymouth . . . *not* to the Nore!"

That set off a chorus of boos, catcalls, and growls of rage.

"We'll have to hold out 'til they've guaranteed *us* the pardon too, presented us with the same terms, and sat down and negotiated with *us* . . . or whatever we wish beyond the Spithead agreement!"

I'll be Goddamned! Lewrie groaned. "Horse turds!" he bellowed, before he could think about it.

Which made them turn and glare at him, every last mother-son!

Ah . . . oops! he blushed; *too forceful.*

CHAPTER TWENTY-TWO

*I*n for the penny," Alan sighed dejectedly, "in for the pound."

"If the settlement satisfies Channel Fleet," he roared, though, "and was done in good faith, then why is it not good enough for the Nore? All any ship has to do is send ashore to Vice-Admiral Buckner and ask for written confirmation of the terms. Then sign them and return to duty and receive the very same terms. *And* pardon!"

"No, no, won't work!" McCann shot back. "Ain't had our chance t'purge our own ships o' tyrants an' brutes! Pardon don't apply here, anyways! They gotta deal with us face t'face and give it to us, and we see they live up t'what they promised Spithead. 'Til we see they'll not stab Brother Seamen in the back, like they done the Cullodens, or if they're schemin' t'go back on it soon as it suits 'em . . . year and a day?"

"Wouldn't trust 'em further than a man can spit!" another sailor cried from the back of the pack below the nettings in the waist.

"Backstab a whole *fleet?*" Lewrie countered, forcing himself to laugh McCann's suspicions to scorn. "That'd be national suicide, and well you know it. Admiralty, Parliament, Crown . . . they agreed to all they could, except for shore leave, because they *need* you! And they'll need you more than a year and a day, the way this war is going, so how are they going to renege on you?"

"No, hold out 'til we get liberal shore leave, what our brothers at Spithead gave up on!" Seaman Bales shouted, striding out into plain view.

"A fairer division of prize-money too. A whole lot more things that Spithead was afraid to demand," he slyly added.

"Like bloody what, Bales?" Lewrie snapped, hands on his hips and pacing forward to confront them, so more hands could hear the dispute. "You men . . . did Admiral Buckner come aboard this instant and offer you the same terms as Spithead . . . how many of you would take 'em *and* your pardon, return to duty, and have this done?"

He was gratified beyond all measure to see tentative hands stuck aloft, like schoolboys who thought they might just know the answer to a "puzzler." More than *half,* Lewrie exulted, more than *half,* ready to cave in, take the liberal terms the government had made, duck out of sight and notice, before they got dragged into deeds which could get them hanged in wholesale lots!

Mates and warrants of a certainty wavered. Lewrie nodded as he took a quick count; a fair portion of the Ordinary or Able Seamen, the Marines, and *most* of the new-comes, the landsmen idlers and waisters . . . new ship, few cliques, no real complaints against *Proteus* of her officers, yet . . . scared men, looking for safety . . . ?

"You're not part of the ship's committee, Captain," Bales cried. "You have no say in this . . . nor any right to demand a division of our house, sir!"

"Turn 'im out!" Yeoman of the Powder Kever shouted. "*There's* a vote t'take, hoy, brother seamen? Turn all th' officers out!"

"He's only doing what Admiralty demands of him," Bales quickly disagreed, "not your *practiced* tyrant . . . but, don't heed him, brothers! There's no proposal from Admiralty to vote on . . . not yet!"

Lewrie cocked a wary eye at Bales, puzzled. Most captains had been sent ashore by their mutineers; he'd be in good company. So why *not?* What motive could this Bales have for scotching that idea?

"Follow President Parker, lads," McCann shouted, sticking his oar in, "don't sell yer birthright f'r a mess o' pottage. We've but to hold on f'r a piece more; we'll win all that Spithead got and more!"

"Vow to hold out 'til it's a proper, written Act of Parliament!" President Parker boomed. "Not only for yourselves, but for your fellow seamen at Spithead, Plymouth, Great Yarmouth . . . overseas . . . !"

"Hold out all summer, do we haveta!" McCann screeched. "We got th' ships; we got th' guns! 'Thout us, Admiral Duncan at Great Yarmouth can't do a thing, do th' Dutch come out! *Aye,* they *need* us! An' we'll make 'em pay a pretty price for us, you mark my words! We sit tight, united as Brother Seamen, 'til Howe'r some other top-lofty lords come wringin' their hands, quakin' in their boots, t'sit down an' deal with us direct! Right, Brother Parker?"

"Absolutely right, Brother McCann!" Parker firmly said.

"By God, we'll make 'em sorry they don't!" McCann ranted on. "We could block th' Thames'n Medway an' starve th' city out! What'll th' high-an'-mighty do, then? Why, we could sail up an' shoot Whitehall t'flinders if they don't do right by us'n th' Spithead lads! Any sign they deal deceitful an' we burn it t'th' *ground* . . . Whitehall, Admiralty, all of it! Raise th' whole nation, an' . . . !

"But it won't come to that, lads!" Parker cried out to cut off McCann before such rebellious talk went any further. For a fleeting instant, Lewrie could almost sympathise with the poor bugger, saddled with such a batch of firebrands! God knew who sat on the Fleet Delegate Committee— United Irishmen, wild-eyed Republican rebels and Levellers, foreign-paid traitors and schemers . . . ? It probably wasn't much fun trying to ride whipper-in to a baying herd like that.

"A little more patience is all!" Parker cautioned, "so they see we're serious, and they'll give in to us, come talk to us. They'll *have* to! We'll get our own terms, winnow our officers and mates, and get our own pardons! A week or more, and it'll be settled. Peaceful!" Parker shouted, rewarding McCann with a warning glare. "And a permanent Act for all the world to see! You mark *my* words on *that!* Unity! Unity, lads! Strike up 'All Hail, Brother Seamen,' there . . . !"

Then he quickly led them into the beginning of a song, which took their minds off fantasies of torches, stakes, or crucified aristocracy.

"Go below," Bales yelled, mustering his staunchest supporters and pointing at Lewrie and the officers aft. "No votes for officers . . . Go below! No votes for officers; go below . . . !" they began to chant.

> *"All hail, Brother Seamen, that ploughs on the Main,*
> *Likewise to well-wishers of seamen of fame,*
> *May Providence watch over brave British tars,*
> *And guide them with care from the dangers of wars!"*

"Might be best, after all, sir?" Lt. Langlie posed. "We don't wish to create a regrettable incident, the mood they're in at present."

"S'pose you're right, Mister Langlie," Lewrie gravelled, loath as he was to be seen to flee. And, admittedly, loath as he was to duck below without flinging them a last, stinging, Parthian shot. He'd never let an insult pass without giving as good (or better) as he got; why change his ways aboard ship, then? But he had no choice this time.

> *"At Spithead, Jack, from long silence was roused,*
> *which wakes other Brothers who did not refuse,*
> *to assist in the plan Good Providence taught,*
> *in the hearts of brave seamen that had long been forgot!"*

"Goddamn them!" Lt. Wyman most uncharacteristically blasphemed. "It's all over, can they not see that, listen to cool reason . . . ?"

"Evidently, not," Lewrie snarled.

> *"Old Neptune made haste, to the Nore he did come,*
> *To waken his sons who had slept for too long,*
> *his thund'ring loud voice made us start with surprise,*
> *to hear his sweet words, and he bid us arise . . . !"*

"Gentlemen," Lewrie prompted, pointing to his companionway ladder, and they sorted themselves out in order of seniority to descend to his cabins. Lewrie tried hard not to glare them all to scorn for a last stinging defiance. Once more he had been bested, scoffed at! And it stung like the very blazes!

CHAPTER TWENTY-THREE

*A*nother bleak morning, another bleak walk after breakfast, upon his usurped quarterdeck, with hands shrinking away from him when he got near them. And, Lewrie sighed in frustration, another damned longboat coming alongside, which had left HMS *Sandwich* minutes before. And, he feared, another harangue by the Fleet Delegates, another excuse for the crew to sing, caper, and tweak their noses at him! A ragged side-party turned out to welcome the visitor; and Bales, Handcocks, Morley, and Kever turned up to greet him. Hands engaged in the task of scrubbing and sluicing the decks, tensioning the shrouds and stays, paused from their labours to see what the occasion was. Rather blearily, Lewrie thought. There seemed to be even more women aboard than the evening before, more strange new faces yawning over mugs of small beer drunk to cut the alcoholic fog from all they'd taken aboard in the previous night's revelries below decks.

Thankfully, it was only a minor functionary this time, Lewrie saw, a common seaman bearing a note. He'd barely gained the gangway and handed the note over to Bales, shared a quiet word with him, then he was off once more, back over the side and into the boat.

"Bosun, pipe 'All Hands'!" Bales shouted. "Don't stand there with yer mouth agape, Mister Pendarves. Don't look to Captain Lewrie when I give you an order, damn yer eyes, he's not in charge here. *I'm* in temporary command. Pipe 'All Hands,' then 'Hands to Stations For Getting Underway!' "

Sounds like an officer, Alan thought; where'd he learn that?

Pendarves was looking up from the waist to the quarterdeck, in a quandary as to what to do. Sitting and waiting for the mutiny to be settled was one thing; getting up the anchors and making sail sounded like a dangerous escalation of this crisis!

" 'Vast, there, Mister Pendarves!" Lewrie barked. "Bales! You will not endanger my ship by getting sail on her. That's beyond your brief. By God, sir . . . explain yourself and be quick about it!"

"Aye, I'll explain myself, sir," Bales shot back, stung to the quick for a rare once; his smirky, superior demeanour pierced. "The ship is ordered to shift her anchorage into the Great Nore."

"Not by any authority I recognize, Bales," Lewrie hooted. "She stays where she is."

"Damn you, Pendarves . . . pipe 'All Hands On Deck!' " Bales roared, as he and his minions stalked from the gangway to the quarterdeck.

"That's *Mister* Pendarves, Seaman Bales," Lewrie corrected, with a great deal of glee for an opportunity to gall the man. "I do believe your Fleet Delegates ordered you to show respect to superiors. Surely, you're capable of following a simple directive . . . ?"

"*Mister* Pendarves, pipe 'All Hands,' " Bales was forced to amend, reddening with anger, "and my pardons to you."

"Sir?" Pendarves said, looking to Lewrie still.

"Proceed, Mister Pendarves," Lewrie allowed lightly.

The more witnesses, the merrier, he silently smirked; *t'see this shitten louse get taken down a peg'r two. I've got to him at last, in public! Stung him so deep, he might make another error?*

The Bosun dutifully sounded the call, and the hands below, with their hung-over "wives," came shambling up into the fresh air, looking as if sunlight and a fresh breeze didn't much agree with them.

"Lads, the Fleet Delegates've sent us a message!" Bales cried.

And Lewrie was pleased to note how much they lacked enthusiasm for that news this early in the morning! Too many special messages, he hoped, too many excuses for ranting speeches, stirring orations, or declarations already?

"Ahem . . . ' . . . to temporary "Captain" Bales, in command of HMS *Proteus* . . . you are required and directed to shift your anchorage from Garrison Point to a position among the Nore Fleet, exercising all due care and caution in the selection of your anchorage . . . ,' " Bales read aloud.

"Dangerous ground, Bales," Lewrie loudly sneered, "your Fleet Delegates parroting real orders . . . they've no power to 'require or direct.' Nor do you. Pretending to be Admiralty or government will cost 'em dear . . . cost *you* dear, and any man who pretends to obey such . . . !"

"We'll take that risk!" Bales snarled back at him, just as loudly. "Fleet Delegates wish us to shift to the Great Nore; then that is where we go . . . sir! Beyond the reach of the fortress guns and such!"

"Out where men who disagree with you and your floating 'Parliament' can't desert, you mean!" Lewrie shot back.

"Go below, Captain." Bales flushed once more, striving to keep his temper. "You've no say in this, no vote."

"You'd shift this ship without putting it to a vote!" Lewrie retorted with a tongue-in-cheek twinkle. "What say you, lads? Do you *want* to be that far from shore, on *his* mere say-so? . . . Fire on civilians ashore later? Sail to bloody France later, just 'cause he . . . !"

"Enough, damn you!" Bales screeched, prodded into fury at last and instantly regretting it, for the low murmur of shock that arose on deck from the waiting hands. "Mister Handcocks," Bales said, calming, "men to the quarterdeck to see the Captain below! And see he remains there 'til I give him leave!"

"Here now, Bales," Pendarves called up from the waist, "ya lay hands on a Commission Officer, and everyone's doomed t'hang alongside ya. Ya swore this'd be peaceful, respectful . . ."

"And it is, Mister Pendarves!" Bales countered. "But for *this* . . . but for the Captain's objections. It's my responsibility. I take it on myself. We're peaceable, so far. I ask you, though . . . who among us is the one trying to stir us up, turn us 'gainst each other, except for the Captain? Any dispute amongst us 'tis his doing! Now, Brother Seamen! We'll go to stations . . . get the anchors up, make sail!"

Handcocks had summoned half-a-dozen hands, the hardest, meanest, and most dedicated to the Cause. Lewrie contemplated further resistance, of taking a cuff or two, perhaps a full beating from them, to spur his crew to mutiny against the mutineers, if that's what it took!

"You'll need the officers," Lewrie suggested slyly, yielding not a single inch, "if you're determined to move this ship."

"Nossir, we do not!" Bales snapped. "We've senior mates aboard, experienced sailors. I've served as Quartermaster and Master's Mate before. I think we're perfectly capable of sailing two miles and taking a new anchorage . . . without the help of you or your officers! Now, pipe 'Hands to Stations,' Mister Pendarves! Jump to it, lads! Sir . . . Captain Lewrie, sir, I'll thank you to leave the quarterdeck. Else whatever befalls you will be your own fault," he added, much softer.

"And none o' *yours*, of *course*, Seaman Bales!" Lewrie sneered, secretly gloating that he'd finessed this nigh to the crucial confrontation that would break the back of the crew's apathy, put steel into the spines of those wavering . . . "Well, if you and the rest of your mutineers are so damn' capable, why don't you put us ashore before you guarantee the noose around your bloody neck!" he hissed with pleasure.

Bales did the very worst thing then, to Lewrie's lights. That subtle bastard regained his composure, stepped so close that Lewrie could smell the reek of his unwashed shirt, and smiled quite malevolently.

"So that's what you wish, is it, Captain?" he whispered. "Well, you'll not get it. Oh no, not you, most of all. I've *plans* for you, I have! No matter how the mutiny falls out. Now, would you be so good as to get your arse off *my* quarterdeck? Out of the way of sailors who know what they're about? Mister Handcocks, see 'im below. Be gentle with 'im, but not too gentle, hey?"

Of all the low lifes they could have clasped hands with, there was Haslip with Handcocks's party of enforcers, with his hand upon the hilt of his (so-far) sheathed clasp knife, with an expression of pure hatred and revenge on his phyz for his ravaged back.

Taking a cuff or two, getting his eyes blacked, or spouting claret from a smashed nose, well . . . that was one thing. Getting his gizzards spilled by a mutineer's knife was quite another! For one, there'd be no opportunity to savour his testimony, or the joy of watching these people go for the high jump from the gallows! For the first time, he felt a *frisson* of pure fear! This mutiny could end a lot bloodier than anyone intended or expected. *His* blood, in point of fact!

"Will ya go below, Cap'um, sir?" Mr. Handcocks asked, seeming about as shaken as Lewrie was that he was offering a threat of violence to an officer. " 'Fore, uhm . . ." he gulped, shifty-eyed.

"For now, Mister Handcocks," Lewrie allowed after glaring hot (and taking several temporising, restoring deep breaths). "For you, sir. *You've* done nothing worthy of hanging for . . . yet," Lewrie lied.

"Aye, sir. Thankee, sir," Handcocks muttered, sounding almost grateful. "We should go, sir," he prompted, as Pendarves and Towpenny reluctantly piped the call which Bales had bade them, amidst the scamper and thunder of feet heading for the capstan, the messenger cables, the nippers, and the shrouds which led aloft to the yards.

They paced aft to that companionway ladder near the taffrails once more, in silence as the afterguard trudged to the kedge anchor cable, to the jears and halliards for the mizzen tops'l and spanker.

"I don't know what led you to take part in mutiny, Mister Handcocks," Lewrie said in a low voice, "what grievances you had that stirred you to rise up 'gainst lawful authority, or take such a *prominent* part in it. How long you helped its planning . . ."

Handcocks merely breathed hard, his gaze fixed shoreward.

"But I warn you now, Mister Handcocks," Lewrie whispered, "it is getting out of hand. It's grown a life of its own, and you have no control over it. Do you have any real say in the ship's committee, it might be best did you speak out for temperance. Threatening a captain will lead to blood, sooner or later. First we move out of gun-range. Next time, will it be the Texel? A French port? Out to fight Channel Fleet . . . now they're restored to duty?"

"Sure I don't know, sir." Handcocks groaned, sounding strangled.

"Maybe we're being shifted 'cause Parker, Bales, and their lot're afraid of sensible hands taking the Spithead offer," Lewrie suggested. "So they don't lose control . . .'cause that's not what their paymasters want . . . a settlement. Their *foreign* paymasters, Mr. Handcocks."

"Sir, if ya *please!*" Handcocks begged as they got to the top of the companionway, all but wringing his hands in abject misery.

"Mister Handcocks, Bales has more in mind than redress of your so-called grievances," Lewrie intimated, striving to sound "matey" and concerned. "Ask yourself what that could be. His dislike of me, however—though I can't recall ever meeting the man before—one would think he held a *personal* hatred. Whatever it is, Mister Handcocks, don't be too caught up in it. This could gallop out of control in the blink of an eye! The Spithead offer . . . it's fair. 'Twixt you and me, I'll say it was overdue, aye. But it's all you're going to get. Don't lose your Warrant . . . or your head . . . asking for a jot more. Or let things turn violent, hmmm?"

"If you'd go below now, sir, Cap'um, sir," Handcocks replied, wincing and bobbing his head in agony. Lewrie gave him a hearty clap of sympathy on the shoulder to buck him up.

And if that didn't light a fire under his "nutmegs," Lewrie told himself, once below and out of sight, I don't know what will. And if he can't take a hint, then to the Devil with him!

"Brandy, Aspinall . . . brimmin'," Lewrie called.

"Aye, sir . . . comin' directly."

'Twas a near-run thing I didn't get beaten senseless, Lewrie had to admit to himself; pushed it almost too far, I did. But at least I made Bales an ogre to the hands; gave 'em another think about how dangerous this is. Put caution in Handcocks, a few others . . . ?

Hmmm . . . this Bales, now . . . Lewrie thought as his brandy came.

He'd revealed that he'd served as a Quartermaster and Master's Mate at one time; might have aspired to Admiralty Warrant as a Sailing Master too? Lewrie pondered, idly pacing his cabins. Must've blotted his copybook though, or lost his patrons when turned over into a new ship . . . lost his rate when a new captain had come aboard with his own favourites in tow.

That would explain his grudge against the Navy, Lewrie decided, but . . . he threatened me, directly! As if I owe him for something from his past? And he'll make me pay, no matter what happens, will he?

"For the life of me, I can't recall . . . !" Lewrie grumbled.

"Sir?"

"Nothing, Aspinall . . . just maundering."

Scotching the cries for putting me ashore . . . as if he's savin' me for something, well . . . Lewrie scowled in thought; *best for him, if he did! I get under his skin, row him to rashness . . . expose his weaknesses or his true motives. Reverse our positions and* he'd *be ashore, in irons, quick as you could say "Jack Ketch!" After a keehaulin' . . . or two.*

It would be so easy for Bales to hide in the Navy, even was he a *Bounty* mutineer! There were hundreds of "jumpers" who enlisted over and over, gave false names to a ship's first officer, got the Joining Bounty, then scampered, to try it on again. And what would he look like without that full beard of his, Lewrie wondered?

And why, in this particular incarnation, did Bales pass himself off as "Bales"—if former deserter, malefactor, or mutineer, he was? Had he served under the unfortunate old man; had he been aboard hard-luck *Ariadne* during the Revolution? Bales appeared to be in his mid-to-late thirties . . . old enough to have been a teenaged topman or cabin servant back then. Hmmm . . . that bore some thinking about.

"Christ!" Lewrie suddenly gasped, coming out of his dark study.

Proteus was underway, her hull timbers beginning to creak as she worked, slightly canted by the wind . . . underway under the charge of the common seamen! And that bastard Bales, or whomever he was!

Lewrie dashed to his after-companionway ladder, rushed up it, to stick his head above the hatch coaming. There was no sentry to detain him, so he cautiously climbed further, to take stance beside the flag lockers at the taffrail and sternpost, expecting the very worst.

Unfortunately, nothing was out of order.

She was well in-hand, under tops'ls, spanker and inner and outer jibs, everything Bristol fashion. And Bales stood with his hands in the small of his back, amidships of the quarterdeck, looking upward and outward with the cool professionalism of the saltiest watch-officer.

It seemed that the mates, the common seamen, *could* sail her . . . anywhere they wished, Lewrie grudgingly decided: Holland, France, over to Ireland . . . the Great South Seas if they bloody wished!

"Damme," Lewrie whispered, slinking below before anyone spotted him and hooted in derision at his surprise and disappointment.

BOOK FOUR

Tua nunc terris, tua lumina toto sparge mari;
seu nostra dolos molitor opertos sive externa manus,
primus mihi nuntius esto.

Cast now thine eyes upon the land, upon all the sea;
whether it be men of my own land or strangers
that are planning secret treachery,
be first to bear me news.
— ARGONAUTICA, BOOK V, 246–49
VALERIUS FLACCUS

CHAPTER TWENTY-FOUR

*I*f *Proteus* had lacked information before, her isolation became even worse once the mutinous fleet had shifted out to the Great Nore. Their "Parliament" had already banned letters to or from shore. Now, 'tween-ship visiting, which was usually allowed, had been cancelled as well. Oh, there was still visiting; but it was done by the representatives from the "Parliament" ship, HMS *Sandwich* alone, the daily parade of rowing boats filled with cheering leaders and sycophants, accompanied by noisy ships' bands, and a sea of gay flags.

Monday the twenty-ninth had been Restoration Day, and to celebrate King Charles II's return to the throne after the end of commoners' rule, the mutiny ships had fired the usual 19-gun salutes and hoisted the royal standards for a time, though the weather was cold and gloomy, blowing half a gale of wind off the North Sea, even harbour waves high enough to stir and rock the line-of-battle ships like fishing smacks. A rather *odd* act, Lewrie had thought, for a pack of mutineers hellbent on *hanging* the monarch, to read their truculent diatribes!

But there had been no Rope-Yarn Day after, no special feasts, no libertymen allowed ashore to carouse and toast the King in the pubs. Once the royal standards had been lowered, they had returned to a lack-lustre waiting, and workaday chores of ship-keeping.

Rumours, mostly third- or fourth-hand, spoke of President Parker and the Fleet Delegates meeting ashore with the Lords Commissioners of the Admiralty . . . others spoke of pilots called aboard to steer them to France . . . six months' arrears in pay to be settled on the morrow . . . the only thing sure was that no one but Parker and the other leading negotiators, and their boat-crews, were allowed liberty in Sheerness. Delegates had made the rounds, dictating a new "regulation" that said a man must apply to the Fleet Delegates for a pass, after approval by his own ship's committee, and the matter decided by Parker himself!

Anchored that far out, the mutineers had also lost the services of the many vendors' bumboats, their pastries, meat-pies, gew-gaws, or smuggled spirits; the shoes, shirts, and slop-clothing better than what Mr. Coote offered; the tobacco, sweets, or treats that sailors bought to liven the dull sameness of ship's fare. Though some pedlars tried to make the long row or sail out to the mutineer ships, their numbers were not a third of the usual, or previous, days.

One thing Lewrie had determined by keeping an eager ear open to the complaints of his crew; what Joining Bounty they had gotten as volunteers had already been spent on slop stores; what little they'd hoarded for contingencies had gone for the wild sprees that had followed the mutiny's eruption. The poor bastards were broke! The bumboaters couldn't squeeze a single farthing more from them; and, expecting the worst from an impatient government, were not of a mind to extend them any credit against future pay vouchers either!

Now that they were reduced to plain commons and the skimpy daily rum issue, whole days of skylarking, hornpiping, and delegates' shouted harangues could not relieve the monotony of Navy routine. Resentments arose too over how long this mutiny of theirs might take before winning the wished-for results; most especially, they resented the strident militancy and "high-flown airs" of the Fleet Delegates of their brand-new "Floating Republic."

And the women . . . ! Lewrie could recall, hugging himself with joy. Article the Third of their compact declared that ". . . no woman shall be permitted to go on shore from any ship, but as many may come as please." When they had been anchored hard by Garrison Point, that had been a lark. Now, though, the women were becoming burdensome, one more irritant.

Proteus had over an hundred "live-lumber," not two dozen of 'em authentic wives who had come out to stand by their real husbands. No, the rest were Sheerness or Chatham whores, the hired doxies and drabs brought out in the bumboats by brothel-keepers, pimps, or boatmen, who got a share of their earnings in return for "passage." The hands *had* been eager to speak up and claim the prettiest and cleanest, youngest and most fetching, declaring them "wives" who'd turned up to stay with them whilst in harbour, to be "kept" on their money and rations. Even some of the most raddled, who were normally turned away, had remained, knowing that someone less choosy would turn up after a few hours down on the gun-deck, and all that semi-public rutting to whet appetites or remove fears; and even honest married men might succumb, the young and inexperienced turned heady with lust! They'd not been turned away by the Surgeon, Mr. Shirley, and his mates, so they weren't "poxed" so . . .

They would usually stay aboard as long as a ship was at anchor and Out of Discipline, as long as their "husbands" had money for their sexual favours and upkeep . . . and not a single minute more.

Now the "fairer sex," even the frailest, sweetest, and prettiest (and there were damned few of those to start with!), were sniping and snarling over being "press-ganged" without pay! They were definitely *not* a pack of shrinking violets to be put off, stalled, or "used," without solid coin either. Born with, or developing by necessity, a grave-digger's chary soul, the average sailor's doxy was a flinty chit, no one to trifle with! Coquetry and languid, lash-fluttering charms of perfumed London courtesans, shammed passion and affection were beyond them. Mostly it was, "Hoy, Jack . . . wanna poke?"

Now, without money to earn, without civilian fripperies off the mostly absent bumboats, kept from leaving as strictly as the sailors, and now reduced to the same salt-rations, tile-hard ship's biscuit, the same pease porridge and already semi-rancid Navy-issue cheese, and with but a *sip* of small beer or a *share* of their "man's" watered grog, they posed a greater threat of *counter*-mutiny than anything Lewrie or his officers could conjure up! Clearly, the "honeymoon" was over. He snickered in private and schemed upon how to turn it to his advantage!

⚓

Lewrie paced the larboard gangway for exercise, all the way to the bower
anchor cat-heads and the break of the forecastle; 'round the belfry, then
down the starboard gangway, aft to the quarterdeck and the traffrails, to
begin another circuit. To be seen by his men, unruffled, calm, and serene,
no matter his predicament; to point out things needing trimming or re-
roving, a lick of paint or tar, to the mates and leading hands; reinforcing
his authority. . . . and eliciting information.

"Mornin', Mash . . . bearin' up?" He would brighten whenever he en-
countered a face he could put name to in his raw, new crew. "Mornin',
Landsman Furfy . . . mornin', Landsman Lucas . . . Bannister. Christ, what
an eye, man! Run into a rammer in the dark, did you?"

"Run outta money, sir . . .'en run into th' wrong drab, sir," the sailor
griped, daubing at his impressive "shiner" with a soggy neckerchief.

"Knocked 'im flatter'n a flounder, sir," Middle Grace chuckled. "Ah, a
fearsome woman. Not one t'cross, Cap'um, sir," he said with a jut of his
chin towards the blowsy blonde who'd mocked Lewrie before.

"Nancy, sir," she named herself, swaying her broad hips at him as she
paced over near the bottom of the gangway lip below him, putting on a
lascivious air (out of hard-drilled habit, Lewrie suspected).

"Aye, I put him down, the 'skint' pup!" she boasted, hands on her hips,
and leaning forward to sport her ample bosom at him. "Ya give me a
dozen lashes, Cap'um? Or a dozen o' somethin' *else'd* be yer pleasure?"

"And my dear wife'd black both *my* eyes, Nancy," Lewrie quipped.

"Give a poor girl a chance, Cap'um!" She pouted, with what she must
have imagined was an enticing note to her voice. "None o' yer lads've
two pence t'rub t'gither . . ."

"You leave 'em anything to rub at *all*, Mistress Nancy?" Lewrie was
quick to reply, enjoying the banter with her. "Even a nubbin?"

By God, scrubbed up, she don't look half *bad!* he thought; tad stout,
but that's teats an' hips, mostly. Blonde, pretty-ish . . . *Gawd!*

She threw her head back and cackled, *proud* that she'd "rubbed" at least
one, two—a half-dozen of his hands down to "nubbins" before they'd run
out of coin. Brassy, bold, fresh-faced, totally amoral . . .

Was a time, 'twas my favourite sort, he told himself!

"Wager *you've* more'n a nubbin in yer britches, Cap'um, sir!" she suggested, drawing a chorus of "ooohs" from the hands nearby. "Care t' *spank* me fer bein' mean t'yer men? Handsome officer like yerself, I'd even enjoy it . . . nor charge ye much, darlin'!"

"Now how could I do that, Mistress Nancy?" Lewrie felt obliged to pout in disappointment. "And a firm, spankable bum I'm certain you own too. But . . . like you say, now the hands are 'skint' . . . how fair d'ye think it'd be for me to savour what the lads no longer can?"

Damme, bet it is! he all but salivated; *now, let's see what they think o' that? Aha! Sage nods . . . bless me . . . old "firm but fair!"*

"Dammit t'Hell, Cap'um . . ." Nancy groaned, swiping at her hair irritatedly, " 'thout they let me'un t'other girls ashore, how am I to keep meself?"

"Well, you've what you've earned . . . to spend on the bumboats," Lewrie suggested, " 'til they let you and the rest go. Did you spend that well . . . there's Bales and the other committeemen. They've still got coin, I'll wager. Planned this for a long time? Probably laid a store o'money aside for it."

"Them with the green cockades?" Nancy sneered, spitting on the deck in derision. "Mouths, they got! Fine words. No nutmegs though. Too busy t'even play wif their *own* cocks!"

Another hearty laugh, this one directed at their "betters." Oh, trust a leery, chary English sailor to turn on those over them as soon as they began to put on the "Qualities' " airs. There was an inbred deference to your average Englishman, be he tar or rural day-labourer, a costermonger or house-servant. He would doff his hat, knuckle at his forelock, and scrape out a bow to gentlemen and ladies; and most of the time (as long as orders were reasonable) would obey. He had trouble with obedience though, when it came to being bossed about by those no grander than he was—or who had risen from *his* level to greatness.

Officers and midshipmen, sailing masters, and surgeons were from the Quality, the squirearchy or aristocracy, the upper level of middling rank—used to being obeyed, and the sailors were used to obeying, and even expected "the Better Sort" to make the decisions. Now, though . . . Another reason for resentment, Lewrie schemed.

Nancy, encouraged by the laughter her comment had got, hoisted the skirts of her gaudy sack gown to display her calves. They were bare, instead of sheathed in the usual cotton or opaque silk stockings . . . slimmer and more alluring than he'd suspected! Clean, too; not smutted with tar or soot. Rather cunning little feet . . . !

"Not even a thumb-worth, Mistress Nancy?" Lewrie pretended to gawp in astonishment. "Not even a nubbin? *Less* than a nubbin? Damme, ye don't think they traded 'wedding-tackle' for green cockades, hey?"

They made sure that every man had pledged fidelity, gave oaths as firm as wedding vows, and sported the red cockade of rebellion . . . but then said that *red* cockades must respect *green* cockades as their superiors—as good as officers.

Nancy gave out a shriek of mirth, which made the rest feel free to roar their appreciation of his jest too.

"Hoy, then!" another harridan bellowed from below him, this one a much fiercer old bulldog, practically towing a rather pretty younger miss with her by the hand. "Daughter'un me, fine sir! Damn my eyes, I won't let *her* spread fer free, nor lift *my* skirts fer nothin' neither! Th' skipper o' this here barge, are ye? Well then, 'thout you pay us t'stay, give us a boat t'go ashore, ya tight-fisted bastard!"

And then, Lewrie sighed, there *were* some who'd skipped classes the day they took up "Deference."

"I have no control over that, Mistress," Lewrie told her, taking off his hat and laying it over his heart to show the old strumpet just how sincere he was. And giving the old bat's fifteen-year-old *protégé* a *good* going over with his glims! "The fellow calls himself 'captain' of 'this-here barge' . . . for now . . . is named Bales. You'd have to take it up with him and his committee. You want pay, you'd best ask of them to give you your daily bread . . . and your daily shilling. Or a boat."

"What good're the likes o' you, then!" the old woman scoffed.

" 'Til this crew accepts the Spithead terms, the pardon, and returns to discipline, ma'am," Lewrie informed her, "there's nought that I can do . . . not with a pistol to my head or a knife in my ribs, I cannot. Me, I'd be happy to oblige you and put you ashore with all your earnings, where you can buy yourself and charming daughter a meal and a bottle, when you wish. But . . ." He shrugged most eloquently. And sadly doffing his hat and making a departing "leg" to Hoary Harridan, Bountiful Nancy, and the Unknown but Luscious Little'un, he departed.

With the gay sounds of curses, slurs, demands, and arguments in his shell-like ears!

Another bloody fire lit, he sniffed; now let's just see who gets scorched by it!

Hands who now couldn't afford to put the leg over, but presented with (mostly) desirable pulchritude everywhere they looked; real wives who wished the paid variety off, 'cause their husbands still had money and didn't need the temptations trolling about for tuppence; mutineer leaders maligned, and another resentment, and suspicion, raised against them. Did they *really* have some hoarded coin and took time from their incessant preaching of mutiny and rebellion to put the leg over one of the whores— especially one of the prettier ones—themselves?

And the disgruntled, "impressed" whores . . . ?

Oh, we're a happy *little ship, we are!* Lewrie chortled silently, *a "tiddly" little ship!*

CHAPTER TWENTY-FIVE

*A*nd, by the time eight bells of the Forenoon Watch had finished chiming, Lewrie was quite pleased to see that *Proteus* had been given a new cause for upset.

The hands had queued up at seven bells, when "Clear Decks and Up Spirits" had been piped for the grog issue. A keg of rum so stout it was almost pitchy-dark and treacly had been fetched up; decorated with yellow paint, the Navy seal, and the ancient motto, "The King God Bless Him." With it had come a butt of water, and the miniature mugs; to be mixed and diluted two-for-one, which would yield each hand the equivalent of a half-pint of grog—all carefully guarded and administered by the Master At Arms and Ship's Corporals, the Purser, and Mr. Shirley the Surgeon. Mutineers or not, the ritual was not to be tinkered with, for sailors were a conservative lot, as ill-suited as a cat to a sudden change in daily routine or surroundings. The new leaders aboard, obeying the stricture in their compact to respect officers and their orders, clung to the notices on the watch-and-quarter bills as to how much grog each man should get; was someone being punished by deprivation; and the agreements among the hands themselves as to whether another got not only his own, but "sippers" or "gulpers" of another man's for sewing up slop-trousers to a better fit, standing a watch, making a useful article, or settling wagers between them.

Usually, it was a cheerful time when the crew lined up to take their ration, jealously watching for the slightest shortage when their measure was poured out. It signalled the end of the morning's exercise at sail-drill, small arms, or gun-drill, and the onset of their midday meal. For rum issue, the off-going watch and the on-coming both mingled for a while, crowding them all forrud toward the foc's'le belfry.

This time, it was even more crowded, as wives, children, and the whores gathered round for their share, wheedling, whining, bawling, or cajoling. If the men didn't have money anymore, at least they had rum to offer— the whores'd settle for that.

"How *are* we fixed for rum, Mister Coote?" Lewrie enquired.

"Twelve weeks' worth, sir . . . at normal rates of issue. Longer, did we water it at three-to-one," the Purser answered crisply, knowing his sums to the groat. "We did not receive our total due before . . ."

"Which'd be cause for mutiny of itself, sir," Lt. Langlie said.

"The pigs," Midshipman Peacham felt free to interject.

"Pigs . . . ah," Lewrie breezed on, as if he hadn't a care in the world. "Reminds me; thankee, Mr. Peacham. Speaking of trough, Mister Coote, how stands our food supply, then?"

"Nigh on the full sixteen weeks, Captain, sir," Mr. Coote told them. "Depending on whether we are responsible for victualling the dependents. With them aboard, sir . . . more like ten weeks' worth. Nine . . . are we profligate."

"Then this could go on forever," Lt. Ludlow gloomed. He'd not made many appearances lately, and when he had attended officers' meetings he'd kept his own counsel, merely frowning, glowering, or grimacing without venturing either opinions or suggestions, or any comments that hadn't been elicited by a direct question. He'd not kept up his toilet either, Lewrie noted. Ludlow's waist-coat was dingy with smut and food-stains, his shirt tanned at collar and cuffs from long wear, and his beard stubble a light coal-dust smear on his chin and cheeks.

"No, not forever, Mister Ludlow," Lewrie countered. "Did any of you take a gander at the shore today? Note what's happening in Sheerness?"

"Uhm . . . that it seems rather quiet, sir?" Midshipman Catterall ventured, "without the seamen allowed ashore . . ."

"Do you lift a telescope, you'll find some pleasing sights ashore." Lewrie beamed. "Now let me ask you all another question . . . What will be served for dinner?"

"Sir?" Had he been driven daft by the mutiny was the look they shared; had *Proteus* stolen the wits of another captain?

"What's cooked for the hands' dinner, Mister Coote?"

"Uhm . . . the usual Tuesday *rota*, sir. Pound of biscuit and two pounds of salt-beef per man per day," the Purser informed him.

"No shore 'Tommy' . . . no beeves or hogs for slaughter," Lewrie pointed out. "Nor will there be in future. Vice-Admiral Buckner and Commissioner Hartwell have not seen fit to deliver fresh victuals out to the ships this morning. Really, gentlemen, you should take more notice of things around you," he chid them with mock severity, tsking a time or two with a sly leer. "Do you look shoreward, you will see soldiers and workmen atop the forts . . . mending what's been neglected for far too long, I shouldn't wonder. Troops of militia and regulars patrolling the streets? Standing guard over the dockyards and quays? You could espy civilians departing . . . evacuated or of their own accord. Oh, there'll be some tavern keepers and whoremongers who stay and reap the bounty from all these soldiers. Soldiers, gentlemen," he said, beaming his delight, "most-like with orders to arrest any mutineer who gets ashore, to cut them off completely. I believe Our Lords Commissioners *have* been down to Sheerness and told Parker and his men to get stuffed! Perhaps it wasn't our *mutineers'* idea to avoid shore, hey? And, gentlemen . . . do you look close, you may see some activity, just a bit upriver of Garrison Point. Boats working . . . looking very much to me as if they're laying a stouter boom across the Medway."

His suppositions *sounded* inspiriting; they all seemed to perk up—yet didn't dash to the bulwarks that instant, looking hesitant. Tell *me what I'm s'posed to think*, Lewrie sighed to himself; *I swear, what a pack of cod'swallops!*

There was a glad interruption from up forrud. Some hands were squabbling over the rum issue! One man had offered half his ration to a whore, but it sounded as if he already owed "gulpers" to one of his messmates, who wasn't going to be shorted. Neither would the doxy take less than a *full* half of a half!

"Don't you see, gentlemen?" he posed to them. "This isn't any fun anymore. They've had their Rope-Yarn days, their drunks, their ruts. They're as broke as convicts. No more skylarking ashore, and no more fresh food either. No more quim, 'less they resort to rape. Have to live on sea-rations, share spirits and victuals with women they can't have, 'less they trade food or drink. Too many mouths aboard and short-commons, if this goes on much longer. Anchored out where it's boresome and there's nothing to do but stew and fret 'bout what Admiralty's doing, when it's going to end. And *how*. Now do you take pains to make 'em see what's going on ashore . . . and why . . ."

"Undermine their morale, sir!" Catterall piped up, tumbling to it at last. "So they give it up, take the pardon . . ."

"So *close* to the Queen's Channel too, Mister Catterall," Lewrie muttered, stepping into the taut half-circle of officers, warrants, and junior petty officers. "Where a crew, a ship, did they get fearful or their commitment to the mutiny had begun to waver . . . might think that escape from the Nore might be the best choice, sirs. As a way to take the Spithead terms, the pardon . . . and signal their denial of the mutiny by a return to duty. *Sea*-duty! God bless the mutinous members of our little . . . 'Parliament,' " he sneered. "Putting us where it'd be easier to sail off . . . when we re-take the ship, sirs."

Mouths gapped even wider, as jaws dropped at the idea. Sneaky grins replaced puzzlement.

"With two two-deckers anchored near us, sir," Lieutenant Ludlow said, with a sneer of hopelessness, "upper-deck gun-ports open and primed to fire on any ship that shows a scrap of sail, tries to up-anchor . . ."

"Damme, Mister Ludlow," Lewrie scoffed. "And here I thought *you* were the firebrand, determined to draw blood t'other day."

"When it seemed we had a *chance* to keep the ship, sir," Ludlow shot back. "Not just surrender her like a craven . . . !"

"Consider yourself under arrest, sir!" Lewrie barked, suddenly fed up with the man. "Go below and confine yourself . . . and your insolence . . . to your cabin! By *God*, you go too far, sir! *Have* done since I came aboard."

Ludlow's jaw found cause to drop, and he visibly paled, like to faint. He seemed to reel or stagger, whether to fall to his knees in apoplexy or take a damning step forward to threaten a superior officer, it could be taken either way. Marine Lt. Devereux reached out to take him by the upper arm, to support or restrain him, this could be taken either way too. "You . . . !" Ludlow blustered. "Now see here, sir . . . ! Ah . . . I see, sir. Un-hand me, you tailor's dummy! Ah. Ah. Very well, sir. I will, as always, obey my captain's orders, sir."

"Very good, sir," Lewrie sniped through hair-thin lips. "Then kindly do as I have ordered, Mister Ludlow."

Ludlow had mastered himself, had control of his body once more, though he never would learn how to conceal the emotions that erupted on his phyz, and those were stony and bloody! He doffed his hat and made a leg in a most-formal *congé,* then turned on his heel to stamp away, after sharing a bleak but knowing look with Midshipman Peacham.

"Uhm, sir"—Lt. Langlie whispered, after a long, embarrassed silence—"though he stated his case, uhm, well, insolently, there *is* the problem of those two-deckers and their guns."

"I doubt they keep a zealous watch, Mister Langlie," Lewrie muttered back. "Too bored. We've not held sail-drill lately, or had our people at the artillery. With the shore cut off from them and our mutinous committee worried, suggestions from us as to drilling back to passing competence might find a welcome ear. No shot, no powder in the guns, but . . . ? Make and furl sail; put men aloft on the yards? If we do it often enough, then it may not draw much attention when we do it for our escape. When we cut our cables."

"No pilot aboard, sir," Mr. Winwood pointed out, lowering his voice to a conspirator's hiss. "Tricky passage: shoals, sands, flats where we could run aground."

"But could you do it, Mister Winwood?"

"Aye, sir," Winwood allowed, and that rather reluctantly. It would be a perfect bitch did they take the ground, and under fire from a two-decker's heavy guns. "The tides, though. Do we sail out with the ebb to speed our way, it'd have to be in daylight, sir. The flood runs at night, and will take us into the Medway or Sheerness. Might be a safer escape, sir, if the government has garrisoned Sheerness 'gainst the mutineers retaking us. Dark as a boot, scudding off a North Sea blow, sir? Harder to shoot at."

"There is that, Mister Winwood," Lewrie allowed. "But we'd have to run past a *great* many ships before we got there. Here . . ."he said, casting a hand out toward the beckoningly empty eastern horizon, "we're less than a mile, mile-and-a-half . . . the Range-To-Random-Shot of an 18-pounder . . . from showing them a clean pair of heels. We're in the outer row of the Great Nore, less than a mile from the buoyed channel. Most of the other ships are streamin' back from a single bower. When the flood runs, they point outward. When the ebb runs, they're facing Sheerness. Sail exercise . . . make a slow way up to short stays, under reduced sail, then furl and fall back. Do that a few times each morning and, sooner or later, they'll take no more notice of us. But one time . . . the last time . . . we cut and keep on going. Turn of the tide, Mister Winwood? With a suitable slant o' wind? Do-able, d'ye think?"

"Aye, sir. Do-able," Winwood replied gravely. But with a nod of conviction and determination.

"The gunboats, sir . . ." Lt. Wyman enthused, almost hugging himself to contain his eagerness. "They've lost 'em, sir. There's no one to chase us, did we get a way on."

On Restoration Day, during the gale, when even massy two-deckers had been tossed about, the eight commandeered gunboats which had been stationed at either end of the fairly snug double crescent of warships had been all but swamped by breaking waves and had finally gone into the calmer waters of the Medway for shelter, just in time for Admiral Buckner to stir himself to action at last and take them away from the mutineers.

"Uhm . . . there is the additional problem of arms, sir," Marine Lt. Devereux sighed, pulling at his nose in thought. "Beyond our own, we've none. Though we *have* identified hands who remain loyal, and we know who supports the mutiny . . . would fight to keep the ship . . . we *are* a bit thin on the ground compared to their numbers. And they now are armed, sir."

Another pesky problem, that; Bales had finally tired of being denied the arms chest keys by Lewrie's aloof truculence and had torn the locks and hasps off the chests with crow-levers from among the gun tools hung over every mess table, to distribute muskets, pistols, and swords.

"Aye, they are, Lieutenant Devereux," Lewrie sombrely agreed. "But then . . . so are the loyal men. Damme, sir . . . they were forced to take the oath . . . they wear the red cockades, don't they? And so do a goodly number of the fearful and the un-committed who'd let themselves be blown will-he, nill-he by either faction. Let themselves be blown to sea, and out of danger, if it came to it. There's a mixture of all factions in every watch, good sir . . . every division or work-party. We know who the ringleaders are, who the firmest supporters are. Do we get the drop on them when the time is ripe, take the deck and keep a fair number of true mutineers below long enough . . ."

"Arms are common, aye, sir." Lt. Devereux pondered, his aristocratic features creased in thought as he pondered something pleasant, put his wits to work on a tactical situation, a lightning raid, a coup. "They *have* to allow all hands have arms, watch-and-watch. Else it . . ."

"Else it seems as if the real mutineers don't trust the rest." Lt. Langlie smirked. "And they can't have *that* sort of resentment in their ranks."

"As if they don't now, sir?" Midshipman Catterall quipped, in *sotto voce*.

"If they don't have it now, we could make sure they do soon," Lewrie hinted. "Do we drop a few sly rumours. There's grievances beyond the mutineers' demands aboard. We must exploit them. We *believe* we know who among the crew we can trust . . . those clever enough to keep mum 'til our time comes. Those who can chat up the rest and sow even more seeds of discontent. The mutineers have helped us in that."

It was goggling time for his officers again, one more reason to stare at him as if he'd grown antlers or broken out in purple blotches.

"They've cut off news from shore, d'ye see," Lewrie slyly explained. "No more rowing 'tween ships to visit cousins, brothers, or old shipmates either. What morale our people have is become entirely internal to *Proteus*. They're already showing signs of boredom with cheering and speechifying. Now what else d'ye think they could get hellish tired of . . . do we put our wits to it, hey?"

"When our chance comes then, sir . . ." Mr. Winwood gravely mused, "shouldn't we get the women and children off the ship? Out of the way of any fighting? It'll require some fighting, I expect, sir. Without their wives, and uhm . . . without the distracting, er . . . that is to say, entertaining presence of the, ah . . . them." Winwood flummoxed, trying to find a Christian way to name that which he disdained.

" 'Thout the whores an' strumpets, Mister Winwood?" Lewrie rephrased for him; taking a bit of joy in twitting the man by employing plainer terms.

"Ah . . . aye, sir." Winwood actually blushed. "Fallen women or not, sir, they are the frailer sex. T'ain't right for them to be exposed to violence, no matter their stripe or station. Without women aboard, would they not become even more dispirited with nothing to do but dwell upon their dismal situation? And I believe Mister Coote will bear me out that they *are* eating us out of house and home, sir. Week or two more of feeding useless mouths and we'll deplete our victuals. Then when we do cut free, we'd not be at our best state for duty."

"Hmmm . . ." Lewrie frowned in thought, clapping his hands in the small of his back and studying the toes of his boots, the tarred oakum seams in the quarterdeck planking. "No, Mister Winwood. Their being aboard and out of reach for want of money is troubling to our tars, so . . . we'll keep 'em as one more cause for upset. If they are eating us out of house and home, then Bales and Handcocks might put them on half-rations . . . put the whole crew on half-rations sooner or later. No quim *and* short-commons? Our jacks'll never stand for that! We've need of the whores, believe me."

CHAPTER TWENTY-SIX

A little after the midday meal had been served to the crew and they lazed in post-prandial ease for a half-hour (during which time the officers dined), Lewrie was surprised to hear a hail from an entry-port to an arriving boat—one which didn't draw the requisite cheers that the delegates prefered. He was making the best the best he could of his dinner, which wasn't much more than the same salt-beef that the hands had fed upon, and was more than happy to abandon the effort and saunter out on deck to satisfy his curiosity.

He was further surprised to see that a bumboat had come alongside. Mr. Morley of the ship's committee was speaking to the hopeful trader and summoning Bales to make the decision about letting strange people aboard. The boat's skipper was bowing, scraping, and gesticulating as humbly as a Levant rug-merchant, pointing overside and leering suggestively. Even *more* whores? Lewrie wondered.

His mate in the boat passed up a wooden cage in which several plump chickens resided, shedding feathers and dung as they swayed up on a light whip, and squawking their unwillingness to be so impressed into the Royal Navy. Their upset spurred other creatures into protests, and Lewrie heard the squeals of piglets. Drawn by gustatory fantasies, Lewrie drifted forrud, fingering his purse for ready coin.

"Well, damn th' authorities, says I!" The bumboatman was crying. "No man'll tell a Willis he can't sellta whoever he wishes, mate. Hoy there, Captain, sir! No more fresh stores t'come. Admiral saysta cut 'em off. Wager a plump hen'r two'd suit ya, sir, whilst yer forced t'wait. Yer officers, too, sir . . . hens, geese, a plump tom turkey fer th' gunroom? Roast piglet wi' cracklin's an' gravy by sundown, do ya buy this hour, sir. Loaf bread, sweet biscuits . . . fresh cheese that'll melt in yer mouth, sir. Hoy, now! Who'll buy . . . does *this'n* let me aboard, hey? Give a poor merchant a chance, willya?"

Full or not on Navy fare, the hands drifted over to see what he had, up on the gangway to peer over the bulwarks, or below its lip to grumble and insist that Bales let him come aboard. Most especially the whores.

"Might not see another, Brother Bales." Handcocks speculated. "Tyrants've most-like scared th' rest o' th' bumboatmen from tradin'. Threatened t'take away their permits, sure."

"Very well," Bales sighed. "No private spirits, mind. We've articles against it, Mister Willis," he warned the vendor. "You've no doxies in your boat, so I can't see the harm. Let him enter!" Bales decreed in a loud voice, like Moses reading the First Commandment, to a glad cheer from the bored crew and the deprived womenfolk.

Willis the vendor and several of his assistants clambered up to the gangway. Some of them descended into the waist to show off samples of their wares. Children began shrieking over gooey sweets or stickily sugared buns they wished. The warship's waist quickly became a village green on Market Day.

Willis the vendor came aft to confront Lewrie and the rest of his officers, who had come up fingering their own purses or delving in their breeches' pockets to purchase those luxuries which enlivened their own lives.

"Oh, sirs, I've so many fowl, I'm chicken-pore, an' they'll go for less'n anybody else'd charge ye, my Bible-oath 'pon it! T'others cut off from tradin' . . . skeered off from tradin' by that Admiral Buckner and that new Gen'r'l Grey just come t'Sheerness with all his soldiers?" The man bubbled most brightly. "Wines, sirs. Brandies, sirs. Not for the likes o' them lads down yonder, but off'cers can have private wine-stocks. Good vintages an' more'n reasonable. Here, Captain, sir. We see ya, all but slobb'rin' over these here fine shoats. Brace of them, good Captain, an' I swear ya could feast fer four days runnin'. Half-crown each, Captain, sir. A crown, th' pair."

"Damme, that's . . . *more'n* reasonable," Lewrie was forced to say.

"Bought up th' stock o' other vendors!" Lewrie could hear a vendor's assistant on the lower deck bawling the explanation. "Bought for a song, when they saw 'twas ruinous for 'em, th' craven poltroons! Bought cheap, sold cheap! Come one, come all. No pushin' there, lad!"

"I'll take the shoats," Lewrie said, looking for Aspinall to come and take charge of them and opening his purse for solid coin. "A brace of geese too. A full pound for all, is it?"

"An' here's yer change, good sir!" The vendor winked, handing Lewrie a folded square of paper. "Shame it is, good Englishmen forced t'use paper money, but there 'tis." He winked again.

Lewrie pocketed the note in his breeches and gave this fellow Willis a dumbstruck nod of understanding.

"No matter th' rest o' th' cowards, sir," Willis assured him, "you can count on Willis's fer *all* yer needs. Be back whene'er th' ole Nore weather allows me, sirs. Keep ya in yer best tucker. Cheer ya with spirits, as good as any fine merchant in London would, and so I will. Good as . . . Willis's *Rooms'd* treat a lodger such'z yerself."

"I know it well," Lewrie admitted with a nod, keeping a grin of comprehension from giving the game away. "But . . . ah . . . ?"

"Thought ya would, Captain Lewrie." This Willis whispered as he twisted his torso to one side to pocket more money from the other officers who'd made purchases. With another brief wink.

"You will come often then, I take it, sir?" Lewrie asked.

"Ev'ry t'other day, do th' weather allow, sir," Willis boasted in a normal voice.

"Good." Lewrie smiled. "I'd *hate* to be deprived out here. Of anything *needful*. A newspaper . . . ?"

"Next trip, sir, or my name's not Willis." The man guffawed, as if at a private jest. "*Zachariah* Willis."

"Ah!" Lewrie nodded, the scales of mystery torn from his eyes.

Of course, every arm of HM government had been sicced on this mutiny, on the Spithead mutiny before it. Nepean had said that agents working for the Duke of Portland, the King's "Witch-Finder" and seeker of dan-

gerous dissidents, had been delving 'round Portsmouth and Plymouth for
signs that the mutiny was foreign-sponsored.

Every arm of HM government, both the spiritual and temporal. Most-
like the Established Church of England had already sent out circulars to
every vicar, urging them to preach loyalty and obedience from their pulpits.
And should a tiny bureau of the Foreign Office be told to delve, to finagle,
undermine, and investigate—perhaps even go so far as to eliminate the
most infamous rabble-rousers, well . . .

Zachariah! A clue to Zachariah *Twigg*, that cold-blooded, ruthless old
cut-throat spy of Lewrie's long, painful, and dangerous association? In
the Far East 'tween the wars, the Ligurian Sea not so long ago in '95
and '96 . . . ! *Someone* official was establishing underground communication to him, to all captains who'd not been put off already. Looking for
information . . . imparting information, encouragement . . . orders? That
folded square of foolscap was burning a brand upon his thigh!

"Pity I have so little to give you, Mister Willis," Lewrie said with an apol-
ogetic shrug. "But I didn't anticipate your arrival. I b'lieve, though . . . when
next you call . . . I'll have a proper *list* of my wants and needs."

"Ah, that's th' spirit, Captain, sir!" Willis cackled with glee. "All brass-
bound Navy like. Can't scuttle 'cross a duck pond without a man havin'
his lists. An' I'll be honoured t'have 'em from ya," he hinted.

Lewrie's lips opened and he felt the urge to take the man by the arm
that instant to pump him for more information or tell him about the state
of the mutiny aboard *Proteus*. But this fellow who pretended to be Willis
took a half-step back, squinted in worry, and gave him a brief but vig-
ourous negative shake of his head.

"See some others've found th' courage t'come out an' trade with the
ships," Willis said instead, further pretending to frown, pointing outboard.
"Hope you'll not be fickle an' let just anybody come sell to ya, sir."

Lewrie looked outward. Despite the likelihood of decent profit, there did
seem to be an increase in the number of traders' bumboats by the other warships now. There were smaller row-boats from Sheerness, Minster, or Leigh
alongside some, crying their fresh-dredged oysters or fresh-caught fish.

"Thrivin' trade, sir," this Willis simpered, "d'spite prohibitions 'gainst it."

"Admiral Buckner's . . . or Parker's?" Lewrie muttered.

"Mum's th' word on that head, sir," Willis responded.

"Smugglin', are you?" Lewrie barked with amusement, and Willis looked like to about jump out of his skin in alarm. In point of fact, Lewrie suspected he had a poor repute with the Twiggs of this world; it was evident this man had been warned he was dealing with a loose-lip, a slender reed. Perhaps he'd been promoted to Nitwit, who was nowhere as clever as he thought himself.

"Well, damme..." Lewrie pretended to sigh in resignation. "How else'd I, or anyone in England, have our tea, silks, or lace without a smuggler at the root of it."

"Ah, ha!" Willis nervously laughed at that, all but shivering in relief (1) that Lewrie had grasped that the bumboats were indeed smuggling, but in the King's name; (2) that despite the reports, Lewrie *wasn't* a raving twit; and (3) that he hadn't gotten him killed—yet! "But a very English trade, sir, hey? 'Long as it *stays* solely English?" he purred in question. After he'd gotten his wits and control of his sphincter back, that is.

Which subtle query gave Lewrie pause. *Damme, this is gettin' a tad deep,* he thought; *bad as spoonin' up some willin' chit right under her husband's nose! How to say it? He's as good as put it to me direct: Is our mutiny home-grown or foreign-brewed? And what do I know?*

"Oh there may be interlopers, now and then, who hope to prosper at it," Lewrie cautiously replied, with wit enough to growl, indignant, "though not for very long. It's a home-grown trade mostly. That's to say, ah...uhmmm..." *Horse turds! Even I can't make sense of what I just told him!*

"Oh, exactly, sir," Willis said, his eyes hooding (and crossing in perplexity) as he could take no clue from that either. "Well, sir, take joy. By yer leave, I'll search out some other customers."

The smuggled letter (for that was what his "change" had been) stated what he already pretty-much knew or had deduced. It began most ominously, though, with... "The Dutch Fleet is ready."

The additional demands of the Nore mutineers had been presented to visiting Lords Commissioners of the Admiralty and had been rejected out-of-hand. The Spithead terms would be all they would receive. And those terms were not the defamed Orders in Council but were legitimate Acts of Parliament for all to read. Copies of the Acts, and copies of the King's Pardon, were being smuggled aboard the recalcitrant vessels at the Nore to convince the deluded or ignorant that they should take them and return to duty, be pardoned, without any hard feelings.

Upon receipt of those, did his crew still refuse to return command of his ship to him and return to discipline, the letter bore specific orders for all captains and officers still aboard mutinous ships to quit their vessels at once and report to Admiral Buckner ashore!

"Damn, damn, damn!" Lewrie sighed, hunched over the letter at the transom sash windows right aft, huddled up in a corner of the settee atop his lazarette stores. How could he leave her when his plots to retake her had barely been set in motion, had yet to bear fruit? he agonised. With the King's Pardon and Acts of Parliament aboard for all to see, there was more than a good chance that *Proteus* would strike the mutineers' flags and hoist her proper colours!

But it was a direct order, scribbled at the bottom with Vice-Admiral Buckner's signature; to dis-obey, did the crew prove obstinate, was to risk not only this command but his entire career!

He crumpled it up into a tight ball, thinking hard; which gay noise brought Toulon from a sound nap atop the wine-cabinet, swishing his tail in expectation of a brand-new, un-munched, un-swatted "toy." He plopped to the deck, meowed enticingly as he hopped into his owner's lap, trying to paw it or bite it from Lewrie's hand.

Lewrie idly stroked him, as he unfolded the letter to give it a second reading, hoping for an escape clause. No, no hopes of that, but . . . information he had leapt over before: Channel Fleet was returned to duty— Admiral Duncan at Great Yarmouth was to sail to the Texel Channel to block the exits of the French-controlled Dutch Batavian Navy.

Channel Fleet would be no help here; Brest, Cherbourg, St. Malo, and Le Havre already bristled with warships, invasion galleys to carry troops, and escorting gunboats. That armada was weather-bound, so far, but was rumoured to be on tip-toes, prepared to descend on Ireland or, perhaps, even on England's south coast. It was vital, therefore . . .

"And blah-blah-blah," Lewrie softly groaned. "Sorry, puss, not a toy for you." To his ram-cat's dismay, he shredded it to tiny bits, before someone else could read it. "Well, you *can* have it . . . later."

He could toss it out the transom sash windows, but that might raise suspicions if someone spotted him doing it. But turned into a heaping handful of foolscap, the letter would do main-well for filler in Toulon's litter box! After a fragrant spritz or two of cat-pee, no spy in the world would even *try* to retrieve it, much less piece it back together!

"Oh, sometimes you're so useful, Toulon," Lewrie told him. "Do you know that? Yayysss, 'oo *are*. I'll give you another sheet to play with . . . would you like that?"

Toulon did, eagerly bounding off to football, pounce, and mutter over a blank sheet, most intriguingly balled; far forrud into the dining-coach and back.

"Damme, and it was such a good plan we had going too," Lewrie sighed, quite bleakly, as he gingerly "disposed" of that incriminating letter's remains.

That late in the afternoon, the tide was starting to turn. His frigate, streaming back from a single bower, was beginning to swing on her cable, turning her stern shoreward as the evening flood tide took her. In the transom sash windows, the alluring vista of an open horizon, the puddled-steel glitter of the North Sea, and freedom, was slowly being replaced by the sight of low-lying fen land to the north—Foulness and Shoeburyness, the villages of Great Wakering and Southend, the partly exposed Leigh and Maplin Sands at low tide.

An embaying fen land—hemming him and his ship in.

CHAPTER TWENTY-SEVEN

*W*hen in doubt . . . mope, Lewrie told himself, of half a mind to begin packing his sea chests. And of half a mind to have himself one more glass of claret and wait 'til after Aspinall and his cook served up that goose they'd cooked for him. A dull rumble interrupted his foul mood though, the sounds of many voices. And a knock on the door.

"Captain, sir?" Mr. Midshipman Sevier cheeped, leaning in the doorway to bare his noddy's face. "Disturbance on deck, sir. They're arguing amongst themselves, and some are calling for you, sir?"

"Haven't built themselves a guillotine out o' bosun's stores yet, have they, Mister Sevier?" Lewrie frowned at him, slumped quite comfily on the starboard side settee with his feet and legs out-splayed.

"Uhm . . . a guillotine, sir?"

"You know . . . King of France . . . chop-chop?"

"Uhm . . . nossir. It's getting heated though, sir. The people wish you to address them."

"Ah, then!" He brightened. Those smuggled Acts of Parliament and the King's Pardon must have encouraged the moderates and faint of heart to relent already! He rose, tugged down his waist-coat, plucked his shirt cuffs, and clapped on his hat.

He emerged on the gun-deck to witness a slanging match between determined mutineers, ditherers, and quitters. They'd formed sides in unconscious scrums, dividing themselves into packs laced with uncomprehending children and hectoring wives and whores pretty-much allied to the loyal side, or the ditherers in the middle, with but a few harpies siding with the committee or the leaders.

They quieted their arguments as he appeared and made his way to the starboard quarterdeck ladder, parting before him, even as Seaman Bales was still expostulating from the nettings overlooking the waist.

"... cutting off all food to us, brothers!" Bales bellowed, to exhort his minions before Lewrie could speak. "Not even their damned substitute flour will they give us! No more candles, rum, small beer! Damme, no more rope, tar, or lumber either."

"Treachery!" the determined side shouted.

"Now you see what our King thinks of us, mates. How little he thinks of you, his long-suffering and loyal tars. How could a loving King deprive you thus, who've served him so well in the past? Or let criminals like Pitt, Henry Dundas, and Spencer try to starve us out to get what they want . . . ?" That drew many boos and catcalls.

Lewrie scowled as he ascended to the quarterdeck. Bales's hot-blooded talk was dangerous dissident cant, the sort that could get any civilian tossed into gaol for treason. He might have something interesting, indeed, to pass on to that Willis fellow when next he came out to offer his wares! He scowled too, because he was loath to be drawn into a noisy *Beggar's Opera*, a bit of political theatre, as it now seemed the mutiny had become!

"But here's your captain, brothers. . . . You wanted him to speak to you, and I'll not have it said your committee, your 'Fleet Parliament,' won't abide by your wishes," Bales hurriedly summed up as Lewrie stalked up to his side, almost shouldering him aside from his rightful place. Bales tossed him a sneerful, high-nosed glare of satisfaction, as if he'd finessed Lewrie into an impossible situation. His smile of welcome, and reason, was a bloody sham for the others.

"Very well, men," Lewrie said, looking out and down. "You say you wish me to speak with you. About what? Out with it."

"The terms, sor!" Landsman Desmond was quick to shout. "Them they got out to us . . . are they true?"

"They are," Lewrie assured them. "Just as Parker told you . . . when he was last aboard. Pay rise and all. Everything Spithead won for themselves is now yours. If you submit and take the pardon."

"Don't say nothin' 'bout riddin' th' ship o' bad officers an' mates," Mr. Morley objected. "Doesn't give us th' liberty we wanted either! What about them?"

"Say 'sir,' Mister Morley," Lewrie chid him, glaring at him as long as it was going to take, 'til he swallowed hard.

"What about them, Cap'um, sir?" Morley blushed.

"You know the objections to shore leave, to inland leave-tickets, Mister Morley," Lewrie explained, turning to speak to them all. "The Admiralty never knows when the foe will pop out. They can't idle their ships with a third or a half of the crews out of reach. They leave it to the discretion of captains. Now I ask you, lads . . . how many of you have ever had a captain that *wouldn't* grant shore leave to those hands he thought he could trust to come back, hey?"

Damned few, aha! he thought; *and so much for how dangerous* that *question was!*

"And how many of you knew men who couldn't be trusted to come back, who were just looking for the first chance to scamper, that *you* would trust?" he dared pose. "Slackers, idlers, backbiters . . ."

Quite a few, it should be said.

"But Spithead put off'cers an' mates ashore, sir!" a foremast sailor queried. "Acts don't say nothin' 'bout it. Does that mean we cain't?"

Lewrie had wondered about that unwritten clause. The settlement had reputedly contained that term, and the last newspaper he'd gotten his paws on, before this mess had started, of course, had decried the removal or replacement of officers the Spithead mutineers had thought as tyrants, cruel floggers, and "drivers." This was dangerous ground. Did he sound approving of it, he'd be labeled a radical himself! Did he not . . . he might lose this wondrous, un-looked-for chance to finagle his crew back to duty!

"Like here, as I recall . . . ," he began, crossing his fingers for luck, "officers were put off at Spithead and Plymouth. Here . . . there are officers who have already gone ashore of their own volition. And I must tell you true . . . does this ship not take down those yard ropes, lower the red flags, and return to duty . . . I am ordered to depart and take all officers and

midshipmen with me. Leaving you your *appointed* captain and mates . . .
Seaman Bales, Mister Handcocks, and that lot. . . ."

He was heartened more than he could have ever imagined to hear so many
voices raised in sudden, distressful woe that he was going to leave them!

". . . every captain remaining will do so, every officer still on mutinous
ships!" he shouted. "The good'uns . . . *and* the bad!" Lewrie added. "Did
Admiral Lord Howe agree to that at Spithead, it was *after* officers had
gone ashore from those ships too. I don't *know* how they agreed to it, how
the lists were made up . . . how they determined which officers did not
return aboard, but . . . damme, lads, d'ye think it's a thing they'd scribble
down for all to *see?*"

Oh, Christ, I've just cut my own throat, he told himself; *there goes my
good odour, my career! I'm* tellin' *'em how to purge officers, pushin' 'em to
winnow the gunroom!*

While they had a hearty laugh and began to hoot, whistle, and catcall
in what he hoped he could construe as appreciation, he dared to glance
over at his officers, warrants, and midshipmen. They looked dumbstruck
by his admission, some outraged, some queasily appalled.

"Now as for the rest of your demands . . ." Lewrie roared, raising one
hand to gather their attention again. "What . . . for ships to be paid arrears in
wages down to six months before sailing. They can't help you on that'un,
lads . . . there's a war on, and England's short of cash. In peacetime, they
might could, but not now. That rise in pay you've *already* won . . . even if
you *never* mutinied . . . thanks to Spithead, that increase for pensioners too,
for sick-berth hands and those crippled to be paid off . . . the increase in rations to sixteen ounces, instead of twelve or fourteen, that takes money too!

"You said you wanted new-come *pressed* men to get two months' advance in pay, like a Joining Bounty for *volunteers.* . . . Admiralty can't afford that either. Back wages and indemnification made to men who've run
once before then gone back in service . . . the same problem with that.
And, an encouragement to bounty-jumpers, who'd do it over and over
again and deprive *you* of funds! Useless damned shirkers the lot of 'em,
and well you know it! Given a choice, would you have a thing t'do with
'em? No, I tell you!"

Damme, I'm rollin', now! Rantin' like a leapin' Methodist!

"Your delegates wanted those jumpers and runners to keep what *they'd* stolen from your mouths when *you* were ready to sign on, serve King and Country, heart and soul! And then . . . *not* be arrested as deserters when justice caught up with 'em! What, you want them *rewarded?* Is that what real English sailors wish . . . or is it some foreign, radical shit someone in Paris dreamed up to undermine the Royal Navy?"

More hoots, more claps and cheers, and cries of "No!"

Damme, he exulted; *no wonder the reverends look so smug. This is* fun!

"You said you wished a fairer split of prize-money," he ranted on, rocking on the balls of his feet, gripping the cap-rail to lean out over them as he got on shakier ground. "Three-fifths 'stead of your two-eights. Well, if Spithead could concede that point, and the prevailing division wasn't cause for them to kick furniture, then should it not be good enough for you?"

Uh-oh . . . losin' 'em.

"Well, as long as a fine frigate such as our *Proteus* is swingin' 'round the anchor in the Nore . . . you're *not* takin' prizes, are you?" he hooted. "You give me my ship back, I'll take you out where we *can* find prizes, scourge the seas, and give you a chance to get bloody *rich* . . . even under the *old* division!"

That got them back. They were, the bulk of them, growling like famished tigers for a chance at pillaging enemy ships. The hard-core mutineers could only glower, grim-lipped, and swear to themselves.

"And the last . . . alterations and amendments in the Articles of War." Lewrie deigned to sneer. "But . . . you'll note your committees and delegates never spelled out what changes or deletions they wished, did they? Because some of 'em are wanted men . . . pickpockets and thieves who've stolen from shipmates before? Duck-fuckers and buggers who prefer the 'windward passage,' who don't want to be court-martialed for it? Maybe it concerns Article Three . . . Holding Illegal Correspondence with Enemies. Article Five, the one against spies or Seducing Letters? Or Numbers Eight or Nine, about stripping anything they want out of a prize, and stripping and abusing people taken aboard a prize? Damme, do away with those, and we might as well hoist the 'Jolly Roger' and become pirates! Is that what *you* want?"

Another loud outburst of "Noes!"

"Is it Twelve they object to, the one against Cowardice in Action, and Neglect of Duty?" he posed, strutting now, as aggressive as a guinea cock. "Fifteen . . . desertion or running away with a ship and its stores? Sixteen . . . the one against desertion itself? Enticing others to desert? Or are they trying to cover their arses by doing away with Nineteen, Twenty, and Twenty-one . . . the ones covering Mutinous Assemblies . . . Seditious Words . . . hiding or covering Mutiny and Sedition . . . *shit-stirring* over unwholesome victuals! They put that in your compact so no one would be punished later? Well, what d'ye think the King's *Pardon* is about, then!"

"Twenty-six!" Bosun Pendarves roared from the base of the main-mast. "Maybe they like to neglect the steering . . . the cunny-thumbed bastards!"

"Twen'y-seven . . . an' we'll all be allowed t'sleep on watch!" a sailor on the larboard gangway shouted.

"So what the Devil is it they wanted, then? Does it make any sense to you, lads?" Lewrie asked them, once that laugh had run its course. "What do your delegates *really* want? Look you yonder."

He pointed ashore towards Sheerness.

"Yesterday, lads, you could see a flag flying on top of a house ashore . . . the flag of the Lords Commissioners of the Admiralty. Lord Spencer was here, I'm told. They came to negotiate, to tell your delegates that the Spithead terms were official Acts of Parliament, show your leaders that the King's Pardon was real. Well, do you see their flag flying now?"

An hundred heads craned to look.

"No, you don't!" Lewrie screeched. "And why is that? Because your delegates spoke *for* you and told 'em to bugger off! That they wanted *more* . . . that *you* wouldn't take the Spithead terms of settlement and wanted to hold out for all sorts of impossible things. That you'd defy your King, turn your back on your Country when it needs you the most, and spurn a perfectly good offer . . . turn your guns upon Sheerness, defy the rest of the Fleet . . . threaten the *nation!* So they had no choice but to leave and cut off the dockyard stores, cut off the ration boats. Wasn't wicked ministers . . . wasn't a tyrannical King caused *that!* 'Twas the pride and arrogance of your delegates . . . !"

"That's enough!" Bales howled, summoning his stoutest henchmen. "Said he'd answer questions, not rant! Lads, he lies . . . !"

"No, let 'im speak, damn yer eyes!"

"Arra, th' Cap'um's talkin' sense!" Desmond countered.

"Give it up!" someone cried. "Give it up! Take the terms!"

"No, you damned cowards! Lickspittles!"

And where's my sword when I need it? Lewrie goggled, seeing a pushing, shoving match break out on every hand. It was happening . . . a sudden, un-organised counter-mutiny!

"Lookit t'other ships! They're striking colours! Runnin' up white flags!" Ship's Corporal Burton screamed. "Givin' it up too!"

It was true! From what Lewrie could see as he whirled about in a furious, dis-oriented fugue that almost made him dizzy, there were at least a half-dozen warships where the same sort of melees were breaking out, where the ominous yard ropes were being hauled down to snake back to the decks, and the unadorned red banners of rebellion were fluttering down, to here and there be replaced with proper naval ensigns and white flags of submission!

Hands were springing to the flag halliards, to the racks of belaying pins or bitts which secured *Proteus's* yard ropes. Just as many were swinging their fists, flailing about with gun-tools or whatever fell to hand to prevent them. The cowards, the confused, or hesitant, the women and children were hanging back, thundering in panicky herds from one gang-fight to another, turning this way and that in response to cries for help from those who'd strike, to bitter battle-cries from those who'd hold out, resist.

"Take her back, lads!" Lewrie yelled, stumbling as someone to his left shouldered into him. He shoved back, faintly recognised one of the afterguard before bringing a roundhouse right fist into juncture with the fellow's skull. "King and Country!" He stooped to pick up the dropped belaying pin the man had been about to cosh him with and waded in on those who were shouting objections the loudest. He heard a rabbity scream, got a quick glimpse of a loyal sailor being stabbed in the belly with a clasp knife. Heard the dread popping of a pistol! *Right,* he thought; *a real battle and no quarter!*

Haslip came at him with a cutlass, lips drawn back in a feral grin, almost hissing with delight. A turn or two, a parry or two, and Lewrie had the man's blade far out from his body. He clubbed Haslip on the forehead as hard as he could and danced away as the man went down like a toppled marble statue, landing so hard on his back that Lewrie might conjure that he'd shatter.

"Piss-poor sailor . . . piss-poor swordsman too!" Lewrie sneered as he traded the belaying pin for the blade. He hobbled off aft, under a mis-directed swing or two, jabbing at shins or knees to gain running room, as he tried to join Lieutenant Ludlow, who had both hands around a man's throat and was squeezing him blue. Midshipman Peacham was partnered with Ludlow, of course, laying about with an iron crow-lever from one of the quarterdeck carronades, and two sailors who'd tried him on were al-ready down and bleeding. "Give it up!" Lewrie urged to all. "Give it up!"

"Rally!" Lt. Devereux was crying. "Rally on me! Come on, men!" And two or three of his Marines were with him, fist-fighting their way forward to reinforce Lt. Langlie and the other midshipmen.

There was a sudden report, the stink of powder, and the fearsome "thud!" of a .75-caliber ball slamming into someone quite near. Another shot, and Lewrie heard and felt a ball sizzle past his ear. Even more shots up forrud, another scream of anguish, almost lost in the high-pitched screams of terrified women caught in the middle of this fight.

Then the deep, door-slam BOOOMMM! of a cannon.

"Drop it, sir!" Mr. Handcocks snapped, facing Lewrie with his own cutlass. "Best, sir . . . really," he wheedled, nothing like aggressive. "We're winnin'. Got th' pistols. Got th' muskets."

Lewrie brought his cutlass up to touch blades with Handcocks's, batting at it to beat it aside, as the Master Gunner retreated, keeping his sword in play, but only on the defensive. Lewrie had no time to sport with him. He launched himself into the drill with a right-to-left downward slash, and Handcocks responded with a two-handed parry, stamping his foot for a backward slash, though yelping and giving ground, never trained in using an awkward cutlass the same as a smallsword, avoiding the point which Lewrie was probing at him.

Another loud cannon boom, then another! Quite near. A splash of water that towered over the quarterdeck, as one of the two-deckers anchored close to *Proteus* started firing on any ship which looked like it was defecting from the mutiny.

"Throw down yer arms 'fore I kill him!" Marine Corporal O'Neil screamed to one and all, holding Midshipman Elwes with one arm, with a wickedly gleaming midshipman's dirk to the terrified boy's throat!

Punctuated by another cannon blast from the two-decker. Which, this time, rattled everyone's teeth as a solid 24-pounder round-shot struck *Proteus* in her timbers in the lower wale below the gun-ports.

Bales strode up, a pistol in his right hand with the lock back at full cock, another in his left at half-cock. He jammed the right-hand pistol hard against Lewrie's skull, stiff-armed, from his side.

"Throw down before I kill *him!*" Bales roared, panting with exertion and emotion, yet grinning like a death's head, and seeming eager for the opportunity. "It's over! D'ye hear, there!" he bellowed, throwing his head back like a wolf at the moon. "By Jesus, does any man-jack continue to resist the lawful committee, I'll put a ball in the Captain's head . . . *hear me?* Surrender, you perjurers! You lying, canting hounds! Run up the red flags 'fore we get shot to flinders!"

Lewrie's cutlass was too long to do anything with it with Bales so close to his right side. He changed hands, laid the blade flat upon his chest, so he could stab to his right with it. He moved it forward, felt the tip meet resistance against flesh, pucker a dingy chequered calico shirt . . . almost begin to grate upon a rib?

"Be the last thing you ever do, *Captain* Lewrie!" Bales grinned, yet almost on tip-toe to back off and still keep his pistol in contact with Lewrie's skull.

"Then it'd be worth it, you shit-eatin' dog!"

They glared at each other, each determined to die if it came to it, neither yielding the other even a blink as they locked eyes in a moment of ultimate truth. Yet, grinning.

Clatter of steel on oak though. Cutlasses, clasp knives, iron marling-spikes, and gun-tools being dropped. The thuds of wooden weapons being abandoned too, as the threat took the last resistance away.

"No, lads, don't give up on me!" Lewrie pled. "We almost had her back!"

"*Too* late!" Bales sing-songed, triumphant.

Lewrie almost wet himself, as he felt something cold and sharp poke at the left side of his neck. Handcocks, with his cutlass. Even if he took Bales with him, he'd still die. He didn't dare turn to look.

"You'll hang for that, Mister Handcocks," Lewrie swore. "Even if you don't hang for the rest . . . you'll die for that."

"Give it up, please sir," Handcocks begged. "Short, sharp . . . but th' donnybrook's done, an' we've th' ship again. No harm done."

"Give it up, you lot!" Bales snapped to the men behind Lewrie. "Midshipman Elwes . . . your precious captain. Think your little band'll prevail? Even if it costs two more lives? Gentlemen, gentlemen! Men most-like dead already here!" Bales cajoled. "For nothing! See the masts? Yard ropes rove again . . . flags hoisted again. *You* made this happen, out of pride and arrogance! Now atone! Give it up!"

Another, final clatter of weapons as they hit the deck; curses as proud men were forced to surrender.

"You last, sir," Bales said, swivelling his gaze back to meet Lewrie's. "Corporal O'Neil, un-hand the wee midshipman, will you? And Mister Handcocks, I'd admire did you step back. Not too far. Surrender your cutlass, Captain Lewrie. It's not as if it's your own sword of honour, is it. Drop it . . . or die. For nothing."

"I'll see you in Hell, Bales," Lewrie spat, knowing he was going to drop the sword and hating himself for it. "Soon as I'm ashore your name'll be known as a murdering bastard. And there's no place on earth you can ever run and hide, not from the Navy you can't."

"I'll take the chance." Bales shrugged, as if was no threat at all.

Lewrie gritted his teeth and straightened himself erect. With a forceful exhalation, he lowered the cutlass's tip to the deck by his left side, willed his fingers to let it go, to clatter on the pristine white-sanded quarterdeck, and turned on his heel to walk away.

To see the pain, the *accusing* pain, in the eyes of his officers! He'd failed! He'd been a coward before them! Better he'd died, with his pride, his honour intact . . . !

"By God, Captain," Lt. Wyman muttered brokenly, with tears in his eyes, one hand out as if to shake. "I am so sorry, sir! I let you and the rest down, but I couldn't see Mister Elwes butchered . . . nor you shot down, sir! Forgive me!"

"Ah?" Lewrie gawped, realising it wasn't accusation he'd seen but commiseration! And the shame of their own surrenders! "You're a brave young man, Mister Wyman, and an honourable one. Had it been a fair fight, without such a dastardly ploy . . ."

Christ, and when did I ever fight fair? he chid himself; *haven't I sneered my whole life at the very idea? Get the knife or the boot in first . . . and make it* look *honourable? Fair fight, mine arse!*

"Almost took her, sir," Lt. Devereux gruffly muttered, coming up to offer his hand as well. "Do better next time, what?"

"Now we know there are more than we thought who're with us," Lewrie agreed, taking his hand. "I count on it . . . as I count on you, Lieutenant Devereux. All of you. For a moment there . . ."

"Took us all by surprise, sir," Lt. Langlie said, staunching a bloody bruise on his handsome brow. "Be better prepared, organised . . . ?"

"Aye . . . though we *are* ordered ashore. I hope there's a next time, but in the face of that . . ." He gloomed, looking about. "How many are hurt? Mister Shirley? Where's Mister Shirley and his mates?"

" 'Ere, sir," Surgeon's Mate Mr. Durant piped up, clambering to the quarterdeck from the waist. He had his leather "butcher's apron" on, fresh from the lower-deck surgery. It, his hands, and rolled-up shirt cuffs were speckled with blood. "The surgeon an' M'sieur Hodson are below, sir. There are several wounded. An' one dead, sir. A man *sous le nom de* . . .'scuse. 'Is name is Beamish. 'E was stabb-ed, sir."

"I saw that." Lewrie nodded grimly. "Uhm . . . the man here who was shot . . . I thought I heard a man being shot too, Mister Durant."

"Ah, *oui*, Captain." Durant shrugged with Gallic coolness. " 'E is ver' bad hurt. Anozzer loyal seaman, *c'est dommage*. Per'aps an even dozen below who need care too? *Et vous, m'sieurs?* Any of you who need care? Lieutenant Langlie, your brow, sir? Lieutenant Ludlow?"

"Nothing to you, sir!" Ludlow snarled. "Bucket o' sea-water's a better cure than *your* sort'd give me."

"Mister Ludlow!" Lewrie seethed. "Mind yer manners, sir."

Ludlow had come up at the first sounds of rioting, had come to fight, which was a credit in his favour. He now bore a bleeding gash on his sword-arm and a bruise on his face which was already yellowing and bluing. Another mark to his credit. Still . . .

"Damn all Frogs, sir . . ." Ludlow went on, wincing as he flexed his fingers in experiment. "Might ask *this'un* where all the radical ideas o' th' mutineers came from. He knew Beamish as a loyal man, and he knew to call the shot hand as loyalist too. Wager anything I have he knew the names of the conspirators. . . . *days* before . . ."

"*Vous minus!*" Durant bristled. "*Vous cochon insultant!*"

"Here, speak English, you damned . . . !" Ludlow barked. "What's he sayin'? Damme, does he dare insult *me?*"

"Mister Durant," Lewrie interceded, "you will apologise to the First Lieutenant . . . for calling him a moron *and* an insulting pig. He is your superior officer and such is not allowed from a warrant mate to a Commission Officer. At once, sir."

Durant simmered, looked fit to whistle like a tea kettle to have his gentlemanly honour maligned—heaved a great sigh, swallowed his pride—and stumbled out an apology.

"And, Mister Ludlow," Lewrie intoned, "you will apologise to Mister Durant for your own harsh words and your supposition that Mister Durant is a traitor or in the pay of French agents."

"Why, sir, I'll be damned if . . ."

"You will, sir! Now!" Lewrie snapped. "Goddamnit! One dead, a man close to death . . . a dozen wounded. We don't have time for any of this petty . . . *shit!* More to the point . . . *I* don't! I expect my officers to behave like gentlemen, to the hands and to each other. *Now* . . . sir!"

"Very well, sir." Ludlow flushed, lowering his chin and turning nigh to burgundy-colour. "Mister Durant, I apologise. My pardons."

"*Merci* . . . M'sieur Ludlow," Durant replied, *most*-stiffly.

"Thankee, Mister Ludlow," Lewrie said, turning to face him. "I have orders for us to depart the ship. All of us. Given the fact that you responded to our melee with alacrity and courage . . . I release you from confinement. Let us pack our chests, sirs. There is light enough for us to get ashore before dark if we leave within an hour. Let me thank you all again," he said, peering at their downcast faces, most especially Ludlow's, "for all you tried just now. But . . . well, excuse me for a moment or two. Dismiss."

⚓

He paced aft to the taffrails, with failed resisters, the faint-hearted, and the sneering victors all giving him a wide berth. He took hold of the cap-rail, gripping the timbers 'til his fingers screamed.

Best chance we'd have . . . the last *chance!* he groaned to himself; *and it's a bloody failure! Have to slink ashore with my tail between my legs.* Ceding the field and the ship to the mutineers, he realised. Encouraging them and their little victory, so they'd be even more obstinate, *less* prone to settlement.

Some distant firing made him spin about, searching for a source.

There!

"Ah, Christ!" He sagged.

Making things even worse for him at such a bleak, low point (was such a thing possible) was the sight of a frigate from the inner tier of ships, flying a Blue Ensign at her main and spanker gaff, with her royal standard at the fore! Sailing into Sheerness on the flood tide!

Escaping . . . as he and *Proteus* hadn't.

L'Espion, he thought she was—Captain James Dixon. He'd wanted to visit her when he had time—before the mutiny had happened—to see if her captain was the same James Dixon who'd commanded a sloop or smaller ship that had taken part in his Turk's Island adventure back in '83 and compare notes and reminiscences about that time . . . perhaps dig up some juicy "dirt" on the way then–Captain Horatio Nelson had bungled that fiasco!

Dixon had managed to overcome his mutineers; *Dixon* had won free!

He went back forward to the binnacle cabinet to study her with a glass. Aye, it was *L'Espion*. And in the yards . . . HMS *Niger*, another frigate . . . that morning she'd been flying the red mutiny flags, but now she also sported the Blue Ensign in defiance.

"Christ, why not us too?" he muttered in self-pity, envious of those two ships, which were now, or soon would be, as safe as houses in the welcoming bosom of the Admiralty; feeling like the weakest, most inept idiot who'd ever put on King's Coat!

He put the glass back in the binnacle cabinet rack and paced to the larboard bulwarks for something to grab onto, scathing himself, as he tried to relive those few breathless moments of confusion, seeking a way he hadn't tried, but should have . . .

He looked down on the waters of the Nore as they flowed and cat-pawed alongside, just beginning to be bloodied by a faint red sunset.

"Lir . . ." he whispered hopelessly. "You're a blood-thirsty sort. This is your ship then? Pagan, vengeful . . . this your way of taking care of another English bastard, same'z the way you sorted out the last'un? Well, hurrah then . . . you won. You really want this ship for yourself, heart and soul? Then stir your salty arse up and help me!"

Daft, he told himself, straightening and peering about quickly, in fear that someone had overheard him and would deem him as lunatick as that Captain Churchwell had been just before he'd fled *Proteus*.

Daft as bats, he silently re-iterated to himself; *pleading to a Celtic sea-god! Might as well read some sheep guts, for all the good that does. Sacrifice pigeons . . . ? No, better that bastard, Bales!*

He's yours, Lewrie silently vowed. *His heart's blood is yours, if you help me!*

CHAPTER TWENTY-EIGHT

By sundown, he was ready to leave, taking his sea chests and a few necessary articles. He emerged in the waist to find another mob assembled to see him, and the rest of the officers, off. He expected to be jeered at by the mutineers, but evidently the brief fighting had battered any taunting out of them, had sobered them to the enormity of what they were dedicated to continue.

"No man t'help 'em," a committeeman cautioned. "Let officers carry their own traps fer once."

"Don't be a *whole* bastard, Lincoln," Curcy, the lamed cook, spat. "Lend 'em a hand, there."

"We do require a working party for our dunnage, Mister Lincoln," Lewrie calmly demanded, boring him with his gaze. "No dis-respect to officers and mates, remember? I certainly will, you know. When this is over."

"Ah, uhm ..." Lincoln grumbled, unable to match gazes with him; perhaps fearing the further consequences and harried by protestations from other crew members. "Right, then ... reeve a stay-tackle aloft!"

"Captain!" A bright call came from the quarterdeck. "Leaving, are you?" It was Bales, damn him! In quite good cheer, come to gloat.

"Seaman Bales," Lewrie coolly replied, turning to look at him, once more detesting that their places were reversed.

"You're more than welcome to stay aboard, sir," Bales told him with a taunting, mocking tone to his voice. "She is still your ship, after all."

"I have my orders," Lewrie snapped, hands in the small of his back. "As I'm certain, Bales, you have yours from your revolutionary paymasters."

"Oh, sir, when will you realise that your crew turned against you of their own accord . . . oppressed too long by too many grievances." Bales sighed theatrically. It would be more political theatre to the last. Lewrie grunted in disgust. "Right, lads?" Bales prompted, but didn't get the "amens" and cries of agreement which he'd expected. "Well?" he posed, and even that left them mute and shuffling in embarrassment.

"Lecture and prose all you like when I'm gone, Bales. But for now . . . just *do* stop yer gob, will you?" Lewrie gravelled.

"A fighter to the end, would you?" Bales smirked, crossing to the starboard ladder which led down from the gangway to the waist. "A worthy opponent to the last. Damme, Captain Lewrie, I enjoy our debates so much, I'm loath to part with you. So . . . I won't."

"I *beg* your pardon?" Lewrie gawped.

"We took a vote, didn't we, lads? Ship's committee all put our heads together and decided we'd take your advice, Captain Lewrie, and purge the ship of officers and mates we wish gone for good."

Knew *I was gonna regret those words,* Lewrie bleakly thought!

"Now we can't do without the Sailing Master," Bales explained, as he clumped down the steps to the gun-deck, taking way between crew-men as easily as a lord strolling down the Strand might part the poor with his walking-stick. "So, Mister Winwood will remain aboard her . . . just in case." He winked at those closest to him, causing sly mirth.

"I shan't!" Mr. Winwood erupted. "Do you try and force me to sail her out, I'll put her hard aground. You'll get no aid from me!"

"We'll see about that, Mister Winwood." Bales shrugged, as if he had no doubts about his powers to coerce when the time came. "We also voted to keep the rest of the officers aboard. As an assurance, if you will, gentlemen, that the authorities ashore realise just how determined we are. Though not all. Oh my, no. Not all. You must go ashore, Lieutenant Devereux. Most of your Marines wished to keep you, but after this afternoon's little set-to . . . you proved yourself just a bit too doughty a fighter.

One too dangerous to keep, nourished in our breast as it were . . . like the proverbial viper?"

"Bales, that well-studied insult will cost you a stretch of the neck, I promise you," Devereux smoothly replied, as if relishing the event already and with the greatest enjoyment.

"Mister Ludlow too!" Bales shouted, lifting his arms to strut out into plainer view, "the worst of the slave-drivers and floggers!" he exulted, to stir up the silent, shambling crew. He struck fire on that stroke, raising grumbles of assent, some glad cries of "at last!" from others. "*And*, his creature Midshipman Peacham too!"

That drew a *much* louder cheer. Ludlow and Peacham protested, their honour impugned to the quick, but anything they had to say was lost in jeers and catcalls.

"Damme, Bales! You can't do this! You can't pick and choose!" Lewrie shouted to make himself heard. "You can't detain us when we've orders to leave either. That's kidnapping, that's . . ."

"Ah, but we like you so much, sir," Bales told him, as the catcalls and verbal abuse heaped on Ludlow and Peacham continued. "We've nothing against *you* or the rest. Adair, he's a likeable fellow. The other midshipmen are good lads," Bales almost cooed. "Midshipman Sevier, that lack-wit? Mister Catterall, he's a jester . . . an empty shell."

"With or without our chests, Bales, we're going ashore. And I dare you to try and stop us," Lewrie threatened.

"Without a boat, sir?" Bales smirked. "And no hand willing to aid you? I say you'll not, sir," he chuckled, his eyes crinkled with mocking mirth. "If I have to lay hands on you, sir. If I have to put a gun to your head . . . again, I'll run that risk."

"What do you have against me, Bales?" Lewrie demanded, feeling trapped again, powerless and utterly frustrated. "You've acted as if this was a personal grudge 'twixt us since you rose up to capture the ship! Did we ever serve together? Did I ever do you or yours a bad turn?"

"Don't know what you mean, sir," Bales taunted, grinning wider. "Rose up 'gainst tyrants, sir, same as the others. Now do you wish to *think* it's personal 'cause you can't feature your 'faithful' sailors turning on you . . . or you're growing fearful at last, well . . . that is *your* problem, sir. *Are* you becoming a bit fearful, sir?"

Damned right I am, Lewrie queasily thought; *but I'll not give him the satisfaction!*

"Oh, don't keep lying to me, Bales. You must've served under me. On *Ariadne,* back in '80, the both of us, under poor old *Captain* Bales. That's where you found your present name, isn't it! Joined the Navy again, under his name, 'cause your own was too well . . ."

"Never heard of him, sir," Bales intoned deadpan. "Never was on a ship named *Ariadne* either," he swore, then turned away to regain the crew's attention and dismissing Lewrie's presence. "Last now, lads! What we agreed to! Who among the officers does the Captain's chiefest bidding? Who worked us harder than the Israelites in Egypt? Harder'n Cuffy slaves cutting sugar cane in the Indies? The Second Officer Mister Langlie, wasn't it? Mister Ludlow's too cup-shot most of the time to work us . . . just abuse us! . . . but Mister Langlie did, so . . . off the ship with him!"

"Oh, I say . . . dammit," Langlie gaped, astonished to be tarred as black as Ludlow. "What utter rot!"

"Didn't none o' *us* vote fer that!" Landsman Furfy complained in a loud voice, speaking for a majority of the hands, who were as astonished by that pronouncement as Lt. Langlie was.

"Damme, don't ya trust yer committeemen, mates?" Mr. Handcocks bellowed. "We'll see ya right, you can count on it!"

"Why would they wish *me* ashore, sir?" Langlie fretted as hands fell to at lashing up Lt. Ludlow's chests. "What'd *I* ever . . . ?"

"Side-party!" Bales hooted. "See the tyrants off with proper honours at least, hey, lads?"

"Damme, I'm no Tartar, no plantation flogger, sir!" Lt. Langlie said, pressed close to Lewrie by the sailors coming to tote the expelled officers' chests. "Ludlow and Peacham I can understand, and good riddance to bad rubbish, frankly, but . . ." he whispered derisively.

In spite of being out-schemed once more by Bales's latest blow to his covert plan, Lewrie allowed himself a *frisson* of relief that Peacham and Ludlow would be gone.

Outwardly though, he gave Lt. Langlie a tiny shrug of agreement, a wee *moue* of disgust. "Because they wish to strip *Proteus* of any officer the hands like, Mister Langlie." He spat. "Anyone with courage or wits or bottom, who the people'd listen to, bring them back 'round, and retake the ship."

"Ah." Langlie winced for a moment. "I think I see what you mean, sir. Me . . . Lieutenant Devereux . . . a compliment really. Sort of."

"No matter," Lewrie cut him off, his mind awhirl to rebuild the shambles of his schemes—and suddenly, chillingly aware of just what sort of lies or half-truths the truculent Lt. Ludlow and his creature, Midshipman Peacham, might impart ashore—to their own advantage, to his detriment! "Look, we've no time to write a report, why it *seems* that I'm dis-obeying orders to quit her, but I am held against my will . . . I *still* have hopes of retaking the ship and will try to parlay becoming hostages into something useful . . ."

"Well, of course, sir," Langlie nodded, encouraging him.

"You must give the authorities a *true* accounting, Mister Langlie," Lewrie bade him in a fierce whisper of his own. "You know all of the ringleaders, who to accuse . . . that most of the crew's wavering, more than a minority loyal . . . !" he rushed out, pressed to furious urgency to say a half-hour's piece in a single minute. ". . . state of rations, how long they could hold out. Names of the dead . . ."

"B'lieve I know what needs telling, sir," Langlie assured him with a firm, determined expression, "to bring our nastiest villains to book . . . where the real infamy lies."

"No matter Lieutenant Ludlow is senior to you and *his* place to make the report, it's vital . . ." Lewrie sped on, stifling the urge to beg as he dropped his carronade-sized hint.

"Rest assured, Captain Lewrie," Lt. Langlie said, coming over all noble, "I'll speak of *everything* infamous aboard *Proteus*. Everyone," he added, with a significantly arched brow.

Thank bloody Christ! Lewrie thought; *ah—t'other thing . . . !*

"Do you come across some *leery* sorts, Mister Langlie," Lewrie rushed out, as if Langlie's assurances that he'd cover his arse for him were neither here nor there, "some civilians who have no business in this, but *do?* They'll be government agents . . . spies . . . same ones who smuggled the Pardon and the Acts of Parliament aboard in the bumboats . . . ask for one going by the name of Willis . . . I think he's working for a fellow I've met before. He'll understand. Tell him I've determined our rebellion is home-grown . . . mostly! But I fear there are some of a more dangerous stripe exploiting it for their own ends. Turning it political. Didn't begin it, I don't think, but . . ." Lewrie stammered in his haste to get it all said.

"Soon as I alight, sir," Langlie declared, offering his hand to be clasped right-manly. "And I'll pray most strenuously for your safety and your success with the hands, sir. I trust I'll serve under you again, sir . . . be proud to. Aboard a free, un-tainted *Proteus*."

"Thankee, Mister Langlie, and I'm certain you will," Lewrie said at last, realising there was nothing more he could do or say. He took Langlie's hand and gave it a welcome shake. "Pray I see you too, sir . . . coming o'er the lip of the entry-port to reclaim your place as her first . . ."

Oops! he grimaced; *what sort o' slip is that? Hmm . . . useful!*

"My pardons, Mister Langlie," Lewrie all but managed to blush. "A thing devoutly to be wished perhaps . . . but best left unsaid. It'd be dis-loyal to Mister Ludlow . . . no matter his temperament . . ." And he attained a gruff sadness for his last, abashed ". . . poor old fellow."

"Thank you, Captain, er . . . I say, thank you!" Langlie croaked, be-dazzled by the possibility of being so honoured, to even *accidentally* be offered the post of First Lieutenant as a mark of his captain's esteem.

I swear I can hear the wheels turnin', Lewrie told himself; *see puffs o' smoke from out his ears! Hooked, gaffed . . . and landed!*

Langlie finally let go Lewrie's hand and stepped back a respectful dis-tance so he could doff his hat in a parting salute, before following his sea chest up to the gangway to take his place in the pecking-order of seniority decreed for the departure of officers. Lewrie was quite pleased to note how many sailors came up to Langlie, how many of the marines approached Lt. Devereux, to share a few last kind words . . . assurances that they weren't died-in-the-wool rebels too, but . . .

You devious . . . shit! Lewrie chid himself; watching them depart. *With Langlie as First Officer instead of Ludlow, would I have even* had *a mutiny aboard? Now if Langlie truly* is *ambitious, his account would expose Ludlow's insubordination. . . . Hell, he needed turnin' out, him and Peacham both! Not*

*just for this ship, but for the entire Navy! Couch my final report the right way,
and I'll purge 'em as good as Spithead ships cleaned out their gunrooms!*

He reluctantly went below to unpack. Once there, he faced his Cox'n
Andrews, Padgett, and Aspinall, who had just released Toulon . . . who
was bristled up and carping angrily at the indignation.

"Almost made it ashore." Lewrie shrugged. "Sorry 'bout that."

"Not your fault, sir," Padgett replied, looking miserable.

"Uhm . . ." Aspinall sighed, scuffing his toes. "Now we're t'be aboard,
sir . . . your goose *is* cooked, so . . ."

"It would seem so, now *wouldn't* it!" Lewrie barked sarcastically.

"Uh, nossir! Meant your supper, sir!" Aspinall yelped. "Meant, 'twas a
shame we'd leave without it, and . . . do ya feel peckish, I can fetch it from
the galley, sir! Be a shame it goes t'waste."

"Oh." Lewrie relented, smiling and blushing. "That! My pardons, Aspinall. But since it seems I'll *not* dine at Admiral Buckner's, by all means,
trot my goose out. I am hungry. Dry too."

"A nice bottle o' your claret, and the goose, comin' right up, sir! And
a tot o' brandy t'tide you over whilst I fetch 'em!"

Now, *what am I going to do?* he asked himself, once he'd gotten his
paws about a large snifter of brandy. *Devereux gone, now Langlie . . . my
stoutest fellow conspirators! Even Ludlow and Peacham! Dim-witted, insultin',
truculent . . . but, bred-in-the-bone foes of mutiny and eager to fight when you
let slip their leashes.* Caused *half of it, but they could've helped put it down.*

I still plan to retake the ship, Gawd! he squirmed at his boasting to
Langlie; *what empty posturing* that *was. As if I have leaders left who could
sway the crew to help me!*

Bales had been right, he determined, wincing again in recrimination,
and hellish-astute too. Those left . . . Catterall, he was very witty and droll,
smarmy-clever. But was he reliable? Adair was promising, a clever lad.
Sevier was a lack-wit, just as Bales had deemed him, with nothing behind
his eyes but rote, dumb obedience. Nicholas and Elwes were too young to
scheme or dissemble . . . they could run covert messages, at best, chat people up. The hands liked them. Would they blush and duck their heads
though, were they put to whispering ideas to *Proteus*'s people in seemingly
casual conversations?

Most likely, he groaned. *Lieutenant Wyman?*

A likely lad, a sweet young fellow too. Reliable, ever cheery, and genuinely liked by the crew; earnest and brave, determined to do his best, but . . . would it be enough? Lewrie could imagine Lt. Wyman uttering "my goodness graciouses" with his eyes blared . . . like a virgin chamber-maid the first time someone put a hand 'neath her skirts!

"We need a half-dozen o' *me*," Lewrie decided in a black humour. "A pack of the *real* ruthless bastards."

Bosun Pendarves and his mate, Towpenny, Mr. Winwood and his mates, that's five men. Mr. Garraway the Carpenter, at least two of his crew, his mate, Jacks? Purser and his assistant . . . Sailmaker, Mr. Reyne, and at least one from *his* crew. Mr. Offley the Armourer . . . twenty-five or twenty-six people, all told? God, it still looked hopeless. The Marines, now . . .

Bales had said that most of the Marines had wanted to keep Lieutenant Devereux aboard—all but Corporal O'Neil the Irishman, one of the United Irish for certain. Three or four of the privates were with the hard core of mutineers . . . Corporal Plympton the Devon man, though, and Sergeant Skipwith . . . *there's* where he should make a sly approach! With twenty to twenty-five of the fourty-man marine complement allied with him, there just *might* be a chance yet.

"Supper's served, sir," Aspinall announced at last.

"Hmmpfh," Lewrie grunted, as he rose to go forrud to his table. Even if it did seem hopeless, at the moment, at least he could keep up his strength . . . for that "later" he dearly coveted.

CHAPTER TWENTY-NINE

*I*t seems there's more than one way to vote yourself out of the mutiny, Mister Pendarves," Lewrie gleefully pointed out to the Bosun and his mate, Mr. Towpenny, as they supervised the gun-deck crew through a rare "River Discipline" sail-making drill. "That's *two* ships gone!"

He said that loud enough to be easily overheard by many of the hands near them, yet casually enough, he hoped, that it would not come across as contrived. It had been hard, personally galling for him, to get this sail-making drill staged. He'd had to point out to Bales that the crew had gone slack, requiring exercise at sea-tasks—practice at what Lewrie had hoped was a rehearsal for their escape—then wait for *Bales* to make up his mind as to whether *he'd* allow it or not!

"Bless me, not another, sir?" Pendarves replied almost as loud, attracting even more hesitant attention, as they'd rehearsed earlier.

"The *Clyde* frigate too, Mister Pendarves." Lewrie shrugged, at a seeming loss. "She isn't in the anchorage this morning. And when I went aloft with a glass, I could have sworn I spotted her anchored inshore. Must have slipped her cables and drifted into Sheerness on the flood tide last night. Now *San Fiorenzo* too. A bit more theatrical that"—he grinned—"but out to sea on the ebb."

The *San Fiorenzo* frigate, originally assigned to carry Princess Charlotte and her new husband, had "eloped" in broad daylight, sailing out to sea

275

where a merchantman had guided her to deep water. She had attracted vicious but poorly aimed and ineffective gunfire from nearby mutiny ships. Stalwart mutineers had crowed over the gunnery display, jeering that such would be the fate of any deserter, and who *wanted* such half-hearted bastards as them anyway! But it had been sobering to *Proteus*'s crew.

And after yesterday's brief counter-rebellion and the restive misgivings his own sailors had felt after it had been put down, by delegate force, Lewrie could conjure it had heartened those gnawed by grave doubts, for *San Fiorenzo had* sailed free. No matter how the ship's committee or Fleet Delegates explained it, everyone could see that two ships had found their courage and their common sense, and were now clear of damnation. That, atop his sailors' misgivings and grudges, were all to the good for his scheme.

Proves it can *be done*, Lewrie gloomed; *to them, and me. Maybe they'll take heart from it, find the bottom to stand up to Bales. Or maybe it's already too late—two ships escape, they're sure to be on their guard now, even stricter than before. Did we lose our best shot at it 'cause we failed yesterday? Buck up, damn ye!* "Now perish all gloom," *and play up* "me-hearty." . . . *We're halfway there; I can smell it!*

His crew *was* acting sullen and restive: moody and grumbling at their drills in silent, wooden obedience; glumly going through the motions with their minds half on their own troubles. Over the necessity of drilling, of course, but . . . for also still being there, trapped and damned by Admiralty, by the nation itself.

"Now, Desmond . . . that's not the way t'belay that clew-sheet . . ." Pendarves grumbled, almost sighing at the futility of teaching hapless landsmen even a tenth of what a crewman had to learn. "Lemme show ya . . . again."

"Morning, Desmond . . . Furfy." Lewrie nodded most sunnily at his Irishmen. They mumbled back greetings, torn between watching Pendarves and the rope-end, and their curiosity.

"Cap'um, sir . . ." Desmond whispered, "is it true, sir, that *two* ships got clean away?"

"Looks that way, Desmond," Lewrie agreed.

"Faith . . . an' d'ye think any o' their men'll be hanged, sir? As they returned to duty now, sir?" Desmond queried, fearful of the other sailors, who might overhear and report him.

"Only the villains, I'd expect, Desmond," Lewrie informed him. "Only the villains."

"Aye . . . them as'd kill a body, do 'e not keep his oath." Furfy almost shuddered.

"There are tyrants," Lewrie muttered, guardedly, "and then . . . there're tyrants, Furfy. It seems there're tyrants *before* the mast too."

Furfy was a simple soul, Lewrie suspected; his large bulk seemed to deflate to half its size as he heaved a helpless sigh but shook his head up and down in agreement, as if completely lost, or doomed.

"Bad as th' Houghers or White-Boys, Michael?" Desmond commiserated. "Join, help out, keep mum . . . or die, 'cause they'll niver let a body go 'bout his own bus'ness nor stand apart."

"I never thought *willing* duty was tyranny though, lads," Lewrie hinted, wondering what in blazes Desmond was talking about. Some anti-English secret societies back in Ireland?

"Broke their Bible-oath they did though, sir," Desmond carped in a louder voice, as they all sensed the presence of a committeeman on the gangway above them. For his own protection, Lewrie decided. "No good'll ever come from such as that, Cap'um."

The committeeman, an Ordinary Seaman named Ahern (another Irishman), gave a faint nod of approval and a sniff of satisfaction before he turned his attention to other things.

"And what's the value of a Bible-oath exacted at the point of a sword, Desmond?" Lewrie posed. "One that'd drag you down to Hell, do you honour it, along with the cynical bastards who bound you with it."

Furfy, the faint soul, automatically crossed himself. Desmond was made of quicker wits though, for he slyly smiled.

"Why, t'would be no oath at'all, sir," Desmond chuckled softly. "Now, was a man t'take an oath worth honourin', Cap'um . . ."

Lewrie wasn't sure what Desmond was getting on about that time either, but he felt it wouldn't go amiss did he reward him a wink and a tap of his forefinger beside his nose before resuming his seemingly casual stroll about the decks, towards the quarterdeck, seeking out Sergeant Skipwith, to see what he might have to say. He found him supervising practice with a quarterdeck carronade. These marines were free of pipe-clayed crossbelts, cartridge boxes, waist-coats, hats, and bayonets of the sentries, though they still wore their short hangers on their left hips, hung from shoulder-belts. Discipline was still at full bore though, for they still wore their hair pulled hard back in a tar-stiffened queue formed over a "rat," and were sporting the cruel stiff leather neck-stocks, no matter that they worked at an un-marine-like exercise.

"Charge with cartridge . . . !" Skipwith intoned, and one man pretended to cradle a sewn cartridge bag of powder into the squat gun bore, while a second man plied the flexible rope rammer down the barrel to seat the imaginary charge. "Shot your piece . . . !" And the first man pretended to heft a 24-pounder ball down the bore.

Lewrie waited 'til they'd gone through the steps of ramming the shot down firm against the cartridge, stepping back and seizing up the run-out tackles, pricking the cartridge bag down the touch hole, priming the flint-lock igniter, fiddling with the elevation screw, tightening the compression baulks to either side of the slide carriage, and pretending to traverse, aim, and fire.

"Three rounds in two minutes, Sergeant Skipwith?" Lewrie asked.

"Detachment . . . , 'shun!" Skipwith yipped, and sprang to quivering attention as if Lewrie had snuck up on his blind side and goosed him. "Aye, aye, Captain . . . sah! Three rounds in two minutes . . . sah!"

"At least, long as you're loading such *heavy* cartridge and shot, Sergeant?" Lewrie chuckled.

"Well er . . . aye, sir." Skipwith darkened, making his gun-team smirk as much as they thought they could get away with. "But I know we'll make three rounds in two minutes when it's for real, sir!"

"I get us out to sea where we can load and fire for real, then we'll see, Sergeant Skipwith," Lewrie said, strolling up to lay a hand on the breech of the short 24-pounder. "I did not time you, but I am certain you were managing quite well, men. As Lieutenant Devereux had assured me you would, even if it is unfamiliar to you."

Hmmm, he thought, three *more* who seem crestfallen at the mention of their absent commander, now that they were freed from the demanding but mindless labour and had time to dwell upon it.

"Marines can do anything, do they put their minds to it, right, Sergeant?" Lewrie joshed.

"Ever and amen, sir!" Skipwith proudly barked, even un-bending enough to display a rare smile of pleasure. "Mister Devereux said we could do it, sir . . . t'help the Captain's sailors out, sir . . . then we will do it, sir!" Of course, given the anarchy of the times, he dared put in a sly dig at sailors (as Marines ever would) that put a beamish glint in every "lobster-back's" eyes, for a second or so, and stiffen their backs with pride as they stood at attention by the gun.

"Been at it long, have you, Sergeant Skipwith?" Lewrie enquired, off-handedly.

"Half-hour, sir," Skipwith told him.

"Well then, I'd imagine a turn at the scuttle-butt, up forrud, would not be sneered at," Lewrie allowed. "Besides . . . all the rumbles are scaring my cat out of a year's growth. Even making *my* gunners go green with envy, hey?"

"Aye, aye, sah!" Skipwith replied, taking the hint. "Squad . . . ! Quarter-hour interval! Dismiss!"

After the privates had sloped off towards the water butts, Lewrie turned to Sergeant Skipwith. "Sorry if I interrupted, Sergeant. And for presuming to issue orders direct, 'stead of through your own officers, but . . . since Lieutenant Devereux is ashore . . ."

"Understood, sir," Skipwith replied, a tad less starched.

"What's their mood, this morning, Sergeant Skipwith?" Lewrie asked, clapping his hands in the small of his back whilst pretending to inspect the carronade. "Any of them wavering after yesterday? An idea of how many of the marine complement we could trust, did we . . . ?"

"Ah, sir," Skipwith gravely nodded, stepping up closer, as if responding to a question Lewrie had posed about the gun. "Beg pardon for sayin' so, sir, but I was *hoping* you were still of a mind to take back the ship. Even if Mister Devereux is now ashore, sir."

"I am," Lewrie vowed, sure he could trust Skipwith to keep mum. "Could have done it yesterday had we known there'd be a scuffle among the hands. Corporal O'Neil, though . . ."

"God-damned Paddy duck-fucker!" Skipwith graveled. "Umm, beg yer pardon, sir."

"Thought pretty-much the same of him"—Lewrie snickered—"when he put that dirk to Mr. Elwes's throat. Many of his sort, Sergeant?"

"Nossir," Skipwith replied, twisting up his face in disgust at that deed's recollection. "No more than a half-dozen, all told, sir. 'Bout five bigger, older men, who know all th' cautions, who've served at sea before, sir. O'Neil one of 'em . . . last'd be a new-come private . . . Private Mollo, sir. Oh, he's a smarmy bastard, sir, a right sea-lawyer, all pepper an' ginger, but the lazy sort. Spotted him as trouble first I clapped eyes on him, sir. Now I thought I knew O'Neil, t'others, but . . ."

"So, they'd be easy to overpower . . . cut out of the pack?" Alan muttered hopefully.

"Aye, sir . . . do we do it sly-boots," Skipwith affirmed. "See, sir"—he flummoxed, ready to run his hands through his hair in frustration—"*most* o' our lads are new-come, straight from bashin' on the barracks square, sir. Hopeless dolts, o' course, sir, when they come aboard, but that proud t'be Marines and eager t'do their duty, sir . . ."

"Open to blandishments from the half-dozen seniors though."

"Green as grass, sir, aye," Skipwith admitted. "Easy-swayed. Caught up in the fun of it, skylarkin' the first few days, sir. . . . We hadn't much hope, the Leftenant an' me. Last few days though, sir, we were close to bringin' 'em 'round. The men look up to Leftenant Devereux, Captain, sir. Firm but fair, he is, and ever a cheery word for 'em. Treats 'em with respect, sir, like they were special already, sir. Oh, but he's a *good* officer!"

And most aren't, I take it, Lewrie could only silently conclude.

"Now though, Sergeant . . . how close might we be?" Alan pressed.

"They're low, sir," Skipwith pondered. "Havin' the Leftenant sent away . . . seein' how far the delegates'll go t'get what they wish too, sir? Told 'em, the Leftenant'd be ashamed of 'em did they keep on with this. Corp'ral Plympton an' me made sure the lads know they're runnin' outa chances t'make him proud . . . be proud of themselves, too, sir. They're close t'givin' it up, I think. Be hard to get anything done on the sly though, sir. Committee has said they won't let anyone assemble below, after Lights Out, anymore. Don't want any of what they call perjurers to the oath, sir."

"But you could still stir the pot, Sergeant?" Lewrie queried. "Into

Sheerness . . . out to sea, either way, depending on when it comes, and the tide state . . . we'll need to be ready to spring into action at a moment's notice. Fiddle with your watch-and-quarter bill perhaps, isolate O'Neil and that Mollo, the others, in one watch . . . ?"

"Half-and-half, sir," Skipwith suggested. "Then it's only three t'overpower on deck, and three t'jump below decks."

"Just as long as they don't get excited and start titterin' in their hands," Lewrie warned. "Give the game away, 'fore . . ."

"Aye, they're young'uns, I'll allow, sir," Skipwith gloomed, "but there's *some* with foreheads bigger'n a hen we could tell off at first," he quickly added, with a hopeful set of his shoulders. "And you know how it is, Captain, sir . . ." Skipwith leered. "As scared of a noose as most of 'em are, now they see how things stand, p'raps they'll be more gulpy-nervous than titterin', an' the ringleaders'd not know the diff'rence. And they *are* Marines, sir. Hard as recruitin' gets . . . desp'rate as we are for warm bodies . . . an' low-down, dumb, an' hopeless as most *recruits* are, sir . . . they are *Marines*. Means they stand head an' shoulders above yer av'rage tar or Redcoat when it comes to wits, sir. Beggin' yer pardon, o' *course*, Cap'um, sir."

"Well, there is that . . ." Lewrie felt he had to admit.

"Won't let you or the Leftenant down again, sir. Swear it. Now they see two *other* frigates managed to cut free . . . well, sir!"

"I'm certain they won't, Sergeant . . . Thankee," Lewrie replied, giving Skipwith's shoulder a grateful squeeze. "You carry on with the undermining and shuffling, and I'll search us out the opportunity. Do you tell 'em I'll move Heaven and Earth to get their officer back."

"Aye, sir, I'll pass that along, sir!"

Pleasin', Lewrie felt like humming to himself as he resumed his strolling, all but strutting with delight; *it's comin' together, maybe as soon as tonight, once it's dark as a boot? Sheerness, or seaward, that's the question. Seaward, I'd prefer, but . . . inshore might have to suit. Look up Mr. Wyman, the middies . . . have 'em in for dinner, aha! Let 'em know we can now count on the Marines, make a final list of friends or foes . . . Hell's Tinny Little Bells! As downcast, as shit-scared! as most of the people look this mornin', we just might* could *pull it off tonight! Backed into a corner, damned by everyone from Land's End to John O' Groats . . . time runnin' out on 'em . . . one word'd send 'em to their knees in gratitude, most-like. We could . . .*

Cheering interrupted him, making him snarl petulantly; a reedy, thin, distant cheering from down the line of anchored ships that began at the far end and swelled towards *Proteus* like the onset of a gale. He went to the bulwarks to see what nonsense had them going this time. Another parade of boats and bands?

"Oh, Christ!" he gasped, espying a cloud of sail offshore. "A glass! Now!" he bade, turning his head to see Midshipman Sevier near the binnacle cabinet. "My glass, Mister Sevier, quickly!"

Once he had it in his hand, he slung it over his shoulder like a carbine and scampered into the larboard mizzenmast shrouds 'til he was above the cat-harpings near the fighting-top.

Dutch . . . French, he fretted, opening the tube out of its full extent. Panting a bit too, and damning the enforced idlness of these last few days; surely it wasn't *his* fault that a brief ascent winded him! There! Enemy ships, come from the Texel before Admiral Duncan could take up his blockade . . . the van division of a feared invasion?

No, they were beam-reaching off a Northerly, which would blow a "dead-muzzler" for the Texel's narrow North shore exit, so they couldn't be the Dutch Fleet.

French then? No again, he grumbled. They'd have had to come up-Channel, first, weather the Straits of Dover, the Downs, and Goodwin Sands.

Channel Fleet, itself, come to shoot the Nore ships into submission? Well, maybe, but the tail-end ships seemed as if they'd come from the North, scudding *off* the Northerly winds before they wheeled about in-line-ahead to follow the others which were coming in for the Queen's Channel and the outer anchorage on a soldier's wind.

"Duncan!" he cried with glee. "The North Sea Fleet, ordered to the Nore to put the mutiny down! *Someone* found his nutmegs, at last! Now we'll see something, by God!"

He lifted his glass again, leaning back into the shrouds, with one arm cocked through the rat-lines, smug with victory, and pitying the poor fools who were cheering the sight of the arriving ships. In a half-hour, when they opened their gun-ports and ran out their batteries, they'd be laughing out the other side of their necks!

"Ah . . ." He shuddered.

Perhaps not.

For atop the on-coming line-of-battle ships' foremasts, he saw a dread, red plain-ness to the flags they flew. No royal cantons, no cross of St. George or St. Andrew . . .

Plain, stark red battle flags—*mutiny flags!*

Aye, the North Sea Fleet had arrived. In open rebellion!

CHAPTER THIRTY

A bloody, unmitigated damned disaster!" Lewrie fumed, pacing furiously from starboard to larboard in the day-cabin of his quarters, while his remaining officers and midshipmen stood or sat.

"Enough to make a man weep, sir," Mr. Winwood spat, looking as close as he'd ever come to letting his despair overpower him. "Thirteen sail of the line they have now. Nigh on ten thousand seamen and marines in rebellion. Encouraged . . ." he trailed off in a sigh.

"There's been battles won with less," Midshipman Catterall had the lack of tact to say almost under his breath, and even Mr. Adair's warning elbow in his ribs only caused him to grunt and glower back in ill humor. *He* was senior midshipman, two years older than Adair, and the cock of the orlop cockpit; ever the nudger, not the nudgee.

"Oh, yes, there have been, Mister Catterall," Lewrie sniped back. "Thank you *so* much for bringing that historical fact to our attention!"

"Uhm, sorry sir," Catterall reddened, trying to pull his head in like a tortoise. He found something intricate in the Turkey carpet's design to be fascinated by.

The heart of Admiral Duncan's North Sea Fleet, the bulk of his two-decker, 64-gun warships—*Montagu, Belliqueux, Repulse, Standard, Lion,* and *Nassau,* along with the *Inspector* sloop and the fireship *Comet*—had come in around 5:00 P.M. the previous afternoon. Captain William Bligh's

HMS *Director* had been part of that fleet, but had mutinied whilst anchored at the Nore, so no one expected that Admiral Duncan had much left to work with, if he still intended to blockade the Texel channels. If it came to a fight with Channel Fleet to put down this mutiny—if one could still call it a strictly naval mutiny and *not* a burgeoning revolution—it would be a close-run thing, even if Channel Fleet owned larger, more powerful 74s, 80s, and ships of the 1st and 2nd Rate, compared to the weaker, shallower draught 64s from Great Yarmouth, more useful near the Dutch shoals.

If it came to a fight, Lewrie glumly suspected, it'd be no fight at all. Channel Fleet might have been saved from mutiny, most of the grievances satisfied. But would that be good enough for them to fire upon other British tars? Should that come, it'd surely be the end of the Royal Navy. Most-like, he imagined, the two fleets would meet and blend, overthrow authority again, and would then be fully provisioned, *at sea!* beyond the reach of reason. Not just the Royal Navy though, oh, no . . . perhaps it would be the tiny spark in the pan, like that one at Lexington in the lost American Colonies, that had begun the revolt against the Crown; and Britain would be torn asunder. Republicans and Jacobinist Levellers versus Royalists; hard-pressed as the commoners were by the demands of the war and the new taxes, it might be wealthy against poor too! The Irish, of course, encouraged to throw off the yoke of English occupation. Scotland too, uneasily forced into submission since the last rising of the clans in "The 45."

"There is the possibility the new arrivals are not victualled as well as the original mutinous ships, sir," Mr. Coote offered in a hopeful gesture. "And with supplies now refused them . . . perhaps they cannot stay here at the Nore for very long."

"I rather doubt that, Mister Coote," Lieutenant Wyman sighed, "though it is wishful. They were to all accounts provisioned for an extended spell of blockade duty off the Dutch coast. From what I heard from our rumour-mill, they defected *after* receiving sailing orders to join Admiral Duncan. Meet him at some 'rondy,' somewhere off the coast . . ."

Lt. Wyman did not wear disappointment well; he looked like he'd aged ten years in the last two days and was not as prone to appearing surprised or startled any longer. Most un-lieutenant-like, he slouched on the starboard-side upholstered settee with his legs out and his hands in his breeches pockets, like one of Hogarth's sketches of an idle roisterer with a killing "head," the morning after.

"And where do they *think* they'd get provisions, with every port closed to 'em, Mister Coote?" Lewrie fretted. "Aye, most-like they *are* well-provisioned for up to six months at sea. Gawd . . . !"

"Can't last that long, can it, sir?" Midshipman Adair queried. "Else the wind shifts, sooner or later, and the Dutch get out to sea. The French Fleet at Brest bound for Ireland . . . we've been fortunate in the weather so far, sir."

"That's so, sir." The Sailing Master nodded, stuffing tobacco into his clay church warden pipe. "But a man who'd depend on weather for his salvation is the hugest sort of fool. I cannot but think that the Merciful Hand of Providence has controlled the contrary winds this long during our travails, sirs—to grant His most favoured nation a space in which to save ourselves. But such Divine Mercy is not forever."

"A tiny space," Lewrie mused, mussing his hair as he came to a stop behind his desk, for a moment envying Mr. Winwood the comfort of his pipe and tobacco. He'd never taken up the custom, and the time he had been forced to smoke, with the Muskogee Indians during the Revolution, hadn't exactly made him a devotee of the Noble Weed. "Is it not true, Mister Winwood, that 'God helps those, who help themselves'? As you say, it's only the fools who lift their hands in supplication, depending on the Lord, not their own efforts, to save their skins."

"Well, there are some believers, sir," Winwood winced, "not in the Established Church, of course, who hold that is the Almighty *truly* 'almighty,' He can do anything, even for the weakest and most powerless. It has been my experience though, sir, that . . . was a man adrift at sea in a small boat amid a raging gale, the Good Lord might look down more kindly on the sort who'd strive in league with Divine Assistance, not lay whimpering in the bilge, sir. Though I must confess the Bible is replete with examples of the utterly hopeless being salved at the last moment, through no action on their part but deep, abiding faith and a fervent prayer." He puffed away quite contentedly, wreathing himself in aromatic blue fumes, after delivering what to Lewrie sounded mightily like a paradox: "This, but on the other hand. . . ."

"Take the case of Abraham, sir, and the offering of his beloved son on the altar in the desert wilderness . . ." Mr. Winwood began to expound.

"You've prayed fervently on this, I take it, Mister Winwood?" Lewrie asked him.

"Well . . . *aye*, sir!" Winwood admitted, as if surprised that anyone might suspect that he had not.

"And I take it that all of you gentlemen, as Christian, English gentlemen, have prevailed upon the Good Lord for guidance and succour, for victory over our foes, and a way out of our . . . wilderness?"

"Oh, of course, sir," they mumbled back, as if by rote, though looking a bit cutty-eyed that they had perhaps *not*, but were making the "proper" noises.

"Then we cannot fail." Lewrie thinly smiled, tossing in a stab at "Hardy, Noble Christian Gentleman" himself. "And, with Divine aid, we will retake *Proteus* . . . God willing," he piously concluded.

And thus endeth the epistle, he sourly thought, having no time for Winwood's parson-like pontificating: *or is it "here endeth"?*

Damme I must *pay more attention next time I'm in church!*

"But . . . *how*, sir? Now that . . ." Lieutenant Wyman waffled.

"Aye, they're encouraged, Mister Wyman"—Lewrie grinned at him—"I'll grant you, for the nonce. I doubt though that these new-come ships are as radical as some. They've not been cut off from news from London and know of the Royal Pardon and the Acts. Their arrival here at the Nore is, I suspect, a *temporary* thing . . . their way of assuring themselves *they're* included in the terms, showing support for the Nore sailors who might *appear* to be excluded for the moment."

Don't know that at all, he admitted to himself; *whistling past the graveyard . . . spinnin' fairy-shite!*

"Doubt there's been much communication 'tween Great Yarmouth and the Nore either . . . they haven't had a chance to take their measure of our mutineers. Once they see what a pack of radicals they are, there's more than a good chance it'll make 'em queasy. We're still anchored out in the seaward row, close to the Queen's Channel. The new-comers are crowded in on either end. We're still dealing with the two ships anchored closest to us. And one of those came within a quim-hair of overpowering their mutineers. Now granted, the *other* one fired into us, but . . . if we continued sail-drill, making up to short stays before backing and filling, we can lull them to think nothing of it, just as we originally planned. We've *most* of the Marines on our side now . . . ready to act the next time."

"Sir, are you sure they're still with us now the mutiny's reenforced and their spirits lifted?" Mr. Coote worried aloud.

"A day or two's excitement," Lewrie said dismissively, hoping that he was right, feeling forced to be optimistic, if only to prevent his officers from sinking into the "Blue Devils." "A day or two more and they'll be back to their doubts and mis-givings, thinking of the courts-martial and gibbets. Here's what we should rumour about: The North Sea Fleet is here so they can be included in the Spithead terms and nothing more. There's no contact allowed with them either, so our hands won't know the diff'rence."

"But they would, sir," Mr. Adair plumbed the fault to it quite quickly, "the Fleet Delegates will swear they're in agreement with all *their* terms."

"Unless they already are, sir," Midshipman Catterall gloomily pointed out.

"You are *quite* the font of cheer, Mister Catterall," Lewrie said rather frostily, delivering a withering glower. "Right, then . . . we say they've been deceived, now they're here, 'cause *they've* no wish to be against Crown and Country or be part of a Floating Republic forever! They're ready to sail to aid Admiral Duncan, even if the delegates, in the pay of foreign powers, wish to prevent it. Plausible?" he asked.

"And our people are already leery of the Fleet Delegates, and their radical insolence to authority, sir!" Midshipman Adair excitedly chimed in. "Why, they already take half what they say with a *handful* of salt! North Sea ships, *and* ours, deceived . . . !"

"That's the spirit!" Lewrie nodded with pleasure. He had put a bit of iron back in their spines and had cobbled together new reasons for his ship's hands to despair once more. "Thank you, gentlemen. I think we should begin spreading our 'moonshine.' And about time for us to conduct sail-making drill, hmm? I'll be on the deck later to see how it goes. Both the sail-drill . . . and our rumour-mongering."

Once they had departed though, he flung himself into his desk chair with a fretful sigh and rang a tiny bell for his steward.

"Any coffee left on the candle warmer, Aspinall?"

" 'Nough for a cup, at least, sir. Comin' right up."

Aspinall delivered the cup, atop a new sennet place mat, as intricate as Holland lace.

"Nice work, that . . . complex," Lewrie idly congratulated him.

"Aye, sir. Some o' the Irish lads're teachin' me their Gaelic knots," Aspinall proudly admitted. Under Andrews's and others' tutelage, Aspinall had become quite good at decorative rope-work, fashioning some brooches, bracelets, even rings, as well as place mats and such. "Some of 'em still know their old ways . . . what they call Celtic. I'll pare a bit more sugar for ya, sir. Won't be a tick."

Lewrie studied his mug, the coin-silver, engraved present from his former Jesters, while Aspinall scraped at the bee-hive–shaped lump of sugar in the small pantry. Hmmm . . .

He stared at the engraving, setting it down to rotate it, with a thoughtful expression; admiring the profile of *Jester* rushing along with all plain sail set, a bone in her teeth, led onward by that mysterious forearm and sword, with the dolphins and seals dancing . . .

"Aspinall . . ." he mused aloud.

"Sir?"

"You associate much with our new-come Irish, do you?"

"Some, sir."

"Are many of *them* in on the mutiny, d'ye think?" Lewrie asked.

"Not that many, sir," Aspinall discounted. "Most of 'em are as poor as church-mice . . . just wantin' decent wages and a chance to get by, sir. Not much work in Ireland, troubles and risin's, and most of 'em wishin' a wide berth o' those, like Desmond and Furfy. Count them with any education on the fingers o' one hand, sir. A chearly lot, I must say, though, for all that . . . singin' and hornpipin' at the drop o' your hat, sir? Full o' grand stories too, sir . . . why, Irishmen could talk the birds from the sky and not repeat themselves for three days runnin', sir!"

"You ever tell them stories, Aspinall? They pump you for information?" Lewrie pressed.

A captain's steward could be an unwitting font of intelligence for the disgruntled; some stewards traded on their access.

"Lord, sir . . . get a word in edgewise! Aye, some. 'Bout how we had a lucky ship, sir . . . and you, a lucky captain."

"Ever tell them *all* about *Jester?*" Lewrie pressed, getting inspired at this welcome news, "and the strange . . . fey things we saw?" He swiveled the mug about and pointed at the dolphins and seals and the sea-god's arm, tapping his finger by them. "And how much do they know about *Proteus?* They came aboard after Chatham. They may not know all her short history . . . her launching, the change of her name, the Irish sawyer and his boy who convinced her to take water?"

"Dribs an' drabs, here an' there, I s'pose, sir," Aspinall said with a shrug.

"That *Proteus* was an ancient sea-god, Aspinall." Lewrie smiled. "A *very* old, shape-changing sea-god. This ship murdered a Protestant, Anglo-Irish vicar. Drove an Anglo-Irish captain ashore, mad as a hatter. But so far . . ." he added, rapping his knuckles for luck, "she has nothing against me. For I've *seen* an old sea-god. *Jester* and me, we were a lucky ship, together. A blessed ship, Aspinall. But, *by whom?*"

"By 'at ole Lir, sir?" Aspinall replied.

"And Lir's an *Irish* sea-god, Aspinall." Lewrie nodded happily. "Lir . . . *Proteus* . . . same old gentleman. Cleared her hawse, *Proteus* did, so *I'd* come aboard her as captain."

God, I am such *an egotistical bastard!* he silently grimaced to himself; *and a damned liar too!*

"Oh, I think I get yer meanin', sir!" Aspinall grinned slyly.

"A proud, willful ship, a *living* ship she is," Lewrie said. "Too proud to let herself be shamed by serving an Anglo-Irish captain. Too proud and haughty to be involved in something shameful either! And . . . too savage in her anger 'gainst anyone who'd let her be shamed . . . in *his* name! Vengeful, arrogant, blood-thirsty . . . a ship to serve chearly . . . in *his* name."

"Lord, sir!" Aspinall gulped. "Talk like 'at fair gives me th' shivers!"

"Your Irish mates forrud . . . they tell their old tales like they half-believed 'em, Aspinall?" Lewrie smirked.

"Oh, aye, they do, sir. Even Desmond . . . best-educated o' their lot, sir. All his songs an' stories . . ."

"You tell 'em *our* songs and stories, Aspinall," Lewrie schemed. "*Jester* and the burial, the seals . . . the seals off Italy the morning we caught that French bastard Choundas. In the Adriatic, at that pirate isle . . . *Proteus* wants out of here, Aspinall, before she's smeared in shame for all time, and no good . . . what do they call it? No good *cess*'ll be in her if she doesn't . . . for any man-jack who doesn't aid her. Or . . . *him,* whose name she secretly bears. Can you whisper that to 'em, lad?"

"Oh, aye, sir, I can," Aspinall agreed.

"You and the Bosun, he already knows her nature. Hunt up Bosun Pendarves, Mister Towpenny . . . they're West Country men almost good as Irish. You tell 'em for me, Aspinall. I can't. 'Twould sound like crowing."

And get me tossed in gaol as a heretic—or Bedlam as a loonie!

"I'll get started then, sir. Iff'n ya don't need nothin' else?"

"No, nothing else, Aspinall. You go visit your Irish friends."

God helps those who help themselves, he told himself after his steward had departed; *now . . . which god, well . . . ! Either one, ya know I'm desperate. And a gallopin' lie in a good cause is forgivable.*

CHAPTER THIRTY-ONE

Another day, another harangue, Lewrie thought with a scowl as he pared his nails with a small pocket knife. The boat-parade of delegates had come with a band, flags, their "green cockade" speakers, and another rant, that just might take up half the Forenoon Watch if past performances were anything to go by.

Must be gettin' dotty, he told himself; *but I'm almost lookin' forward to the "entertainment!"* He sat, most *un*-captainly slouched, in his personal wood-and-canvas folding deckchair of his own devising . . . feet up on the compass binnacle cabinet, conveniently near the speaker so he could hear all that transpired . . . yet far enough away to disclaim any *real* curiosity— enjoying the wan sunlight and fresh air, should anyone enquire. Lazily, as was his secret wont.

"Now, hark ye, t'what those cringin', *cowardly* tyrant ministers from London have sent us, thinkin' we'd cringe an' knuckle under," the idiot McCann raved from the forward edge of the quarterdeck, brandishing a sheet of paper over his head. "Ahem!" he announced, lowering it so he could read it. "George Rex . . . '*Whereas!*'" he bellowed, ". . . 'upon th' rep . . . rep-resent . . .' damme."

Lewrie had himself a pleasing smirk of glee over McCann's nigh illit-erate ignorance, well hidden by the shade of his cocked hat.

"'. . . of Our Lords-commissioners of Our Admiralty respectin' th' proceedin's of th' seamen and Marines on board certain of Our ships at th' Nore' . . . hah! *All* ships at th' Nore, an' more to come, count on't, lads! Here, uhm . . . where th' Devil was I . . . ? Ahem! 'We were pleased to command Our Lords-commissioners of Our Admiralty to signify to th' seamen and Marines Our gracious intentions, ex . . .' hmmph! '. . . under Our sign m . . . man'—means he writ his name—then, '. . . bearin' date at Saint James's th' 27th day of May instant; and, *whereas* . . . ! Our right trusty and beloved . . .' Devil take 'em! He says Earl Spencer, th' Lord Arden, and Rear Admiral Young are 'trusty,' th' old half-wit. Loony as a bedbug, an' ever'body knows it! Here, someone with good eyes, *read* this shitten thing! Brother Bales, you're a scholard, ain't ye?"

Bales, Lewrie noted, was ever eager to step forward and bask at centre-stage. A quickly whispered conference, McCann's tarry finger on the place he'd left off, and Bales began to declaim.

". . . 'did cause Our gracious intentions, expressed in Our declaration, to be signified to the crews of Our ships at the Nore, and did require such crews to return to their due obedience accordingly; and, whereas it has been represented to us, that some of the crews of Our said ships have been desirous of returning to their obedience, accordingly, but have been prevented from doing so by violence . . .' "

"*Who*, by Jesus?" McCann howled, peering about the gathered hands as if seeking witches in New England, making the crowd of sailors balk and cringe. "No one *I* know wants t'return t'duty, by God! Violence . . . twaddle! We're free men here, of our own free will for th' Cause!"

Then why, Lewrie almost chuckled to himself, did Fleet Delegates now travel in very well-armed packs, escorted by weapons-heavy guards!

"Read on, Brother Bales! Read on!" McCann boomed.

Bales shrugged, then turned back to face the crew below him in the waist, crowded on the gangways. "Ah . . . 'doing so by violence, and others of Our ships in the actual discharge of their duty having been fired upon, and attempts having been made to prevent some of Our ships from proceeding according to the orders of their commanders, and whereas such continued perseverance in rebellious and treasonable attempts . . . against Our Crown and dignity . . .' " Bales began to mutter and frown at those words, and Lewrie perked up his own ears; "Rebellious" and "Treasonable" were not words idly bandied about!

"Louder, damn ye; we can't hear!" some hands demanded.

"Uhm, ' . . . after repeated admonitions and offers of Our gracious pardon, render it necessary for Us to call on all Our loving subjects to be aiding and assisting in *repressing* the same!' Listen, mate, we best not . . ." Bales fretted, turning to McCann, as if pleading to leave off.

"Go on, Brother Bales . . . louder! What's it say, then?" McCann insisted, oblivious to the consequences. Bales dashed a hand 'cross his brow as if sweating lead pistol-balls. He peered about the deck for a bit of help, it looked like, someone with sense he might appeal to.

Lewrie lowered his feet, blew breath on his now-trimmed nails, and sauntered a few feet further forward, suddenly filled with hope as he realised that the King's letter was an ultimatum!

Bales heaved a petulant, despairing shrug, then continued where he had broken off. " ' . . . We have thought fit, by the advice of Our Privy Council, to issue this Our royal proclamation, and we do hereby strictly enjoin all Our admirals, generals, commanders, and officers of Our forces by sea and land, and all of Our magistrates whatsoever, and all others of Our loving subjects . . . that they in their several stations do use their utmost endeavours, according to the law, to suppress all such mutinous and treasonable proceedings, and to use all lawful means to bring the persons concerned therein, their aiders and abettors to . . . to justice!' "

Some few still dared to boo or hiss like geese; the rest stood rooted by alarm; it *was* an ultimatum: His Majesty's patience had come to an end!

" ' . . . and We do hereby strictly enjoin and command all of Our loving subjects whatsoever not to give any aid, comfort, assistance, or encouragement whatsoever, to any person or persons concerned in any such mutinous and treasonable proceedings, as . . .' " Bales paled, " 'as they will answer the same at their peril; and also to the utmost of their power, and according to the law, to prevent all other persons from giving any such aid, assistance, comfort or encouragement. Given at Our court at Saint James's, the 31st day of May, 1797, and in the 37th year of Our reign! G . . . God save the king!' "

"What?" McCann erupted in spittle-flinging fury. "God-*damn* th' ol' bugger, is more like it! Listen, Brother Bales . . ."

"It's what's written here, you fool!" Bales screeched back at him. "See it? It's how *any* royal proclamation ends, damn your eyes!"

Glorious! Lewrie felt cause to exult in his heart; oh, thankee Jesus . . . maybe Lir, too! They should *never* have read that to the mutineers!

When the Crown spoke of Rebellion or Revolution and portrayed the mutineers as Treasonable . . .! That could get *hundreds* hung higher than Haman! And to order the entire nation to deny any mutineer aid, comfort, to deem anyone who did as co-conspirators!—like the Romans Lewrie could recall from his schooldays—exiles had to leave the furthest border of the Empire and never return, shunned as lepers and denied all aid on the way—"neither fire, nor food, nor forage," he thought the phrase was— or end up nailed to a cross, exile and aider alike!

The King demanded that family, neighbours, friends, wives, even shop-keepers, publicans, and *whores* shun the mutineers now; the children flee from their father's sight, lest they be tainted and taken up!

Opportunity! Lewrie exulted; *look at 'em waver, even the stout radicals . . . grim as a cartload of condemned men on the way to Tyburn and the gallows!*

"Empty threats, I tell ya!" McCann ranted, too stupid to realise the harm he'd done his cause. "The common folk are with us! We got th' North Sea Fleet, in spite of any royal decree! Thirteen ships of th' line, strong enough t'sail right up t'London Bridge, smashin' all th' forts along th' way! Take th' arsenal at Woolwich, all th' guns, shot an' powder . . . gather up th' soldiers too, just ripe for comin' over to us, and don't ye doubt it, brothers! They're tremblin' in their boots!"

And you're whistlin' past the graveyard, Lewrie thought!

"Now, lads, I'll show ye how our Floatin' Republic answers those high-flown tyrants an' butchers! Wrote in *plain* English, not all that 'gilt-an' beshit' . . . ahem!" McCann said, producing another letter.

"Brother McCann," Lewrie could hear Bales urge, laying a hand on his arm to dissuade him. "It's too much for them; they're fearful . . ."

"Let 'em stew an' fester on the King's writ, Brother Bales? No, they shan't. This'll nip fear in th' bud. Are *you* growin' fearful, Brother Bales? Turnin' cool to th' Cause, backin' off like Parker is? Mayhap this ship should elect *you,* day-t'day, like we do him! Nossir, lemme go . . . *ahem!*"

McCann shook loose of Bales's restraint, and drew a deep breath.

"My Lords!" he roared, " ' . . . we had th' honour t'receive your Lord-ships' proclamation, for we *don't* conceive it t'be his Majesty's, accompanied by an insipid address from Admiral Buckner. They met with th' fate they justly deserved! How could your Lordships *think* t'frighten us as old women in th' country frighten children with such stories as th' Wolf and Raw Head, and Bloody Bones . . . or, as the Pope wished to terrify th' French Republic with his famous Bull at th' beginnin' of th' Revolution! Know, gentlemen, that we're *men!* Men long tried for courage and per . . . perseverance in a cause *not* altogether so interestin' to ourselves as the present. Shall we then now be induced from a few paltry threats t'forsake our glorious plan, an' lick your Lordships" "—he paused to titter—" *'feet!* . . . for pardon an' grace, when we see ourselves in possession of thirteen sail of as noble ships as any in his *Majesty*'s service! And men not inferior to any in the kingdom! Do we demand anything but what justice licenses, and preservation approves?

" 'Th' few reasonable articles we've presented to your Lordships *should* have been attended to in a *respectful* manner, otherwise by your deferrin' it a few days longer, some *others* may pop up their terrific heads t'stare your Lordships in the face! We have nothin' more t'say but hope you will take th' necessary steps to save the country from a Civil War, which may end in th' ruin of yourselves, and uneasiness in our Gracious Sovereign, to whom we have ever been and will be loyal . . . whilst there's a chance of our grievances bein' addressed.

" 'With regard to our havin' fired at th' *San Fiorenzo* . . . be it known to you that we are very sorry that we could not *sink* her! As, without regard to th' league she had entered into with us, she basely deserted. We wish your Lordships likewise t'observe that th' Article Number Six shall extend to *all* persons condemned to imprisonments, or any other punishment by th' sentence of th' court-martial, as well as to prisoners who have *not* been tried, and that all persons now aboard labouring under any such sentence be from this time entirely free! We have th' honour t'be, your Lordships' very humble servants, th' seamen of th' fleet at th' Nore!' "

God, Lewrie shuddered in awe; *now you've* really *stepped in the quag . . . right up to your eyebrows! I wouldn't post a letter like that to a dead lawyer! Threatening civil war, my Lord! If the King's proclamation hasn't taken the wind from their sails, then that damn-foolery surely did! Of all the belligerent, bone-headed . . . !*

Chatter was breaking out on every hand again, and the stunned mutterings pro and con swelled up from the gun-deck, out of his sight. Lewrie began to walk forward, into that maelstrom of doubt, sorting his thoughts for a choice, telling phrase or two which would scuttle Bales, McCann, and *Proteus*'s mutiny once and for all.

"No, keep him back, there!" Bales cried, wheeling about as one of his minions tugged at his sleeve to point out Lewrie's intentions. "Not this time, you don't. See 'im below," he ordered those supporters on the quarterdeck. "He's nothing new to say to us. I'll not have it! All officers, mates, and midshipmen will go below now!"

And before the crew knew he might have spoken, before most even could espy his presence, Lewrie was seized and hustled aft to the companionway near the taffrails, and down the narrow ladder to his cabins. The arched, cross-hatched timber hatch-cover was slammed down over it a moment later, as Lewrie stood massaging his arms where they'd taken hold of him—though with a lot less violence than he'd expected from them. Fear of the consequences, Lewrie suspected, now the consequences had risen gallows high?

The door to the gun-deck slammed open against the partitions of the chart-space, and Aspinall, Padgett, and Cox'n Andrews were hurled inside to join him. In the few bleak seconds allowed him, Lewrie got a glimpse of sailors gesticulating and jabbering back and forth, angry fists being shaken in faces, some making push-off gestures of conciliation as they argued for or against continuing the mutiny, amidst wails from the confused womenfolk.

And McCann's voice, which soared over them all, rasping harsh and shrill, so loud his words could clearly be made out even through the thick deck timbers overhead . . . "Spread th' ships out so we really give' th' lyin' bastards summat t'think about! We . . . !"

"Dey threatenin' t'flog any mon who goes against de oath, sah. Douse him in th' sea," Andrews carped, rubbing his arms as if to wipe the mutineers' taint off, not to ease bruised flesh. He was scowling hellish-angry; even after years of freedom after running away from his slave-masters on Jamaica, he showed an aristocrat's loathing for being pawed at.

"Ssshh!" Lewrie bade him, pointing a finger aloft.

". . . won't issue rations; then we'll *take* what we need!" McCann was bristling. "Hundreds o' merchantmen, every day! Navy storeships be fair game too, a feast bound upriver t'London in every bottom! By order of th' Fleet Parliament, we'll starve London, swing th' people . . . !"

"Oh, Lord, that's revolution for sure, sir!" Aspinall gasped.

"Hush!" Lewrie snapped, all but cupping his hands to his ears.

". . . anythin' perishable's free, but grain, coal, anything else, we'll stop here in th' Thamesmouth, lads! Brother seamen in merchant ships, they'll side with us, o' course they will! By next week, we'll be twenty thousand, thirty thousand strong . . . in a fortnight, we'll lay our guns on alla London do they not give us our due! Brother Bales . . . ! Up-anchor an' make short sail for . . ."

The rest trailed off into gibberish, then nothing, when McCann stopped talking for the horde and directed softer comments to Bales. Lewrie dropped his hands to his sides and lowered his gaze to stare at his tiny clutch of loyalists.

"Oh, Lord, sir," Aspinall said again, in a wee-er voice. "They really mean'ta start a rebellion. Damn' *traitors* they are! Were, all along, sir, an' just hidin' h'it 'til . . ."

"Hark, sah," Andrews said, cutting him off, cocking his head to one side. But they could all hear the drum of horny feet on oak decks, the rustle and thump of coiled sail-tending lines being taken down from the racks of belaying pins and dropped on the deck where they'd feed out smoothly; the preparatory creak of rope as men scampered up the shrouds and rat-lines to the tops and upper yards, the groan of the capstan as it was slowly rotated to free its drum before the messenger cable could be led to it and wound about it so the ship could be heaved into short-stays above her bower anchor. *Proteus* trembled gently to the movements as Bales and his mutineers prepared her to get underway.

Lewrie went forrud to the door and pulled it open to look out at what was going on, hoping someone, anyone, might put up strong objections, but . . . worried as they seemed, they were still cowed by rote duty, cowed by force of arms and the threat of punishment from their rebellious leaders . . . the habit of obedience drummed or lashed into them . . . damn' em.

"Nossir." Landsman Haslip leered at him, with a musket held at port-arms across his chest. "You stay b'low, sir," he insisted, taking stance to block Lewrie's exit. At his shoulder was Marine Private Mollo, also armed with a musket. "An' no talkin' neither. Don't 'ave no need o' you, sir . . . none a'tall." He grinned evilly.

The deck was its usual bedlam, of course, as gangs of men stood crowded together at jears, halliards, lift-lines, clews, and sheets, and no ship ever had room on deck for all of them to work at once, not with all those men at the capstan, the nippermen along the messenger and the heavier cable. It was shoulder-to-shoulder, as dense as the packing of slaves on a "black-birder" on the Middle Passage, and with so many women, and a fair number of children, aboard taking up precious deckspace . . .

"Here, now!" the old trollop with the passable daughter yelled, advancing on the doorway, and Lewrie felt a sudden flood of gratitude that Mollo and Haslip were armed; she looked so angry and full of lust for blood, she'd turned plummy-purple! Daughter, and that Nancy, were close on her heels, followed by at least a half-dozen more ship-wives, all howling bloody murder! "Git out me way, ya God-damn' bean-pole! I wanna word with 'at useless cap'um, yonder!" the old harridan shrilled.

"Aye, he's got some 'splainin' t'do!" Miss Nancy threatened.

Damme, wonder why I ever thought she was toppable, Lewrie thought with a *frisson* of dread; *now she looks like death's head on a mopstick!*

"Let us in there, damn yer blood!"

"Why . . . go right in, ladies," Haslip snickered, half-bowing to them and doffing his tarred hat. "You go right in!"

In the face of that, Lewrie retreated to the middle of his day-cabin as about ten women swished in like a Macedonian phalanx, bristly and out-of-sorts.

"Arrr . . . *some* live better'n others, I do declare," Old Trollop remarked, looking 'round at the furnishings. Lewrie kept a harder eye on the Lissome Daughter, who was picking things up and valuating them; books, plates, cups, spoons, napkin-rings . . . anything that wasn't locked up or nailed down, and several others were coughing, strolling, and "shopping" too; a sure sign they'd practiced the shop-lifting "lay" a time or two together.

"We'll frisk you down when you leave, ladies," Lewrie declared, "so you might as well leave my things be."

"Aye, an' I'll jus' bet ye'd enjoy th' pattin' down," Lissome Daughter tittered.

"Depends on how *you* might enjoy it, young miss." Lewrie grinned.

"La, what a cheeky ol' bugger ye are!" She coloured, swishing her skirts impishly. "Fetchin', though . . ."

"An' take 'at spoon out your apron pocket," Aspinall warned.

"What do you wish of me?" Lewrie asked.

"First of all, Cap'um . . . how 'bout ya trot out some grog? We're dry as dust," Miss Nancy demanded, "an' them sailors o' your' won't go shares no more."

"Ah." Lewrie glowered. "*That* all?"

"Nossir, it ain't," Old Trollop thundered. "We wants t'know what's t'happen to us, dammit! What-all that speechifyin' was about."

"Aye, does that mean they'll hang us as traitors'n rebels if we stay out here?" Nancy frowned, hands on her hips in a full aggressive fishwife's stance. "Mean, do we let 'em top us, we're guilty of givin' comfort an' such, so we get took up for't?"

"Ah!" Lewrie glimmed, his eyes crinkling with un-looked-for inspiration. "Uhm, Aspinall . . . do you and Andrews fetch out the barricoe of wine from the lazarette . . . the, uhm . . . claret. Mister Padgett, may I prevail upon you to break out all my cups and glasses? I doubt I've seats for all of you ladies, but . . ." he said invitingly, waving a hand about the cabins.

"Claret, well now!" Several oohed or ahhed. "Ain' niver had a claret." "Sure ye ain't got no gin?" one of them had to carp though.

They shoved dining table chairs out in the open, tried to shift his desk chairs but found they were "fiddled down"; filled the settee to starboard overfull, even perching on the arms, and clucked and put on airs as they got their glasses, mugs, or coffee cups filled from a hastily decanted pewter pitcher, getting "lordly" for lordly guzzle.

Well, burgundy, Lewrie sniffed to himself, *not good claret, and I doubt they'll know the diff'rence. Gad, look at 'em slosh it back . . . that five-gallon barricoe'll be gone in an eyeblink!*

"Now, ladies . . ." he began, accepting a sherry glass full of the wine himself—to be "chummy." "I have to warn you . . . what our King said is that he no longer looks on this as a mutiny but as an armed rebellion against the Crown. And anyone who persists in it is labeled a traitor to King and Country from the moment it was read. Just like readin' the Riot

Act before the soldiers come to clear the streets . . . once you hear it you have no more excuses for creating a disturbance."

"God o' Mercy, they'll string us *all* up!" one of the older ones wailed into her hand, her fine "claret" forgotten and her eyes red.

"Tosh, ya silly ol' cow!" Nancy gravelled, tossing her chin and her hair. "Won't hang poor whores, 'cept those that sided with rebels! Transport some maybe . . ." she said, level-headedly, "examples, like."

"Gawd, I don't wanna go t'no New South Wales!" Lissome Daughter whined. "T'other end o' th' world, nigger savages an' snakes . . . tigers an' dragons! I seen 'em in a book, I did! Real dragons, with tongues o' fire! An' coal-black murderers wif pointy teeth too!"

"Hmmph!" Lewrie heard Cox'n Andrews sniff in disdain. He gave him a shrug, to commiserate with him over the pig-ignorance of whores.

"Oh, worse than that." Lewrie winced, almost sucking wind between his teeth, trying to recall all he'd seen in the Far East or in a recent account of the flora and fauna of that part of the world.

"Lord, what'd be worse, sir?" Lissome Daughter blubbered.

"Sea-snakes, long as this ship," Lewrie intimated forebodingly. "Crawl right out of the water and swallow folk whole. Poisonous snakes, but with mouths that big, it doesn't matter much, now does it. Snakes and scorpions on land, spiders big as soup plates . . . poisonous too, I read. Crocodiles fiercer than the ones in Egypt . . . plagues of flies as bad as the Bible. A lot of sickness. Can't even wet your feet in any stream 'thout you get bit by something. Can't sleep safe . . ."

They sat gap-mouthed, looking physically ill.

"An' that whatchyacallem they read, h'it says if we be took with rebels, we're rebels too, then?" the red-eyed one sniffled.

"That's what it meant, yes," Lewrie sadly intoned. "Means any person who sells 'em anything, associates with 'em, or even knows who they are but doesn't speak up, will be called a rebel too. Can't hide 'em out from the law either. If you don't stop *others* from helping them, that's enough for a court to rule you guilty. Just like it urged me to do my utmost to quash them and take back this ship and return it to proper duty."

Proteus was shimmying now, heeling over a few degrees from upright as she paid off from the breeze under the barest amount of sail, making a queasy leeway, not yet under helm control.

"Hoy, where they be takin' us then?" Old Trollop barked, getting to her feet in a huff. "Dear God, not t'France, surely!"

"No, just a bit across the Great Nore," Lewrie patiently explained, putting on a sad smile to calm her. "Recall what that delegate said ... about blockading London? They're shifting ships so they have a line right across the Thames approaches. Further apart, d'ye see ..."

Further out from each other, he schemed hopefully, where they'd have to guess the range and would have to be quick off the mark to hit *Proteus* with their first un-organised broadsides, before she got far enough away to show them a clean pair of heels! Far enough that it would take too long for a re-enforcing boarding party to come help their mutineers, should they overpower them? Aha!

"*We* didn't want no part o' this, Cap'um, sir!" Nancy insisted. "Kept us aboard, press-ganged! Wasn't our doin'! You could speak up for us, couldn't ye, Cap'um Lewrie?"

"Kept us broke an' poor as them, th' shitten cheats!" one more spoke up sarcastically, one of the more pragmatic variety. "Here! We could go 'board them new ships, 'long as this'n writes a letter to th' magistrates, tellin' 'em we're innocent. 'Long as we're kept out here, why can't we turn a shillin'r two, I ask ye? We gotta eat!"

"No visiting 'tween ships," Lewrie pointed out quickly. "That's one of their rules. Besides ... the way I hear it told, the North Sea ships came *here* to get paid, 'cause *they're* stone-broke too!"

"Ya mean they're 'skint' too?" Nancy sneered. "Gawd, I just knew it. E'en with our gowns on, we're just fucked, is all."

"Wouldn't be th' first time *that* 'appened, Nancy," Old Trollop hooted. "Wi' half our trade 'knee-tremblers' in an alley! Cheap shits, too cheese-parin' t'rent a room, an' all that tar an' splinters from crates'n barrels on me bum, come mornin' ..."

No, he didn't particularly wish to picture *that*—ever!

"Gawd, whatever'll we do then?" Lissome Daughter blubbed, tears streaking her face. "Hung or transported fer life. Oh, we're jus' whores, not like respectable folk, so they won't care if they string us up by th' dozen! After we done so *much* fer th' Navy too!"

"You can help me," Lewrie suggested, "help me take the ship."

"*Wot?*"

"Do something *else* for the Navy, ladies," Lewrie muttered covertly, suddenly inspired as he paced out between them. "You know who the real hard-bitten mutineers are as good as us. You live a rough life . . . cheats who won't pay first, pimps trying to recruit you, and take all your earnings . . . others of your sort who'd fight you for the good corners, the better taverns, right? Don't you have to carry some . . . uhm, 'persuaders,' for your own protection?"

Aye, they allowed—yes, they did. Coshes, leather sacks full of lead balls, Dago or Spanish knives that flipped open, or wickedly sharp shaving razors. Lissome Daughter brought forth a pair of hatpins and rewarded him with a happy nod of understanding. Lewrie rewarded her with a beamish leer and a sly-boots chuckle. Lissome Daughter sprang to her feet and walked right up to him, all smiles.

"Lor', Cap'um Lewrie, sir!" she gushed, throwing her arms about him, going on tiptoe to kiss him on the cheek. "Feller smart'z you, a fine gentleman, I just *knew* you'd find a way t'save us!"

"Well, thankee, uhm . . . don't b'lieve I ever caught your name . . . ?" Lewrie blushed, quite happy to return her warm, promising embrace.

"Sally Blue, sir," she giggled, swaying back and forth as if it was a dance. "Sally fer me name . . . an' Blue fer me eyes."

"Well, uhm . . . well, pleased to make your acquaintance, Mistress. Sally Blue, rather. Well, uhm . . ." he flustered, wishing he was alone with her, and the rest shooed out to commit mayhem that instant. She took the hint and flounced quite coquettishly back to her wine glass, with a practiced but fetching gleam in those blue eyes of hers.

"Now give 'im 'is bloody watch'n chain back, Sally," Mistress Nancy wryly sniggered. "Gawd! Men's brains . . . !" They all shrieked.

All Lewrie could do was shrug haplessly as Sally Blue returned his watch to him. He felt like patting himself down, just to see what else her clever fingers had pilfered. The coy little minx!

"So yer sayin' . . ." Miss Nancy puzzled, after draining off her wine and beckoning Aspinall for a refill. "With us, you'd have more'n enough t'overpower Bales an' his lot, that right?"

"Assumin' they keep their brains where it seems I keep mine," Lewrie confessed with a disarming, sheepish grin, "aye."

"So do we come over all lovey-dovey an' swoggle 'em, you'd clap 'em in irons an' take your ship back," the buxom lass conspired. "Keep some of 'em below . . . an' busy long 'nough . . ."

"Exactly, Nancy. To a Tee." Lewrie smiled.

"Then ya put us ashore, 'cause we ain't gonna stay out here not a minute after," Nancy declared for them all, turning to see them agree with her, "not with ev'ry hand turned against us if we stay longer than we have to."

"We take her back, Nancy," Lewrie promised. "I'll see that you all get ashore and back to your own beds. Back to making money. With a letter to Admiral Buckner, praising you for what you did for me, with all your names on it. Why, you might even be called heroines! Get your names in the paper, thanks of the Admiralty, the King . . ."

That would mean sailing in towards Sheerness. He regretted it, but if that's what he had to do to gain allies . . .

"Fiddler's Pay," Old Trollop snorted in derision. "Thanks an' wine, an' then . . . get out th' door. Hmmph!"

"Aye, Cap'um Lewrie . . ." Nancy smirked at him. "That's all well an' good, but . . . times is hard, an' money's short. So . . . what's in it for us?"

Uh-oh! He flinched.

CHAPTER THIRTY-TWO

*T*he mutinous ships at the Nore were now arrayed in a single long line, right across the navigable waters of Queen's Channel and Thamesmouth, with a half-mile separation between ships. *Proteus* hadn't gone very far, and was in fact now directly North of Minster and Cheyney Rock Oyster Ground; and when the ebb ran, she streamed back from her anchor into the Queen's Channel, into deep water, with her stern half facing the inviting escape route into the North Sea. Several smaller warships patrolled the inner and outer face of that barricade to stop and inspect the papers and cargoes of every vessel that tried to sail up or down the great river. So far, McCann's ravings hadn't come true; no provisions from civilian merchantmen had been removed and shared out to those ships short of supplies. Of course, Lewrie was now beginning to understand, just like there were tyrants, and then there were tyrants, there were delegates, and then there were delegates, and McCann didn't speak for them all—thank God.

Proteus began her ship's routine at daybreak, with the hands up to scrub decks and stow bedding. There would be no more drills though; Bales had had enough of those and was leery of any more sail-making.

After the decks were spotlessly sanded and sluiced to pristine white, perhaps as a way to regain the crew's lost enthusiasm for the evolving mutiny, Seaman Bales decreed a day of "Rope-Yarn" sloth and led them

into the requisite morning "three hearty cheers" before dismissing them
for their breakfasts and got back what sounded a bit like proper *elan* in
their open-throated response.

"Rope-Yahn, sah." Andrews smiled, ducking back into the cabins.
"Evahbody gon' caulk or idle."

"Aha," Lewrie sighed, looking glum. It was perfect, the enforced half-
mile separation, the crew restive and gnawing on their worries, and now
idled for the day. Plenty of reason for any sharp-eyed watcher to nod off
and let his guard down, plenty of time for his new "vanguard" of prosti-
tutes to insinuate themselves with the diehards and dis-arm them . . . one
way or another. He looked at Wyman, Winwood, and his midshipmen,
who were aft to breakfast with him. There would never be a better chance,
not in a month of Sundays, yet . . .

He fretted his mouth, gnawed at his lips in indecisiveness. It could still
fail, go horribly wrong, and more innocent men be killed or injured, more
loyal hands hurt and let down by a second failure. After scheming for so
long, feverish for an opening, if they tried again and were beaten again,
there'd never be another hope of salving *Proteus*.

What they pay detached captains for, he writhed in silent agony; *be
king and foreign minister and God all rolled up into one, with yer head on
the choppin' block if you're wrong! Come on, ya damn' fool! A bit o' backbone . . . a pinch o' wits!* Say *something. They're waitin'.*

"Forenoon . . . or wait 'til the First Dog," Lewrie muttered just to fill
the echoing void, to temporise a bit more while his creaky wit churned.
"Try to sail past the guns of the rest . . . with frigates and a sloop of war
patrolling inshore? I fear it'll have to be mid-morning, gentlemen. No
chance to retrieve Lieutenant Devereux and Mister Langlie 'til this is done
and we can put back in for 'em."

"But do we proceed, sir?" Lt. Wyman dared press.

"Aye, we do." Lewrie sighed, feeling like it was wrung from him on
an inquisitor's rack. "Alert Sergeant Skipwith and Mistress Nancy. Charge
your pistols and hide them on your persons. Swords might alert them.
Let's say, uhm . . . six bells of the Forenoon. With a Rope-Yarn Day,
they'll begin queuing up forrud before the rum-cask comes up in no particular order. With nothing more'n grog on their minds, we must hope.
Six Bells, gentlemen. Aye . . . let's proceed with it."

Gawd! he shivered as they departed, flopping half-limp into his desk chair; *I'm trustin' to luck, Marines who can play-act innocent, and a pack o' whores!* But he opened the mahogany box on the desktop and extracted two long-barreled, single-shot pistols to clean them and charge them, and check their flints and mechanisms. Andrews set to at his second set of double-barrel Mantons, and Aspinall and Padgett got busy with Padgett's two small, single-barrel pocket pistols.

"You hear me shout, Andrews, you come running with my hanger," Lewrie bade him. "Your spare cutlass, since you know how to use it. I will trust you, Aspinall, to guard my back with one pistol, and you to my other hand, Mister Padgett. Close-in belly shots, no tricky work."

"Aye, sir." Padgett nodded in his lugubrious, quiet way, with a fine sheen of sweat on his forehead already and his long, clerkish, ink-stained fingers juddering a little in fearful foreboding.

Daft! Lewrie deemed it; bloody, ragin' daft! Still, by 11:00 A.M. there'd be some fewer mutineers aboard. Mr. Handcocks and Morley would be aboard *Sandwich* for the daily wrangle, and they'd take a boat-crew with them, about half of those the diehards. Six or seven less for them to overpower, so . . . Christ, so *hellish* daft!

Half-hour to go to the appointed time for the uprising. Lewrie posing at music by the taffrails, since it was a dry day with no rain, some sunshine, and a bit of wind. Wind square out of the North, about perfect for a ship bound out so she could beam-reach at first to deep water, then haul off to Large or Fair down the Queen's Channel. Bosun Pendarves had been told off to take and hold the forecastle with some few trusty men, to cut the anchor cable and hoist the inner and outer jibs, so *Proteus* would bear off to her larboard, South-facing side, and drift. Mr. Towpenny and a few more would hoist the spanker from the mizzen to get some drive on her. Let fall the fore and main-course to hang loose-braced and baggy for speed and not worry about the tops'ls or t'gallants 'til they'd gotten the last of the mutineers subdued.

With a brace of long-barrel pistols shoved down into the back of his breeches under his uniform coat, sitting on the flag lockers wasn't the most comfortable thing he'd ever done, as he tootled away on that tin-whistle of his. Louder than his usual wont, to sound casual, and harmless. "Derry Hornpipe," "Portsmouth Lass," "Tomorrow Shall Be My Dancing Day" . . . he ran through his repertoire (and a damn' thin'un it was!) of the old, old airs, the Celtic, Gaelic, West Country tunes he knew.

Lt. Wyman, as jittery as a whore at a christening, sawed away on his violin, with its case ajar at his feet, where he'd concealed a brace of his own pistols in addition to the pair he'd secreted under his own coat. He struggled in mid-saw, uttering a shuddery, "Uh-oh!" for approaching them on the quarterdeck were a clutch of Irish hands, and Lewrie wondered if a cry of, "I didn't do it!" might help, as his tootling faltered to a stop.

"Beggin' yer pardon, sir," Desmond said, doffing his hat and making a short bow. "Know we ain't t'be on th' quarterdeck without an off'cer's leave, sir, but . . . d'ye know a slip jig, sir?"

They haven't tumbled to it yet, thankee Jesus! Lewrie shivered.

"A slip jig?" he managed to enquire with forced cheer.

"Aye, sir . . . slip jig or hop jig, they calls 'em. English don't allow our music played back home, sir, but there's times we sneak away an' play 'em still . . . in a remote *shebeen*. Here's one, sir, by your leave?" Desmond smiled, producing his lap-pipes. Furfy was with him, along with Ahern, Kavanaugh, and Cahill, and they took seats flat on the deck. The ship's lamed fiddler joined them. "One o' th' easier ones t'play, sir . . . called 'Will You Come Down t'Limerick.' You'll master th' tune easy, Cap'um, sir . . . Mister Wyman, sir."

It was a catchy tune, though a difficult one to follow, for the tempo changed several times, throwing Lewrie and Wyman off, so for the first few minutes they sat with their hands in their laps.

"You try her now, sir," Desmond urged, as Furfy swayed and beat the time on his meaty thighs, and the other three began to dance stiff-armed but footloose. They were beginning to gather a crowd of sailors who had nothing better to do on a Rope-Yarn Day and temporarily allowed access to the quarterdeck by their leaders.

Lewrie shared a sick look with Wyman as they lifted their instruments, thinking they were exposed and a step away from being seized and disarmed. And, for the short meantime, mocked and derided!

"A fine auld air, sir," Desmond rhapsodised, as he pumped away with his elbow to stoke the *uillean* pipes in his lap, keyboarding the notes.

"Suitin' for lads who cling to th' auld ways an' legends. An' tales o' th' auld gods, sir," Desmond added, when he saw that his hint wasn't broad enough. "Seen *selkies* for real, have ye, Cap'um Lewrie? Arra, yer a blessed man, sir. An banshees in th' riggin', croonin' th' poor lad a *keen*, ah?"

"Aye, pretty much like that," Lewrie replied, hiding his gasp, still not knowing if he was being twitted or re-enforced.

"For th' auld god who can't be named, sir . . . and for his ship," Desmond muttered with a proud smile and an affirmative nod of his head. "Do ye let us play an' sing our auld songs, sir, and we're yours. You say th' word, Cap'um, an' we'll be like th' 'Minstrel Boy' I spoke t'ye of . . . 'our swords at least thy right shall guard . . . an' *one* poor harp t'praise ye.' " Desmond shrugged modestly about his talents.

"My word on't," Lewrie blurted out at once, in spite of a nagging fear he was exposing the plot to a clever burrower.

Desmond widened his smile and gave one more cryptic nod as his lips encompassed the mouthpiece of his pipes; and when Lewrie looked up, Landsman Furfy, that simple soul, was beaming fit to bust.

We can't fail now! Lewrie thought in secret glee as he essayed a passage of "Will You Come Down to Limerick" on his tin-whistle; *with a fair portion of the Irish lads with us . . . who can be against us?*

"Boat ahoy!" though, was shouted down over the larboard side.

"Delegates!" the boat's bowman cried back. "*Proteus* delegates!"

Damn, damn, damn! Handcocks and Morley returned, and at least four mutineer oarsmen in the boat-crew with them! A cause for another speech or harangue, with all hands summoned on deck to listen, and no chance to delay or dis-arm their supporters below.

It had certainly drawn Bales already, with Haslip, Mollo, and a few committeemen up from a meeting on the berth-deck. Men who held arms at their sides or in their belts by dint of long custom by now.

They played through the rest of the tune, and Desmond began to rattle on about another he particularly liked, whilst Handcocks and his partner clambered aboard and had a few words with Bales on the gangway. Try as he might, Lewrie could not help riveting his gaze on them to see what would happen. Which was pretty-much nothing after a minute, for they broke up and drifted away, as lackadaisical as anything.

Still ignorant of what we've planned. Lewrie sighed in relief.

Then Bales looked over his way at the impromptu concert, and he smiled; one of his astute, knowing, and pleasureably evil smiles, which made Lewrie come within a cropper of filling his breeches in terror!

He knows! he chilled; *or he has somethin' wicked in mind.* And he didn't know which was worse to fret over!

"Uhm . . . you called it . . . ?" Lewrie made himself ask.

" 'Molloy's Favourite,' some name it, sir . . . 'My Sweetheart Jane' it is to others," Desmond replied, tossing a worried look over his shoulder too.

"By, God, you perjurer!" someone roared a moment later, just as Desmond and the ship's fiddler could begin to play the old reel. "No more heart for it, have ye? What's *this*, what's *this*, then? Pistol in yer pocket, have ye? What for, ye damn' traitor?"

"Oh, Christ." Lewrie sagged, feeling physically, spewing ill.

Corporal O'Neil and a sailor were manhandling Private Pope up from below, shaking him back and forth between them like a ragdoll in a hound's jaws, up from the midships hatchway!

"By God, I'll see ya flogged for it!" Morley was bleating as he scampered nearby. "Seized up an' dunked from th' main-yard 'til yer lungs pop! Here, Brother Bales!"

Lewrie's party scrambled to their feet, Lewrie hissing at them and crooking a finger to draw them close about him. He drew a pistol and handed it to Desmond; Lt. Wyman gave up one of his to Cahill, and used his toe to open his violin case to extract the other pair.

"Keep 'em well out of sight, lads," Lewrie cautioned. "If we don't have a chance, hold onto 'em for later," he said, walking forward to the quarter-deck nettings. He saw Andrews below, through the opened skylights, gave him a confirming nod to summon the others.

"Arming yourself against your shipmates, are you?" Bales asked loudly. "Bosun, plait me a 'cat.' You'll flog him raw."

"Douse him overside from th' main-yard!" Morley objected.

"I'll not do your flogging for you," Pendarves countered, his arms folded cross his chest.

"By God, sir, I tell you you will!" Bales yelled. "Or *you'll* be tied to the gratings, and we'll have ourselves a 'bloody' bosun in another minute. All hands! All hands on deck! Muster aft to witness punishment!"

Christ, it's over! Lewrie groaned, nigh to tears, with his face screwed up. No, *by God. What . . . ?*

Sally Blue had climbed to the top of the midship companionway, her hair undone and long down her back, her sack gown held up with one hand over her breasts for modesty as she came up to watch the show. A moment later, Miss Nancy, the blowsy blonde, came up to stand beside her, re-dressing herself hurriedly as well. But they were *smiling!* Tipping him the wink too! And with the smile of a sweet-souled innocent, lissome little Sally Blue drew a finger cross her throat, dropped Lewrie a curtsy, and let go the top of her gown to hang 'round her waist, and stuck her tongue out at him impishly as that exposure took the interest of the hands already on the gun-deck!

Spec-*tacular* young bouncers! Lewrie exulted in spite of the circumstances and encouraged by that hussy-ish demonstration (about as much as he was *going* to be encouraged) cleared his throat and drew breath.

"You shall *not!*" he bellowed in his loudest quarterdeck voice, hands in the small of his back (close to his remaining pistol). "You will flog *no* man aboard this ship! *You* do not have the authority or the right. You never had . . . and you never *will!* Not over *my* people!"

Political theatre to the end. He snickered as he went over near the larboard ladder to the gun-deck, looming over the upraised grating where O'Neil and the other mutineer were stripping Private Pope of his waistcoat and shirt, waiting to seize him up.

Bales glared up at him, disliking their respective positions.

"We shall, Captain Lewrie, for an example." Bales sneered back.

"You've brought shame enough to this proud new ship, you shit," Lewrie snapped, taking the steps one at a time, slowly, eyes ahead and seemingly paying no heed for his balance as he descended. "Taken her into a mutiny, shunned a good settlement, as good as declared war upon your King and Country . . . beguiled good men to folly, ready to drag 'em all down to Hell with you, 'long as you don't go alone, you . . . !"

"Seize him, stop his gob!" Bales snarled. "We've not time for his lies! By God, do it! By God, better we flog *him!*"

Just like McCann, he'd made a serious error, though Bales had wit enough to realise it. It was hard to miss, for most of the hands catcalled or booed Bales's order and his threat. No one rushed over to seize Lewrie either, and almost everyone studiously kept their hands in their pockets, or peaceably at their sides, as he continued down to the foot of the gangway ladder to confront his enemies.

"What's in it for you, Bales? What makes you so dead set on the ruin of this ship and every man in her?" Lewrie scoffed, certain he'd have the upper hand, after that wink and smile, after Desmond's pledge of support. He took time for a slow scan about the deck and was glad to see that more than a few of the diehards were not present. "French money? Treason? Revolutionary fervour? Hatred for me personally? Whatever it is, it clouds your judgment, leads you to violence. You men there, turn Private Pope loose! Mister *Devereux*'d be ashamed . . . was a man of his flogged for no good reason!" he bellowed, using Lt. Devereux's name like a magic talisman.

"Shut up, shut up, you . . . !" Bales cried, drawing his cutlass and raising it on high, taking a step forward as if he'd strike Lewrie down! "You bastard!" he screeched, panting hard, his neck corded in emotion.

"Here, now!" Mr. Towpenny shouted, elbowing his way forward to take Bales's sword arm. "Got no use for ya, Bales; but ya harm Cap'um Lewrie, an' ya lay ev'ry man-jack in a noose for murder!"

"Let go of me, you arse-kissing dog!" Bales whirled, shoving Towpenny off him and lowering the cutlass's point as if to skewer him. Lewrie was jostled from behind, almost drew his pistol in fright, but it was Desmond and Furfy, Ahern, Cahill, and Kavanaugh coming down the ladder past him to take guard on his right-hand side . . . as they'd promised!

"Aye, show yer colours at last, Bales!" Twopenny taunted him, baring his chest to dare him to stick him. "*That's* yer Floatin' Republic,' ain't it! All yer talk o' votin' an' debatin', an' it comes t' th' power o' yer sword. You ain't no man t'follow. *D'ye hear, there!*" he roared as if to summon all hands on deck. "Ya want t'hang for *this* bastard's spite? Turn him out! 'Fore ya share his ruin!"

"You're a loyalist, Mister Towpenny. You got no right t'tell us how t'conduct ship bus'ness," Haslip sneered, coming up with his clasp knife drawn to defend Bales. "Do for 'em both, like ya said, man!"

"Vote, vote, vote!" Desmond began to chant, arm-swinging at his fellow Irish to get them to join in.

"Shut up, you witless Paddy!" Bales snapped, turning his sword on him. "By Christ, we'll stick it to the end! I'll do for any hand who won't keep his oath. Now get back to your cabins, Lewrie, before I take my pleasure of you *now*, and be sure of it at last!"

"Nope . . . don't think so, Bales," Lewrie said, with a shudder of commitment. He had at least ten loyal people close at hand, his whore platoon had kept several of Bales's hottest below, and the Marines on the gangways were fidgeting with their hanger or bayonet hilts, cutting their eyes at their foes. "Or whoever you really are. You hate *me* . . . *!* It's personal!" he shouted loud enough to carry. "You don't give one wee *damn* for anyone else. To hell with you! Lads . . . !"

"Shut up, you monster, *shut up!*" Bales screeched, turning back to Lewrie with his cutlass raised again.

"*Strike!*" Lewrie howled, digging desperately under his coat to free his pistol, scared he'd get skewered before he could, or shoot his own arse off if the mechanism got hung up on his waist-coat belt. The cutlass tip came nearer as Bales began to lunge, his face constricted by fury, as he realised Lewrie *had* organised a rebellion, despite his watchful guard, his superior wit, his thought-out plans. . . .

"I'm *Rolston*, you whoreson!" he howled, stumbling forward, off balance a bit from being jostled. Lewrie flicked up his left hand, parried that wicked blade off with his *penny-whistle*, and his foe goggled in stunned dis-belief!

Rolston? Jesus, o' course! Lewre goggled himself. *Rolston?*

Almost chest-to-chest, Bales—no, Rolston!—gaping that he'd been denied his long-sought vengeance by a tin penny-whistle, as Lewrie raised a knee and got him a good'un in the nutmegs, which whooshed the *last* startled air from the man's lungs! Then Desmond and Furfy leaped into the fray, pawing Bales/Rolston down and piling on to drag him to the deck and seize his sword-hand. Lewrie at last got his pistol out, shoved over near the larboard ladder rails, and leveled it at Corporal O'Neil, who was ready to skewer him with an infantry hanger. The dog's-jaws already back at full cock, a hasty trigger-pull . . . BLAM!

And Corporal O'Neil's rage was quite flown away—along with the back of his head, splattering gore and brains on the other mutineer who'd been holding Private Pope. He'd lost his stomach for mutiny and dropped his weapon, raised his hands, and knelt as Pope scooped up both pistol and cutlass and gave him a boot in the belly before spinning off in search of someone else to fight!

A fight, By Jesus, yes, Lewrie crowed to himself, seeing melees on every hand. Old Trollop and Sally Blue whacking the stuffing from a mutineer who'd displeased them or cheated them most-like, swinging sand-filled leathern coshes with Amazonian howls of glee! Some of the waverers, the sheep-in-the-middle, bleating in alarm and backing up to the trunk of the foremast, hands conspicuously empty and un-involved! Bosun Pendarves on the forecastle, hewing about with a tar-paying iron loggerhead as the Armourer, Mr. Offley, was hacking at the bower cables, and four men, defended by Pendarves, hauled away lustily to hoist the jibs! And Andrews, eschewing his pistol but clashing his cutlass against Mr. Morley's!

Lewrie stopped to pick up the cutlass at his feet, pulling like he'd jerk a turkey leg off the carcass to wring the leather wrist strop from Bales's/ Rolston's hand and making him howl, while Desmond and Ahern lay atop him to keep him out of action.

Aha! Lewrie espied Haslip and stalked after him. Haslip had no taste for danger, like all sea-lawyers, and gibbered in spittley panic as he back-pedaled. Before Landsman Furfy came up from his offhand side, that is, plucked a pistol from Haslip's nerveless fingers, and lifted him high in the air as easily as if Haslip was a kitten! The Irishman gave him a fearful shaking, then took a deep swing like some foredeck hand ready to swing the lead to sound the water's depth, and *hurled* Haslip, screeching thin and rabbity—Gawd, Lewrie could not quite feature it, but Haslip cleared not only the lip of the gangway but the larboard bulwarks as well, blubbering, "I cain' *swim!*" before he dropped from sight, followed by a most-welcome, but mortal, *splash!*

"Spanker!" Lewrie roared, dashing back to the quarterdeck in a giddy, bounding rush, where he could see better. *His* quarterdeck once more, where he could *command!* Robbed of re-enforcements, taken unaware and surrounded by secret defectors, all but the last of the mutineers were now out of it: dis-armed and held down, out cold, or bleeding on the decks and gangways. "Mister Towpenny! Hands to the fore-course halliards! Hands to the starboard braces! Mister Pendarves, sheets! Jib sheets! Sheet home, and flat-in yer jibs!"

With a groan and a gun-shot-like pop, the bower cable parted in a flurry of dry rope-shards and slithered out the hawse hole and over the side. *Proteus* was free of the ground! HMS *Proteus* was *free,* and paying off her bows to point South towards the Isle of Sheppey, paying off and shuffling alee as the out-rushing tide took her! Backed jibs were barn-siding taut, bellied out, the spanker above his head winging and flutter-ing as it soared aloft, the gaff-jaws and wood-ball parrels groaning and squeaking as the upper gaff scaled the mizzen as high as the cro'jack yard. Bowsprit jutting upward, sweeping Sou'easterly to parallel the Queen's Channel.

"Mister Winwood, sir!" Lewrie called out. "Lay her head East-Sou'east. Mister Towpenny, the fore-course, smartly now! *That's* the way, my bully lads! That's the way, my Proteuses! Haul away all!"

He couldn't help giggling, stamping his foot, and flinging wide his arms to hoot and howl to the heavens as *Proteus* began to gather way, singing along with the beginning notes of a ship under sail, with the gurgle and chuckle of salt water 'round her rudder and transom post and under her forefoot, the apparent wind just beginning to whistle in the rigging! "Free, by God! *Free!*" he bellowed.

"Sir," Mr. Winwood said, coming to his side. "Don't know the channel all *that* well, sir. Hoped we'd have a pilot aboard. Do you allow me to steer more Easterly, out to mid-channel? Hate to take the ground. An outbound ship to guide us, like *San Fiorenzo,* t'other . . ."

"Anyone know the Queen's Channel good as a harbour pilot?" Lewrie roared down to the gun-deck, where the Bedlam was at its greatest, with mutineers herded to one place, sail-handlers trying to do their work in the room remaining, Mr. Shirley and his mates poking and prodding those still down on the deck, and a pack of loblolly boys traipsing along in their wake with their narrow carrying-boards.

"Er . . . know it pert' well, Cap'um!" Old Man Grace shouted back. "Me an' me son been up an' down it fer years, sir. Not in a big ship, but . . ."

"Come up here, Seaman Grace, you and your son! Hell, bring the grandson too! Assist the Sailing Master 'til we reach deep water."

"Aye, aye, sir!"

Skreakings and squeals of the *lignum-vitae* sheaves of the pulley blocks as the fore-course finally reached its limit of travel and the main-course began to ascend too, more squeals as the brace-blocks to the courses took a strain, as the braces were trimmed in to cup wind.

BOOM! From astern at last, and a few seconds later a cannon-ball went shrilling past *Proteus*'s starboard side, very wide of her and hopelessly high. The ball's first graze raised a feathery plume at least a quarter-mile beyond and well alee.

"Showin' 'em our stern, Mister Winwood. Aye, Easterly, as much as you wish," Lewrie agreed, crossing to the binnacle rack to fetch a telescope. He could see several ships near their recent anchorage that had opened their gun-ports; but it was a haphazard thing, as irregular as a beggar's teeth, and he doubted if they'd get off a killing broadside before *Proteus* got out of range. BOOM! another piece spoke, but it was a forecastle carronade on one of the 64-gunners, not a long-range gun. This ball was closer to line-of-aim, but couldn't even begin to reach her and fell very short, not even skipping near.

"Sergeant Skipwith?" Lewrie demanded, pacing back to the hammock nettings.

"Aye, aye, sah!" Skipwith said, stamping to attention.

"You and the Master At Arms, the Ship's Corporals assist Mister Offley. I want all our mutineers taken under arms in chains at once!" Lewrie ordered. "Especially *that* bastard!" he said, pointing at Bales with the tin-whistle, which was by then pretty-much the worse for wear.

Rumbold, Smyth, and Mash, Mr. Handcocks, Mr. Morley, and Private Mollo, two of the Sailmaker's crew, Bales, and two other of the Marines, a few more faces he'd come to loathe by then, scooped up from where they lay or slumped on the deck, some dragged up from below already in irons, hooted and jeered by the victorious doxies who'd bamboozled the lot of 'em. Seventeen, altogether, less Haslip and O'Neil. He hoped *Proteus* had enough restraints to hold them. If *Proteus* had sailed into Sheerness through a blizzard of gunfire, he'd have been able to dispose of them with the authorities. Now, though, escaping to sea, he was stuck with them and he doubted his died-in-the-wool mutineers would go quietly. They'd finagle and whisper, perhaps cry out to the rest of the crew for help, try to turn them back into mutineers and free them, retake *Proteus* . . . Bales especially. There were a whole nest of vipers in his breast, and he needed to be shot of them as quick as he could. *How, though? Hmmm . . . good question*, he mused.

More cannonfire, as *Proteus* got a bone in her teeth and began to put on speed, gathering way out into Queen's Channel, beginning to bend her course a touch Sutherly at Elder Grace's suggestions, sailing Large off that North wind, and the sea round her peppered by misses still, but more guns were now involved. And there was a mutineer frigate far up near The Warp, off the North shore, that was speeding down on *Proteus* to intercept, abandoning her clutch of ten or twelve captured merchant ships to punish a defector.

"Mister Wyman?" Lewrie snapped, turning to his Second Officer.

"Aye, sir," Wyman replied, still smiling dreamily over retaking the ship.

"You are now my First Officer, Mister Wyman," Lewrie said.

"Ah . . . I see, sir. My goodness gracious!" Wyman sobered. That was an onerous job of work he hadn't thought to expect, sure that Lieutenant Langlie, or even Ludlow, might return aboard.

"Get sail on her, Mister Wyman, quick as dammit!" Lewrie said. "Before yon rebel frigate catches us up. Tops'ls and t'gallants. The foremast first, to lighten and lift the bows.

"Er . . . aye, aye, sir!" Wyman goggled, then gulped, reset his hat, and cupped his hands round his mouth. "Hoy, there! All topmen aloft! Lay aloft, trice up, and lay out! Free tops'ls and t'gallants! Smartly, foremast . . . hand-somely, main and mizzen!"

Lewrie looked aft. That frigate off his larboard quarter seemed to be gaining slightly, though not yet within range of her foredeck chase-guns. Heavier stuff was peppering about astern though; someone had gotten a 3rd Rate's lower-deck 32-pounders in action at last and three or four round-shot went moaning past *Proteus*, rustling the air with the sound of ripping canvas, to splash about a quarter-mile ahead of her bows. Turning to follow their flight, and seeing those towering plumes of spray, Lewrie could see several merchantmen far beyond, out to sea, some coastal fishing boats slanting in towards the Thamesmouth or the Medway. Or at least they had been, until they'd seen firing and gotten a fright, for they either fetched-to or broadened profiles even as he watched, steering clear of something they didn't wish to be involved with.

Coasters! Lewrie thought; *find myself a coaster, warm him off of the*

Thames, and get him to land my chained mutineers somewhere else . . . turn
'em over to a civil magistrate, if not a Navy officer. Where's the Impress
Services; they'd suit? Harwich, Whitstable, Herne Bay . . . bloody Margate?

" 'Ere!" Miss Nancy was crying, scampering up the starboard ladder to
the quarterdeck, with several other doxies in tow. "We're goin' *out!* We
wanna go back t'Sheerness, Cap'um, not t'*sea!*"

"Aye, what're ya playin' at, sir?" Sally Blue's mother carped. "By God,
didya play us false, I'll have yer gizzard!"

"Ladies!" Lewrie boomed, spreading his arms in greeting, just as chearly
as anything to placate them. "You did it, by Christ!"

Mr. Winwood could be heard uttering a scandalised groan.

"My undying thanks to all of you!" he pressed on quickly, taking off
his hat, making a formal leg to them. " 'Twas a fearsome and brave deed
you did in your King's, and Country's, service; and I will be sure to list
each of you by name, with the firmest recommendations to Vice-Admiral
Buckner, the First Secretary to Admiralty, Mr. Evan Nepean . . . aye, I'll
write 'His Nobs' King George himself, swear I shall! telling them what
splendid, patriotic women you are. And honour our pact, I assure you.
But . . ." he said, straightening and pointing astern, "we aren't out of the
woods yet. We almost lost again, and it was happenstance that we beat
'em down when the tide was running *out*, not in. I *will* set you ashore . . .
promise! But we have to get out of the range of their guns first. Wait 'til
dusk, no longer. Swear it."

He didn't think it would go amiss to walk amongst them (though he
suspected they still had their impromptu weapons about their persons),
bestow kisses on work-hardened hands, buss cheeks on the younger—and
cleaner—and speak a few personal words of congratulations and gratitude.
Sally Blue responded most eagerly, flinging her arms 'round him again,
and he patted (well, perhaps stroked as well) her slim back as she jounced
atip-toe and squealed nicely. It seemed to mollify them.

"Oh, give 'im 'is fob back, Sally," Miss Nancy chuckled when they'd
untangled from their embrace, relenting to his logic.

"*Sorr*-eyy." Sally Blue blushed quite prettily. "Habit, like."

"Right, then, Cap'um Lewrie." Miss Nancy shrugged. "We'll wait 'til
dark."

"You kill any of 'em, Miss Nancy?" he had to ask.

"Hurt a few, I reckon." She shrugged again. "Aye, one o' them com-mitteemen . . .'at Kever feller? Ravin' 'bout settin' light to th' powder store, 'fore he'd let th' ship be took, so . . ." She drew a hand across her throat, though not with as much enthusiasm as Sally Blue had the moment before the counter-mutiny had erupted. "Lost int'rest fer quim too quick; couldn't 'old 'im back."

Lewrie nodded, thinking on how he'd manage *Proteus* as a fighting ship without Master Gunner, Mate, and Yeoman of The Powder. *Oh shit,* he suddenly realised; *we could've been blown higher'n a kite! I do b'lieve I need me a sit-down. And who slit Kever's gizzard for him? You, Nancy?* he wondered. *Damme, don't* know *why I ever thought her attractive. There's some women just* too *dangerous t'mess with!*

He looked aloft, saw the tops'ls on both fore and main drawing, the fore t'gallant heaving upward from the fighting top, almost in position, half-open and flagging like a rattle of musketry. He turned to look back towards the Great Nore. What cannonfire directed at *Proteus* from the anchored ships wasn't reaching them and was tailing off in a weary accep-tance—and it had never been more than half-hearted. The frigate to her North still stood on, though slanting more to the Sou-Sou'west, back into the Queen's Channel, as if she was breaking off pursuit too.

Can't trust their own hands to chase us too far, Lewrie realised with joy; *'fore they get ideas about escape in their heads too!*

"Things well in hand, Mister Winwood?" he asked, walking back to the helm where Winwood was buried in his charts, and the two Grace men were craning their necks and conferring on where the next deadly shoal might be.

"Good as may be expected, Captain," Winwood allowed, not quite sure he liked being counselled by two common seamen; wasn't he Sailing Mas-ter, the Admiralty-chosen sage responsible for safe navigation?

"In th' main channel, sir." Elder Grace grinned. "An' clear o' th' worst bars an' shoals, so far. Markers an' buoys'll see us right."

"Very well, Mister Winwood, Seaman Grace. Carry on." Lewrie nod-ded. "And, thankee . . . thankee both. Or, all three, that is," he added, as their son/grandson crooked his neck to follow Winwood's finger on the chart, between their legs, seeing a wonder he'd not suspected could be pictured or written down, that lore he'd learned from the cradle, most-like. "For your loyalty and steadfastness through all our troubles. I believe, Mister Winwood, we'll be needing a replacement for your Irish Master's Mate, Mister Nugent?"

"Well, aye, sir." Winwood frowned.

"Move one of the quartermasters up, one of the mates to replace that'un . . . and Mister Grace here," he nodded at the elder, "advanced to Quartermaster's Mate?"

"Very good, sir." Winwood nodded, whether he liked it or not.

"And Young Grace, sir!" Lewrie said, squatting down. "Mister Peacham is ashore . . . permanently, pray Jesus. For the short time we must promote Mister Catterall an acting-lieutenant, Mister Adair, too, as Third Officer. That leaves an opening in the midshipman's mess. Would you be interested, Master Grace?" he asked the boy. "Try your hands as a trainee midshipman?"

For a poor fisheries lad with no hopes of a naval career, it was a miraculous bolt from the blue. Aye, he was *more* than eager!

"Good, then," Lewrie said, rising to his feet. "Carry on, Mister Winwood. Make us a good offing, but we'll lurk off to the South, for a while longer. Deep water off Herne Bay, Whitstable? By dark, we'll close the coast and land our prisoners and civilian women. Should we not come across a coaster or large fisheries boat, we could pay to put them ashore."

"Aye, aye, sir." Winwood perked up, glad to be rid of the women at last.

"Know most of 'em, sir," Elder Grace supplied, still peering at the seaward horizon with one hand shading his eyes. "Beg pardon, but do ya wish, it'd be best did I hail 'em. They know me, but they'd run from a Navy ship, expectin' a Press Gang, sir."

"Very well, Grace, we'll do it that way." Lewrie nodded. "I'll go below for a moment then. Mister Wyman? You have the deck, sir. I have much to write 'fore dusk, and little time in which to do it."

Proteus had been slowly hobby horsing over the tide-run, surging a bit to the press of the winds. Now her bows lifted as a wave, a *sea* wave, crested below her cutwater and broke to cream down her flanks. A cheer went up, for she was now truly free and halfway to salt ocean.

"Mister Wyman!" Lewrie roared. "Haul down those yard ropes . . . haul down those red flags. Mister Catterall? Fetch out a Red Ensign from the aft lockers and bend it on. Put us back under *true* colours!"

He went forrud to the edge of the nettings to look down on his crew. It was a thinner crew than before, barely the numbers he needed to work her or fight her, and God knew when he'd get more, especially sailors he could trust implicitly. Perhaps the entire Navy would have that problem from this moment on, no matter when the Nore mutiny was over. And it would be over, he was mortal-certain. With his crew as a guide, there weren't enough wild-eyed radicals to sustain rebellion, when that wasn't what the most had sworn on for. Days . . . weeks even; but sooner or later, it would be over. He just hoped it ended before England's enemies took advantage of it.

They stood on gun-deck or gangways, now the topmen were down off the upper yards, looking to him their captain. Proud and pleased; the sullen, who still might prove untrustworthy; the frightened and confused, who'd always wavered in the middle . . .

"Thankee, lads! Thankee," he said, taking off his hat in humility. "We're now returned to duty. The Spithead terms are yours. See you *yonder!*" he cried, spearing an arm aloft.

Red Ensign at the mizzen peak, where it belonged.

"H . . . M . . . S *Proteus!*" he roared. "Won back from the brink of shame by *men!* A proud ship . . . *redeemed!* A proud young frigate, manned by a proud crew! Mister Coote, sir? I note it is now a quarter-past noon. B'lieve 'Clear Decks And Up Spirits' is late, sir! We'll splice the main brace! Proteuses, ladies and wives, alike!"

That raised an even greater cheer.

"Slate's clean again!" he shouted, as they began to queue up at the foc's'le belfry. "And nary a man who returned to duty will ever be charged, you hear? Now when you drink . . . drink to yourselves. Drink to success for our ship! May her fame never be tarnished again!"

CHAPTER THIRTY-THREE

$\mathcal{N}$igh to dusk and HMS *Proteus* lay fetched-to a scant five miles off Herne Bay and Whitstable. They'd come across a Margate lugger two hours before, had had to run her down and fire a warning shot to bring her up, then perplexed the very Devil out of her captain by having Elder Grace call over to her, for he'd known her identity as soon as her patched sails were close enough to fill a telescope.

"Hoy, Jemmy Vernish! Ye want t'make some money?"

Aye, Captain Vernish did and had come aboard to haggle out the price for carrying prisoners, despatches, and whores into Whitstable: prisoners dumped on the local magistrate, whores wafted upriver behind the Medway booms to Sheerness in shallow oyster dredgers owned by men whom Middle Grace recommended.

"Glad you have 'em chained, Cap'um Lewrie"—Vernish had smiled—"for my own piece o' mind . . . and, for the constable at Herne Bay. Not one you'd call a capable feller, God help him."

Despatches! Lewrie and Padgett had scribbled away in a fury, and a flurry of ink to get them all done in time. He wrote to Admiralty, Admiral Buckner, even the King, as he'd promised, praising the loyalist hands who'd stood by him, naming those who had wavered but rallied to his side—and damning the prisoners, citing their crimes. He urged for Langlie, Devereux, and *most* of the others sent ashore to be sent posthaste to Whitstable, swearing he would patrol close offshore, to await their arrival as long as he could.

As for Lieutenant Ludlow and Midshipman Peacham, he strongly hinted at their assignment to another ship, since their brusque and abusive dealings had been partly responsible for stoking the fire of mutiny in the first place, despite his cautions to modify their behavior . . . the reassignments and acting-promotions he had made, being very short-handed . . .

And, short-handed though he was, and his crew inexperienced or not, he wrote that, barring orders to the contrary ". . . it is my intent to remove my ship as far from mutinous assemblies as possible, 'til my taint is scoured away by dint of routine Discipline, and Instruction in seamanship restores her people to complete Obedience. Therefore, once my officers are aboard, I shall sail at once for the Texel to bolster what few ships Admiral Duncan has got, shorn as he is for the moment of two-deckers. I see this course of action as my bounden Duty, in such parlous times, with the threat of battle or invasion ever before us . . ."

God, but I'm a toadyin' wretch! even *he* groaned as he read his prose; *what a canting bastard! But it will read well with those who count,* he told himself. *And I didn't trowel it on* too *bloody thick!*

Recommendations for his "distaff" re-enforcements, his whores; a draught on his funds to his solicitor, Matthew Mountjoy in London, to pay them, or their representatives, a certain sum each. *Hmm,* Lewrie thought; *and a rather handsome sum it was too!* Thirty-two women, at £5 per . . . that atop the pound note he'd slipped each one after they'd made it to sea, *and* the five shillings per for passage with Vernish . . . *and* the money Padgett would carry to buy their further passage back to Sheerness too! *And if Padgett thought he was going to enjoy his short voyage with 'em, then God help the poor lad!*

Finally it was done, and all but the personal copied into his letter books, with Padgett aided by Mr. Coote's Jack-In-The-Breadroom clerk, who would spell Padgett until he could return aboard. He still had to update his watch-and-quarter bills, of course, but that could surely wait . . . Lewrie rather hoped he'd get Langlie back as his First Officer quickly . . . then he could saddle *him* with the drudgery! That's what First Lieutenants were *for*, by God, Lewrie could gladly contemplate!

Proteus heaved and clattered slowly on a slack sea, now that the tide had turned for the night and sundown reddened the western skies; laying cocked up to weather near Captain Vernish's dowdy old lugger—which went by the grand name of *Marlborough*. *Proteus*'s boats were hard at it, stroking over to her filled with iron-bound men. Some waited on the larboard gangway for their turn in the boats. Pleading . . .

"Sir, Captain Lewrie, sir," Mr. Handcocks smiled sheepishly with his wrists before him. "Hope ya put in a good word for me, sir. Didn't mean no harm, ever. Stood up for sailors' rights, sir, same as ev'ry other hand. Didn't *wish* t'be a delegate, sir, but th' lads chose me an' I couldn't say no, now could I, sir? Keep' 'em on th' straight'un narrow?"

"It's over, Mister Handcocks," Lewrie grunted, having no wish to bandy words with the man. "You, a man with years at sea, Admiralty Warrant . . . God help you, Mister Handcocks, for I can't."

"But, sir!" Handcocks began to beg, then broke off as he got his pride up, biting back what else he might have said, gnawing on his cheek lining, as stoop-shouldered as a man already convicted.

And there was Seaman Bales . . . Rolston, really. Lewrie had *yet* to dredge up his Christian name, after all these years, when they had been midshipmen together aboard HMS *Ariadne*, under *Captain* Bales, so long ago in 1780! Bales, even in chains and shackles, still exuded an air of coolly aloof superiority, a sneering "damn yer blood" glint to his harsh phyz. Even without the beard, Lewrie would have had no clue as to who he was. Perhaps someone else in the Navy might've. Lewrie had made sure that his report had contained Bales's secret identity . . . with what few hints he'd gleaned about his prior service, the boasting he'd made when first they'd shifted *Proteus* to the double crescent anchorage, that he'd once been a Master's Mate.

Bales/Rolston glared daggers at him. Lewrie felt happy enough to return him what was known in the Sea Service as a "shit-eatin' grin."

"You really plan this, Rolston?" he idly enquired, taking a few steps closer. "Right from the start, did you? One of the schemers in *Sandwich?*"

"Why should I tell you *anything*, Lewrie?" Rolston sneered back. "*Keep* wondering . . . and the Devil take you, as I'm sure he will sooner or later."

"Rather think he'll see you first, you dog." Lewrie continued to grin, enjoying goading him. "Did you really come off a frigate up at Chatham . . . *Hussar*, was she?"

Bales sniffed in derision, but nodded in the affirmative.

"Just an Able Seaman . . . after all these years," Lewrie taunted. "Found your proper level, I s'pose. Yet a naval career begun with such promise . . . my, my," Lewrie snickered, rocking on the balls of his feet. "Keith Ashburn . . . you remember Keith, don't you, Rolston? Post-Captain into the *Tempest* frigate. And that was in '94 in the Med, so he's sure to have risen higher by now. Young Shirke, I heard he got command of a brig o'war last year . . . made Commander. Even Bascombe, that idiot, *he's* a Lieutenant too. Yet you, on the other hand . . ."

"You ruined my career for me, you sonofabitch!" Rolston growled, lifting his shackles as if he still wished to strangle his tormentor but was held by the Marines as his side.

"Ruined it yourself, Rolston . . . when you pushed that topman off the tops'l yard."

"I never pushed him; he fell!"

"Gibbs, that was his name, aye," Lewrie chirped. "Been ridin' him for weeks, puttin' him up on charges as I recall, threatened he'd be flogged, were he the last man off the yard again . . ."

"He fell. He was clumsy, I tell you! *You* were the one called it murder, starting your vicious rumours, backbiting in our own mess . . . !"

"Never a bit of it." Lewrie frowned, though that *was* close to how he recalled it, for he'd taken an instant dislike to Rolston, the moment he'd shown up with *Ariadne*'s boat to fetch him out to the ship his first morning in the Fleet. "You were guilty as sin."

Never came right out and said *it, mind*, Lewrie qualified; *but I did beat all 'round it! Take him down a peg . . . got out of hand.*

"By God, I'll settle for you yet, Lewrie! You always were the worst sort of bastard!" Bales snarled.

"Aye, and you tried, right after Captain Bales chid you to take better care of your people aloft! Came at me with your dirk . . . in the midshipman's mess, 'fore a half-dozen witnesses!" Lewrie retorted, in sudden, gloating heat. "Tried to murder *me*, by God! *That's* what got you broken, Rolston. That's what cost you your career! Signed aboard another ship under another name, did you? Rose to Master's Mate, did you crow . . . well, what stupid, criminal thing did you do there to end up nothing but an Able Seaman? You try to murder someone else?"

"Go fuck yerself . . . mate." Bales chilled, closing down against any more abuse. He glowered at his wrist shackles for a moment, shook them as if seeing them for the first time. Lewrie had almost turned away to other things, but was caught by a harsh mutter.

"Whip-Jack sham of a sailor you were, Lewrie. Still are for all I know." Bales spat, shrugging as he realised his defeat. "Come with your rich purse, your allowance, your lordly airs . . . your nose in the air, and your hands soft and clean! Nothing but sneers for the rest of us, the ones who *cared* for a commission. God, I can't tell you how *much* I despise you! You and all your privileged sort! All I ever *had* was ships and the sea, and hopes to advance, but you scuppered those, didn't you? Ran into your sort all my born days, thinking men before the mast less than *animals!* Tools that speak, long as they don't dare speak *back!* Ludlow, you . . . you're all alike when you get down to it. Cruel, dismissive, sneering . . . officers!"

"Ah, but *you* wished to be an officer, Rolston!" Lewrie snapped, seeing how he could stick the last inch of spite in and give it one last twist. "All you are is envious, not admirable. All your years before the mast and hating every minute of it, every man-jack you had to serve with and play up matey . . .'cause you were never matey with any one, as I recall, Rolston. You despised 'em most-like; you *seethed* at being ordered about by mast-captains and mates who didn't have a tenth o' your intellect, didn't you. God help the Navy had *you* made a commission, for you'd not have been a whit kinder to a ship's people than Ludlow was. You *are* a Ludlow, deep down, Rolston. Onliest trouble is you never had the *chance* t'be a bastard! I took joy of suspecting that you pushed Gibbs, aye, 'cause I didn't like you then, and I don't like you now. If that spurred you to try and kill me, then it was the best service I ever did the Navy 'cause it kept you from abusing sailors . . . maybe even killing more of 'em as the *worst* sort of officer!"

"Listen, Lewrie, you . . . !" Rolston blanched.

"Gag him, Private," Lewrie ordered his marine guard, " 'til he's aboard the lugger. I think we've all heard enough of this murderous bastard's guff!"

The boats were now beginning to transfer the doxies, leaving the prime ringleaders for one last, well-guarded load. Lewrie went over to say his last goodbyes. Since they were *expensive* goodbyes, he felt he should get his money's worth! He took a soft, bosomy hug from Miss Nancy, pecked her on the cheek, and wished her well, assuring her that his solicitor would have their money ready for them. And did Nancy actually return to Sheerness for a pay-out with the others, he would be *damned* surprised. He'd heard of honour among thieves, but how far that stretched, well . . . Perhaps they'd go in a well-armed committee, keeping a wary eye on each other 'til they had bank notes in hand?

"G'bye, Cap'um Lewrie, sir," Sally Blue said, most mournfully, working up tears in her eyes as she came to take her turn down the battens. She'd gathered up her few pitiful belongings in a scraped-bald carpet clutch-bag and was turned out in a fresh gown and hat Lewrie had not seen 'til then. Scrubbed up, too; and even in the nigh-darkness, she looked as chaste and missish as any squire's daughter of a Sunday.

She opened her arms, but Lewrie was twice-bitten and thrice shy by then. Yet the woebegone disappointment on her gamin face caused by his refusal made him relent, despite his fear of being pick-pocketed to instant poverty. He smiled, cocked his head, and held out his arms in welcome. She stepped close and, to his considerable alarm . . . and sudden thrill, it must be admitted . . . ground her things and groin against him with a puckish twinkle, bestowing a gentle buss near Lewrie's gawping lips.

"So long, Sally Blue," he said, still trying to stay aware where her free hands might roam. "Take ye joy . . . Have a safe voyage, and a good life after. Thank you again for all you did to get me back my ship. Never forget you, m'dear . . . there's a sweet young chit."

"You come back to Sheerness, Cap'um Lewrie," Sally Blue whispered hot and alluring in his ear, enveloping him in a faint hint of a fresh-dabbed scent in her hair, "you come look me up at Checquers, th' public house? Sometime at th' Crown an' Anchor, but that's no place fer a fine feller like yerself . . . Jus' leave a note. La, yer *such* a kind an' gallant gennleman . . . don't git much chance t'meet such in my line o' work. What ya said ya wrote them swells 'bout me?" she cooed as she fell back a half-step to lay hands on his shoulders and look up searchingly into his eyes. "Don' forgit h'it's Sally Caruthers, not Sally Blue . . . same as ya wrote down to yer banker man. Send fer me an' I'll come runnin' . . . an' I'll treat ya to a wondrous time whene'er yer in port. 'Long as ya don't ask me t'come out t'your ship no more. Kinda lost me taste fer that . . ." Sally said with a frazzled *moue* and a gentle chuckle.

"I quite understand, Sally . . . Mistress Caruthers." Lewrie smiled back as he let go of her, stepping back to doff his hat to her as fine as he would to any lady-guest. "We'll see, perhaps . . ."

He did not say that most-like he'd never seek her out or send her a bidding note . . . but then, he didn't exactly say that he wouldn't either, for she was a wee, fetching thing, slim and pretty, like a rose grown on a dung-heap, and sure to be as bouncy and exuberant as a half-broke colt.

His hands felt the need to twitch though, to see if he still had his watch, chain, fob, coin-purse, pocket-knife, loose change, his silk handkerchief, his breeches' buckles, or even his horn comb! She laughed again at his strangled look, a quite fetching titter as she looked him up and down as if to fix him in her memory, biting on her lip.

"No fear, Cap'um Lewrie, sir." She beamed. "Didn' take nothin' . . . Not this time. You're too fine a man t'pilfer. Well . . . bye, Cap'um Lewrie. Fer now?"

"Adieu, Mistress Caruthers." He bowed. "Milady."

"A . . . ah-doo, Cap-tain Lewrie," she pronounced more or less correctly, dropping him a deep curtsy and a graceful incline of her head that would not have been out of place on the Strand, or at St. James's Palace. ". . . 'til we meet again, good sir," she hinted from beneath her bonnet's brim.

Ah, a sweet chit, he thought as he handed her to the entry-port gate, as she swept her skirts to turn outward and lower herself over-side by battens and man-ropes. *Tryin' t'gain manners and style. I just* might *look her up . . .*

"Arr, ye keep yer fuckin' eyes awrf me bum, ya googlin' shits!" Mistress Sally "Blue" Caruthers chid the boat-crew below, as she heard their appreciative moans and whistles. "Ain' none o' yew gettin' e'en a 'finger-lark,' so hush yer gobs!"

Then again . . . perhaps not, he sighed with a wry grin.

At last, the final boat-load of women and sailor's children had gone. The darkening seas were getting up a tiny bit more boisterous, and the wind was backing from due North a wee touch more with each gust . . . presaging a switch to Nor-Nor'east in an hour or so perhaps. Lewrie was anxious to get underway, make an offing from the shoaling coast before he was caught on a lee shore at night. And it would be safer for the lugger to get into port before the rising, shifting wind raked up rollers over the bars, which might poop her.

The last boat-load, though . . . he simply had to stay on the gangway to watch Handcocks, Morley, and Rolston go, along with two more of the green-cockaded committeemen. Everyone did, it seemed. No sailor wore their red cockades any longer. Once *Proteus* had escaped for sure, her wake had blossomed with their discards, and their frigate's creamy stern-froth had resembled a sea-bride's train on a bloom-strewn church aisle.

Bales . . . he was *still* unable to call him Rolston! His ancient dislike of the boy he'd been so long ago had been dismissed from Lewrie's ken ages before . . . he despised the twisted, jealous, radical hell-spite the *man* had become in his latest guise.

"Once the boat's returned, Mister Wyman, ready the hands to recover the boats and stow them on the cross-deck tiers," Lewrie said.

"Aye, aye, sir," Lt. Wyman piped from the companionable dark. A number of hand-held muscovy-glass lanthorns along the rails threw amber-yellow moon-glades so the hands could see what they were doing, and Captain Vernish's lugger's lights competed to turn the patch of sea between them into a gently heaving, glittering sheet of molten gold.

Him and the others gone, Lewrie decided as the ringleaders got pushed to the open gate of the entry-port, *then this ship'll be clean, untainted . . . like I told the hands, the slate erased. Then we make of her what she should be. What* Proteus *deserves to be,* he mused.

Handcocks went down the battens, chains clinking at every step. Then Private Mollo, stripped of his red tunic, for he didn't deserve to wear a real Marine's jacket. Morley next, complaining and whining, as he descended to a sure death a few days or weeks away, once the Court Martial Jack was hoisted at the Nore.

The crew lined the larboard side, perched in the lower shrouds, or hung half-over the gangway bulwarks for a better view of the departure of their tormentors, their fallen heroes. A few of the stauncher loyalists hooted softly as they left, some of the particularly threatened or browbeat, but most were still just too numb—or too unsettled—to utter a peep.

"Go on then, ya bugger," Corporal Plympton urged Rolston, the last of them. "Think we got all night for th' likes o' you?"

Rolston would go game. He sneered a faint smile of disdain for the gathered seamen, chin-high and clearly disgusted, as if to wonder out loud why he'd ever thought he could make a revolution with such a poor grade of malleable clay, trying to stare individuals down, and make them duck and cringe in shame they'd failed him. Stiffly, he shuffled in leg and wrist chains, his back straight, as if he was determined to face his music with the innate superiority and courage of a Commission Sea Officer, a cultured, educated gentleman—which to his lights he'd always been—but for Admiralty's "Guinea Stamp." He twisted his neck, straining the cords of his throat like a man fighting a tightening noose, and his badly tied gag fell away.

"Damn the lot of you!" Rolston gravelled, silencing what half-hearted jeering there'd been. "Faithless cowards. Weak as water. To think I believed you were men worth saving! But you never were. You will always be sheep . . . you'll *always* buss the rich folks' arses."

He turned his back outwards, shuffled his feet so the chains on his ankles wouldn't tangle on the entry-port lip, took hold of the man-ropes, and began to descend, glaring fire-and-brimstone at them. Lewrie stepped closer to the port gate to make sure that Rolston was well and truly going away, happy to see the back of him.

Lewrie felt a brush along his right boot, heard a faint grumble in Toulon's throat as he moaned and spat, as if even a cat could recognise evil when he saw it.

Clank-shuffle-thud . . . clank-shuffle-thud, Rolston jangled, taking his eyes off the unfaithful sailors to peer over one shoulder, to see where to place his feet below the gun-ports and wale; and men in the cutter were shuffling to make room for him on a centre thwart. He glared back up once he was sure of his footing, stepping down with an old sailor's expertise, now he'd found a rhythm.

"Oowww!" he yelped, of a sudden, and his hands on the man-ropes flew open, his eyes widening in surprise.

"Shit!" Softly, from the bow-man in the cutter when he let his boat-hook slip off the dead-eyed shrouds on the main-chain platform and the cutter began to drift free, though its stern was still secure to a painter. He stabbed out and down . . . and missed!

Rolston stabbed out too, got his right hand around a man-rope, with a petulant frown and child-like purse of his lips at almost falling, getting dunked, eyes slit upward to see if anyone had dared kick him or prick him.

Then *Proteus* heaved a bit, as a rogue swell lifted her, rolled to larboard as if bowing alee. Below, the oarsmen were dipping their free-side oars at Andrew's direction to stroke her back to the hull where the bow-man could hook on once more, but it was as if everyone had caught a cramp as their looms tangled in confusion. *Proteus* . . . a few degrees from horizontal, and Rolston's feet went out from under him as if the battens were slick with tallow or hoared with sea-ice!

He dangled by that one hand, swinging his feet for a place to stand, swinging his left arm to a grip on the left-hand man-rope, then the right one below his precarious grip.

"Aahhh . . . !" he yelped again, as the seamen on the bulwarks and shrouds gasped or moaned with alarm. Bosun's Mate Towpenny scrambled past Lewrie to the top step of the battens to reach down, when no one else looked like they'd help him. "Well, damme . . . !"

Toulon moaning and spitting, bottled up and arch-backed. Leaping atop the bulwarks before Lewrie and balancing easy on four close-placed paws.

"*Ahhh!*" Rolston cried again, his right hand flying open as if he'd grasped a red-hot poker. And fell, his yelp of pain and incredulity turning to a thin, disbelieving scream. He plunged into the gilt-lit sea in a huge eruption of foam and spume, like a moth seared from the air into a blossom of yellow flame-points in a chandelier! Down Rolston went into the gap 'twixt ship and cutter, oarsmen and bow-man swinging oars out to probe for him underwater, for him to grab, should he meet up with one.

As the splash plume subsided like a guttering candle flame, the mutineer corked back to the surface, as most divers must at least once, hands stretched high as if in supplication. He heaved a great gasp of air, even as another wide welter of spray erupted 'round him—as if a beast had risen from the great deeps, expelling its whale-breath after an abyssal sounding.

"*Nnoo!*" Rolston screamed, disbelieving, *accusing* eyes locked on Lewrie, above him, cut off suddenly as he was dragged back down in an eyeblink by the weight of his shackles and chains.

"Holy . . . !" Lewrie gasped, feeling his nape hairs bristle with a sudden terror. He barely heard the shocked tumult that gusted through his sailors, barely heard the long, eerie moan from his cat, right by his left elbow, over the distant, rushing ringing in his ears.

All that remained was a spreading, fading grey-white target of roiled water, with a bull's-eye of the palest, winking lanthorn-amber . . . like a sea-beast's eye, that faded away to ripples.

Lewrie turned to see many of his hands crossing themselves or standing gape-mouthed in awe . . . looking at *him*. There were whispers . . . soft, sibilant sighings and almost-words he strained to fathom that came on the fickle night wind.

"Ah . . . hmm, then," Lewrie finally managed to say, removing his hat to swipe at his hair, that felt clammy and suddenly cold on that night wind from a gush of funk-sweat.

"Reckon he's a goner, sir," Lt. Wyman ventured to say, breaking the spell.

"Very well, Mister Wyman. Let's be about it then. Finish the ferrying, quick as you can, Andrews; then we must get underway. This wind is backing," Lewrie ordered, clapping his hat back on and placing his hands square in the middle of his back. "Take the ship's boats in tow for the nonce. Ready to make our offing, are you, Mister Winwood?"

"Aye, sir, but . . . some of the people are saying the most blasphemous, un-Christian things, sir. Pagan sea-gods and vengeance . . ."

"I'm sure 'tis nothing of the sort, Mister Winwood," Lewrie said, sure he was lying through his teeth.

"We should put a stop to it, sir, at once!" Winwood insisted, as prim as a slapped vicar. "The simple minds of your common sailor, and so many superstitious Irish aboard, why . . ."

"Have we learned nothing, sir?" Lewrie asked him. "Our common sailors are nothing *like* simple or child-like; we just saw that at the Nore and Spithead. Do the people come to believe that *Proteus* had an odd birth, an air of mystery about her . . . a *soul,* if you will, what's the harm in it? Perhaps they'll serve her more chearly for that."

"From fear, Captain?" Winwood countered, nigh to scoffing.

"*For* the ship, sir . . . if she demands it," Lewrie allowed, turning to stroke Toulon, who was now washing himself as if he hadn't one care in the world. "Pride, stubbornness . . . that's more important among them than Navy, King, or Country . . . the ship, and their mates are paramount, if you get past all the patriotic cant. Shame of failing mates, good officers like Lieutenant Devereux for our Marines, that makes 'em toe up and stick it in a scrap. Discipline and fear of punishment . . . that only goes so far. But it doesn't *inspire* them, Mister Winwood!"

Winwood got cutty-eyed, seeing his point, but not liking it.

"We'll not encourage such moonshine, sir. But *let* 'em have a spindrift, and a sense of bein' unique men servin' a unique ship. In the long-run, it really doesn't signify."

"Uhm . . . very good, sir." Winwood surrendered, though dubious.

Let him think what he likes, Lewrie thought, turning away to see to getting his ship underway. *I begged God—and Lir—the both of 'em, to get her back. I promised Bales's . . . Rolston's heart's blood for it. Whichever answered my prayer, well . . . that don't signify either. As long as I have a* proud *ship!*

EPILOGUE

Forsan et haec olim
meninisse juvabit.

Perhaps someday it will be pleasant
to remember these things.

—Virgil

$\mathcal{H}$MS *Proteus* lay peacefully at anchor in the port of Harwich, up the coast from the Nore. She was finished with provisioning, and her people were Out-Of-Discipline, after six rugged weeks at sea, off the Texel. Six weeks they'd bluffed with but a handful of ships to shut the door on the Dutch, with Admiral Duncan's two or three liners anchored almost aground, right in the channel, and *Proteus* and a few other frigates or sloops further out, flurrying bogus signals to a pretended "fleet" under the Northern horizon. With battle expected daily, Lewrie had found his external bogeyman, the roweled Spanish spur that focused his crewmen on learning their trade as quick as they could. Now she was of passing professionalism—still with some raggedness about her, of course, but Lewrie reckoned that she'd just about do. So when she had been relieved by the Nore ships, the re-assembled North Sea Fleet, which had given up their mutiny not ten days after *Proteus* had escaped, everyone had been more than grateful for a spell in harbour.

The skylights were open to cool his great-cabins as he worked, and he could hear the voice of Lieutenant Devereux drilling his Marines on the quarterdeck above him, the clomp of booted feet as they sweated through close-order under arms. Music drifted up from the berthing-deck where the hands idled with a new lot of temporary "wives."

"Down By The Sally Gardens," he recognised, pausing in his writing, smiling to himself since he'd learned a thing or two himself, learned to play a few new airs on his battered, but straightened tin-whistle.

"Boat ahoy!"

"Aye, aye!"

"Marines! By the left . . . quick-march!"

Though the crew had settled into a trouble-free Navy routine—for the most part—summoning Marines to the entry-port boded ominous. That "Aye, aye!" might mean the presence of an officer in the approaching boat. Or it might be Thomas McCann, come back from his tar and chains! There was a stamp by the door, the rap of his sentry's musket butt. "Midshipman Nicholas . . . SAH!"

"Come."

"Captain, sir!" Little Mr. Nicholas burst out, flushed and excited, "the First Officer Mister Langlie's respects, sir, and I am bid to inform you that we've a visitor arriving . . . a soldier! A real general, he appears, sir!"

"Good, God," Lewrie replied, with a frown, startled to his feet, and grasped for his coat that hung on the back of his chair.

He only knew one general . . . his father! And what the Devil was *he* doing in Harwich? Lewrie feared the worst; there had been no fresh letters from Anglesgreen since he had taken *Proteus* over to Holland . . . whilst recent bumf from his solicitor, tailor, Coutts's Bank, chandlers, and such had come aboard with Langlie and Devereux. Despite his own letters home, there'd been no replies, and he could explain that away only so long with the urgency of the spring planting season.

He dashed out of his great-cabins, up the starboard ladder to the gangway and entry-port, as the Marines formed up and Lt. Langlie had Bosun Pendarves shrilling like a starved harpy on his silver call to assemble the crew. "Present! Ship's comp'ny . . . off hats, face to starboard, and . . . salute!" Langlie bellowed.

A cocked military hat loomed over the lip of the entry-port, the bosun's calls tweetled a long, complicated trilling . . . gold lace then appeared. *Damme, it is my father*, Lewrie thought with a deeper frown.

Sir Hugo Saint George Willoughby got safely to the deck, almost spryly, gaily, and stepped inboard, grandly doffing his hat to one and all, with a condescending smile on his phyz, like a hero might at the theatre, cheered and clapped for his most recent exploit and basking in his glory from a loge-box before the curtain rose.

"How-dy do, sir . . . Charmed, I'm certain, young sir . . . ," Sir Hugo said, as officers and midshipmen were named to him. "Ah!" he finally cried, "*there's* my son. Embrace me, lad . . . and give ye joy!" making Lewrie feel like a schoolboy just back from his first term at boarding school. And about as embarrassed.

"What in the world are you doin' here? What's happening at home? You'd not come 'less there was something horrid . . ." Lewrie babbled as he suffered himself to be bear-hugged, bounced and dandled, thumped on the back so hard, for a moment he could conjure that someone had died and left him a *huge* bundle; he could not imagine his father acting so "paternal," else!

"Patience, lad," Sir Hugo muttered in his ear, "and all will be told. Everyone's well. No worries on that score." He released Lewrie at last, stepped back, and whinnied louder for everyone's ear, "Why, I haven't seen you in *ages*, and here you are, back safe . . . and famous, I am bound! I'm dry as dust too. Warmish summer, ain't it. Good t'see me, too, eh wot?"

"We can retire to my cabins," Lewrie said, getting the hint. "This way . . . Father. Lookin' fit and full o' cream, as you always do. What about some champagne? Aspinall, break out some 'bubbly.' "

The drunken old fart! Lewrie thought.

"Ah, capital, my boy . . . simply capital!"

"Well, aren't ye goin' to congratulate your *pater*, me boy?" Sir Hugo asked, once they were below and out of public view.

"Uhm . . . for what, sir?" Lewrie had to ask, pouring him a glass and keeping his eyes fixed on his sire. It was an old habit—*always* know where his paws were, else he'd pick you cleaner than Sally Blue—and twice as neatly!

Sir Hugo smirked as he reached up to tap his gaudy epaulets.

"Major-General, me lad, just as I told ye, haw!" He beamed like a well-fed buzzard, "Thanks of Parliament too."

"Ah . . . congratulations," Lewrie replied. "Just who'd you kill?"

"Haw-haw!" Sir Hugo guffawed, tweaking at the fabric of his new and fashionably snug breeches, "No, for my duty suppressing your Nore mutiny. Arrived just after your ship scampered . . . under General Grey and Buckner's replacement, Admiral Lord Keith."

"Keith Elphinstone, when I knew him at Toulon," Alan supplied, handing his father a tall stem of champagne. "Balls of brass too."

"The very one," Sir Hugo quite cheerfully agreed. "I brought our Yeomen Militia up t'London, got brigaded with some Kentish regiments, and got the brigade when the first'un fell off his charger . . . howlin' drunk. Man can't handle his drink surely can't handle his troops."

"First *I've* heard." Lewrie found cause to snicker, despite continuing fears that a tragic shoe was about to be dropped. "Though that tipple was as important to the Army as gun-oil."

"Bit of a muddle for a while," Sir Hugo preened on. "One damn' regiment went surly on us near Woolwich . . . some others traipsed into camp with only half their muster. Rot, sir! Radical, Republican rot, worse'n ever I'd imagine in England! But we put it right, stiffened the Tilbury forts' garrisons, reclaimed some ships that had mutinied . . . *up* the Thames . . . marched down to Sheerness and put spine in the town. Damme, though!" Sir Hugo wheezed in pleasing reverie, "missed the sight on the King's birthday, Alan! Everyone firin' th' hundred-gun salute . . . mutineers, too, damn their eyes . . . made the ramparts at Garrison Point collapse! *One* gun would've done it, and thank God we never had t'cannonade the mutineers for real!"

"But it's over, now," Lewrie said, sipping at his own champagne and feeling impatience to get past the "pleasantries."

"Almost. Some courts-martial still a'waitin'. Hellish docket, d'ye see. That Parker fellow went for the high jump. After that, we marched off for home. Got presented at court, my way back through the City, when the Thanks, and the promotion, came. 'His Nobs' the King, he thinks high of you . . . that letter you wrote him."

"He *does?*" Lewrie could only gasp.

"Well, those whores of yours became, ah . . . 'certain loyal and patriotic women of Sheerness,' but . . . all in all, he thinks you're th' knacky sort. Never hurts . . . when he's in his right mind, that is."

"Well, well . . . !" Lewrie had to gasp again and sit down.

"Now . . . about personal doin's . . ." Sir Hugo said, sobering and cocking his head at Aspinall, who was puttering and hovering.

"Aspinall, do you go on deck, for a while. My father and I wish to chat private for a spell," Lewrie bade, tensing once more.

"Damme, never saw ye as a ship captain, Alan . . . in the Far East, the best ye had was a dog's manger for quarters," Sir Hugo said, as he peered about appreciatively, not innocently though—there was a tad too much of the smirk to his face for that. "Navy lives right well, I must say!"

" 'A poor thing, but mine own,' " Lewrie quoted, shifting uneasily in his chair.

"Fine, quiet . . . damn' near stylish place t'put the leg over any willin' mort, I'm bound." Sir Hugo leered on. "Damme!"

Toulon, attracted by Sir Hugo's idly swinging, highly polished boot, had come to greet the new face; he leapt into Sir Hugo's lap and swished his tail right-chearly, reaching up to bat at those glittery gold epaulets with their tantalising gilt cord tassels.

"Nice, kitty . . ." Sir Hugo glowered. "Now, bugger off!"

Damned near cross-eyed in perplexity, and with a tiny "ummph" of disappointment, Toulon did, though Sir Hugo hadn't moved a muscle.

"Father, what . . . ?"

"Always were fonder o' quim than yer av'rage feller, I recall," Sir Hugo frowned, studying his son over the rim of his glass. "*Mad* for it, from yer first breeches."

"Right, so . . . ?" Lewrie attempted to bluff.

Christ, who blabbed? was his panicky thought though; *and just which "liaison" of mine was blabbed* about? *Did Sophie, that . . . !*

"Just after Caroline fetched Sophie and your kiddies back to home, there came this damn' letter. Damn' good hand, expensive paper . . . one o' those catty things from 'a concerned friend.' Someone hates ye worse than Muhammadans hate roast pork!"

"What the Devil d'ye mean, someone hates me?" Lewrie flummoxed. "*Lots* of people hate me, I'd expect . . . God knows why! Whatever did it say, then?"

"The court takes note ye didn't try t'deny it straightaway," Sir Hugo quipped, looking coolly amused.

"Well, how can I do that when you've yet to tell me *what-the-bloody-Hell's-in-it?*" Lewrie snapped back.

"It described, ah . . . yer 'diversions' in the Mediterranean. A certain sham Corsican countess, no more'n a common whore, named Phoebe Aretino?"

"Oh!" Lewrie felt the need to gasp again. "Shit!"

It was out at last! Lewrie had himself a *deep* draught, going icy inside.

"Then, t'make matters worse, some Genoese mount, Claudia . . . *however* d'ye say it . . ." his father prompted, scowling.

"Mastandrea," Lewrie croaked, "Claudia Mastandrea, but she was secret government business, a French spy, and . . . !"

"And you were ever the patriotic sort." Sir Hugo felt the need to cackle. "Court also takes note ye know the lady in question. *Knew,* rather . . . biblically. And the worst part . . ."

"Worst?" Alan sighed. "Jesus!"

"Last year, when your ship was in the Adriatic," Sir Hugo went on relentlessly, "you rescued some Greek piece, a widow once married to a Catholic Irish trader . . . in the fruit trade, it said?"

"Currants," Lewrie weakly supplied without thinking.

"Right, then . . . sweet currant duff." Sir Hugo sniffed, as if it was all a titanic jest. "Took her t'Lisbon 'board yer ship as a cabin guest . . . Saw more of her in Lisbon too, 'fore she took passage to her in-laws in Bristol. Yer nameless informer knew all that, her new address . . . and the fact that when the Widow Connor turned up on their doorstep, she was 'ankled.' "

"What!" Lewrie yelped, his features paling whey-ishly, and just about ready to tear his hair out in consternation. "What? Preg . . . no! We, I . . . that is, uhm . . . !"

"Thought I taught ya th' value o' *good* cundums, Alan, me dear," Sir Hugo sighed, worldly-wise, as if disappointed in him. "Venetian or Dago made, were they? Hard t'find at Lisbon? When I was hidin' from creditors in Oporto, they surely were. Damn all Romish countries and their meddlin' priests . . ."

"P . . . pregnant?" Lewrie could only splutter. "Impossible, for I had three-dozen of Mother Green's best, I assure . . ."

God, he thought though; *that* first *night, we didn't! Too mad for it, right after I rescued her from the Serb pirates! One bloody, incautious night, just the* once . . . ? That was simply *too* unjust!

Despite his predicament, for a glad second or two, he recalled summer-sheen sweat and slippery bodies, going at it like stoats, quiet whimpers instead of wee screams, so her son could sleep through it in his hammock . . . God, at least four bouts or more!

August, that'd been—Theoni had taken ship from Lisbon in October and wasn't showing *then!* He caught himself counting the months on his fingers.

"Fine thing t'master . . . mathematics," his father commented, in a hellish-pleased humour, as if scoffing a cully who dared to be half the man that he was. "Mistress Connor was delivered of a healthy boy, your informer says . . . Papist baptised, though. *Alan* James Connor, do ye see. Hellish coincidence . . . ain't it."

"Dear Lord," Lewrie said, topping up their glasses.

"Bein' in *trade* an' all," Sir Hugo sneered, "the Bristol branch of the Connors can add too, and knew there was no way their dead son could've quickened her, so . . . her new in-laws truckled her right out, soon as she bloomed. The damn' foreign chit, and what can ye expect of Dago trash? Damme, the Connors must be *rollin'* in 'chink' t'have such touchy morals . . . never could afford 'em, me. But Mistress Connor has her dead husband's half-share o' th' currant trade, plus a good claim on *their* share, with a wolfish lawyer. She lit in London, livin' just as high as any righteous widow. Your 'concerned friend' knew her address there too. Looked her up on my way back to Anglesgreen, your dear wife bade me."

"You what?" Alan said with a wince, sure the game was up after all this time. At *Caroline's* urging? "She *did?*" And did his father try to put *his* leg over? "How was she? How did she . . . ? Is he really?"

"He has your eyes," Sir Hugo cooed.

It was true, then; after all these years, he'd sired a bastard . . . one he *knew* of, at any rate. One he had to own up to . . . well, there'd been Soft Rabbit up the Appalachicola, but he'd scampered long before she'd borne his git . . . on King's business!

"Fetchin' wee lad," Sir Hugo said, holding up the bottle to see if they'd need a replacement soon. "And I'll give ya points, me son, for taste. A dev'lish-handsome woman is Mistress Theoni Connor. Those big amber eyes, almond-slanted and all, her chestnut hair? And still trim as a spinster lass, despite bearin' two 'gits.' "

"So . . . what *did* you tell Caroline?" Lewrie enquired, crossing his fingers for luck; feeling the urge to cross his legs too!

"Partways, the truth," Sir Hugo replied, taping his noggin and looking especially sly.

Lewrie felt like putting his head on the desk and blubbing.

"Partways, lad." Sir Hugo chuckled. "Whorin' runs in the fam'ly blood . . . so does artful lyin'. Told her, yes, she's a newborn and she did name him after you . . . but for savin' her and her son, Michael, from rape and butchery . . . for helpin' her t'Venice to cash in, thence t'Lisbon and the packet ship for Bristol. Out of gratitude! But I also said I didn't see a bit of resemblance."

"Thank bloody Christ for that!" Lewrie whooshed in relief. "I mean . . . thank you, Father!" That was hard-wrung from him; Lewrie could not recall too many benefits he'd ever gotten from the man to thank him *for!*

"Lied main-well, if I do say so m'self," Sir Hugo told him, as he smiled. "Your ward, Sophie, did too."

"Sophie? Hey? She never knew Theoni, so . . . Oh! Phoebe!"

"Aye, *that*'un," Sir Hugo chuckled. "Poor chit got flustered . . . when home, remember, does Sophie begin t'babble more Frog than English, she's up t'somethin'. But Sophie assured Caroline this Phoebe chit was just a seamstress and maid from Toulon . . . came aboard your ship as a refugee with hundreds of others, and served Sophie 'til she got off at Gibraltar. Your cabin was arseholes and elbows with *emigrés*. No privacy anyway."

"So what did Caroline make of all that?" Lewrie dreaded to ask.

"That there's a damn' sight too *many* women so 'grateful' to ya t'suit her. Allowed that it all *might* sound innocent . . . you bein' so manly and fetchin', or so she said. But there's a bit too *much* of it. Said maybe the damn' letter was from some termagant mort you'd *spurned* . . . !"

"Oh, *good!*"

"Should there actually *be* one in that category . . . hmmm?"

"Forehead creased?" Lewrie asked, crossing his fingers again.

"Nigh a *yard* deep," Sir Hugo related. "Muttered somethin' like 'where there's smoke, there's fire.' More fool you, me lad, marryin' a *shrewd* woman. I'd o' cautioned ye t'stick with 'stupid' if I knew you felt the marriage itch. Slack-wit women may fluff up 'jealous' . . . never for th' right reasons, thank God, so ye can get away with more. Now, Alice, Lord . . . I could've had her maid in the soup tureen, and she would've said the tang was off, was all."

"So Caroline's mollified? Completely?"

"Well, let's say she almost *was* . . .'til your solicitor wrote to her," Sir Hugo said, beginning to smirk and chuckle under his breath as he topped their glasses with the last of the bottle.

"Beg pardon?"

"Needed seed money, day-labourer's wages. Feller said that she couldn't get as much as she'd requested since ye'd promised one-hundred-sixty pounds to some Sheerness women for, ah . . . 'services rendered.' "

"But that was for helpin' me . . . they weren't . . . I never!"

"Stap me, didn't I caution ye. Quality beats Quantity all hollow, me lad?" Sir Hugo had the cruelty to hoot in high humour.

"Thirty-two of 'em, surely the number *told* her it was preposterous . . ." Lewrie spluttered some more, growing numb.

"I'll not get in the middle o' that 'un," Sir Hugo vowed.

Aye, it'd look that way, wouldn't it? Lewrie sighed to himself; *I am so well and truly . . .* ruined! *Do I go home, I'll most-like be shot on sight! Her brother, Governour, always was toppin'-fair with pistols!*

"We need another bottle," his father pointed out.

"Gad, yes . . . I expect we do," Lewrie replied, stumbling over to the wine-cabinet and fetching one himself, stripping the lead foil off and fiddling with the cork.

"Oh, give it here, cunny-thumbs. I know my way 'round a cork," Sir Hugo crankily told him. "There . . . d'ye see? Slap, twist . . . pop!"

"Think it's safe to go home?" Lewrie enquired, once re-enforced.

"Not if you care for breathin', no . . . not for a while. Gathered from the keyhole like . . . things'll be more'n a *tad* frosty, for quite a spell. 'Time heals all wounds,' they say though. She'll still write . . . though she suggested separate letters to yer children so ye and she can thrash things out in private missives. I also gathered she's of a mind that your Navy can *have* ye . . .'twas best you're at sea and absent. At least a year in foreign climes, she said t'me direct. I did fetch a letter along. Sorry, lad. Tried me damnedest, but . . ."

He slid a rather slim letter across the desk, making Lewrie lean far back from the edge, half expecting it to burst into flames!

"And whilst I was passin' through London on the way here, Alan . . . I also stopped off t'see your mistress. She bade me bear a letter to ye as well."

"She's *not* my mistress!" Lewrie felt need to growl. "I've not seen her since Lisbon, not heard a word . . ."

"Oh, is she *not?*" his father drawled, amusedly. "May have little need o' yer *loot* . . . Hindi word for plunder, by-the-by . . . but I've ears, me lad. I know th' sound o' fondness when a lady speaks of a feller . . . how she asked after ye an' all?" he added, softer, more kindly.

He slid the second over; this one was thicker—much thicker.

And which'll I end up readin' first? he asked himself, fearing to touch either, yet unwilling to shuffle them into a drawer *together.*

"That damned 'concerned friend' letter," he said instead, "is there a single clue as to where it came from, who wrote it?"

"No return address o' course," his father said, with a shrug of his shoulders, making his epaulets dance and glitter. "As I said, it was a good hand, quite cultured, in fact. Costly paper, but no identifying seal in the wax. Who might've known about your Mediterranean doin's?"

"Lucy Beauman . . . old amour from the Caribbean," Lewrie confessed, "Lady Lucy Shockley now . . . she was there in Venice. I turned down *her* advances."

"Well, *there's* a wonder!" His father hooted once more.

"Married woman, throwin' herself at me, and havin' it off with another Navy officer, Commander Fillebrowne, at the same time!" Lewrie spat, railing at Lucy's morals.

"Oh, such shameful doin's." Sir Hugo mocked.

"Well, I quite liked her husband."

"Could she be your anonymous correspondent, then?"

"Doubt it." Lewrie frowned in thought, all but chewing a thumb nail. "A bold, florid penmanship, as I recall . . . rich as Croesus even when single, but . . . *sheep* could spell better than she could! Well . . ."

"Hmmm?" his father prompted, with a purr.

"Fillebrowne. Clotworthy Chute diddled him with some expensive 'instant' antique Roman bronzes. You recall Clotworthy from Harrow?"

"Unfortunately yes, I do," his father said with a grimace.

"Fillebrowne bedded Phoebe, after we fell out. Boasted of it, to row me. How he learned of Claudia though . . . that was before his ship and mine served together . . . though *Phoebe* knew of Claudia. Hell's Bells, yes! 'Twas the reason we parted! I couldn't tell her it was orders!"

"And knows nothing, ah . . . *recent*, with which t'plague ye?" his father asked, almost looking relieved. "Beyond Mistress Connor?"

"Not a damn' peep," Lewrie declared, rather relieved by such a revelation himself. "If not him, though . . . I can't imagine who'd be such a bastard . . . or bitch."

"Mistress Connor herself? More fond o' ye than she lets on?"

"Oh, surely not! Might as well accuse Harry Embleton!" Lewrie scoffed. "And he hasn't a clue, a decent hand . . . *or* the wits!"

"Well, p'rhaps this'll blow over then, given time. And when back in Anglesgreen, I'll tell Caroline how aggrieved ye were by her suspicions . . . how sunk in th' 'Blue Devils' . . . took 'all aback,' as I think you sailors say?"

"That'd be a wondrous help, Father. Thankee."

"And . . ." his father began to coo again, "when passing through London, on the way, as it were . . . might there be anything you'd wish me t'say to th' handsome Theoni Connor?"

"I . . . !" Lewrie began to say, staring off at the forward bulkhead, where his wife Caroline's portrait hung in the dining coach. "I don't know quite what *to* say . . . she deserves more than . . . I mean. Give me her address. A letter'd be best. A few days' time to think about it, then write to her before we sail for the Texel again. Besides," he attempted to make a jape, "I know *you* of old, dear Father. I'd never put it past you not to inveigle your way into her good graces, and her bed, out of familial, paternal . . . duty!"

"If you think I'd do that to th' only son I *care* t'claim, then you've worse problems than a suspicious wife, my son," Sir Hugo said, with a wry shake of his head. "Were I not comfortably . . . ensconced, as it were, already, I'd be sore tempted, I admit. Odd, though, that you would come over all possessive of her. That's what I mean when I say you've a worse problem. Not her . . . *your* bastard either. Guilt and a sense of responsibility towards them doesn't quite explain the sound of your voice. Oh, my son, my foolish son!" he gallingly mocked.

"Rot!" Lewrie shot back, "Mine arse on a band-box!"

But he found himself diverting his eyes from that portrait on the partition; found himself, instead, passing a hand over his eyes as if to block it out.

Gawd. Lewrie squirmed in the beginning throws of agony; too scared t'really face either, read either letter! What t'do, what t'*do?*

Get mine arse to sea, *that's what!* he told himself; *there's the Dutch, sure to sail out sooner or later. Th' Frogs, ready to fall on Ireland, or us!* Poor Proteus, *still so raw and barely battle-ready! Compared to those problems, what matters my puny . . . ! And if* Proteus *isn't ready, then Caroline, Theoni, my children, her child . . . what if England's conquered, what life would they have if my Navy doesn't . . . ?*

He almost gagged and wished he could throttle himself.

Oh, right, he chid himself, chagrined; *try t'couch it so* noble! *Such* ragin' *patriotic twaddle . . . what a lecherous fool I am. And in it for sure now . . . up t'my eyebrows!*

He prayed that *Proteus* would be ordered back out to sea instanter; to the sea, his final, perfect haven . . . where a man had a chance to *think!* Where, it would seem, a man was *safe!* Where he had no opportunities for stirring up *more* trouble for himself! Hopefully for a long time to come.

AFTERWORD

I've always liked to open things with a bang, which is why this installment of the Alan Lewrie saga began with the Battle of Cape Saint Vincent on Valentine's Day, 1797—quite apt, that holiday, in light of Lewrie's later troubles with "the Fair Sex."

Saint Vincent was the first great break-out event in the career of Horatio Nelson. His actions were totally unheard of and a reason for a court martial and firing squad at the taffrails, à la Admiral Byng, had he failed. Nelson's solo charge into the teeth of the larger Nor'west part of the Spanish fleet, so they could not shake themselves out in battle order, or close the gap behind Admiral Jervis's fleet, confounded them. He risked their over-whelming fire, yet boarded and captured one, *then* used her as his famous "Patent Bridge" to cross and board a second, larger line-of-battle ship that had come to aid the first!

Nelson was promoted to Rear Admiral and became a household word, got command of a squadron of his own, and began to apply a unique "all-or-nothing" style of sea-fighting (all three good for his craving for glory!), beginning an unbroken string of lopsided, annihilating victories. That's not to say that I *still* don't think Nelson was about three hotdogs shy of a picnic, at times.

⚓

The economic problems when Lewrie got home were true. Taxes were high, wages had not kept pace, the Industrial Revolution had been jump-started by the need for *mountains* of war *materiel*. Almost overnight, a tranquil, pastoral, rural England was ripped from its doldrums into the Steam and Machine Age, and with Enclosure Acts stealing poor crofters' common lands drove a horde of displaced farm workers into the cities and manufactures. Later, this exodus would give rise to the squalor, wage slavery, oppressive day-labourer poverty, and other evils resulting that Dickens wrote of in his condemning novels of the 1840s and 1850s.

With all this upheaval, following democratic revolutions in the former American Colonies and the republican revolt in France, and now being exported by force-of-arms by French conquests to the rest of Europe (mostly welcomed in the beginning by the Common People who got con-quered!) it was no wonder that England and the British Isles looked more than ready for a social explosion from the bottom up!

The only people who could vote were those who earned, or owned property worth, £100 *per annum*. In some "Rotten Boroughs," and in more than a few normal, the number of voters were as few as thirty, perhaps twelve, or a mere three or five! The power-holding voters elected their own kind—the educated, land-holding, well-to-do, even the titled, or the sons and son-in-laws of such, who were easily controlled. The so-called House of Commons was hardly representative of the vast bulk of voteless commoners back then; though there were some progressive New Men who championed commoners' rights, such as Sir Samuel Whitbread, "the Ale King"—who was *rumoured* to have been seen conferring with some mu-tineers near the Nore in the beginning!

There was already an uprising in Ireland, without the expected French arms and troops, and Anglo-Irish tenant landlords, overseers for the ab-sentee landlords (such as *Proteus*'s first captain), and Protestants were being burned out or "refugeed" to Dublin. The "Houghers" and the White Boys that Furfy and Desmond mentioned were irregular partisans (pre-IRA) who punished the rich, oppressive, and uncaring; burning, plundering, and ham-stringing (houghing) livestock. British troops and Anglo-Irish militia units quite gleefully returned the favour all over the countryside. The Irish language, music, legends, dances, and the Catholic religion were banned; their bards, priests, teachers, and leaders reduced to being homeless "hedge-folk," liable to arrest, hanging, prison terms, or transportation for life overseas. All while the songs and stories of Ossian and O'Carolan were madly popular with the English! Great stuff for making the British Isles feel special, and different from "feelthy frog-eatin' Frenchies"—but not good enough for their original owners, the Irish and the Scots!

Binns, Thelwall, Place, Priestley, and Thomas Paine (now exiled in France!) were merely a few of the influential men who spoke and wrote for more freedoms, and were harried by the Crown, every meeting broken up by hired government mobs ordered by Tory government ministers like Pitt and Dundas, and prosecuted by the Duke of Portland. Men like the poet Samuel Coleridge, a huge admirer of the American and French Revolutions, saw which way the wind was blowing and ducked for cover— silenced and intimidated. Reformation of politics wasn't fashionable any longer—and was too dangerous for dilettantes.

The real danger came from the many more anonymous writers and printers of penny tracts, of a true rebellious, blood-thirsty nature, who called for real radicalism—even if everything had to go up in flames!

And as industry grew by leaps-and-bounds, so did the first tentative workers' guilds (not *owners'* guilds) and trade unions, although the government had outlawed them. Many a tavern, pub, music hall, coffee house, and printing shop was a forum for dissent and a fertile Petri dish for revolutionary fervour.

In the spring of 1797, therefore, England had never been closer to massive uprisings of the Mob, the Have-Nots, the Voiceless. And the war had just resulted in the introduction of the first-ever income tax! Even middle-class shopowners and tenant farmers could be dis-affected!

Which is why books like James Dugan's, *The Great Mutiny*, and Mr. Johnathon Neale's, *The Cutlass And The Lash*, which cover the Spithead and Nore mutinies, are not catalogued under Naval History, but can be found under Industrial Relations!

⚓

The first mutiny in Channel Fleet at Spithead and later down the coast at Plymouth scared the Be-Jesus out of everybody, though it was, as I wrote of it, a rather respectful and dignified "jack-up," a strike *without* smashed machinery, punishment for scabs (for the simple reason that no one in his *right* mind would trade places with sailors, in those days!), or threats against the nation. No one was hanged when it was over, and the principal organiser, speaker, and representative—Valentine Joyce—went on to participate in many battles. There was no talk of revolution. The Duke of Portland's agents sifted and probed all over Portsmouth and could find no sign that it had been sponsored by anyone ashore, or from overseas either.

The Spithead Mutiny was well-organised; the ships involved were united by prior service and contact because they had been based together, sailed together, and worked and fought together for several years.

Admiral Lord Howe—"Black Dick, the Seaman's Friend"—met a respectful, pleasant reception when he went down, at long last, to sit with the delegates and settle things. Whatever sentiments among those (for the most part) worthless Quota Men or the infiltrators from the United Irishmen never arose. It *was* strictly over conditions, money, shore leave, and such that they'd mutinied, and they were intelligent enough to keep it that way.

By the way, the pay rise wasn't much, a few more *shillings* per month for all. The Victualling Board still tried to foist off their flour for fresh meat, but the weights and measures were altered, and they got rid of the worst officers—Lord Bridport among them. All officers had been sent ashore at Spithead and Plymouth, and Admiral Howe and the delegates listed officers and mates to be denied a return by the *posts they held*, not their names. Without formal courts-martial and lower-class common seamen as witnesses against the Quality, their reputations remained intact. And, as I related, it only applied down at Channel Fleet, a thing only to be abided by HM government once!

This caused problems later. If Lieutenant Algy Whiphand was the First Officer of HMS *Flagellant* and got turned out because he was *born* a brutal, wall-eyed bastard, he's still free and in good odour with Admiralty when assigned to another ship, since his *name* was not put on paper, only his position. And, years later, if he runs into some mutineers from *Flagellant* aboard HMS *Pederasty*, and he has a *long* memory, then God help the former mutineers!

There were also some senior officers who got "yellow squadroned" as unfit for future sea commissions; the Spithead Mutiny at least weeded out a fair number of "gummers" and overaged ninnies who weren't worth a pinch o' pig-shit already, and action was taken about the *real* bastards who delighted in abusing their crews. But it didn't cull many of the middle and lower ranks, who'd go on to command ships later—those who were of the "off-with-their-heads" persuasion to start with, and were utterly convinced, after the mutinies, that their sailors were the scum of the earth forevermore.

Lewrie met quite a few real people in this book, such as Commissioner Proby at Chatham, who really *did* christen HMS *Bellerophon* on a night of winter gales, *after* she'd launched herself! Whether Proby really believed the sentiments I gave him (for dramatic effect) I do not know, and I'll thank his family to keep a cool head and lose the phone number of their solicitors if I portrayed him as more romantic or mystic than he really was. Evan Nepean's descendants too.

Vice-Admiral Buckner and Commissioner Captain Hartwell at the Nore were real people too. Poor Buckner, he really *did* command all, and nothing, no matter his vaunting title. Admiralty lost patience with him 'round the beginning of June 1797, and shipped Admiral Lord Keith down to dictate in their name, whilst still signing orders in *Buckner's* name; but the old fellow was relieved soon after it ended.

Thomas McCann and Richard Parker . . .

In Dugan's *The Great Mutiny* (the year-long loan of which I am most heartily grateful for from Bob Enrione's personal collection!) Thomas McCann was limned as a loose cannon. He'd been in HMS *Sandwich* but had been sent ashore to the naval hospital for skin ulcers, where he railed against almost everything, though his main complaint was the quality of the beer, and hoisted a red flag from the hospital's roof! McCann was such an irritating and fiery rabble-rouser that, towards the end of the mutiny, he was kicked off his own ship, and none other would accept him aboard, sure every man-jack would be hanged if found within a mile of him. And he *was* the irksome sort who could turn missionaries into mass-murderers!

That incident when McCann demanded the arms-chest keys—that really occurred, but aboard Captain William "Breadfruit" Bligh's HMS *Director* (3rd Rate, 64-gun). Bligh told him rather calmly (given his allergic reaction to mutiny by then!) that he couldn't have them, and McCann went bug-eyed, "snot-slingin' " nuts, howling, "By God, was *I* in *Director* I'd have the arms-chest keys!" Though he was, at the moment, aboard that ship and armed to the teeth to boot!

Richard Parker was a more enigmatic character, because no one I could find for research knew much about him. Richard Parker had entered the Navy young, had been a Master's Mate, perhaps a Midshipman, and was reputed to have gained a Lieutenant's commission, before challenging his captain, Edward Riou, to a duel! Dismissed from the service, Parker tried his hand as a private tutor, teacher, and schoolmaster, essayed a few commercial pursuits, but failed at each. He last enlisted under his own name in Scotland, was now married, and deep in debt. He wangled a £30 Joining Bounty to support his wife while he was at sea—a main-well job of negotiating, that—and was in HMS *Sandwich*.

There is no record that Parker ever called *himself* the President of the "Floating Republic" or Admiral of the Nore Fleet; he must have had *some* sense, after all! He did sign himself as the President of the Fleet Delegates though, which was enough to get him hung in the end.

After being tossed out of the Royal Navy, Richard Parker simply must have been infected with radical (small R) republican grievances. As a failed "gentleman" who could not make a decent living, his grudge against Society must have been stoked by London Corresponding Society newspapers and tracts, to a certain extent—though not, perhaps, as red-hot as Bales's/ Rolston's grudges. In fact, compared to the majority of the Fleet Delegates, Parker might have been considered a *moderate!* He was educated and literate, more so than the rest, able to pen a telling letter, and the perfect choice of the wild-eyed radicals who appointed him spokesman and president. Later, for trying to quell the greater foolishnesses of his fellow delegates, he was punished by the end of his presidency every night at eight bells, *re-elected* every morning at eight bells, so they could keep him under their thumbs!

It was Parker, though, whose limited knowledge of legislation and his misperceptions, (from what I could gather) who led the mutineers into thinking the Acts of Parliament settling the Spithead Mutiny were mere Orders-in-Council or, even if a real Act or Acts, good but for a year-and-a-day. Poor, mis-guided fellow—he even failed when acting as his own attorney at his court martial; victim of his belief that he was capable. And a man who did not lead, quite as much as he was pushed from below!

"A British naval historian told the author (James Dugan) in 1963, '. . . Ah, the Nore! Nobody will ever understand the Nore!' "

Compared to Spithead, the Nore Mutiny was a dis-organised mess and a lot more violent. None of the mutineers were as familiar with each other as the Channel Fleet and Spithead ships had been. The comment has been made that Spithead was "leaders looking for supporters" . . . whilst the Nore was a disgruntled "herd" looking for leaders; and they found people like McCann and Parker and other firebrands—to their great loss.

It was brawling and violent from the outset, with other ships and the shore being fired upon. Just after *Proteus* escaped, and those last few North Sea Fleet ships from Great Yarmouth had come down to be part of the mutiny, effigies of Pitt and Dundas were hung from the yardarms aboard HMS *Sandwich*. Waverers, "Perjurers to the Oath," and the remaining midshipmen, petty officers, and senior Marines were ducked by hauling them up "two-blocked" to the main-course yard, then let go to sink deep in the harbour water as punishment. Some were flogged, as Rolston threatened, and shown round the anchorage with cries of "here is a bloody sergeant (bosun, midshipman, etc)."

For a time, it looked as if the Nore Mutiny *might* topple the government. A regiment near Woolwich and the Arsenal *did* wobble in their discipline and loyalty; troops in Sheerness and Chatham *did* commingle with mutineer sailors. Ships anchored below the Tilbury forts on the

Thames, not twelve miles below the Pool of London, did join the mutiny. At one time, seventeen ships of the line and well over ten thousand men were involved, blockaded London's vital upriver imports, the downriver export trade, and seized nearly two hundred merchant ships.

Lewrie was lucky in escaping when he did, for a few days later, the ancient navigators' guild, the Trinity House Brethren, removed all the buoys, light ships, beacons, and channel marks near the Nore in the night and extinguished the lighthouses.

None of the merchant ships' crews joined hands with the sailors at the Nore though, and no foodstuffs were taken out of the captured ships; the lack of supplies helped end the mutiny. Despite the boast that McCann made that the "people are with us," after the King's Proclamation of 31st May (quoted in full, thankee very much!) the merchant sailors wouldn't even allow mutineers aboard their anchored ships, sure they'd be hung with them.

The Nore Fleet *did* try to sail out *en masse*. Vilified in newspapers, from the pulpits, knowing there would be no sympathetic civilian or Army revolt, the Green Cockades erred badly by announcing that they would steer course for France and join *their* Navy! But when it came down to it, most of the Nore sailors, even some of the initially determined hands, were simply too used to being True Blue Hearts of Oak and Englishmen, unable to turn real traitors, become life-long deserters . . . or sever ties to home, and kith and kin, forevermore. It is said that some sail was freed, but not set, and just as quickly was brailed back up again. No capstans turned to raise anchors, just as Lewrie's crew did when he ordered *Proteus* to set sail when the mutiny began!

As a *final* resort, the Nore Fleet split into five distinct camps or schools of thought. The largest group voted to stay in the Great Nore, surrender, and take their chances. A smaller second group was of a mind to sail out for Cromarty Firth in Scotland, far from authority's initial reach, and make up their minds what to do later.

Some wanted to sail for Shannon, and become a quasi-Irish Navy, to join the expected French invasion when it came. If all else, they thought to sell off the ships, guns, muskets, powder, and shot for what they could get to help arm the Irish countryside—then melt into the civilian population with the profits.

There were two other camps, both forlorn and deluded by rhetoric right to the end, of a mind for more radical things—or simply too stark-staring "bonkers" to recognise reality if it crawled up to bite them on the ankles!

One group actually believed that they could continue a rebellion by sailing over to the Texel to seduce Admiral Duncan's few remaining warships into joining hands with them, then sail back down-Channel to the French port of Cherbourg, and become an English Republican squadron of the French Fleet!

The last group, spurred by thoughts of the *Bounty* mutiny, with heady romances of lusty native girls (perhaps by back copies of the *National Geographic*, and the Discovery Channel!) had a thought to sail to some nebulous "New Colony," wherever and whatever *that* was, beginning a new life of buccaneering and, "Arrh, yo-ho-ing!"

But at the very last, none of them hoisted anchor for any purpose; they all ended up surrendering.

If you think that the tortured rhetoric that the mutineers used sounded a lot like the sort of Socialist Revolutionary, Bolshevik, or People's Liberation Army cant one might have heard in St. Petersburg in 1917, and in Havana or Pyongyang today, I'll admit that I was amazed too, when reading their writings or recorded speeches. It was Trade Unionism, "All hail the proletariat!" to a Tee! And "the Floating Republic" had an eerie similarity to George Orwell's novel *1984*, or his *Animal Farm;* Green Cockades were better than Red Cockades—"two legs good, four legs better"? Perhaps while delving among the stacks of the London libraries, Karl Marx found his "lingo" for Communism in the annals of the Nore!

At the Nore, people had been wounded and killed. Damning insults had been uttered, a republic had been proclaimed, and a rebellion urged, civil war threatened in the mutineers' sneering response to the King's Proclamation (*also* quoted *verbatim*, thankee!) and broadsides fired, so there was little mercy for the Nore mutineers. Crown, Admiralty, and Society had been humiliated and taunted enough at Spithead; they were not about to swallow a second, more dangerous dose! Had the mutineers not been drunk on their own words and fantasies, the Nore might have ended much sooner and a lot more peacefully, but their truculence was their doom.

McCann, Richard Parker, and dozen of others were hung as *rebels*, as well as for being mutineers. Others were transported for life, got long gaol sentences—a stalwart few committed suicide. In the end, most sailors returned to duty, with the gains that Spithead had gotten them and they had already possessed *before* rising their only comfort—except for the part about removing officers and mates that did not apply to them.

I hope no one minds that Rolston (even I can't recall his first name from *The King's Coat!*) served as a stand-in for Richard Parker . . . and got what Lewrie thought both deserved. But trust Lewrie to have a *host* of people in his past who wish to slip him a bit of "the dirty" and give him a comeuppance, a talent pool upon which I may happily draw to challenge, confuse, and plague him. But what would life be like if things ran as smooth as a Swiss watch *all* the time, hmm?

And we've plagued him pretty sore, by now, ain't we! Old foes, new foes—it was looking rather neat, with Lewrie-1, Baddies-0, 'til that letter showed up. Was it really Lady Lucy Shockley *nee* Beauman, or Commander Fillebrowne? A lark played by Clotworthy Chute or Lord Peter Rushton? A skewering connived at by Harry Embleton and Uncle Phineas Chiswick; Zachariah Twigg and his spy minions run *amok* in his dotage? Could it possibly really be Theoni Connor . . . even Phoebe Aretino, who wants him back . . . Claudia Mastandrea, still in the pay of French schemers? Admit it, you didn't think of those, now, did you!

Well, no matter for now. He's truly in the "quag," 1797 and 1798 will be an adventurous time.

And even I can't wait to find out what happens!